DEICIDE

Tim Hawken

First published in Great Britain 2013 by Dangerous Little Books
This edition was published 2021 by Seahawk Press

(C) Copyright Tim Hawken

Cover art by Menton3
Cover design by Xavier Davies

ISBN-13: 978-0-6482558-7-1

"And there was a war in heaven. Michael and his angels fought against the dragon, and the dragon and his angels fought back. But he was not strong enough, and they lost their place in heaven."

REVELATION 12: 7-8

1

SITTING AT CASA DIABLO, my closest allies surrounded me. Could I trust them all? Charlotte was at my immediate right, an angel fallen from Heaven back into my arms. To my left sat my most faithful adviser and friend, Smithy, the elderly pilot who was as wise as he was kind. Mary Magdalene, Clytemnestra, Marax and the Pure Seven made up the rest of the council. Twelve in total: twelve dark apostles, seated around a food-laden table for our meeting. An ostentatious throne sat empty at the head, its red cushions cold and dusty. I refused to sit there despite some protests from the others. Rather, I sat in the middle, so I could be amidst the discussion instead of directing it. All present had proven true to our cause so far, but their number unsettled me. Memories of the Last Supper spun in my mind. Jesus' words came back to me in a whisper: 'One of you will betray me'. Was I to have the same fate?

I shook my head. No; I was in charge of my own destiny. I was a creator and a destroyer alike. Asmodeus had made me in his image: his true son. I was powerful, able to control the elements that made up existence. Unlike my hated father, I was intent on creating truth and freedom in the universe. All he stood for were lies and oppression. We had to stop him.

Our first mission was successfully complete: the barrier separating Heaven and Purgatory had been demolished. With the help of the prophet Zoroaster, we destroyed one of the two filters, which separated the realms of the afterlife. Our initial goal had been to take down the wall between Purgatory and Hell, but I could not stand to bring more souls into this fiery pit of sin. We had freed the innocent souls of Purgatory and allowed them to enter Paradise against God's wishes: against Asmodeus' wishes.

He is not a God. I thought to myself. *He is an abomination*.

Only one more obstacle remained: we had to bring down the gates of Heaven once and for all, so the lost souls of Hell could rise up to claim

1

their own right of equality.

"Our only way to Heaven is to go through Earth," Clytemnestra growled in her demonic tone. Even now, the unearthly pitch of her voice seemed askew with her femininity. Were it not for her sharp teeth and black gums, she could have passed for human. She held a piece of uncooked meat in her hands, but did not eat. Shadows roamed up and down the walls behind her, where a row of fire torches cast their light about the room.

"We cannot ascend to Earth without bodies to be born into," she continued. "I have asked all the shamans and necromancers I can think of. They all say the same thing: there are Hellmouths where the entry to above is possible, but without an earthly vessel to contain our ethereal souls, we would just be sucked back down into the abyss."

"What about possession?" Marax said in his subhuman growl. "It has worked for others before."

"Only in rare cases," Clytemnestra replied matter-of-factly, "and it's too problematic. There are families, priests. We cannot hope to possess entire cities. Only weak souls who are open to total control accept possession for any length of time. We do not have that. Most would resist and we would be confined to wrestling with their spirits."

"Michael can make us bodies," Charlotte said confidently, leaning forward in her seat next to me.

I gently wrapped my clawed hands over her fingers. My body was part demon, part human: a sign of defiance against our creator. My fingers were sharp talons. My ears curved into sharp points, tinted red on the ends. My teeth were that of a wolf's. Charlotte's smile was the same as mine: fanged and deadly. It did not diminish her pure beauty. The change had happened when she decided to hold hate against Asmodeus in her heart, so she could come to Hell to be with me. I loved her all the more for her commitment.

"There are too many problems with this plan." Smithy got to his feet beside me. He let his old eyes linger on each of those present. "We can't take millions of hellish souls to Earth and hope to somehow sweep up to Heaven. There are too many innocents there that could be harmed."

"Most humans on Earth are far from innocent!" Marax snapped from his seat. The hulking wrath demon had once been the head juror in the tenth circle of Hell. His vicious pursuit of blind justice often clouded his thinking.

"But some are," Smithy pressed, raising his voice over Marax, "it's not right. We're not prepared. We would be marching into battle blind. And what do we do once we are in Heaven? Just charge the gates? It's madness!"

2

"Do you have a better plan?" Clytemnestra cut Smithy off. "Since Lord Michael returned, the barrier of Hell has been fortified even further from above. There is no way we can take a direct route to Heaven. We must use Earth."

"There is always another way," Smithy bristled.

"Then what is it?" Marax joined Clytemnestra's argument. "You do nothing but find fault in other people's ideas."

"Enough!" I said finally, slapping the table with irritation. After returning to Hell, I had enjoyed a blissful few days reuniting with Charlotte. Now the sharp reality of our situation hung in the air. We were all trapped here, hoping to somehow overthrow a powerful enemy, without any idea of how, or when, it would happen. On top of that, all of the demonic souls in damnation were restless. They had heard that the wall to Purgatory had been dismantled, but the ringing reply was not one of joy. The question being shouted loud and clear in the streets was: what about us? Something had to be done quickly, or the tension in Hell might boil over to something even more sinister. It was no environment in which to be mounting an attack.

Another problem remained too. In the past, Asmodeus had infiltrated Hell in disguise. He had made himself into a Bishop and gained our trust. How he had done it was still a mystery. The fact that he could do it again weighed heavily on my mind.

"Smithy is right," I said firmly. "A blind charge is not the answer. I cannot create millions of bodies for a mass resurrection to Earth anyway. Unless a soul is implanted into a womb it is impossible to fuse a soul with a new, fully grown body."

"But you were reborn to Earth when you went back for Gideon," Charlotte said softly next to me.

I looked at her, surprised. It was easy to forget that I had shown her my memories. My wife now knew me more intimately than I ever thought possible. She knew my thoughts, my desires. She even knew my greatest fears, ones I would never voice aloud. Her blue eyes shone with knowledge; they gleamed with certainty. She had been lost in Limbo for so long that I couldn't believe she was finally at my side again. Sometimes in bed I awoke with a start, grasping to make sure she was still there. I would never leave her again.

Mary shuffled uncomfortably, clearing her throat. I had lost myself in Charlotte's gaze. Reddening with embarrassment, I looked down. Mary had confessed her love to me while we were in Purgatory with Zoroaster. She was a close friend and it wasn't fair to throw my connection with Charlotte in her face. Mary was over two thousand years old but, where

3

most humans' emotions grew weary with age, hers had only become stronger with time. Her deep red hair and emerald eyes made her look like a goddess of passion. In a sense she was.

"It won't work again," I answered slowly. "I was reborn into my own body, not one manufactured after the fact. Asmodeus is the only one who has been able to replant his soul into a new vessel and he is fractured. His mind is not stable."

"But it's possible," Clytemnestra pushed. She placed the piece of meat she was holding into her mouth and started chewing.

"With time," I confirmed, "with help."

Clytemnestra raised a dark eyebrow, but before she could ask the question, Smithy interjected.

"We have another issue we haven't discussed yet." The pilot was still standing. He moved across the table and leant over to take a pot of tea in his hands. As he poured the steaming liquid into a cup, he looked to Mary.

"Mary, there is the question of how we get to Heaven from Earth once we manage a resurrection. We can't just take my helicopter, that's for certain."

Mary laughed at his joke, her hearty amusement easing the tension in the room.

"I know what you're thinking, Smithy," she said. "And the answer is I'm not completely sure, but I do have some theories. I believe there may be a way. I'd like to do some more research first."

"If you believe with conviction, it will become truth," seven voices chorused from across the table.

I looked over to the Pure Seven. They had been sitting perfectly still until now, eerie to behold. They were like seven gothic statues, each a single color of the rainbow. Each color represented the sin that they had chosen to become completely. Lust was blue, Wrath red, Pride violet, Avarice yellow, Envy green and Sloth indigo. Even though they were individuals, they always spoke as one. They were all perfectly formed angels, with claws similar to mine. None of the angels ate, except for the orange, Gluttony. Now that it was animated, it took food from the platter in front of it and constantly shoved it into its mouth. It swallowed without chewing, gorging itself upon everything at hand without spilling a morsel. Once, the Pure Seven had been followers of Zoroaster, pledged to discover real truth in the universe. Now that Zoroaster was in the other realm, they deferred to Mary. It was curious that Asmodeus had not already driven Zoroaster out of Heaven, but the old prophet had said that unless he directly opposed him, Asmodeus could not cast him out without losing the support of the good souls there. I only hoped that he was still with our

4

cause, gathering an under swell of support for us. I couldn't rely on that however.

"I think the world has had enough blind faith," I said to the Pure Seven. "We need objective proof. I want to seek the truth as much as you, but we need to know, not just believe," I turned back to their new master. "Mary, what do you need?"

"To go back to my map room and consult a bible."

"That book contains nothing but lies!" Marax rumbled from his seat.

"You would be surprised at the amount of truth in there if you care to look," Mary said curtly.

"Do what you need to do, Mary," I said to her. "Does anyone else have anything to add?"

Clytemnestra nodded gravely.

"You're already aware there is unrest brewing in the streets, Lord Michael. We must do something to stop it; otherwise there will be a riot. It doesn't take much for demons to resort to murder and looting."

I bowed my head. Did they not understand that we were doing all we could? The masses weren't stupid, but they could be ungrateful. It was also a reminder that perhaps some of the souls in Hell did deserve to be trapped here, but I had to believe they could change. I wrestled back my anger. If I was to lead these people I had to make them trust me. If I kept them in the dark we would never see the light together.

"Very well. You and Marax take the Pure Seven and spread word that I will give an address on the Great Lawn at week's end. First, I need to try to make a friend see reason and come to our side."

"Who?" Charlotte asked, sitting up straighter.

I drew in a long breath and stood.

"The Perceptionist."

2

"I WANT TO COME WITH YOU," Charlotte said, grabbing my arm.

It was now just her, Smithy and I left in the war-rooms. The rest of the council had gone to spread the word of my impending public address; it would at least buy us some time. Smithy stood calmly to one side, waiting for us.

"I know you do," I whispered. The truth was, I felt nervous letting her out of my sight. "But I need to go alone. The Perceptionist is a fickle creature, I don't want to upset him in any way."

Charlotte sighed her acknowledgement that she knew I was right.

"Smithy will look after you while I'm gone." I continued. "I trust him with my life. He can take you on a flight over the city and show you your new home from the skies."

"I've already seen it through your eyes," she reminded me.

"Then see it through your own," I persuaded her. "I need you to make your own mind up about things. I need an honest opinion not clouded by my perception. Please, go with him and learn about this Hell we live in. I'll meet you at Mary's when I get back."

Smithy stepped forward on cue, his face splitting into a fatherly grin.

"I'll take good care of you m'lady. We can even go to the casinos and have a flutter if you want," he winked at her cheekily.

"No trouble," I cautioned him. "Just stay in the air and keep her safe."

"Aye, Aye, Captain."

I looked to the clock on the wall. It was not a normal timepiece. Instead, it was split into six sections, a single black dagger revolving slowly around to each point. The marks represented something more important in Hell than time. They showed when the next wave of The Guilt would wash through the underworld. That horrible control mechanism Asmodeus had created was still alive and torturing the souls down here. I still hadn't been able to formulate a mass solution for it. I was safe since The Perceptionist had built a barrier of reason around my heart. I had painstakingly done the same for Charlotte, but it had taxed me. The Pure Seven saw the truth of their actions and so felt no guilt. Mary was the same. Smithy, of course, had refused, saying he deserved the shame of his sins. I wondered if he was right and I should have left us all open to it, but I could not afford to be lost into the oblivion of forced remorse, risking exposure every time the fires swept through. The clock was almost to the next mark.

"Smithy, you'll need to wait for a little while until you leave," I said, indicating the time.

He nodded in appreciation. I turned away and leant in to kiss Lotte goodbye. She kissed me and whispered in my ear.

"I'm stronger than you think. I can look after myself."

"Then please look after Smithy for me, my warrior." I hugged her tightly. "I'll see you soon."

Leaving the room, I strode out into the foyer of Casa Diablo. Renaissance and romantic era artworks stared forth from the walls. It sometimes disturbed me that my taste in art was so similar to Asmodeus'. I could not bring myself to take down the pieces of genius. The medieval weapons once on display had been removed by the demon caretaker, Azazel, and replaced with statues of previously conquered gods like Zeus and Odin. Sometimes I wondered if they were all simply forms of Asmodeus, given a different name. Either way, he would one day be a part of mythic history just like these deities. The tall oak doors to the foyer sat open, giving way for me to walk down the long rows of steps to The Great Lawn. This was the scene for my original sermon, where I had reluctantly announced my claim to the leadership of Hell. I hoped that my next speech would be as successful in galvanising the intentions of the population of this forsaken place. At the edge of the Great Lawn, a new suburb of Hell was being constructed. Half-finished concrete edifices sat like grey ghosts, waiting to be occupied. Structural steel beams protruded upward from the larger buildings, in readiness for more floors to be added. They looked like twisted metal crowns. Workers milled around every site, hammering, digging and building. Before, the Forest of the Damned had covered the mountainside, but I had released the tortured souls of suicide from their wooden prisons and cleared the dead trees to make way for development. Now, new homes were being built for them and the other damned people pouring into this domain everyday.

Clytemnestra had dubbed the development Hope. If we could fulfil the change it represented, none of us would have to hope any longer; we could just be. At the foot of the mountain, our city shone with its neon lights and blazing red streets. The suburb of Smoking Gun gleamed in the middle, its casinos symbols of the sin that had trapped everyone here. I would love nothing more than to tear them all to the ground, but I had to let people make their own choices. If I forced ideologies on people, it would only serve to make them cling to old, comforting ways. True revolution of the mind would only come from reason and debate, not violence and terror.

Flares of color started to burst around the horizon and a roar of flames crackled to a deafening howl. I watched calmly as the firestorm of Guilt exploded over the city. Death, smoke and horror blasted upon Hell. It may have been my imagination, but it seemed The Guilt had become more intense since we brought down the barrier of Purgatory. The chorus of tortured souls wailed into the sky, trapped in the visions of every sin they had ever committed. I closed my eyes and fixed my attention to their sorrow. This is why I was doing what I was doing. Nobody deserved this, day after day, year after year, millennium after millennium, forever. Finally, the assault passed and Hell simmered back down to its normal, yet still terrible, self. The lights of Smoking Gun shone once more.

Casting my eyes beyond the city centre to where the lights turned black, I set my sights on my destination: the suburb of Satan's Demise, home to The Perceptionist. I needed to persuade him to come to our side in this struggle. Harnessing this Elemental's unimaginable power was the only way I could see for us to succeed in defeating my father. The Perceptionist remained the only being in existence that hadn't actually been created by Asmodeus. The Perceptionist had created himself.

Summoning elements of air around me, I rose into the sky. Flutters of blue molecules swirled around me in a cocoon of levitation. Sweeping the winds at my back, I blasted down the mountain, shooting across the heavens of Hell. Sparking fire underneath me, I formed a comet's tail and let it sizzle in my wake. Anyone looking up would know for certain that the Lord of Hell had returned, and that I was not scared to enter the darkest part of our savage home.

MARLOWE SAT in front of the insipid yellow door, with a glowing sword resting across his legs. He looked up calmly as I floated down into the lane he had been set to guard. Raising my hand in silent greeting, I allowed the elements of air to scatter and felt solid ground rest beneath my feet. Marlowe stood and nodded his head. Without a word, he opened the door and walked inside, leaving it open for me to follow. I had no doubt that he had been told by his master I was coming.

I closed the door behind me as I entered the home of The Perceptionist. This small grey kitchen was a gateway to The Void in which he spent most of his time. Marlowe laid his sword to rest against the wall, next to a man who continuously rocked back and forth, staring into space. This figure was Germaine, an ex-pupil of The Perceptionist's who was driven insane by the might of his own power. Germaine had withdrawn into his own mind and now remained just a quivering husk in the corner. He was a reminder that self-control is the most powerful thing anyone can possess. Germaine had been in that exact spot when I had first come to seek guidance from The Perceptionist, all that time ago. So much had changed since then, but he had remained constant, trapped in his own personal hell.

"So," Marlowe said, taking two goblets from a cupboard and putting them on the bench next to a bottle of red wine. "The prodigal son has returned."

He rested his fingers lightly on the bench, while pouring both of us a cup of the crimson liquid. I stood quietly, unsure what to say, watching the wine sluice into its vessel. I wanted to embrace my friend, but didn't want to make the first move. Finally, Marlowe offered me the drink and grinned. His smile spread wide to show his brilliant white teeth.

"It's good to see you! I'm glad I didn't have to save you from the Barghest outside this time. Those horrible little creatures seem to be breeding. I hear you've been busy, Lord Michael." His tone suggested he thought the title was more amusing than impressive.

Relaxing, I took the cup that Marlowe still held out for me.

"Just Michael is fine thank you, Marlowe. Cheers."

We clinked glasses and sipped the wine, holding each other's gaze. Setting the drink down on the table, I walked in and hugged the man who I had met when searching for the prophet Phineus. I clapped his back, then took a seat, leaving him towering over me.

"How are you these days, Marlowe? Any news since I saw you last?"

"Ha!" He threw back his head. "My life as a bodyguard for someone who doesn't need one has been painfully quiet. The only news worth talking about is what I hear you've been up to, breaking down God's creations and asserting your authority on us as your subjects."

"You know it's not like that," I began to protest.

"I know not to believe everything I hear on the streets," he said, sitting down opposite me. "So tell me yourself. Are the rumours true?"

"Partly," I nodded slowly. "It's correct that I have taken control of Hell, but reluctantly. I tore down Asmodeus' barrier between Purgatory and Heaven, sending the souls there up into Paradise. Most importantly, I have Charlotte back. She is with us down here."

Marlowe smiled as though he already knew as much. The company he kept accepted no lies. My friend was just being polite.

"And you still wish to destroy Asmodeus?" Marlowe asked.

I nodded slowly.

"I want to create a level ground for everyone. No more manipulation by the All Mighty, if that's what you want to call Him. I want people to rule their own lives."

"Easier said than done!" Marlowe exclaimed, taking another sip of his wine. "I admire your intentions though. I suppose that's why you're back here? Seeking a way to kill the unkillable?"

"I want The Perceptionist to join our cause," I confirmed. "And I would like you to stand with us as well."

Marlowe spat his drink back into his cup with surprise. He wiped the drips off his bearded chin with his black sleeve.

"Having me join you is one thing. I would gladly come with you for an adventure, if my master would give me leave to do so. Convincing him to actively interfere in the world will be next to impossible."

"He has come out into Hell with me before. I see little difference between him teaching me and helping to lead others on a similar path."

"I'm not sure he will see it like that."

"He must. I can think of no other way we can win otherwise," I said seriously.

"Maybe he will be able to at least divine another way for you, then." Marlowe stood. "He has enough eyes to see what others can't."

Marlowe plucked his sword from its resting place next to Germaine. Lazily, he swept it in a circle in the air. With a tearing noise, a blue portal split open in the middle of the room. Marlowe poured himself another wine.

"I'll do my best to finish this before you get back," he winked.

4

AS I STEPPED OUT of the swirling blue portal, it collapsed back into itself and disappeared. Vacuous silence drifted about The Void. Blackness stretched into nothingness. This place was a simulation of the universe before God had illuminated existence with Creation. It was the true home of The Perceptionist, where not even time moved forward and his only company was the elements that floated in this endless space.

"Hello?" I called out expectantly. My words were smothered into a muffled whisper as soon as they left my mouth. Something didn't seem right.

Forcing my body to relax, I eased my mind into the elemental view. A flood of molecular light sifted over me. Millions of minuscule points of light glided listlessly around The Void. They were like fine grains of speckled glitter dispersed in water, moving without aim. Using my powers, I called a bouquet of colors into my hand and melded them into a brilliant orb. Fusing elements of fire, gas and liquid to each other, I built it until it was as large as I was. Letting the structure go, I shifted my vision back to normal. A bright sun rose above me, sending a penetrating light outward. No matter where The Perceptionist was in The Void, he would see this and know I had arrived. I looked around, waiting for a response, but only stillness answered. Keeping alert, I waited patiently, hoping for something to happen.

As I was about to call out again, a faint buzzing sounded in the distance. It was low but constant, like humming forks of electricity. I concentrated harder to see if I could hear where it was coming from. Gradually, the buzzing grew louder. As it did, I could make out popping and crackling like the noise of an arcing power line. My body began to grow warmer, the air around me heating up. I still couldn't make out the source of the change in The Void. Squinting around me, I tried to figure out how this was happening, but couldn't discern any change in my immediate surroundings. Then, looking upward, I saw it: a dark ball of energy was shooting through the emptiness toward me. Its blackness stood out against the nothing of The Void like a blurring ink stain. It was scattering all the other elements in its path, sending them fizzing off into space as it speared forward. The thing approached at blinding speed, the force gathering momentum as it came. The air grew hotter and hotter; the elements around me shuddered with friction, charging to become like the heart of a lightning storm. My eyes grew wide with fright. If I didn't do something I'd be consumed. On an impulse, I pushed the sun I had created toward the object, hoping to slow it down. My star shot forward, rushing to meet the missile that was almost upon me. With a jarring impact, the sun exploded into a supernova of energy, knocking the unknown meteor off its collision course and blasting me backwards, down into The Void.

I gripped frantically at the elements as I soared through space, trying to slow my fall. I shook my head, blinking my eyes from the dazzling light that had showered away from the thing.

What was that? What's going on? Where is The Perceptionist? I thought.

Hundreds of other jumbled questions raced instantaneously through my head as I fell.

Regaining my blurred sight, I searched to see what was happening. The thing was still moving next to me, just a few feet away. Its trajectory and speed matched mine, falling at the same pace. The strange object was double my size and oozing an aura of death. Forgetting my descent, I threw a barrage of fire into the dark mass, trying to push it away. The red flames were absorbed into it, making the ball spark with blue voltage as it sucked in the roaring blaze. Other elements around us spun away, hissing, like the object was repelling them. I pushed more fire outward, injecting heat into the ball. Watching closely, I gasped as each separate element turned into nothing as it touched its surface. The thing wasn't absorbing the fire at all; it was cancelling it out into oblivion. Anything that came into contact with the surface of it simply disappeared.

Scrambling to get away from the thing, I spread air elements between us, pushing myself back. In horror, I watched as every azure molecule I manipulated was sucked into the ball and destroyed. Each time it enveloped an atom, the object was drawn closer toward me. Switching to a pure elemental view I tried to see what I was up against. The thing itself was almost indescribable. Instead of being woven from normal elements, it seemed to be made from nothing. No, it was less than nothing, constructed from little holes burrowed into reality to expose an emptiness beyond anything tangible. It was made up of anti-elements. This was anti-matter plummeting through The Void beside me!

I summoned everything I had to hand and hurled it toward the mass: earth, air, fire, water, hate, anger, love, fear. It was all erased into nothing. But as the elements shrunk into death, the ball was getting smaller too. My attack was working.

Doubling my efforts, I pulled every atom close to me and flung them to their destruction. Zapping the molecules of life into subtraction, the anti-matter shrunk backwards and began to take a definite form. The black hole gave way to a humanoid shape. Arms and legs appeared from the darkness. An eye blinked out at me. Then another and another. White skin leeched between colorful irises as I poured the last of my strength to dissolve the deadly substance. A familiar form of intelligent eyes shook off its cloak of shadows: The Perceptionist.

Slamming into an invisible wall, my fall exploded into a world of pain. Air wheezed from my lungs, the impact crushing all of the wind out of me. I choked and gasped, clutching at my body in agony. My muscles throbbed from shock. Struggling to breathe, I grasped at my powers to draw energy and healing inside me. Plucking elements of oxygen and life from The Void, I sucked calming warmth inside my being. Spreading from my middle out, I let my breathing become even and my body regenerated quickly. It returned to normal with the molecular flow, but my mind was still reeling. I rolled onto my back and looked up to see a thousand eyes boring into me with a piercing glare.

"You were not invited," The Perceptionist rasped in his emotionless whisper. "But now that you're here, Michael, I am going to kill you."

5

BEFORE I COULD EVEN SIT UP, a blast of light shot forth from The Perceptionist's hand and pummelled into me. Again I was falling. The shaft of energy sliced at my chord of life, as the force of it pushed me down into The Void. I struggled to stop the energy pushing me backwards, but couldn't. There was nothing tangible to hold onto. I wasn't falling because of gravity; I was being propelled downward into the yawning nothingness below that stretched on forever.

Why?

The question echoed inside me. The Perceptionist had never been outwardly kind, but he had never been hostile toward me. He had helped me. He had guided me to become powerful. Now my teacher was using the elements to rip at my soul and dismantle my essence. His invisible hand was searching inside me, looking to pull away what made me human. In a desperate act of self-preservation I shot hate at the force that was penetrating me. The powerful element of emotion severed the attack, making it recoil backward. I almost cried out with relief when: smash! Again I thundered into a barrier and all air exited my body. This couldn't be real. How could I stop this nightmare?

The Perceptionist's eye-covered body landed noiselessly next to me as I used my last ounce of grasping wit to heal myself again. I would have been unconscious, or worse, had it not been for the technique this creature had once shown me. Holding my palm up in defeat I moaned.

"Stop, please."

"You will have no reprieve from me, Michael," his voice invaded my mind. "You have interrupted my solitude for the last time. I should have done this the first time I met you."

Sweeping my arm to the side, he raised his palm and slapped me on the face. The stinging blow shocked me more than any other attack could have.

15

Water filled my eyes as he slapped me again. It wasn't meant to kill me. He was humiliating me on purpose before he ended my pitiful existence. Again his hand came up and whipped down to snap my face to the side. Anger welled inside me. How could this be happening? It wasn't right. Another slap cracked my cheek. Another. Then another.

Fury clicked inside me. As The Perceptionist raised his palm again, I caught his hand mid-swing. With a roar I stood to meet my attacker.

"Enough!" I yelled.

Kicking with lightning speed at his belly, I wrapped my foot with a charge of wrath. The blow landed with a detonating blast. It resonated outward, sending a shockwave through The Void. The Perceptionist should have sailed away like a ragdoll. Instead, he stumbled backward slightly before standing tall again. Not waiting for his response, I screamed murder, opening my mouth and letting the pestilence of my emotion surge outward. Rage swelled out of me, swarming with hatred and malice. The dark elements came from deep within, like shards of deadly glass. I directed them towards the eyes of The Perceptionist, wanting to worm the molecules into his body and cut off his life as he had tried to do to mine. The blind emotion swirled towards him, but before the stream could reach him, The Perceptionist scattered himself to the wind. Countless lights burst apart in a technicolor spray. The sparks of my attack shot harmlessly away into the dark as I felt new elements clamp around me. Eyes clouded my vision and burrowed around my brain. The Perceptionist was trying to enfold me inside the elements of his own body.

As he forced his mind into my throat, I thought I would gag on his spirit. He expanded himself inside me, possessing me. Struggling to break free, I tried to turn my body into fire. Pushing fierce heat to every surface, I wanted to burn him away. Even if it killed me, I would make him suffer for this. But, before I could turn myself to flame, he let go - as if he knew what I was going to do. Blessed freedom sung into my pores.

I dropped to my knees, panted for air and looked up raggedly, staring at the master of the elements, who stared back at me. He just waited, while I recovered.

Hoping to take him by surprise, I lunged forward quickly. He met my charge with a blast of wind, stopping me short. Again with a yell, I tried to swing a fist forward, but he wrapped my arm in an immovable cocoon of elements. As I attempted to send a weave of hate toward him, I felt a wave of love cut it off; he was anticipating my attacks before I had even thought of them. I was held fast by an all-powerful being who would surely end my life at any moment.

I waited for the moment to come... but it did not. The Perceptionist just stood there, his eyes taking in my confusion. With a flick of his wrist he sent healing elements inside me. As the relief washed through my body, the sound of chirping birds filled the air. It was him laughing. I closed my eyes. *Was this over?* Strength began to return and with it a feeling that this had been some kind of test – a test that I had failed.

"You do not fail if you learn something from your mistakes," The Perceptionist's whisper echoed around my head.

My eyes snapped open. He *was* trying to teach me something. This *was* a test. I watched him, trying to reason out why he'd attacked me. I had been so helpless. The line of thought tumbled through more questions and conclusions until I realized the true puzzle I needed to solve.

"How can you defeat somebody who can see the future?"

The Perceptionist whispered the thought before the idea could fully form inside me. Hopelessness sunk into my body, knowing his very next sentence was going to be a hard truth.

"When you face Asmodeus and try to kill him, the result will be the same."

There it was. The lesson I needed to learn from all of this. I was still helpless when it came to fighting a true Elemental. There could never be any chance of success against someone so great.

"I wouldn't say you are helpless," my teacher leaned in and touched me gently on the chest. "Just misguided. Now, relax. If I wanted you dead, you would never have even seen me coming."

6

THE DANGER HAD PASSED, but I was still rattled to the core. The ordeal The Perceptionist had put me through was only a test. My teacher was now seated like a calm Buddha in front of me, his palms upturned. Elements spun around his fingers, always ready to be commanded.

I pulled myself up slowly, resting my elbows on my knees. My wits were frayed. Keeping my eyes down, I paused for a few breaths, letting the silence reassure me that another storm wasn't coming. Eventually, I straightened and crossed my legs as well, sitting to match my master's pose.

Our physical positions made a mockery of the power difference between us. Our postures were the same, but his dominance was evident. I thought I had become strong, but I was still a baby compared to him. I wondered if he was now even more powerful than Asmodeus. My intuition told me yes.

"Before we begin," he said in his penetrating whisper, "I must make it clear that I will not join you. And before you protest, I say this is unalterable. Let us not waste energy arguing. By the time you leave me, you will have all you need to complete what you wish, without me at your side."

My disappointment sunk through my lungs like a cold mist. I would have felt much more confident going into battle with him among us. I didn't want to accept it just yet, but it wouldn't do me any good to argue for now.

"I need to learn how to make material bodies, so we can be resurrected back to Earth," I ventured instead.

His chirping laughter made me feel stupid for stating my intent, which he clearly knew already.

"For a visionary leader you can be quite short sighted. A solution for that small hurdle will present itself sooner than you imagine, without my help. No, I will show you what you really need: to cloud your future from your enemy."

My heart leapt with possibility.

"I can block Asmodeus from reading my fate?" I asked. "How?"

The Perceptionist paused, glancing out into The Void with all the eyes on the left side of his body. A single line of white shone from the distance, turning into a solid beam, which moved forward and entered his temple on that side. From his right temple sprang another set of light beams. These were different colors, fractured and splintered, heading off in every direction. They looked like pulsing arteries, or tentacles reaching out into the unknown.

"I have shown you something similar before," The Perceptionist said.

I did indeed recall the roadmap he had shown me when explaining past, present and future.

"To one side is your past: irrevocable. A single path," he reminded me. "This has already happened so there is no variation. But the future," he held out his right hand, indicating the tangle of beams shining from his mind, "still has many options. Your pathway is affected not only by your own decisions, but the decisions of others. There is no certainty here. Destinies collide and clash all the time. This is when new futures are formed."

The jumble of options spreading out on The Perceptionist's right actually made me feel better. They were a mess. There were so many unknowns that no one, not even Asmodeus or The Perceptionist, could guarantee any outcome with one hundred percent accuracy.

"You are correct," The Perceptionist nodded, reading my thoughts. "but you are also wrong in a certain respect."

Doubt crept into my gut.

"Watch," he whispered. He closed his eyes and concentrated. The tentacles that leapt out of his mind started to shrink. One pathway grew thicker and shone brighter. The other lines around it were drawn together to form one, thick cord. Its intensity was so stark that it made the other offshoot tendrils burn away. Where there were forks before, now only one certain route remained.

"Is that my future?" I asked.

"No," The Perceptionist said. "This is just a demonstration." He paused and let me study the path. I stood up and moved closer, walking around and through the beam he had created. When I concentrated I could see that there were still some other options, but they were so dark and shaded that the glare of this one way simply overshadowed all others.

"Why is it like this?" I asked.

"Because you are a powerful being. Your will dominates all the others around you now."

As I watched, more of the darker paths surrounding the main one became fused with it, making the centre stronger still.

"Imagine those other lines were the destinies of other people, all separate lives, sometimes joining for moments, and other times splaying apart. Some lives never meet. However, at certain times throughout history there is a cataclysmic event so large that everyone becomes involved. When it is a person of unparalleled greatness like yourself, others are content to drop their personal projects and join with that leader's vision. This is an overwhelming strength if you wish to form lasting change in the universe, but it may also be your biggest weakness in defeating Asmodeus. Because the path is so strong, it makes it easier for him to see what will happen."

I studied the line again. No matter how bright it was, other minor options still surrounded it.

"But you say this isn't my future. This is just a demonstration," I said.

"Yes."

"So how can I stop it from forming like this? How can I make it more unpredictable, but still reach the same end goal?"

The Perceptionist lifted his right hand and the lights evaporated. He turned his head toward me and I thought maybe, just maybe, his lips turned up in a smile.

"Now you are starting to ask better questions," he said, indicating for me to sit once more.

7

"PUT SIMPLY," THE PERCEPTIONIST SAID, lifting his hand and locking his fingers in the peace sign, "there are two ways to foster uncertainty." He let one digit fall and pointed to me with his index finger. "The first is to put your trust in others."

"I do." I started, but he cut me off.

"True trust. Not just a confidence that they follow your plans and do what is right. You must let go. Tell them where you're headed and ask them to help you get there, without them having to tell you how they will get it done."

I lowered my eyes. I wasn't sure if I could release so much control of this. There was too much at stake. I needed to know we were doing things the right way. The Perceptionist was correct: I had faith in my friends, but not blind faith. That had gotten me into trouble before. It was true that letting multiple people have serious input into the way things were done could help develop alternative paths, but if we acted independently of each other we could very well just be stabbing in the dark. The old adage "united we stand, divided we fall" came to mind. We had a united purpose, but I always thought we needed a united pathway to achieve it as well. I looked back up to my teacher.

"What is the second way?"

"Stop yourself from knowing what you intend to do."

What?

I knew better than to question The Perceptionist's meaning, but it must be impossible to complete a plan that I didn't know the details of.

"Not impossible," The Perceptionist read my open thoughts. "It has been done before."

I stared into The Void again, looking at the expanse of nothing for an answer. The elemental lights of an entire universe spread into the distance.

My mind wandered to what I knew about the beginning of Creation, about what my enemy was capable of. The form of Asmodeus filled my mind's eye.

I remembered that he could truly deceive anyone: even himself. At the beginning of time, God split his personality into two beings. He blocked a portion of his mind off and trapped that second, evil self in the Underworld. This was the beginning of Asmodeus' fractured nature and the origins of Hell. For millennia he had fooled himself into thinking Satan was his enemy, when in fact they were the same person. I saw the possibility here, that perhaps I could rearrange my thoughts in a similar way. However, the danger this presented shook me. I didn't want to risk destroying my true self like he had.

"My father did it once," I said. "I can't end up like him." The Perceptionist nodded at my concern.

"You do not need two bodies," he said. "Just two minds."

Two sparks zapped upward from his fingers. Twin human outlines shimmered between us and melded back into one before disappearing. I let the residue of what had occurred clear from my vision.

"I don't understand." I blinked. "How can one body contain two minds?"

"I will show you," he said, raising his arms in the air again and summoning the molecules of life around him. Working with a feline grace, The Perceptionist wove a model of a full-sized man in front of us. The base elements of a physical body encased emotion and reason. Rather than spark the being alive with a soul, he left it dead, but glowing. I could see inside its structure and make out the veins and capillaries coursing through it. The nerve endings pulsed with electrical charges, spreading down from the brain. They were not true thoughts, just an animation; another demonstration The Perceptionist produced for my benefit.

Raising his finger in the air, my teacher sent golden light into the brain: rationality. The body twitched with the infusion of latent intellect. The light followed the electric pulses around the body.

"Now," The Perceptionist began. "Witness an example of the body in true instinctive action."

At his words, energy formed, not in the brain, but in the centre of the body. It zapped outwards in a lightning blast. The pseudo-man lifted his arm then dropped it again. A leg rose and then went limp. Each movement spread so fast that the energy forming and the action taking place happened simultaneously.

"Such action is rarely, if ever, present in humans. You are more measured creatures who require reason and emotion to drive your thoughts. This," he said, waving his palm, "is normal human action with premeditated thought."

The golden light in the man's brain stormed together with new emotion, which The Perceptionist manipulated with invisible strings. The ideas mixed together slowly. Thin, preliminary vibrations reached from their cortex, out to all of the muscles in the body. These weren't full beams, more like probing energy lines that looped through the body and then returned to feed back into the brain again, creating a cycle of pathways. As the sequence repeated, a true thought of intent finally formed and brilliant colors of action zapped outward. The man began to dance, like a marionette.

"The more complex the action, the longer the feedback loop needs to be," The Perceptionist explained while the man danced. "Human bodies actually send off signals that they are going to move before you are even consciously aware that you've made the decision to move it."

In awe, I watched the display again as it was repeated from scratch. If this was true, then even trying to strike someone with a fist could be seen full seconds, if not minutes before it happened. It was astonishing. This was why The Perceptionist had been able to counter my strikes before I could get close to him. He could see in plain view what I was going to do.

"Yes," he nodded. "And just think how easy it would be if you weren't working from impulse. If you had meditated thoughtfully on how you might defeat me, if I was watching you closely, you would never be able to even get near me. It's not just about physical action either. If I watch closely I can see thoughts working inside the mind. I can see plans being made."

"And Asmodeus is watching?" I asked.

"You have the luxury of being in Hell, where he cannot see for now. Remember, he made it originally as a shield to his own abilities. This is why you succeeded in Purgatory; he could not see into that realm through the shroud of the filters. However, he could always come back into Hell to spy. He has done this before."

"How?" I asked, hoping my teacher would have the answer that always plagued me.

"I don't know. He has shielded himself well. What I can tell you is that, even if he doesn't come to Hell, as soon as you step foot on Earth in plain view he will have the capability to know your plans. Should he be watching when you enter the material realm, he'll be able to track your progress and figure out your path. As I have said, any ideas you hold in your head can be divined into future action with strong certainty because of your strength of will and the effect that has on others. I must stress that futures are never completely certain, because of free will, but some futures are much more likely than others based on your thoughtful intent. You can always change your mind at the last moment, but then that would make it impossible to follow a plan and have it work as a long-term goal. Other people near you can distract Asmodeus' focus also. A mixture of intentions can often cloud the certainty of the future, but only if you relinquish your influence over those people. When Asmodeus came to Hell to steal your keys to the gates, the quick actions of your pilot friend helped save some hope. If you put true faith in others, this often pays dividends."

I sat back and pondered what I was being told. If I wanted to defeat Asmodeus, it could not be on a whim. It must be carefully considered. I couldn't see how just letting others do the work for me could ever succeed. They might assist, but I had to help guide them. The brute force inside me dictated that I had to know where to focus my energies. Could I somehow take control, but without knowing it? At the moment we were able to plot against him because we were in the relative safety of Hell. Still, the only conceivable way to Heaven was through Earth, and there I would be exposed. The answer to the problem was still out in The Void somewhere. I was confused. If I was to separate my thoughts into two separate places, how could I follow a plan?

"You leave your day-to-day self intact," The Perceptionist followed my train of thought. "Your short term plans, your individual nature – they all remain the same. What you understand as your conscious self stays as it is. However, your forward thought formation, the element of your brain that will create an ultimate solution, can be locked away. This part of you will plan on its own without being inhibited by immediate problems, or letting the rest of your conscious mind know."

The idea was baffling, but as I let the theory settle inside me I knew it could work. It was like Freud's idea of the "unconscious mind", which affects how we act without us really knowing why. However, this version was smarter and would only drive action when I let it.

"Very good," The Perceptionist clasped his hands together. "You can create a separate intellect, which is a force hidden to everything else. Then prying eyes cannot penetrate it. Not even yours. When you are ready for this part of yourself to become known, you slide the division away and let it take hold of your body, like instinct. If it is constructed well, some portions of your intent can be leaked through to your frontal thought to help you move in the right direction, without you completely understanding why. When the time is ready for attack, you let the thoughts spread instantly to your limbs from the centre, not from your brain. They will then be instantaneous and harder to combat."

The idea now seemed not just plausible, but credible. I was to keep most of my brain as normal, but split the other, scheming side away. In a sense it would be like an extra kind of "gut instinct" that could help guide my actions.

"But how do I lock away potent thoughts like that?" I wondered.

"With emotion."

I looked to my master. The golden glow of rationality was bursting inside him. It was not muddied with the color of emotions like a normal being. He had no love, no hate, no anger and no joy within. He was all intellect, but only because he had made himself that way. It hadn't always been the case. Between our first and second encounters, The Perceptionist had changed his body at will. He had separated emotion from himself and grown other senses which he didn't have before. He had thought that by stripping the disruptive force of emotion away he would be able to interpret the universe more clearly. It had always horrified me that he had destroyed that part of his nature. All my happiness and motivation to find Charlotte had come from emotion. I refused to think of it as a disruptive force. Emotion made me human. I could never give that away.

"I haven't let emotion go forever," The Perceptionist stared at me. "I simply find it useful to have peace to think. It's the struggle between the two opposing natures of rationality and emotion that makes most people unhappy. Take the struggle away and you find peace."

"Struggle is all I have to keep me going," I whispered.

We lapsed into silence and watched each other. I looked at the atoms of my teacher. It was quite beautiful seeing a being so complex, yet so simple in its direction. Perhaps my attachment to emotion was misguided, but how could I ever give my love for Charlotte away in a puff of smoke? It was unthinkable. Looking at his physiology, an epiphany hit me like a bolt. Of course! Emotion clouded intellect! If I were to build a barrier of pure emotion around a separated nerve centre of ideas, it would be hidden from anyone hoping to peer in, including myself. That was how I could separate my two minds. Perhaps that's why Asmodeus could not see through the barriers of the realms either; the weave of emotion through the centre was too strong to penetrate. It certainly made sense.

"You didn't even need me to show you the way," The Perceptionist said softly. "Your past experiences are helping you find new ideas. This is what I have wanted all along, not for me to tell you, but for you to recognize the answers. I hope you will unfold more ideas, and that one day you will show me perfection. I pray you can think of something I haven't been able to conceive."

Perfection. I remembered his quest. So, he had still not found it.

"I have not." My master closed every one of his eyes and stood quietly for a moment. Elements of light vibrated around him in a shudder. "This is why I choose not to interfere directly with the outside world. I am hoping perfection will come to me. It is nowhere I can see within myself, as I had once hoped. Please bring it to me."

"What if it doesn't exist?" I asked sadly, wishing I could somehow repay all that he had given me.

"Perfection exists," he said with certainty. "If it doesn't exist, then it is not perfect."

I shook my head. Perhaps so much intelligence was a form of insanity.

"Obsession is not insanity," The Perceptionist whispered. "Not when you know your goal is out there somewhere and you can have it if you are simply persistent enough."

I thought of my own obsession: to kill our creator; to produce peace and equality. I knew it was possible. A question which had been bothering me came to the surface of my mind.

"What was that dark matter you used against me? Could I harness it to destroy God?"

26

8

"NO." THE ANSWER WAS DIRECT.

Annoyance prickled my skin.

"Do you not think I'm capable enough to wield it?" I asked.

The Perceptionist shook his head.

"You misunderstand me. I say no because you cannot harness it to destroy Asmodeus. The reasons are two."

I furrowed my brow. I was certain those mysterious non-elements were the key to killing my father. However, The Perceptionist could not be lying.

"I can see you already understand that this dark matter is what might be called anti-matter by scientific minds," he whispered.

I nodded my head slightly to show that I did.

"So you will know, then, that it cannot exist outside of The Void. You saw how it was dissolved by the elements you threw at it."

"It was not the only thing that dissolved," I corrected. "They destroyed each other."

"Exactly. It is a simple mathematical equation: negative one, plus one, equals zero. Therefore, a negative element cannot exist inside a universe that is substantive. As soon as anti-matter touches existence, both cancel each other out and return to being nothing."

Sweeping a blank space before him, The Perceptionist began to make a new model to illustrate his point. It was a mini replica of the known universe, spherical in shape and around three feet in diameter. Inside, Heaven and Hell surrounded Earth, swirling in both sublime paradise and deadly fire.

Separating the two ethereal realms was the barrier, swirling endlessly in its dark weave, keeping Heaven above and Hell below. The representation reminded me of a smaller version of Mary Magdalene's map room, where I had first been taught about the barriers separating each of the main realms.

However, in this version Purgatory no longer existed as a totally separate realm. It was now part of Heaven. This was a model of how things were at present. It was terrifying to see all of Creation squeezed into something you could lift above your head. I felt like a giant contemplating a toy. Without pausing, The Perceptionist shifted the model slightly to one side. Then, putting his hands together in front of him in a prayer position, but with the fingers pointing forward instead of up, he pushed his arms out. The movement caused a hideous ripping noise. Hundreds of thousands of new elemental lights rippled into life on one side of The Perceptionist's hands and anti-matter shuddered into existence on the other. He was tearing The Void into two. From nothing, something sprang into existence on one side, and less than nothing was born on the other. For every new molecule that was created, its black antithesis was also made.

"Be careful not to touch them," he whispered.

I shuffled backwards to remain clear of any stray pieces of the deep blackness. With morbid fascination, I watched as my master used his mind to shape the new dark matter into a long spear-like rod. The other positive elements he repelled away, making sure the rippling surface of his new anti-creation only touched space.

"Your universe is made up of something. Earth, Heaven, Hell; they all have an atmosphere. Air has particles. Hell has heat. Every part of the God's Creation has some kind of material that makes up its existence. It is not like this void, where I have created nothingness and then added a few elements to manipulate separately. The universe we see in front of us here is almost totally comprised of elements, with only tiny pieces of space in between. If you were to introduce dark matter into the atmosphere of the realms, you won't be able to control it. You risk total annihilation of yourself and everything you love."

To punctuate his comment, The Perceptionist flung the spear he had made into the heart of the model of Creation. As the rod pierced the sphere, it chewed away at the fabric of existence. The hole it created made the rest of the elements cave in on themselves in a chaotic embrace. What had been the world became just another scatter of elemental illusion, without construction or meaning. The puddle dissolved away and The Perceptionist moved his hand to scatter the elements again. We sat alone once more, master and student. I saw the terrible risk I would be taking if I tried to control that weapon. Yet still, I didn't want to let the possibility fall.

"What if I were to contain it somehow, in small amounts, and introduce them to Asmodeus' body? What if I was careful enough to draw him out into the far reaches of Creation, so as not to disrupt the fabric of the universe?"

"You forget that Asmodeus created himself from nothing," The Perceptionist said. "Like me, he spawned his own consciousness and formed a body afterward. He existed outside of the universe you know because he created it and then made himself a part of it. If you try to annihilate his spirit, he would find his way back eventually. There is no way to end him entirely, without him coming back again. If you risk fighting him with dark matter, you risk destroying everything you love for nothing. If you want to end his reign over the souls of existence, you'll have to find another way."

"Tell me how." I asked desperately.

"You will come to solve the answer yourself," he said, like it was an easy thing to do. "The instinctual reason you shut off from the outside will hold the key. By the time you leave here all will be set. Your journey will reveal the solution."

Clapping his hands, a rumbling wave of sounds whooshed around us. Millions upon millions of emotive molecules rushed to surround my body. I watched as every rainbow color of feeling gathered, ready to be commanded to their task. They sparkled with their eternal potential. It was time for The Perceptionist to show me how to become a split being.

"When you get back to Hell, inform Marlowe that he has my permission to follow you," he said. "The rest of our conversation from here will only be a part of your subconscious intellect. You will not even recall that you have done this, otherwise you will be discovered. All you will know is that you are on a set path, and it is the right one. Trust your intuition. Trust your friends. You will not do this alone."

Flaring emotion around his limbs, The Perceptionist stood. I mimicked his motion and prepared to weave the elements by his side. I needed to do this with him, so I would understand how to undo it when the time came.

"We will see each other once more, Michael," he whispered. "And that will be just moments before you take your last breath. I will not have time to say this then, so I say it now. I will miss you, my friend." He reached out and touched an eyeball on his right hand onto my forehead. After that, all went dark.

9

I STUMBLED BACK INTO THE GREY KITCHEN feeling disjointed. My head buzzed and my eyes stung. Struggling, I fell forward. The scrape of a chair sounded and suddenly Marlowe had me in his arms.

"Michael?" he said, his breath hot on my neck as he fought to keep me up. "Michael? What's wrong?"

It was like his voice was coming at me from underwater, but I understood the meaning. I was not frightened. *Trust your intuition. Trust your friends.* The thought was more of a feeling than anything. Inside I felt completely assured, I just needed to regain control of my limbs. Searching around myself from within, I crawled to the surface of consciousness. I saw the light and reached out towards it with my mind, rising to the surface. Sensation came rushing back in like a gasp of air. Sight, hearing, smell, taste, touch: I was back. It was as if I had been battling a bad dream and had abruptly shaken myself awake. As I blinked my eyes, the dream faded away from thought and all that was left was a brick in my stomach. My surroundings flooded in around me. I had a feeling that something had changed but, no matter how hard I tried, I couldn't grasp what it was. All I could remember were blurs of a conversation where The Perceptionist had shown me the dangers of trying to use anti-matter. Even that didn't seem truly important right now.

"Michael?" Marlowe steadied me on my feet and held me at arm's length.

I looked at him, and the world seemed normal again.

"Marlowe," I smiled. "I'm back."

"I can see that," he said, looking concerned. "But are you really? All of you? What happened?"

"I…" I paused. I didn't quite know what had happened, but knew that I shouldn't say it in those exact words. "I got what I needed. I'm fine, really."

And I was feeling fine. I felt great. The disorientation I had experienced just moments ago had dissipated and immense confidence filled me. I had a mission to complete. My wife and my friends were fighting for the same cause. The smaller answers would come as long as I pursued the end goal. I knew it. I felt it.

Cautiously Marlowe let go of my arms. I grinned at him again, remembering something.

"Your master said you were free to come with me," I told him. "It would be an honour to have you join my inner council. I need people I can trust. We all do. Will you help us get rid of all divisions in this life, so we can have a chance at harmony?"

"Of course," Marlowe answered without pause. He stood to his full height, his hand gripping the sword next to him. "What is our plan?"

I stared into space. No answers came. Racking my brain, a slight amount of nervousness crept into me. Before I came here, I had wanted to know how to create bodies for a resurrection. It was the crucial first step in our plan. This question was unanswered. I felt that it was only a hurdle, yet it was still one we had to overcome.

I looked over to the table, where two glasses of red wine rested.

"Perhaps I should fill you in on our situation?" I offered, motioning for us to sit.

Settling back down opposite me, Marlowe sipped his wine as I explained the state of play. He interrupted at times to clarify who our allies were and what our options were moving ahead. I told him my history and of the events leading up to the liberation of Purgatory. In the end, we were back to the beginning of why I had come to see The Perceptionist.

"I need to find a way to build bodies on Earth, that will enable our souls to be born into them," I explained. "It wasn't something our master could give me the answer to, but we will solve the problem."

Marlowe gripped his cup and took a thoughtful swig.

"I'm not sure I have any answers for you," he murmured.

"I do," a voice said from across the room.

We both turned and Marlowe leapt to his feet in surprise. A gaunt man, with dishevelled hair draped around his face, stood shakily in the corner. He was dressed in bare rags. Ribs showed through his skinny frame, but his purple eyes glowed with power. It took me a moment to realize who it was.

"I will build your bodies for you," Germaine croaked.

"GERMAINE?" MARLOWE UTTERED IN SHOCK. "It can't… You can't."

"I can and have, mon ami" Germaine smiled a crooked grin and looked at me.

From my seat, I nodded my head in a silent hello. I did not feel any malice coming from this man, yet Marlowe's reaction kept me on guard. This was the quivering husk who had sat catatonic in the corner every time I had come to see The Perceptionist. Now he was standing in front of us, seemingly back from the dead. I looked to my African friend, but he only stared at our unexpected guest with trepidation.

Turning back to Germaine, I studied him. He was hunched yet still quite tall, his frail body wasted away from inactivity. His legs were like two withered sticks, holding up a chicken carcass body. Dark brown hair fell in tangles around his shoulders. A short, patchy beard made it look like he had dirt covering his face. Still smiling, he showed broken rows of teeth. He looked like a beggar, although still quite youthful. I altered my vision to take in his elemental makeup. Cascades of emotion flowed all around him. His whole body was shades of rainbow desire: hunger, lust, ambition. I struggled to find the golden light of rationality but there was not even a sliver to be seen. It was as if he was the opposite of The Perceptionist: an animal in human form.

"What you see is an illusion. A désguisement." Germaine stepped forward, jolting me back to my senses. "There is thought inside here. Perhaps too much." He tapped his temple with long fingers.

As he tapped, the rush of emotion moved aside to reveal a glittering mess of consciousness. There was no beautiful pattern like there was when seeing The Perceptionist's mind. This was a chaotic tumble of gold. Germaine tapped one more time and snapped the window to his workings closed. He took another step closer.

Marlowe moved forward as if to stop him, but I put a hand on my friend's sleeve.

"It's alright, Marlowe," I said, the calm of my voice echoing the ease I felt within myself. "There is no danger."

Germaine turned his mouth up in a grin again and cocked his head to one side as if listening for something.

"Hmm, are you sure there's no danger, Michael?" he said in a rough croak. "You've been fooled more than once before."

This time Marlowe did advance, drawing his sword and letting the tip come up to Germaine's throat. The ringing of metal hung in the air.

"How would you know that?" he hissed at Germaine.

Holding his hands up in peace, Germaine spoke quickly.

"I heard you talking, that's all. I hear many things. Like right now." He pulled back his ragged hair and hooked it behind his ear. "Your brain whispers that you think Asmodeus sent me. But you know just as well as I that The Perceptionist wouldn't let that happen so close to The Void."

Marlowe shuffled his feet as if preparing to strike.

"Wait, Marlowe." I said softly. "I think he's here to help us."

The two stood, facing each other, holding their ground. Germaine's purple eyes were spilling over with power, yet he kept still. I watched on, waiting for them to relax of their own accord.

"Look," Germaine said. "We can play this game and pretend that you're in control here, Marlowe, or we can admit who has the real upper-hand."

To prove his point, Germaine leant forward and pressed his neck into Marlowe's sword. Instead of piercing his skin, the blade melted backward, turning to vapour. Instantly, Marlowe roared and charged at Germaine, but before he could get his hands around his neck there was a cracking sound. Marlowe was stopped in his tracks, held by elemental bonds, which Germaine flexed with his mind.

"Stop!" I jumped to my feet.

Before I could do anything, Marlowe let out another cry and a green light splintered out of his mouth, into Germaine's chest. Flying backward, the frail man hit the far wall with a thud. Marlowe advanced quickly, drawing his hand through the air as a new sword appeared from nowhere in his fist. He held the tip to Germaine's throat again.

"Both of you stop!" I repeated.

Germaine began to cackle with insane laughter, holding his sunken belly as he looked up at the towering African. Abruptly, he stopped short and was perfectly composed.

"You've learnt a few tricks, old friend. Please, I do not want to harm you, mon ami," he said. "Although I can't blame you for wanting to hurt me, after what I did."

"What?" I said, stepping forward for the first time. "What does that mean?"

Marlowe sheathed his sword slowly, never taking his eyes off Germaine. A flash of pain spread over Marlowe's face, as though he was remembering a past trauma. He gained control of his emotion before clearing his throat and staring stark hatred at the man on the ground. At the look, Germaine recoiled further against the wall, hanging his head and bringing his hands up to cover his ears, like he could hear the African's loathing and wanted to block it out. Without shifting his deadly gaze as much as an inch, Marlowe told me the reason for his savage reaction:

"This beggar tried almost murdered The Perceptionist."

11

GERMAINE SLUMPED ONTO THE GROUND against the wall, relaxing a little now that Marlowe had put his weapon away. I was still trying to process the exchange of power between the both of them. Germaine had controlled the elements. Marlowe had broken their bonds. There was still so much I didn't know. Marlowe's voice interrupted my thoughts.

"Michael, do you recall that Germaine was The Perceptionist's student?" he asked, glaring down at his subject.

"I do."

"Well, he used the lessons bestowed upon him to try to kill his teacher."

Marlowe stalked back to the table, never taking his eyes off Germaine, who remained silent. He picked up his glass of wine again and took a sip. I eased back into my chair, feeling that any immediate threat of them fighting again had passed. I waited patiently for a proper explanation. Marlowe sat down slowly, his eyes glazing over, as though he was gathering a scene in his mind. After a few moments he focused once more on Germaine, shaking his head in disgust. Finding the right words, he began to tell the story of how this strange man had come to Hell.

"I had been with The Perceptionist for nearly a hundred years, guarding his domain, when a man with violet eyes walked casually into Satan's Demise. He was dressed like a French aristocrat from the 18th century, with jewels embroidered into his coat. He seemed so out of place in Hell that I didn't approach him at first. He looked clean. From the building tops I cautiously followed his progress as he made his way steadily toward this alley. When the Barghest arrived I thought he would be consumed. The hellhounds circled him, but he calmly took a flask from inside his coat and sprayed water into their midst. Afraid, they ran away. I understood then that this person was more than he appeared. He knew things that others before him did not.

"I stepped down to confront him. He did not even flinch at my approach. To my surprise he announced confidently that his name was Germaine and he wanted to exchange knowledge with the only being worthy to teach him: The Perceptionist. Naturally I scoffed at his demand, but then I heard my master's whisper fill the air: *let him come.* Over the next few years Germaine took up residence in these rooms. I learned that he was once a famous alchemist who had lived five lifetimes on Earth before being killed by thieves hoping to steal his secrets. Germaine had no special powers, other than the extraordinary knowledge that he held in his head. He was an expert on every subject, from history to music and, of course, alchemy. He could play the violin like The Devil. He told The Perceptionist of the world and of the ways of man on Earth. He spoke about the psychology of humans, how we are motivated by greed and desires, but that we are unique from other animals because we have the will to suppress these traits if we have proper cause. He spoke about jewels and their special properties, how they could bend wills and cause wars. He told how he had cheated death by discovering the elixir of life.

"All this knowledge was a new way of looking at existence that The Perceptionist hadn't contemplated. He was grateful to have Germaine as a companion. However, because Germaine had no ability to see the elements, The Perceptionist could not instruct him on their manipulation. He did not have the power of God in him like you do, Michael."

For the first time Marlowe took his eyes off of our guest and looked at me. He cleared his throat and continued.

"What Germaine lacked in ability, he made up for with ingenuity. He realized that perception is a chemical process as well as a sensual one. He mixed liquids and potions to expand his sight. He ingested substances to grow his ability to hear and see the invisible world. Initially these drugs helped him. The elements became clear and, because he could sense them, he could manipulate them. His power grew. The elements of air, fire, water and earth bent to his command, then the other molecules of life followed. The Perceptionist was proud of his student. He showed that mere humans could rise above their bodily make-up. That potential was only bound by thought.

Then, the cracks began to show. Germaine would become unresponsive for days at a time, muttering to himself, arguing with nobody. He would then snap out of it and launch back into his teaching, constructing creature bodies, creating souls, searching for the meaning to life. Every now and then he would slip, but he would cover it up saying that he was simply deep in thought.

"One day the hallucinations started: he began shouting and throwing things. I tried to calm him, but he cast me aside like a doll, saying I was trying to steal his secrets like a common thief, that I was an ally to the demons in the room. But it was just him and me. There were no demons. He would have killed me, but The Perceptionist stopped him. It was a wakeup call to all of us. Germaine was pushing the limits too far. He needed rest. The Perceptionist stopped teaching and looked inside Germaine to find that his own thoughts were being projected back into him as voices from the outside world. He was indeed talking to himself. He just couldn't distinguish that from actual external conversations. It was something not unlike what doctors on Earth today term Schizophrenia.

"Deciding he could find a cure, Germaine worked on his potions again. He stumbled upon a mix that stopped the voices, but they cut off his ability to sense the elements as well. He was devastated at having lost the precious gift he had gained. He wanted to stop taking his cure, but The Perceptionist wouldn't let him, saying that if he could not control himself, he could not control the universe. Falling into depression, Germaine sat in this kitchen. His will to live faltered. He barely moved, he just scrawled notes on pieces of paper, trying to find a solution that would mean he could keep his wits while still expanding his senses. Nothing he tried worked. Just before he gave up, he found it. If he mixed the dose of his cure with a dose of the chemicals which had made him that way in the first place, he could maintain his powers while suppressing the voices. Or so he told us. Little did we know there was still one malicious voice that broke through the wall: it was the true devil within.

"This voice convinced him that it was real, a keeper of the key to the universe. After all, Germaine hadn't been able to see the elements before and they turned out to be real; why shouldn't this personality be real too? The voice advised him to keep this information quiet, in case The Perceptionist found out and halted his training again. Once more, Germaine manipulated the elements. He wove new terrors that The Perceptionist hadn't thought of before: bonds that shifted out of your grasp when you tried to move them and mutated to seek out your weaknesses. His ideas astounded the both of us. He was a genius. A mad genius. His potent thoughts were beginning to rival the creative ability of The Perceptionist."

I looked at Germaine and he smiled slightly at the compliment. But the change was only brief as he realized the darkest part of the tale was about to come.

"One morning, Germaine came to me, excited." Marlowe went on. "He said he might have found a key to unlock even more potential, but he needed me to go and find something: the Jewels of Blood, he called them.

He said that The Furies in the Necropolis possessed them and that if I sought them out, I'd be able to convince them to give me just one. He mapped out where I needed to go and sent me off. I was just as excited as him to see if new things could be brought into the world. I should have been suspicious. I should have known something was wrong, but my enthusiasm blinded me from asking the obvious questions. His knowledge had always been accurate and he hadn't had a lapse that we knew of in over a year. I barely made it to the outskirts of Satan's Demise when I heard the scream in my mind.

"It was my master. Something was dreadfully wrong. I rushed back, but as I reached the alley a silent force made me pause. It wasn't a voice, but an intuition that said, Be careful. Be silent. With as much stealth as I could gather in my frantic state, I re-entered this kitchen. What I saw was ghastly. Germaine had trapped The Perceptionist in one of his mutating chains. Every time The Perceptionist moved to escape, the wrap that Germaine held him in adapted to hold tighter."

Marlowe looked over to Germaine with death in his eyes. The man just stared back with sorrow. He hung his head as Marlowe resumed with acid on his tongue.

"My master was paralysed on the ground while this monster was cutting out his eyes. One by one, he was amputating The Perceptionist's vision. As he cut each eye out, Germaine sliced his own body with the same dagger and inserted them into his skin. All the while he was saying, Now we can see like you can see. I was overwhelmed with rage. Germaine was so distracted with his surgery that he didn't hear me pull out my blade. I struck with so much anger that I sliced his evil head clean off his neck. As his shocked face bounced at my feet, Germaine's spell was broken and The Perceptionist let out a wail of agony."

Germaine let out of groan of his own from the corner then, as if adding to the story. Marlowe paid him no attention. He now had his gaze fixed on mine.

"I had to pluck the eyes out of Germaine and put them back where they belonged. The Perceptionist healed slowly and we contemplated what to do with Germaine's head and body, which I kept separated so he couldn't re-form and attack again. I wanted to burn him and scatter him to the winds, but The Perceptionist couldn't do it. He needed to know why his student had turned on him. We pieced Germaine back together and watched him regenerate. It is the curse and the gift of Hell that our bodies can do this. The screams were like music to my ears. I hated him for hurting the one I had sworn to protect. But then the screams turned to whimpers as he realized what he had done.

"Germaine confessed about the voices. He apologised. He wept. And then *the voice* began to speak for him. It was as though its personality had possessed him. It told of its plan to overthrow Germaine's body and laughed; it was going to rule the universe with a fist of blood. That's when The Perceptionist reached out and found the thread of thought that made his student into a puppet. He tore it out and ripped it apart. Germaine's brain began to collapse; the voice had been a part of him, after all. All the voices, every thought he had ever had, turned in on him. I never thought I could feel sorry for Germaine after what he had done, but in that moment I pitied him. He was devoured by his own ideas, and the purple light that had shone so brightly in his eyes went out. He was gone.

"The Perceptionist tried for decades to revive him, but could not. He said that too many doors had been thrown up against the outside world that could never be reopened. He gave up, and left Germaine there to remind himself to never take on another student. To never interfere with Creation again."

Marlowe stopped, letting out a sigh. He reached out for the wine bottle, but it was empty. Again he looked over to Germaine.

"I don't know how you found your way out, Germaine, but I'll be damned if I ever trust you again. Time might have helped me forgive your actions, but I cannot forget them."

I sat back in my chair, looking from my friend to the man in the corner who was barely a bag of skin and bones. His eyes told me everything I needed to know. They told me that he was powerful and dangerous. But they also showed me he had control, for now.

"Nor should you forget," Germaine said, frowning. "We must remember the mistakes of the past or we learn nothing. I was wrong and I know it."

Marlowe stirred, but I halted him with a glance. I wanted to hear what Germaine had to say. I signalled for him to continue. He propped himself up a bit straighter against the wall and then pressed on.

"I have had a long time to dwell in my mind and sort the lies from the facts, the true voices from the faux one. They seemed so real, but in the end I discovered that the only voice in there was my own. As much as I didn't want to take responsibility for these thoughts, where else could they come from but inside of me? I have always had a particular way of thinking. It's hard to explain, but I have always looked at the world as an obstacle. It was how I knew that the voices were mine. They talked about conquest and dominating what can't be controlled. They never spoke about anything new, not in all the time I was in there. All that time I ran away and they called after me. I am sorry Marlowe. I was erroné." He looked at the African with pleading eyes. "I was trapped inside that embrace of madness, fighting against the evil. At first all I could do was shut them out; I created a maze of emotion in my mind to separate off the insanity. I burrowed inside myself and hid there. But now I have conquered the voices that wanted to conquer me. They have no sway over me anymore."

"How?" I asked.

"Your voice was the first true voice I had heard in a long time, Michael. That first time you came here with the Prophet Phineus it echoed inside me."

I looked at him, probing too see if he was telling the truth.

"Oh yes, I'm being honest," he nodded quickly. "Your puissance roused me. Even then, before you knew who you really were, I could feel it. It sang through my skin and penetrated to the middle of the labyrinth in which I hid. The vibration of your energy was like a signal to me. It showed me that the outside world was still there waiting. I could feel your sway, even after you left. Power is attracted by power. Ever since then, I have used that connection to feel my way out, using it as a guide to come back to the surface. Now I am here and I want to make amends. I want to redeem myself. I can help you achieve what you want. The knowledge I have can help you."

"Why should we trust you?" I asked.

"Because I know more than anyone what it's like to be trapped and I want the same thing as you do: freedom. I don't want to dominate. I want to let things go."

I looked to Marlowe, who shook his head with dark eyes. There was only one way to find out for sure. I walked over to Germaine and leant down. Placing my hands on either side of his head, I said "let me in."

Closing his eyes, Germaine opened the gates, and a terrible crash of thoughts welled up into me. In flashes, what Marlowe had told me came to life in vivid detail. Screaming commands to do others harm shouted in my ears. Pleading whispers to kill myself hissed through my veins. Sweating, I dug deeper, through hate and anger and confusion. Twisting through the chaos I finally found what I was looking for: the calm centre. The truth to who Germaine was. I found hope.

Please, his steady voice said with conviction. *Let me build your bodies for you. Let me show you I can be the man I once was.*

Letting my hands fall limp, I fell backwards. Germaine gazed at me steadily. Marlowe rushed next to me, propping me up.

"Michael? Are you there?" he said with deep concern.

"Yes," I answered. "We both are. It is not comfortable inside his mind, but he is sane. I believe Germaine is with us."

"Are you sure? Are you sure he is in control?" Marlowe asked.

"No," I admitted.

I had entered others' heads before: Judas' and Smithy's. This time was different, though. It was not cohesive or ordered. Germaine's insides were a knotted jumble that only the owner could truly find his way around. I knew that deep down he was a kind soul, but layers of filth were streaked all over. I would have to be careful that this tainted side didn't creep into dominance again. At least he knew that he was at risk of losing it as well. Somehow it made me feel better.

"We must have faith in some things if we're to overcome the faith of others," I said to them both. "I choose to rely on people. We have to give people the opportunity to be better than they were. Otherwise we are just like Asmodeus."

Marlowe did not seem convinced, but he helped me to my feet before assisting Germaine to his.

"You can help us, Germaine," I said. "And I will help you in return. I can help keep the voices at bay. We will get you to realize your full potential."

"Thank you," he replied. "The best thing for me is to stay busy. So let us start gathering the things we need."

I looked at him quizzically. I had not expected him to need anything but the elements.

"There is only one type of thing I actually require," he smiled. "We need go to The Furies and find the Jewels of Blood."

12

MARLOWE'S CHAIR CLATTERED TO THE ground as he leapt to his feet and drew his sword.

"You really are insane if you think I'm going to fall for the same trick again." Marlowe said icily.

I could see the anger that he had been holding back burst through his normally cool demeanour. Germaine stood as still as a post, his purple eyes steady on mine.

"Michael, it is not a myth. The Jewels of Blood are not something I made up."

"You're out of your mind," Marlowe cut in.

"I have never been so clear," Germaine snapped. "I might have been tainted back then, but I tell you, this is the only way."

I held out my hand and covered the tip of Marlowe's blade with my fingers. Watching Germaine to see if I could perceive any deception, I probed into him. I listened. There was nothing but him in there. No other voices echoed out to me.

"How, Germaine?" I asked, content that he was indeed telling the truth. "Why do we need these jewels?"

He looked to Marlowe who was still shaking with rage. The African's whole body was tensed into a ball of death, ready to strike.

"I can build bodies without them, but we would be powerless inside them once we get to Heaven. You, Michael, would still have your gift. Yours is built into your soul, but not the rest of us. The ethereal bodies we are in now can be manipulated. I was able to take elixirs to help my perception here in Hell and I still went mad. A body of true earthy flesh could never heal from that. It could never regenerate. Without this you would be leading a pack of lambs to slaughter. You need troops who can withstand Asmodeus' forces on an even plain, not be torn apart like bread and sent screaming back to Hell."

I turned his words over in my head. He was right that we had to keep our souls encased in flesh when we entered Heaven. To change that would simply have us sucked through the filters of sin and returned to Damnation. Still the plan had holes, ones that needed to be filled. Mary said she might know a way to help us ascend to Heaven. There was one other question at the forefront my thinking, however.

"How would these jewels help us?"

Germaine licked his cracked lips and shot a glance at Marlowe, who held his sword firm.

"They are made from the bloody tears of The Furies, who are primordial Goddesses," he explained in a rush of words. "You might have heard them called the Erinyes as well. The Furies were created when the world was new. They were formed accidently from the pure blood of God, before he split his soul. Their female forms bubbled up from God's softer side, but their hearts were hard as stone. The story has been twisted into Roman and Greek mythology. They are patrons of female revenge. What I believe is true in these myths is that when these Furies cry, the essence of what makes them powerful seeps out in their tears – the Jewels of Blood. It weakens them greatly, so they hoard the Jewels. They ingest them again to regain their strength. If we can tease out just a handful of drops I can make some of us part gods, like you."

"If their blood would work, then why not mine?" I pressed him, needing to be sure.

"Like I said, your power is in your soul. Your blood has traces, yes, but you are still part human. Any strands of the element needed that I could siphon out would just weaken you and then be diluted further inside the others."

"And if we got these jewels, we could make stronger bodies for all the souls in Hell?"

Germaine let out a half-cackle before stopping himself.

"No, you misunderstand. We can gather enough for a small force, maybe five or six of us. With that many we at least stand a chance at overpowering Asmodeus long enough to break down the walls between Heaven and Hell."

"How?" Marlowe cut in.

"I have no idea," Germaine replied evenly. "That is for Michael to show us. The bodies are what he needs me for."

I held my breath, sifting through the ideas that were flooding my brain. There were possibilities, but the path wasn't clear. Deep from within I felt a shift inside. A warmth spread through me. My intuition told me Germaine was right. Action was needed to move us forward and this course would help our momentum.

"Marlowe," I said with authority. "Put away your sword. We need to go and speak with Mary."

13

MARLOWE, GERMAINE AND I FLEW OVER Hell in a triangle formation. I was the spearhead at the front, holding the other two with a wrap of elements, pushing us through the sky. Germaine said he could fly on his own, but I needed him to save his strength. I was still wary that letting him tap into his powers would draw him toward the tainted side of his personality. I didn't want to risk that for mere flight. I would only do so for our attack.

The darkened buildings of Satan's Demise faded beneath us and the glow of Smoking Gun shone ahead. The beacon of sin rose up in all its hideous glory. Zipping through the concrete skyscrapers and over casinos, I darted toward Magdalene's Mansion. Seeing the red glass building up ahead, I began to slow. Far below, people milled like scurrying ants. Cars sped around each other on the lawless roads. It was curious to me that, despite all these souls having eternity to live their lives, they still rushed around in a daily hustle. Old habits died hard.

Skimming up towards the rooftop of Mary's, I set us down gently. Two familiar demons stood sentry at the door that led down into Hell's largest brothel. The first was Forneus, a blue lust demon whose body had weeping sores from head to toe. The other was deep orange with a drooping potbelly and bulbous head as wide as his gargantuan stomach. From even this short distance he looked like a deformed hourglass with legs.

"It's good to see you, Wharton," I raised my hand in greeting. His fat face split into a grin at being addressed by name. "You too, Forneus," I nodded.

"Greetings, Lord Michael," Wharton said in a deep baritone voice. His triple chin wobbled as he spoke. "I assume you've come to see Madam Magdalene."

"Yes. These are my friends Germaine and Marlowe," I said, motioning to the men who stood silently at my back. "Is she here?"

"She has been in The Chamber of Maps all day," Wharton confirmed. "I can take you down."

Forneus turned and opened the door, but stayed at his post as Wharton led us down some stairs, into the cool halls of lust that were Magdalene's Mansion. This high up, there weren't any pleasure rooms, just a bright corridor leading to an ornate gold lift. The four of us gathered inside its roomy interior and Wharton pressed a button with an eye symbol on it. Without thinking, I pressed the ground floor as well. I stared at the glowing 'G' for a few moments.

"Marlowe, I need you to please go with Germaine down to reception," I said finally, turning to my African companion. "There will be a woman on reception called Oba; please ask her to summon the pilot called Smithy, my wife Charlotte, and the demon called Clytemnestra. Once they arrive I'll ask you to make the proper introductions before coming to find us. You met Smithy with me once before and Charlotte will know who you are already," I added, remembering that she held my memories. "You'll have to explain about Germaine, though."

Germaine cleared his throat. "If you don't mind, I will explain myself."

"So, you can tell lies?" Marlowe scowled, puffing his chest out to assert his dominance. He was the perfect person to watch over Germaine. He would never let his guard down in trust, as I might.

"So I can tell *my* truth," the powerful alchemist next to me snapped.

Wharton shuffled his feet with uncertainly, his eyes firmly planted on the ground. I suppressed a thankful sigh and took on the demeanour of leadership.

"You'll both do as I say." I stared them down. "Marlowe, you will introduce Germaine as an ally and he will tell his story. You'll be there to make sure he doesn't embellish anything. Understood?"

They both nodded. "Wharton," I said loudly.

The glutton demon jumped at the mention of his name. He looked up with fear on his face. The elevator slowed to a halt and opened up into a marble corridor. This was my stop.

"You'll go with them too and make sure Oba gives them the help they need."

"Yes, sir." Fat wobbled all over his body as he nodded his head furiously.

"Good. I want all of this done quickly. Don't keep me waiting." I left the elevator and let the doors close behind me without looking back. Hearing the lift starting to descend again, I felt myself relax a little. Being a leader still didn't sit well with me. I struggled telling people what to do.

Yet, this was my duty, and duty was never about doing what you wanted. It was about doing what was needed. Even if I didn't feel like it inside, I had to project an aura of untold strength and constant certainty. At times I was even beginning to believe myself.

Turning to the left, I looked up. Ahead was a golden door with a sculpture of the circular eye of the universe above it. Wharton had called this place The Chamber of Maps. I simply knew it as Mary's map room. Wharton's name for it was more fitting for the stunning feat of engineering I knew I was about to walk into. Striding forward, I came to the door quickly. To the side of it were the stone steps that Judas, Mary and I had come down the first time I had entered here. The memory sent a pang of pain through me. Judas. He was still frozen in a constant state of sleep for helping me. How many others would suffer a similar fate or worse? Their souls weighed on my shoulders. Soon, I would be able to lift them off and send them to Heaven. First, I needed to know how we would get there.

Without further hesitation I pushed open the doors and entered a micro-universe. A perfect replica of the Earth revolved in front of me. Its green and blue surface, shadowed by swirling white clouds, curved upward ten feet into the air. The southern hemisphere sunk below into the clear glass floor. Above, the Heavens shone in their infinite beauty; stars and rainbow nebulae twinkled right up beyond sight. Bridges of silver light spread through the expanse that represented our eternal goal, like spirit laneways holding the answer to existence. Hell was at my feet as I walked inside. With each step, it churned below in its black and red anger. Mary sat cross-legged at the base of Earth, where the equator fed into the floor. She had her head buried in a large bible and was reading intently.

"It's nice to see you have removed the grey of Purgatory here as well," I called, to let her know that I had arrived.

Paying me little attention, she held up her hand for silence. I walked to her side and stood above her, waiting, a little annoyed at her dismissal of me. Without looking up from the book, she read aloud to me:

"And Jesus said unto them, 'It is not for you to know times or seasons, which the Father has set within His own authority. But ye shall receive power, when the Holy Spirit is come upon you: and ye shall be my witnesses both in Jerusalem, and in all Judaea and Samaria, and unto the uttermost part of the earth.' And when he had said these things, as they were looking, he was taken up; and a cloud received him out of their sight. And while they were looking steadfastly into heaven as he went, behold, two men stood by them in white apparel; who also said, 'Ye men of Galilee, why stand ye looking into heaven? This Jesus, who was received up from you into heaven shall so come in like manner as ye beheld him going into heaven.'

Then the disciples returned they unto Jerusalem from the mount called Olivet, which is nigh unto Jerusalem, a Sabbath day's journey off."

"The Ascension of Jesus?" I asked her, knowing from my schooling that this was a passage from the bible that told of how Jesus rose from his grave after his crucifixion and went up to Heaven forty days later.

"I was there." She looked up, her emerald eyes full of certainty. "It's exactly how it says it happened. We were at the Mount of Olives and Jesus was taken to Heaven in human form. He was still flesh, Michael. This was after he'd resurrected himself back into human form."

"And you think we might be able to follow in his footsteps? Go to Heaven from Earth in our bodies?" I asked, with hope rising inside me.

"I think so. The 'men in white' who appeared after he left were angels. They said when he returned to Earth he would come the same way. Why else would he have to return in the same spot unless it was a dedicated pathway between realms?"

I sat down next her, gripping her arm excitedly.

"Are you sure? If you were there, why did you need a bible to remind you?"

"Because of this," she said flipping the pages toward the beginning of the book in her lap. "I thought I had read about another reference of a ladder to Paradise. I was right. Listen:

'Jacob left Beersheba and set out for Haran. When he reached a certain place, he stopped for the night because the sun had set. Taking one of the stones there, he put it under his head and lay down to sleep. He had a dream in which he saw a stairway resting on the earth, with its top reaching to heaven, and the angels of God were ascending and descending on it.'"

Mary looked up with fervor in her eyes, then read on. "There above it stood the Lord, and he said:

"I am the Lord, the God of your father Abraham and the God of Isaac. I will give you and your descendants the land on which you are lying. Your descendants will be like the dust of the earth. You will spread out to the west and to the east, to the north and to the south. All peoples on earth will be blessed through you and your offspring. I will watch over you wherever you go, and I will bring you back to this land. I will not leave you until I have done what I have promised you." When Jacob awoke, he thought, "Surely the Lord is in this place, and I was not aware of it." He was afraid and said, "How awesome is this place! This is none other than the house of God; this is the gate of Heaven!"

48

* * *

Mary snapped the book shut as an exclamation point to the sentence. She raised her hand and touched the giant globe next to us with her fingertips. It twisted on its axis with a rush of wind. Land masses spun before us. Clouds parted and the Middle East came into view. The Earth expanded to rise before us, revealing an aerial view of modern day Jerusalem. Our vision swept down even further, to a circular courtyard with tall, brick walls of grey and white blocks. In the middle was an octagonal building made of the same stone. It had a domed roof and, on each of the eight walls, was an archway. Each arch was filled in with stone, except for one.

"This is the Aedicule of The Ascension," Mary said. "It marks the bottom of Jacob's Ladder. Our pathway to the gates of Heaven."

I stared at the globe in awe. Our future was mapped out right in front of me. This was our destiny. My mind spiraled into thoughts and possibilities, but I wrestled it back to the moment. We had to take this one step at a time. Germaine would help resurrect us to Earth and we would climb up further on this ladder to meet Asmodeus.

"And where would we rise up to Earth?" I questioned.

Mary flipped her fingers in the air and the globe shifted again slightly. It came to the very bottom of Greece, on the edge of the Mediterranean Sea.

"The closest Hellmouth is in a cave at Taenarum. It's at the bottom of Cape Matapan. From there it's a short journey across the sea to where we can land on the shores of Israel. It won't be easy entering what is basically a perennial war zone, but it won't be the hardest part of our journey."

My eyes were drawn back to the point of the Aedicule of Ascension and then to the glowing Mary. She had found our path and I had found a way get to it. I wanted to spill out our plan to her, but instead I just took her hand and squeezed it in solemn appreciation. A smile split her face at the touch. Her fingers wrapped around mine and held my hand in her lap. Wavy curls of red hair draped around her alabaster skin. She was a vision. In another world we might have been more than friends, but in this life that could never be. I was content with that; Charlotte was all the love I could ever desire, but I could see in Mary's eyes that she ached for more. Her eyes – her bottomless, green eyes – I lost myself inside them. They were oceans of jade passion, her pupils black like obsidian. She smelt of jasmine flowers; the scent was intoxicating.

"Michael!"

Charlotte's voice jerked me back into the moment. Mary's grip on my palm loosened and she leant back, smiling as my wife entered to room. Smithy, Germaine, Marlowe and Clytemnestra followed her.

"Lotte," I said, looking up, momentarily confused.

"I'm so glad you're all here," Mary said, standing. "I was just telling Michael that I've found a way we can move from Earth to Heaven in bodily form."

Lotte's eyes narrowed for a moment on Mary, before Smithy moved between them and came to shake my hand.

"That's brilliant, just brilliant!" he said with glee. "And we will have bodies, thanks to our new friends here! We should have some cups of tea to celebrate."

"Germaine told you already?" I asked, letting go of Smithy's hand and sweeping in to hug my wife.

I kissed her on the lips and held her tight. Any accusation she held in her eyes melted at our touch. I held her close to me with one arm and nodded my hellos to the others. Clytemnestra had a concerned look on her face. Stress lines crowed out from the corners of her eyes and her mouth was pursed tightly. I looked at her questioningly, but Mary interrupted me before I could ask what was wrong.

"How are you going to make the bodies?" she asked.

Germaine stepped forward. His scraggly appearance made him look unhinged, but his gaze was clear. He reached out a bony hand to Mary. She offered hers and Germaine bowed to touch his lips gently to her skin.

"Miss Magdalene," he said in a honeyed tone. "I apologize for my state of dress. I haven't had time to gather proper attire. My name is Germaine and I am a fellow pupil of The Perceptionist's. I am at Michael's service and yours."

"He will build our earthly vessels for us," I offered.

"Yes, but first we must find the secret ingredient," Germaine added.

Mary raised her eyebrow at me, seemingly unsure what to make of all this, yet keeping her cool composure.

"And what is that?"

I explained the details of why we needed the Jewels of Blood. Mary listened quietly. Lotte still clung to my side while the others gathered close to listen to the story again. Smithy smiled along with the details as if I was telling a bedtime story.

"We just need to figure out how to find them," I finished. "Germaine knows where The Furies live."

"Actually, I'm not sure that information is still current," Germaine said, looking sheepish.

"I know." Clytemnestra stepped forward. The look of worry in her face had fallen away and was now replaced with a fierce determination. "They live in the underground Necropolis. If it means we will destroy that liar Asmodeus, then I will face them again."

"Again?" Smithy and I asked at the same time.

The others looked on, waiting for the response. Clytemnestra's face dropped momentarily, but she regained her steely look and reached up to the tight bun of hair at the back of her head. In one swift movement, she pulled the dagger that held it together and slid it free. Black waves of shiny hair swished down around her neck and face. Through the curly mess she peered out and held the dagger forward, hilt first.

"They are the reason I am in Hell. This is the weapon they gave me to murder my son."

14

LOTTE GASPED next to me at Clytemnestra's macabre pronouncement. She had murdered her own son? There was silence in the Chamber of Maps as the Earth revolved slowly next to us.

"Don't you all look at me with judgment in your eyes," Clytemnestra said in her low growl. "You're all in Hell for a reason. I am no worse than you."

"But your son?" I asked horrified. "How? Why?"

Regret dimmed Clytemnestra's glare, but she clenched her jaw.

"I killed my husband as well."

This time I let out a gasp. This was someone in my council from whom I took advice. I had given her control of Hell. She must have seen scorn in my face, because she suddenly looked afraid.

"My Lord, please. You of all people cannot condemn me. You're the only man who has given me trust in all my days. Will you at least try to understand?"

I thought for a moment, frozen. How could I justify a crime like that? There was only one way. I had to live her memories. No. If all of us were to trust her, then we must all see what she'd done. Only with perfect understanding could you look beyond good and evil and see acts without judgment.

"Very well," I said stepping forward. "Will you open up your mind to us? Will you let us know what you have known?"

She looked tentative. The dagger stood rigid in her grasp. Her knuckles turned to white, she was holding it so hard. Drops of blood escaped from beneath her fingers. She looked me in the eyes and nodded.

"Everyone," I said, looking around, "stand back. We are about to enter Clytemnestra's world."

I held the hilt of the dagger with one hand and put my other over her bleeding fist as our companions stepped back to form a loose circle around us. Channeling the correct elements in a blast of light into us, I delved into her mind. Spinning downward, I was drawn into a lucid scene. It was as if I was an omniscient presence, seeing all as a third person, but knowing and feeling all of Clytemnestra's senses. I projected the vision out of me, so it became real for everyone else to see too.

Clytemnestra lay in wait with blood thumping in her ears, hidden behind a marble column. She could barely hear the splashing water of the bathhouse, or the giggles of her husband's whore as they echoed off the marble walls. Throbbing hatred pounded through her body.

Inching around so she could see them, Clytemnestra pushed her black hair out of her eyes. The chamber was empty aside from the two lovers, who were careless in their lust. The sight of the pair almost made her lose control. They gasped in a writhing embrace, clutching at each other in the rose-petal water, their slick skin glistening in the candlelight. Both were smiling, while all Clytemnestra felt was pain. It wasn't that they were naked together. Jealousy played no part in this. An older and deeper wound ached inside her. The need for revenge was hotter now than it had been, even ten years after it had happened. The sore had now festered to be an all-consuming fever.

Almost a decade before, her husband, Agamemnon, had left for war. He was Commander of the mighty Greek armies and King of Argos. His power was only matched by his ruthlessness in battle. Before he had sailed away with the legions, he had committed a crime that no mother could forgive. To make the winds blow true and take their warships to Troy, Agamemnon had offered a sacrifice to the gods: their virgin daughter, Iphigenia. While the blood of that sweet girl had congealed on the sands of Aulis, the brute had left to spill even more innocent life.

In the years that followed, Clytemnestra was almost driven mad. The grief she felt at losing her precious one had tipped her toward the abyss of insanity. The only thing that held her together was the thought of revenge. Every day she had prayed that her husband would be safe. She wanted him unharmed, so she could be the one to slide the steel in his heart. Every waking moment was spent dreaming of this day of reckoning. In his absence she had managed their kingdom with a cold hand. She closed herself off from any new love. She had taken a partner to satisfy her sexual needs, but she never let any happiness into her heart. Even Clytemnestra's remaining two children: her son Orestes and daughter Electra, became strangers. She never said it aloud, but every time she looked at them, they reminded her of that day. Both had their father's eyes. Eventually she had sent them away, to be schooled in another city.

Now the day of reckoning had come. Agamemnon had returned, victorious. With great fanfare he had reclaimed his rightful throne next to his wife.

He had greeted her as though nothing untoward had passed between them. Clytemnestra played her role while the wheels of vengeance turned behind her glassy eyes. She had stepped aside, as was her duty, and pretended that all was forgotten. As if she could ever forget. His silence on his deeds made her even more furious.

Agamemnon had not come back alone, either. As part of the spoils of war he had taken a concubine, Cassandra. She whispered in his ear constantly and shot smirking glances at the ice queen of Argos. The further insult provided a bitter righteousness to Clytemnestra's thoughts.

A squeal of pleasure brought Clytemnestra out of her brooding. Her eyes narrowed in focus, as if she was only now seeing her prey properly. The axe felt like nothing in her hands. It was an extension of her body. Picking up the fisherman's net that lay at her feet, she waited a few more pounding heartbeats. It was time.

Rushing out from behind the column, Clytemnestra let her instruments of death be her voice. Agamemnon let out a cry of surprise and the net was cast over them. The naked lovers squirmed to free themselves in a splashing tangle, but it only served to ensnare them further. Clytemnestra brought the axe down with a cold smile on her face. Again and again she chopped, not uttering a noise, except for the occasional grunt of exertion when blade struck bone and she had to wrench it out again. The act of murder was finished in seconds, but Clytemnestra continued to strike at their bodies like a crazed woodswoman. Only when a finger floated to the surface did she pause in curiosity. It was her husband's. A gold wedding band was still wedged on it. Bobbing in a sea of red was the severed stump of their original union. It was finally over.

****

Clytemnestra sat on the throne next to her lover, the new King of Argos. Today was a day of audience, where the rulers listened to the people and helped resolve their disputes. A larger crowd than normal had gathered to see the royal couple who had married just weeks after the unexplained demise of Agamemnon. Rumors of how Clytemnestra had killed her former husband were rife in the palace, yet no one challenged her directly. The righteousness she had felt in her actions had quickly melted into sorrow. The murder had not brought her precious Iphigenia back; it had only made the painful memory rise afresh to the surface. She slumped in her seat now, lost in her thoughts, barely hearing what the people had to say.

The new King handled most of them with barely concealed indifference. One by one he resolved their petty problems and sent them on their way. It was only when he raised his voice in surprised anger that Clytemnestra lifted her head to see what the commotion was about. Her heart froze. It couldn't be. Agamemnon stood before *them with a sword is his hand and hate on his face. A hooded cloak lay crumpled on the ground next to him. Twenty soldiers stood in support at his back. How had this happened? From where had he appeared? He was dead!*

The roar of confusion in Clytemnestra's head was matched by the clamor at her side. Her lover was on his feet, yelling, gathering his own soldiers to his side.

"Your father is buried, Orestes. He passed away in his sleep. You have no claim to the throne. Your mother has married me!"

Orestes? The fog of disorientation cleared and Clytemnestra realized what was happening. This wasn't her dead husband. It was her son. He was the exact image of his violent father the day he had gone to war. He had come to claim his birthright. He looked at her with familiar eyes and mouthed the words.

"Mother. Did you do what the people are saying? Did you slay our king? My father?"

The accusation, spoken with such venom, made her hackles rise. The indignity of all that had happened to her, boiled again to the surface. This man had no right to judge her decision. He might be her son, but he didn't know her. He didn't know anything. She had done what she had for his sister. She had revenged a girl in a society that prized men over women. Clytemnestra couldn't explain that Agamemnon deserved to die. How could she justify it to a world that automatically leant more weight to the father than the mother?

Clytemnestra stood in anger. She stepped down from her place on the throne to stalk into the middle of the stand off. Ripping the bodice of her dress, she exposed her chest to her son. The soldiers murmured at the insane display. She came to stand toe to toe with Orestes, who watched her actions in horror. Spitting with fury, her rage spewed out of her mouth.

"I sacrificed that murderer like the animal he was. If it's a crime to kill a beast, then find me guilty. Stab me through the heart, as he did Iphigenia. But know that if you take my life, you will pay for your actions."

Orestes' face fell at her words. He looked into her eyes with regret, before his face turned hard.

"I cannot let a traitor to the throne live. Go to your grave in peace, Mother."

"There is no such thing as peace!" she screamed, as the sword sliced into her breast.

Clytemnestra's eyes faded to black as she watched her son's soldiers swarm over the King's guard. The smell of death filled her nostrils, as it had too many times before.

****

The taste of metallic blood splattered onto Clytemnestra's lips. An angelic woman bent over her, crying red tears that fell into her open mouth. The liquid fed strength and energy through her limbs. Clytemnestra sat up. The scene around her was a black and white battle, swirling in silent violence. She could see in slow motion the wispy form of Orestes making her lover kneel, before he sliced his head clean off. Dark floods of death spilled on the floor. It all happened in a noiseless, far off reality, that was still somehow all around her.

"Sister," the angel at her side said, putting a hand on her face. "We are here to grant your wish."

Two other angels came into view, dressed in robes of red. They had beautiful faces, but their eyes were bloody crimson, not just the irises: the entire eye. They smiled with pointed rows of white teeth, framed by black gums.

"You have been scorned by man, who has seen you as weak. You rose up to fight him and won, only to be pushed back down by none other than your own son. Do you want to show the world that a woman is worth more that?"

Clytemnestra turned back to the ethereal battle around her. Soldiers sliced at each other. They killed and stabbed and hurt. An eye for an eye. A tooth for a tooth. They were tearing each other apart. If she stepped in, maybe she could stop it. Women could do better than this.

"Take this dagger," the angel said, holding out a silver blade. "Pierce man's heart with it and drink his blood. With this power inside you, you will live forever and throw down the patriarchy that enslaves us. Have your revenge."

"Who are you?" Clytemnestra asked in a daze.

"Some call us The Erinyes. Others, The Furies. We are the answer to your prayers. You asked us with your soul to make right was has been wronged. We are here to answer that call."

The angel pressed the hilt of the dagger into Clytemnestra's palm. The metal was warm in her hands. As she gripped the handle tighter, it began to grow hot. The temperature flooded up her arms as she got to her feet. Her anger came back. Color returned to the world and everything spun into furious motion. Steel rang upon steel and cries of war echoed around the room.

Suddenly, Orestes was right before her. He turned his head and stopped. Surprise sparked in his eyes. Before he could react, Clytemnestra thrust her dagger through his chest. Blood trickled out of his mouth and down his neck. The noises of the battle stopped as the soldiers turned in wonder.

Clytemnestra watched the red life seep from her son. The only sound was him choking. His eyes looked up questioningly as he flailed to grasp at the dagger in his heart.

"Now drink," a voice whispered in her ears. "Drink his blood and live again."

But Clytemnestra could not drink. All she could do was watch, as she saw another one of her children die. In her haste and hate she had become just like the man she had despised so much. She had sacrificed her baby, and for what? Life? The power of violence and destruction?

This was not the way, she thought.

Looking up she saw the three Furies watching on, waiting for her to do her part. She shook her head at them and in one swift movement slid the dagger from Orestes body and plunged it into her own. The screaming rage of her angels was the last thing she heard before Hell.

The grinning face of Asmodeus stared down at Clytemnestra.

"I could use a woman like you," he said. "Together we can work towards a better future."

The deceit of his words should have been apparent, but, after so much darkness, Clytemnestra allowed herself to hope that the truth had finally arrived.

I was bowed on one knee as the scene dissipated. Clytemnestra cried on the ground in front of me with renewed grief. I placed my hand over her face to calm her.

"The truth has arrived, Clytemnestra," I said. "It has just taken longer than you thought. You have known sorrow and anger like all of us. You have made bitter choices, but I can't blame you for doing what you did. I know that you want to make amends."

Her crying quieted to a low sobbing. The others watched in silence. Tearing my eyes from this powerful woman, I looked up to the other great females in my life. Mary and Charlotte both stood unwavering.

"Both of you will come with us to The Furies," I said. "I think more than one man could be unwise. Are you ready?"

"Yes," they all said, as one.

15

MARY, CHARLOTTE AND CLYTEMNESTRA stood with me at the mouth of a narrow black cave. Teeth of rock speared up in front of us, making the entry tight and menacing. A howling of souls blew up from inside. I could feel the haunting breeze on my face. It wasn't hot like the rest of Hell's air. It was cool and damp. The sound, which came up with the wind, was like the terrible wailing of someone who had lost everything. I knew the sound well. It had issued from my lips when Asmodeus had first torn Charlotte away from me. The memory sent shivers down my spine. I reached out to feel my wife's arm, just to make sure she was still there.

"This is it," Clytemnestra said. "The Necropolis has been a secret refuge for the females of Hell since time began. Those who don't want to live on the surface come down here under the protection of The Furies. I'm not sure how they will react to your presence, Michael."

"I'm not going to let any of you walk into possible danger without putting myself on the line as well," I said. "Surely they will respect that."

"We'll see," she said, stepping forward to squeeze into the cave. Mary quickly moved in behind her, as bold as ever. Charlotte next. Finally, I pushed my way into the interior, sliding through feet first. My heels came down onto soft dirt. Using some elements of light, I illuminated the cave. We were crowded into a small antechamber of black rock. Ahead was a head-high tunnel, burrowed down steeply into the earth. The walls of the tunnel glowed softly with a green light. Stepping toward the source of the glow, I could see it came from a fuzzy moss which covered the cave. It seemed to grow thicker and brighter further down. Without a word, Clytemnestra moved past me, into the passageway. With her in the lead, we marched in single file downward. There were no twists, no turns: just one long corridor heading directly down. The noise of melancholy cries echoed constantly around.

It wasn't long before I saw where the cries were coming from. Every three feet along the passage, small were shelves cut into the cave walls. Placed on each one was a severed human head. All of them were men. The blood from their necks seeped down the walls, covering the green moss, which cast its unearthly light. The blue lips of their mouths were all open, issuing forth the same horrid wail. Most of the men had soldier's helmets on: some ancient, some new. Many had their eyes sewn closed and their ears hacked off. Others were barely recognizable as heads at all.

"They're a warning," Clytemnestra called back over the noise. "Some fools have been lured by the thought of fresh female souls to rape down here. They never get far, though. The women in the Necropolis are fiercer than you think."

I glanced at one of the faces as I went past. As if my look were a trigger, its dead eyes opened. Inside were bloody sockets, writhing with living veins. The sight made the breath catch in my throat. It reminded me of the eyeless face of the prophet Phineus, before I gave him his sight back.

"They're alive," I said, shocked, before I could stop myself.

Of course they were alive. Nothing truly died in Hell. Charlotte looked to where I was staring and gave a start. The man gazed at me and his cries turned into words.

"Help me; save yourself," he said in a gurgling voice.

I swallowed my fear and moved on, pushing Charlotte along ahead of me. She pressed her hands over her ears. Mary was walking with her eyes trained forward. I didn't blame them.

As we descended, the roof of the tunnel began to get higher. The ghastly sight of the heads became fewer and fewer until there were none at all. The horrible noise faded to eerie silence. The cool breeze still wafted up in our faces. It must have been blowing that awful sound in the opposite direction. The walls eventually splayed out wider and we were able to walk side by side. My thoughts turned to the others back on the surface. I had sent Germaine, Smithy and Marlowe up to Casa Diablo, to begin making preparations for the resurrection. They would also arrange the grounds for my coming public address. I had to placate the souls of Hell once again. At least this time I would have something real to say. We had a plan. Change was coming.

"It's not long now," Clytemnestra said. "When we emerge, we're going to keep walking straight. This is a city in itself, but there are no cars like there are up top. The streets are cleared for walking only. We will head directly to The Mausoleum, in the centre of the city. It's best we hurry and don't talk with anyone." She looked across to us, holding authority in her voice. "Michael, keep your head down. Mary, Charlotte, let's all group around him, so he's at least a little hidden. We don't want to cause a stir before we have to."

Mary turned her face to mine.

"Let's hope that pretty hair of yours makes you fit in," she smirked, trying to lighten the mood as always.

Her comment gave me an idea. Weaving fabric from the elements close to me, I manifested a wide, black scarf. I then wrapped it around my head, concealing my face from view.

Charlotte nodded in approval.

"Remind me to ask you for one in blue when this is finished," she smiled. "Perhaps silk, though."

Before long, the tunnel gave way completely and opened out on a small ridge of rock. There was a pathway to the side, which meant we could amble down to ground level. For now, we paused with our feet at the rooftops, staring across the expanse that was crammed into a gigantic cave. I couldn't see the end, but the sides were within the edge of my vision. Pieces of soiled wood, scraps of metal sheeting and carved rocks had been used to build an extensive slum city, which filled every last inch of space in the cave. I had no idea where they had scrounged any of this stuff from. Perhaps the women brought what they could when they fled here. The result was a mess of recycled materials stacked haphazardly to create small homes, piled over the top of one another, each pressing hard to maintain an illusion of personal space. Right out in the middle of the slum was a white building. It stood out like a gleaming palace amidst the squalor. I knew without being told that this was where we were heading: The Mausoleum.

"Welcome to the Necropolis," Clytemnestra bared her razor teeth at us. "Keep your head down, and make sure you don't step in anything."

16

WE ENTERED THE NECROPOLIS without any greeting or ceremony. Nobody stopped to say hello or ask questions, but I could sense that many eyes were watching us. Women sat or stood along the edges of the streets, which could be better described as passageways, wide enough for two, possibly three people to walk side by side. The shacks of the slum rose up on either side, giving an oppressive feel of being closed in. The smell was intense. Human filth and sweat mixed with the tang of cooking spices. Makeshift awnings hung overhead in odd places, so that at times you had to duck your head to go under them. Fat, black wires sagged from building to building, buzzing with electricity.

My companions crushed against me, like bodyguards protecting a celebrity. We would have drawn attention, had not everyone in the street been forced to bunch up as they bustled past each other. Every corner had some kind of hole-in-the-wall store that sold supplies. Food here. Clothing there. There was a hairdressing salon barely the size of a cupboard. I had thought it was crowded in Hell City. This was another level again. The close quarters made for slow going. We picked our way through the throng and passed an obese hag. The sickly smell of perfume failed to mask the even sicklier smell of rotting flesh on her breath. I did my best to avoid eye contact with anyone, in case they somehow noticed something was amiss.

Like the women pressing into my sides, a growing sense of unease nudged at my skin. I couldn't quite place what it was, but there was something else different about the people here. I snuck glances at them as we moved on, trying to figure out what it was. I passed an elderly Indian woman dressed in an orange sari. I saw her look at Charlotte and nod with a sturdy razor-toothed smile. Another lady, who must have been well over six feet tall, wearing all black leather, flashed the same grin a moment later. That was it! There were no demons here. At least not full ones. At outward appearance, every single woman was... a woman. There were no disfigurements; no different colored skin tones; nothing. The only sign they weren't totally human was their teeth. They were the teeth of The Furies, the same as Clytemnestra's: pointed tips protruding from coal-black gums. Each one of them had a proud look about them as well. Despite their poor surrounds, they held their heads high and their shoulders square. They bore their environment with a sense of dignity, like this was where they had chosen to be. They owned it. I began to take in the faces differently. They weren't necessarily people to be afraid of, unless you tried to take away what they felt they had built and earned. They were just like the souls in Hell, the souls in Purgatory and the souls in Heaven. They simply wanted to feel they belonged somewhere. The difference was, these women did belong here. They embraced their fate. I wondered if I asked them to join our fight, would they laugh and say they didn't need the barriers to come down? I suspected most would just turn their backs and stay with their sisters, as they always had.

Clytemnestra guided us well, leading us around a dogleg and through a short open space. I could see though a gap in the rooftops that we weren't far off our destination. I felt a tug at my arm. Thinking it was Charlotte, I turned my head. A teenage girl, barely eighteen with grey eyes, dark skin and a metal stud in her nose was there instead.

"Would you like to come and look at my jewelry?" she said in a clear voice.

I paused for a moment, before shaking my head slightly and trying to move on. Her grip on my arm tightened.

"Please, ma'am," she said. "It's good quality, I swear." Mary and Charlotte both turned.

"No thanks," Mary said. "We're in a bit of a hurry."

"Are you new here?" the girl narrowed her eyes at her.

"No," Mary said defensively.

"Then smile at me." Now the girl seemed to be getting angry. The pressure of her fingers on my arm grew tighter again.

Clytemnestra stepped forward, flashing her teeth quickly.

"My friend said we're in a hurry," she growled. "We don't have time to shop. I'm sorry to be short, but we must go."

The girl's eyes dropped in deference at Clytemnestra's confident tone. She bobbed in a half curtsy.

"Of course, ma'am," she said apologetically. "Maybe later, then?"

"Yes, perhaps later." Charlotte said quickly, taking my arm out of the girl's grip and steering me away.

I breathed a sigh of relief. It was a helpless feeling not being able to do or say anything, but stay silent and nod. We were just about to delve into another narrow street when the same dark-skinned teenager blocked our path again.

"Look," Clytemnestra said. "I said we don't have time, for…"

"You don't understand," she said, holding out her palm.

"Your silent friend forgot this."

Sitting on her outstretched palm was a plain golden ring.

"Listen, I told don't you we don't want any jewelry," Mary said.

I barely heard her. My eyes were locked on the ring. My heart constricted at the sight of it. Instinctively I ran a thumb over the fingers of my left hand. There was nothing but skin.

"We don't wear wedding rings in the Necropolis," the girl continued in a loud voice, which started to draw attention. "They are a sign of slavery. Why would both her and the blonde one break our traditions?"

People close by stopped at the words. A ripple of murmuring spread out quickly around the crowd and suddenly everybody was looking at our small party.

"How dare you judge two women's love?" Clytemnestra rumbled. "You would think to deny them the right to do what they want? To declare their honor to each other?"

The girl barely paused, before she raised her finger and pointed at me.

"There may be a lot of smells down here that I can't stand. But none is worse than the stench of man!"

The last word was yelled so loud that it reverberated off of the walls around us. Every woman's face was turned to mine. A low hiss started to sound as every one of them peeled back their lips in disgust.

I dropped my scarf down to my shoulders and the hissing turned feral. Clytemnestra pushed my shoulders. "Run!"

17

LIKE AN AMBUSH OF RABID TIGERS, the women descended. Sharp teeth gnashed toward me in a blur of anger. I started to run, but in the small space filled with people it was impossible. My companions tripped over each other in an attempt to flee. In a ball of panicked confusion, they only served to slow us down. A set of incisors sunk into my arm as the teenage jeweler savagely mauled me. I lashed out in pain. A sonic blast swept from my arm. The elements at my call tore into her face and sent her sprawling backwards, bowling over a group of would- be attackers to the ground.

"Get down!" I yelled to Charlotte and the others.

Gathering a force of wind, I sent a cyclone of power ripping away in all directions. The destruction was instant. Teetering homes fell, as pieces of loose sheeting peeled away in the gale. The savage women of the Necropolis howled in rage as they struggled to keep their feet, watching their homes disintegrate. I cut off my attack. I did not come here to demolish their lives; I came for help. If I kept this up, there was no way The Furies would listen to reason. Thinking quickly, I turned back to my friends. Eyeing our path toward The Mausoleum, I pushed a targeted weave of elements forward to clear the way, careful not to touch the buildings on either side. We didn't need an avalanche of rubble on our heads. Still, the bodies of women tumbled to the sides, crashing it walls that rattled menacingly.

"Go!" I waved forward to my friends.

Helping Charlotte and Clytemnestra up as I ran, we rushed in a flurry to the tight alleyway. Mary gasped closely at our heels, a whirl of red hair and terror. Behind her, the deadly women of the city regrouped and began their pursuit. With a curdling scream, a body dropped toward Clytemnestra from the building above. The cry alerted her and she was able to step aside as the girl struck with a mighty slap into the ground. Spreading a thick sheet of air over the top of us, I continued to run. I dare not push the same force field behind, lest I clip the trailing Mary, or lose focus on what was in front. I couldn't risk tearing this place apart, spoiling our future hopes.

Leaping over an upturned cart of vegetables, we hurtled towards our destination. I could see it ahead, the gleaming marble white giving me faith that we might come out of this unscathed. Another woman thudded onto my shield above. From the right, a petite Asian leapt out of a side alley with a knife gripped in her fist. She swung the blade towards Charlotte. Without even breaking stride, my wife blocked the thrust and cracked the woman in the jaw with her other clenched hand. I wanted to yell in triumph, but a scream from behind stopped me. Mary.

Looking back I watched the tall woman in black leather we had seen earlier overtake my friend. The leather-clad Amazon bit hard into Mary's calf, mid-tackle. They rolled forward, scrambling and scratching at one another. I skidded to a halt, ready to go back and save her, but was dragged forward by Clytemnestra.

"If you stop, we're all lost!" she yelled.

I hesitated as two more attackers piled onto Mary, gouging their fangs into her skin. Blood misted into the air, fanning upward with the sound of Mary's pain. She writhed underneath the predators, trying to break free. Her fearful eyes locked onto mine.

"Michael!" she pleaded.

"Michael!" Charlotte's voice echoed, pulling me the other way. Clytemnestra tried to pull me back, but I shook her off.

"No," I spat. "This stops now."

Anger seeped over my vision, pinpointing the heated bodies struggling on top of my friend. I could see the singular being inside each of them. Squeezing on their life forces, I dragged them up, suspending them separately in the air. I could see white lights of souls hurrying in for support, but pushed them all back with my force of will. Booming my voice outward, I made my intention clear.

"If you don't stop, I will end these fiends' existence. I am the Lord of Hell and you will obey my command."

A hush fell over the alley. Movement ceased. Shifting my vision back to normal, I saw a crush of women dripping from every space around. They all eyed me with an equal measure of awe and contempt. I allowed my hold on the souls in my grasp to loosen, dropping them to the ground. The bloody mess that was Mary barely twitched amongst them. My heart cried out in sympathy, but I steeled my resolve.

"Now," I said, breathless. "I have come to see The Furies. Only they can judge my right to be here."

"We have already judged," a trio of voices said behind me.

I turned to behold three fearsome angels, with bloody eyes staring death into me. One held Clytemnestra by the throat. Another had Charlotte. The one in the middle took a step forward. They all oozed with primal, elemental power.

"If you do not bow down immediately, your concubines will know all the wrath of nine hundred thousand women scorned."

18

I GLANCED FROM CLYTEMNESTRA to Charlotte and then to the Fury who stood before me. My companions were held fast by her sisters. The one holding Clytemnestra drew her hostage's dagger out held it to her throat.

"If you do not bow down, I will flay this one's skin off, while you watch. Then I will do the same to your wife."

The tip of the knife glowed with a blue heat. I could see the Fury push some kind of dark energy into it.

My heart told me to kneel immediately, but my pride kept me on my feet.

"I did not come here to fight you," I said through gritted teeth, talking as much to the women surrounding us as to The Furies in front. "I came here to ask for your help."

The hideous laughter all around made it clear how stupid I sounded. I had just wiped out a swathe of their homes and threatened to destroy their souls, and I wanted their help?

The middle Fury stepped toward me and snapped her teeth. I held my ground as she spoke in a guttural voice.

"You come declaring you are the ruler of Hell and that we should obey you. We do not obey men who think they are above us. We do not obey men at all."

She swept her hand down, bringing with it a cascade of atomic weight onto my head. The force should have flattened me into the ground, but I pushed back, using every ounce of talent I could muster to stop it from bending my knees. Those looking on would have seen nothing, yet in the elemental view, I could behold the oldest and most basic of elements crushing from above. Had it not been for the sophistication of The Perceptionist's training, I would have been squashed by its sheer dominance. The Furies did indeed hold a depth of force that was hard to comprehend, but I used delicate weaves to dismantle what was on top of me, so it fell to the side like invisible water. The Furies' faces turned a shade paler, but remained still.

Then I did kneel, needing my action to show I truly meant my words.

"I do not think I am above you. Any of you." I shouted, letting everyone present hear me. "I spoke in anger before, but listen to me now as I speak with a clear head. I am on a path for true equality for all: men, women, lost souls and those who are better off by disposition. We all should have freedom."

The sneer of derision that came out of all three Furies stopped me short.

"Do you truly think we are all equal?" the one who held Charlotte spat.

"He does!" Charlotte said defiantly, from her grasp.

"I was not asking you," The Fury said, jerking back Charlotte's hair so she let out a cry of pain.

I held my anger, looking at the crowd of women first and then staring back at her evenly.

"Yes," I said. "We are all equal."

"Then why don't you let your wife be the ruler?" she answered, shaking Charlotte like a puppet. "Why isn't she the decision maker, then? Why not let her dictate your direction and carry out your plans?"

"Because he is stronger," Clytemnestra spoke in her low growl. "He has the power of God in him."

"God's power?" They all asked in unison, before the middle one continued. "So, if you have more power and you are better than others, then how can you be equal?"

"We are equal in rights," I answered.

The response was met by a murmur from the crowd.

"You are either trying to fool us, or you fool yourself," the middle sister silenced everyone. "Power and rights go hand in hand. You cannot have more power without more right to life. The strong have more and the weak settle for less because they have to. This is how it is and this is how it always has been, no matter how much you deceive yourself."

"That is not true," I said, standing again.

Rather than moving backward at my motion, the entire press of women moved forward slightly. I rose to full height, to show I wasn't afraid.

"I have the strength to take what I want."

With a sweep of my arms I flung a spray of elements outward, pushing The Furies backward and pulling Charlotte and Clytemnestra to my side in a blinding instant. I held the three bloody angels at bay with force for a moment, as a clamor of cries echoed around. Shock at the speed of what I had done spread onto Charlotte's face, which was now next to mine, while Clytemnestra grinned with her razor teeth.

"I have the ability to take, and yet still I ask!" I yelled, releasing my hold on The Furies and dropping to my knees once more. I held out my hands to show I meant no further violence and they paused. Their stillness rippled around through the rest of their fearless subjects.

"Do you really think that brute physical might is the same as true power?" I asked The Furies, but speaking to everyone there. "I need the knowledge of my friends to guide me. I need the passion and kindness of my love. I need the wisdom of age."

Without looking behind me, I lifted the crippled form of Mary out of the pile of bodies that still lay on the ground, using the elements to do my bidding. Sending healing into all of the other women as well, I helped their regeneration, easing the pain of it. The women surrounding us all murmured in surprise as their comrades awoke peacefully and rose. Mary's eyes sparked into a rush of questioning as I set her down next to me. She wobbled on her feet and Charlotte helped steady her, while I continued.

"You say that the weak have to settle for less, but look around you. Some of you are physically weak compared with others, but you have not settled for less. I will not pretend this life is glamorous, but you have more than those in the city above because you have created it for yourselves. You have a sense of safety. You have a sense of freedom not known in the rest of Hell. I can see it all in your eyes. Despite holding some kind of sin to keep you in Hell, you choose not to direct it to your friends here. You support each other, rather than take from the ones who might not be as strong. Do not speak to me of power and rights being the same thing. You are an example of how this kind of co-operation can work. Do you think that everything comes from physical might, or inner strength, or knowledge alone? All are forms of strength and, just because I may have one, does not mean I don't need to ask my companions for help with the others. That is true power and it can only come with unity."

Stunned looks from the eyes of the women of the Necropolis gazed out to me. Their mouths settled into pursed lips that didn't dare raise the question, which The Furies had to voice for them.

"So then, what is it you would ask of us, Ruler of Hell?"

I paused, nodding to Clytemnestra, who I knew would phrase it better than I could.

"All we ask for is your trust, and your tears."

The Fury who had held the dagger to Clytemnestra's throat came forward with it. She threw it down to the ground so it bounced in the dirt at my feet.

"You can have neither."

19

"NO!" CLYTEMNESTRA GROWLED as she swept up the dagger, rushing forward with it as if to stab her prey.

The other two Furies gathered quickly and sent a rush of primeval elements into Clytemnestra. It punched her in the chest and she fell backwards. Mary yelled out for me to stop, but I lunged forward ready for a further attack – which didn't come. The act had simply been a defensive move. Skidding to a halt, I forced myself to calm. I looked back to Lotte and Mary, who were now bent over Clytemnestra. I watched the three Furies as they mustered their pride in front of their followers, who all bristled with indignity, waiting for the command to act. There was none. The Furies did not want total destruction here any more than I did. Going back to my companions, I knelt down to search Clytemnestra for serious injury. She was stunned, but okay, still clinging to the dagger in her white-knuckled fist. We helped her back up and our small group huddled together, to await what happened next.

"Honeyed words do not taste as sweet to us as bitter action," the lead Fury pronounced to the crowd. "This man just told us what we wanted to hear. But do we trust him?"

"No!" came the firm response of feminine voices.

"This woman used to be one of us, but her rash emotion, which has always been her weakness, has shown their true intent. Should she be punished?"

"Yes!" an even more urgent call chorused from all sides. "Yes," The Furies hissed as one.

I tensed, as the same Fury who had thrown the dagger to the ground came forward and plucked it from Clytemnestra's fingers. I held my friend's arm, so she would not lash out again. Red, lifeless eyes stared into mine as the Fury held up the dagger. A black light of hate became infused

71

inside it, creeping out of this demon's skin and into the blade. She spoke, in an ugly rasp, pressing the hilt into my hands.

"Take this dagger, Michael. Use it to cut off the life chord of your servant's soul. If you kill her, we will weep for her. You can take the tears and use them how you wish."

The whole crowd fell dead silent at the pronouncement. I blinked as Clytemnestra turned to me. Her eyes were brimming with tears, but they were the saltwater tears of humanity. She fell to her knees and started to unbutton her shirt, exposing her chest as she had exposed it to her son during her final moments on Earth. This time it was done with serenity.

"Do it, Michael," she said. "If it means you will be able to meet Asmodeus on our terms, then I will welcome nothingness."

I felt both Charlotte and Mary come to my shoulder. My wife's fingers clutched at my elbow, but I didn't need her action to spur me on. Holding the dagger, high so all could see, I took my own emotion and pushed it into the steel. The pink of love cancelled out the hate, until it was just a metal instrument in my palm. I then let it crumble into dust. Looking down to Clytemnestra, who still knelt, I took her hands.

"The only thing that dies today is this cycle of revenge within our own fold."

Raising my head, I spoke to The Furies as I helped my friend rise.

"You know who the real enemy is and it is not Clytemnestra, nor is it anyone who lives in this realm. It is Him. The first He who would subject you to his reign: Asmodeus. Until you can see that, we will all be slaves. Now, let us go in peace and I will promise that if I can find a way to defeat him, I will do everything in my power to preserve all you have built here."

The blood that usually clouded The Furies' eyes cleared for a moment. The red pushed away from the middle to reveal the crystal blue of human-looking irises. They stepped forward as one, cupping their hands beneath their chins. Rare smiles touched the three avenging angels' lips and tears of crimson trailed down their cheeks, turning to jewels as they fell into their open palms.

"Now you have our trust," they whispered as one. "And our tears."

20

I TAPPED THE POUCH, which was held securely in my pocket in a shroud of elements. The Jewels of Blood jingled inside. Hope swelled in my chest, not just because we had a key piece of what we needed, but because of the departure the women of the Necropolis had given us. An honor guard of over half a million people had lined the alleys and rooftops of their slum, as The Furies walked us to the mouth of the tunnel that led to the surface. No one cheered; they just held their hands in a prayer position on their chests – a spiritual salute of solidarity to our cause. As our party left, we each turned and mirrored the salute. Where there had been trepidation and fear on our entry, there was hope and confidence in our departure.

Now, I stood on the balcony overlooking The Great Lawn. Clytemnestra walked the grounds below with the lightness of someone who had just been freed of a lifetime of guilt. She was preparing with the keeper of the house, Azazel. The stream of pilgrims had already started the long trek up the mountainside. The first of them would be here in a matter of hours. I watched as the tide of souls rose up slowly from the city. I needed to make final preparations myself.

Back inside the war rooms, Marlowe watched closely over Germaine, who wove elements together to create our bodies. Smithy sat in the far corner, also watching. Rainbow lights spun into flesh. Bones gathered, tendons formed, skin peeled over the muscles of the frames. These were earthly bodies: ones that didn't belong in Hell. They were for Earth. I could see by their makeup that, if they were left too long down here, they would burn and putrefy in the heat.

Germaine had woven a bed of cool air to encase them. There were six in total; the same amount of jewels The Furies had gifted us. Each body was in the likeness of those who would ascend on our mission: Smithy,

Charlotte, Clytemnestra, Germaine, Mary and Marlowe. There would to be a body for me too soon enough, but I didn't need a jewel to have the power to bond with it. That power was innate within my soul. Germaine would teach me how to fuse the power with flesh and I would build my own human shell. Marax and The Pure Seven would stay behind; they were to help carry out the plan I would announce in my latest sermon. I was ready to hand the souls of Hell the purpose they so badly needed.

Germaine looked up from his work and the lights faltered. He sealed off cool air around the bodies.

"Hello, Lord Michael," he greeted me. "I hope you like my work. I have come as far as I can without the jewels. Do you have them?"

"Yes, we were successful," I nodded.

Marlowe's white grin split his dark features. It was eerie to see him animated in his ethereal form and have another lifeless corpse almost identical on the table next to him. I noticed with some amusement that Germaine's body was more youthful and handsome than his emaciated spirit that stood before me. I wondered why he hadn't healed automatically back to his normal state, now that he'd come back to consciousness. Perhaps the body was a reflection of the chaos that he struggled to contain inside him. Smithy nodded wisely at me from across the room, as if he already expected we would have no problem in our task. He may well have heard the tale of our journey already. We had been back for barely a day and word seemed to spread like wildfire within our camp. It was both a blessing that I didn't have to recount the story to everyone first hand, and a curse that rumors were quickly embellished to become beyond fanciful. Marax had asked me earlier if it was true that I had flattened the entire Necropolis before rebuilding it again. When I said I had not, he thought I was simply being modest.

"Can I have them?" Germaine asked, stepping forward. "I'd like to start adding some preliminary emotion and spirit to prepare these shells for rebirth."

The wary look on Marlowe's face made me pause. Smithy shifted in his chair, but remained silent.

"Why can't you add a small amount of emotion without the jewels?" I queried. "I thought these jewels were to be added right at the final moment, to give the bodies more godly power, not human emotion."

Germaine nodded eagerly, licking his lips as if he'd anticipated my concern.

"Yes, but I need to use the jewels to have the personal power to do it. In my current state I can only manipulate the base elements. I dare not take any potions to expand my ability. We know how that may end." He let the pause after his sentence complete the explanation.

I looked to Marlowe to get his thoughts and he shook his head almost imperceptibly. I thought on the dilemma. I would have to give the jewels over to Germaine eventually, if we wanted our souls fused with these bodies with power, but I wanted to hold off longer. I put my hand into my pocket and let my fingers rub over the precious blood crystals.

"You can have one for now," I said finally. "This one is your jewel. When it's time for the resurrection, you and I will complete the fusion together with your lead. I'm trusting you with this."

Plucking one of the tear-shaped jewels from my pocket I held it up. It sparkled, not from the light in the room, but from the power within. Germaine's eyes widened in anticipation and he once again licked his lips in what seemed to be an almost automatic nervous habit.

"Keep it safe. We don't need to start the next step until after the sermon. I want you, Marlowe and Smithy to take these bodies and have them on display on the large balcony above the lawn. Make sure they look powerful and prestigious. I want them to be a symbol of our achievement. Stay up there and wait. All our high council must stand behind me while I address the crowd. I'll go up and get Charlotte."

Smithy snapped off a rigid salute, worthy of an old soldier. The seriousness of the action was offset by his constant grin.

"I'll see you on the balcony," I said, glad that he was on our side.

Walking through the maze of corridors in the mansion, my nerves started to flutter again. In little under an hour I would be standing before millions of souls. I felt as out of place addressing them as their leader as I did in these luxurious surroundings. I was a street kid and a fighter, not a general; certainly not a lord. Charlotte was insistent that we take the largest room in the palace as our bedroom. She said it was to present an image of power, more than to be comfortable. I was learning from her that occasionally outward appearances could be just as important as inward confidence when it came to leadership. Sometimes one bolstered the other. Charlotte surprised even me with her insight. I thought I had known every side of her and yet an assured confidence in how to lead had sprung from somewhere I didn't know existed inside her.

I stepped past a marble bust of the artist William Blake and rounded the corner to our door. Opening it inward, I almost fell backward at the vision that greeted me. Charlotte was just zipping up a black dress, which clung tightly to her elegant figure. The length of its silken folds reached down to her ankles, but splits up each side revealed her legs to the upper thigh. Red roses were embroidered in fine detail along the neckline, which swept dramatically down in a deep vee to the base of her sternum. The fabric covered each of her breasts just enough to avoid exposing too much, but the effect was scandalous to me. My innocent Lotte looked anything but. She looked like a sophisticated queen of desire, comfortable in her own skin. She looked utterly captivating. My eyes must have been bugging out of my head, because she gave me a demure smile and spun around in her red high heels.

"Isn't it gorgeous?" she laughed. "Clytemnestra had it made for me."

I opened my mouth to speak, but my throat wouldn't produce any words. I just stood there, staring. Eventually, I worked up enough saliva to gulp.

"Good," she laughed. "Speechless is exactly what I was going for. It's important to get that out of the way now, before you have to address the entire population of this world."

She stepped to the side to indicate a suit lying on the bed.

"I had Azazel tailor this to your size. It's something fitting for one who needs to present the ability to control the universe."

I didn't think it was possible, but my eyes went wider still. There was no way I could wear something like that. It was a black, military dress suit. Silver trim lined the collar. Down the centre length of each sleeve, a long row of colorful eyes were sewn into the fabric, right down to the cuff. They looked utterly lifelike, but were only two dimensional, as flat and thin as the cloth they were a part of. On the breast was pinned a row of circular medals, also each an eye. Four of them were held by ribbons, each a color of the base elements: Fire, Earth, Water, Air. On the other breast was a single badge: The Universal Eye. It was the same symbol as above the door of Mary's Chamber of Maps, the iris of the Earth framed above by Heaven and below by Hell. There were two perfect circles around it: one white, one black, touching without a gap between. I understood the meaning: a united existence, for every shade of soul. On the lapels were two silver pins: the silver sickle of death on the left; the tree of life on the right. I walked over and placed my hand on it. At my touch, the eyes on the sleeves blinked and roamed around the room, as if searching for hidden enemies. The effect was disturbing.

"I..." I began.

"You'll look every bit the Lord of Hell in it. I know it's not your normal style, but you being comfortable is much less important right now than you looking strong. Everyone will understand the elemental symbolism of this. They know the source of your power and what you hold control over."

"Is it really necessary?" I said, knowing inside that I wasn't going to win this argument.

"Do you think kings and queens enjoyed wearing what they did?" Charlotte said, putting her hands on her hips. "Heavy crowns and ridiculous robes?"

Her fingers touched the skin at the top of the fabric slits on her thighs. Her appearance, and the effect it had on me, was more than enough of a message to realize aesthetics were incredibly potent.

"Napoleon understood the need for pomp and he was one of the greatest military leaders in history," Charlotte continued. "Hitler built a whole movement behind a manufactured image of might. Despite his message of hate, he was able to enthral the masses through grouping around art and symbolism. Think how much of an impact this could have when the message is good and just."

I sighed. Hitler. Napoleon. They would probably be out in the crowd somewhere today. Those men who did evil things would not have entered Heaven easily. Every other warmonger, tribal chief, soldier and bloodthirsty warrior in history, famous or not, were likely out there as well. I had to get them behind me. Despite their past, we had to move to the future together. There was no other way. I had the tired and the poor, but I also had the evil and strong; the tempest-tossed, huddled masses ready to rise up and be free. I couldn't pretend everyone on our side had perfect intentions. Our goal was salvation, though, and I would do everything in my power to ensure it was achieved the right way.

Picking up the jacket, I swung it over my shoulders. "Help me button it up, would you?" I smirked.

She grinned in triumph and stepped toward me. Her heels were high enough that we stood eye to eye. She grabbed the lapels of my new coat and pulled me into her lips. I let myself succumb to their soft love. I felt a passionate heat for Lotte that had impossibly grown stronger. She pulled back and smiled. Her eyes lit up with the genuine nature that I knew her for. She was still the girl I had met what felt like ten lifetimes ago: that girl and more. Lotte snapped together the jacket up to its collar with deft fingers, then sealed the top with another kiss.

"If you're lucky I might unbutton it later as well," she said cheekily.

I looked her up and down and made a show of exhaling, fanning my face.

"You're lucky I'm letting you out, dressed like that." I said.

"Like you have a choice in the matter."

"We all have a choice," I said in mock seriousness, "that's what we're fighting for."

She slapped my chest playfully.

"Come on, Lord Michael. It's show time."

21

I STEPPED OUT ONTO THE BALCONY to a deafening roar. The teeming crowd of demons and people below boiled with energy at the sight of me. At my side, Charlotte stood, waving regally to all, showing that the stories were true: she had come down from Purgatory and was now with her love again.

To my left were Clytemnestra, Marax, Smithy, Germaine, Mary and Marlowe: my trusted guard. On the right, the bodies Germaine created were suspended upright, like impossible mannequins ready to be spurred into action. There was a glowing light around them. I saw Germaine had added the dazzling elements for extra effect. On the roof behind us, The Pure Seven sat: a septet of colorful gargoyles, watching as sentinels over the proceedings. As one, they fanned out their angelic wings and the crowd erupted again. Waves upon waves of people were spread out upon the lawn, flowing down the mountainside. Not a scrap of ground could be seen. The crush of souls all looked up, trying to get a glimpse of their leader. I wondered if there could possibly be more than a handful of people left in the city below: probably not.

I glanced at my watch, making note of the time. There wasn't long before The Guilt would wash over the gathering, but I had enough time to make my main pronouncement. I held up my hands for silence and the masses obeyed. Their instant response gave me an extra surge of confidence. Amplifying my voice with the elements, I spoke to my people.

"Friends, I thank you for making the choice to come here today. It is a show of your collective freewill that cannot be underestimated."

The crowd yelled their gratitude back up to me and I pressed on.

"We have a journey to take together. No doubt, you have heard that we succeeded in destroying the wall between Purgatory and Heaven. We made a tough decision and freed other struggling souls into the eternity of

78

a bountiful paradise."

Below, the noise erupted again, but not all of it was encouraging. I could see frustration on some of the faces.

"I know some of you think that we should have brought Purgatory here. That we should have swelled our strength in Hell for the war we know is coming. But ask yourselves, is it justice that those people be forced to live in this Hell? This heat? This guilt? To live in this small space that struggles to contain our numbers now? No!" I answered for them. "We now have allies on the other side. They know what we have done for them and they know what is coming next: salvation for all! When the final walls fall, they will fight with us!"

The din that met my passionate announcement was overwhelming. The feeling of hope coming from those who had known none for so long sunk through my skin. I could feel their expectation growing. The mess of bodies all squirmed and writhed, raising their arms to me in supplication. My stomach churned with disquiet. I did not want to be adored. I wanted them to make hard choices for the betterment of themselves.

"That salvation is closer than you think. You can see my advisors at my side. This is my council of truth."

I swept my hand across to my left and let a trickle of the elements escape my fingers. The weave spread across my friends and formed new clothing on each of them: uniforms of white to mirror my black shimmered over their bodies like an illusion, before turning solid. Instead of the four medals of the elements I had on my own chest, the Universal Eye was emblazoned on both sides of theirs. I then motioned up to the Pure Seven, turning their hair white, but leaving their bodies the color of their chosen sin.

"These are my generals. They will command the seven Legions of Sin. Those among us who have given themselves to Lust, Avarice, Sloth, Pride, Gluttony, Envy or Wrath, you are now part of the Armies of Hell. We are at war!"

At my words, the Angels of Sin above me took flight and swept low over the crowd. The frenzy of zeal below reached close to breaking point and the jaws of every demon in the crowd gnashed and howled in delight. I raised my voice again, to ensure the emotion didn't spill over further.

"Marax. Step forward!" I said, looking to my left, as the people settled slightly.

The muscled demon of my companions did as I asked, his chest puffed out with pride.

"To those of you who house a hotbed of conflicted desire inside; you who enjoy multiple sins: this is your new captain. You who are deformed physically from your relentless needs; you who have taken the hybrid shape of human and beast: you are my black legion."

Again, a surge of belonging lifted up in shouts of approval. The darkest demons in the crush below beat their chests, signifying they knew who they were.

"Those who are still more human than demon," I continued. "You are the Legion of White and will have me at your front line when the time comes. Together our nine circles of Hell will defeat the liar who constructed our prison: Asmodeus!"

The sound of the enemy's name drew screams of hatred. I had this gathering in the palm of my hand. I reached out and squeezed Charlotte's shoulder.

"Now!" I boomed, quieting the congregation of millions. "I know there are soldiers among you; great leaders in your own right. There are warriors, thinkers and strategists. I ask you to reveal yourselves to your generals over the coming days. We have declared war today, but the battle is yet to come. This is a time for preparation. We must unite and train if we stand a hope of overcoming the most powerful being alive."

At my words, the crowd hushed completely.

"Yes. I admit we face a strong foe. We cannot pretend he is weak. We cannot fall prey to prideful hubris. We are the underdogs. We are the underworld. But we have purpose. We struggle here while the others rest above. We are hungry."

"Yes!" individual shouts rose up from below.

"More than that, we know he has a weakness!" I answered. "He is afraid. Asmodeus knows we are coming, and if he doesn't he soon will. He has spies here. I know you are out there listening. So hear me now."

Dead silence fell below.

"We are snapping at your heels, Asmodeus. Eternity will not hide you from us. These powerful bodies to my right are our secret weapons to bring down your gates. Your days are numbered!"

I let the glow around the bodies shine brighter and brighter until it would have been like looking into the sun to behold them. In a searing blast I let an atomic wind radiate out from them. The shockwave struck awe in everyone present. I didn't need to explain what the bodies were for. The mystery would amplify the confidence in our soldiers that they were indeed instruments to be fearful of.

I let the crowd settle of its own accord, and was about to deliver the final lines of my speech when a commotion below drew my attention. A group of demons were pushing their way to the front of the grounds. One figure among them stood out to me above the rest: Balthazar.

I should have known that this public address could not go without incident. I watched as the form of my old opponent, the man who I had killed in my earthly life and fought again in The Pit, strode forward. At his back was a group of almost a hundred other souls. Their number amid the millions looked tiny, but I knew if there was enough unrest to gather this many people, there were more out there who could be swayed. All eyes were trained back up to me, seeing how I would react to this disturbance. On the fringes of where I could still make out individual faces in the crowd, confused whispers were rippling backward. I held up my arms once more.

"Someone has come forward to speak," I announced. "Before, their voice would have been squashed by Asmodeus. That deceiver would have not let everyone be heard. But we need the truth of every side if we are to move ahead. Please, listen to this man."

Spreading down tendrils of elements, I helped Balthazar's voice rise up so everyone present could hear. I even projected an image in the sky, so they could see his face. Charlotte gripped my arm.

"What are you doing?" she whispered.

"What's right," I reassured her. "We can't oppress any of these people any longer."

I looked down to the black creature who I had beaten twice before. My heart pounded in my chest. I would need to have good answers for anything he had to say.

"You are all fools if you believe this weakling!" Balthazar's growl echoed around.

Shouts of anger sprung up in my defence, but not all the calls were in my favor. I waited for him to continue.

"Michael says he will free us of Hell, but what has he done so far? Nothing but talk! He has selfishly rescued his wife from Purgatory and squandered a chance to fight Asmodeus head on. He is the one afraid. He is pitiful."

Charlotte bristled next to me and shouted that he was wrong, but the rest of the crowd, which was already in upheaval, drowned out her cries.

"We are only beginning our journey," I retorted with a magnified voice, glad that my tone remained calm. "What do you expect in mere months when this system has been eternal? This course is not easy, but we are on the right path. You speak of the events in Purgatory with all the authority of someone who wasn't even there. These people are not stupid. We will not hear your poison rumors."

Balthazar raised a clawed hand up to me, shaking his head.

"They are not rumors. They are the truth: your precious truth." He spat on the ground like the word left a bad taste in his mouth. "Asmodeus made the entire universe in six days and then rested. You have done nothing but rest since the beginning. When will you start working for your people? If you are so powerful, then why do we still all suffer The Guilt six times each day? If you think you can bring down the walls of Heaven, why not stop our suffering first?"

I was about to open my mouth to reply when a movement flashed in the corner of my eye. I turned to see a red jewel appear in Germaine's hand as he stepped forward. The blood crystal dissolved in his skin as he leapt over the railing with a curdling cry of anger.

"No!" I yelled.

Marlowe reached out to grab him, but it was too late. The figure of Germaine clad in his new white uniform dropped like a burning meteor. He struck Balthazar with such force that it buried a crater into the ground and sent everyone close by careening back like dominoes. I started to jump over the railing, but Marlowe and Smithy heaved me back.

"You can't dirty your hands with this!" Smithy hissed heatedly in my ear.

His words made me pause. Below, the dust was settling and a purple glow emerged from the crater. It was the figure of Germaine, and suspended above him the limp body of Balthazar. With a sudden spray of elemental power, Germaine splintered the demon's body apart. Blood splattered his face as the fragments of gore rose further into the air. The only part still whole was Balthazar's head, which was frozen in a death scream. Germaine's voice shuddered outwards. Its cadence sent a shiver through my body. It was like twenty voices, all rasping over each other, but speaking the same words.

"Our Lord Michael saved me from madness," he said. "He saved me from myself. Now I repay that kindness. This is a rat I hold in my grasp: a squirming voice of dissent that we must shut out. I know what it means to listen to voices of evil and be led astray. We cannot let that darkness taint us. The liars belong in oblivion. This is what will happen to anyone who chooses to take the wrong path and stand against my master!"

A throb of energy welled inside Germaine and I could see he was about to obliterate Balthazar's soul, as I had done once to Gideon's. I could not let that happen.

"Germaine, stop!" I screamed with every ounce of authority I had.

The wild figure below did pause. He looked up to me.

"No, Michael," he rasped in his multiple voices. "This must happen."

Flexing his power again he let a shower of white spiral upward. It pushed inside the soul of Balthazar, but instead of separating, the swirl of his being glowed in a divine color I had only seen once before. It rejected Germaine's advance and shot the elements back down, burying his body with a reverberating thump into the crater behind him. The pieces of Balthazar's bloody body still hung in the air and all around a deep malevolent laughter rose in cackles. It was not the laugh of Balthazar. It was the laugh of my father.

Asmodeus was here.

22

I WATCHED ON WITH THE SAME HORROR as everyone else, as Balthazar's body started to meld together to reveal its true form. Asmodeus. His terrible laughter continued to ring through the air. My father's hated face formed into a broad and spiteful grin. The laugh from the sky took its place deep in his throat, ringing out to us.

"Smithy, Charlotte, Marax." I said, just loud enough for them to hear. "Take the bodies inside with you and lock the doors tight. Marlowe, no matter what happens, don't let anyone get into the castle. Stay at my back."

I didn't turn to make sure they did as I asked, but the shuffling of feet let me know they were at least moving. I only had eyes for my nemesis.

"Oh, Michael, my son," Asmodeus said, still hovering high in the air with a white glow around him. He held out his arms in mock disappointment. "You've been a very naughty boy. What happened to 'Obey thy father'? I have given you so many chances."

"You have given me nothing," I said through gritted teeth.

The masses on the ground where all screaming and pointing, some trying to run away from what they assumed was going to be a bloodbath. Hysteria gripped them.

"My children!" Asmodeus spoke down to them in a commanding tone that made them pause in their tracks. "I am not here to hurt you. I am here to make you an offer."

The people's demeanor below turned to one of hesitation. Was this right? He wasn't there to cause them pain?

"We don't accept offers from the one who invented deception," I boomed in response, trying to win back their confidence. "Be calm. This charlatan does not have the power to harm you all, not while he has me to deal with. If we all rise up together we can end him here and now."

My words seemed to galvanize the people. They started to muster together, looking up in anger, even shouting abuse skyward. I felt Mary and Clytemnestra come to my side in a show of strength. The Pure Seven had formed a rank around Asmodeus in the air, ready to strike at my word. What was I waiting for? I should end it now.

Seemingly reading my thoughts, Asmodeus held up his hand and smiled.

"You do not want blood on your home soil," he said, almost like a friend trying to persuade me. He pointed to the horizon. "In but a few minutes The Guilt will sweep in from the heavens and all of these souls will be helpless. I could slaughter them all before you could even reach me, and you know it."

I continued to hesitate. Was he right? His words were like a spear of indecision wrenching in my gut. I felt an odd wave of emotion that made me look around with elemental vision. I saw that Asmodeus was pouring waves of doubt into the crowd, making them second guess everything I had told them. It was even affecting me. Using my own power, I pushed confidence back out, to try and combat his subtle attack. The twist on his lips showed me he felt what I was trying to do.

"As I said, I come in peace," he pushed on, looking around to the people beneath him. "I want to offer your disciples a deal. A treaty." He watched to make sure everybody was listening.

Those gathered had all paused, but were still on guard for trickery. I could see a shudder of movement stirring inside the smoking crater that Germaine had disappeared into. With distrust inside me, I still waited to hear what Asmodeus had to say. What kind of treaty?

"I offer you peace," he said, turning his palms up to show he was telling the truth. "I shall promise to stop The Guilt, if..." he paused for effect. "If, you all turn on Michael right now and overthrow him. I bequeath Hell to its souls without the device that haunts your minds. You will be able to live without your suffering and not even have to fight for it. Now, swarm the castle!"

There wasn't a breath of wind or noise on the mountain. Not one demon moved. They were frozen in their tracks, standing firm. Asmodeus looked around in surprise at the lack of action. Sneering, he turned his attention back up to the balcony. He spotted the two women at my side.

"Clytemnestra," he smiled his fake grin, "Mary. If you agree to betray this leader of yours, I will give you anything your heart desires. Bow down to me now and I will grant any wish you like. Would you like to rule Hell as I once did? Do you want me to awake Judas?"

I could see that once again he pushed a wave of deception towards us, trying to magnify the emotional power of his words.

"Never!" Clytemnestra spat back at him, before I could even react.

Her defiant words were like a catalyst for all the other souls. They started to shout and scream up to him. The elements oozing out of his body cut short.

"Liar! Liar!" the crowed taunted. "Kill him!"

Asmodeus' grin turned into a scowl. He pointed down to the demons and people below.

"Just remember. My offer stands. If the battle becomes too hard to fight, I can end it with the wave of a hand."

The groaning rasp of Germaine's many voices rose up from the crater below.

"You do not rule us anymore, you powerless god." "Then you truly are damned," Asmodeus spat.

The flares of Guilt flashing on the horizon caused a shout of terror in the crowd. Some of the darker demons started to hold their ears, screaming.

"No," I said, gathering a force of deathly elements at my back. "They are free!"

Bounding forward, I kicked off from the railing and shot towards Asmodeus with the all the speed I could muster, spilling elemental powers from my very pores. He met my attack head on and we collided in an explosion of light. Both of us bounced away from each other from the impact. The Pure Seven, who were still on hand, scattered aside as well. Their screeches barely registered in my ringing ears as I tumbled backward, pain burning in my chest. I managed to grasp a hold of the air around me with my mind, and stop my fall. Asmodeus was like a mirror image across from me. He regained control of his own descent and we locked eyes, both clenching our fists in hatred. I could see the flames of guilt crashing in behind him. In barely a moment, it all happened: The souls at our feet collapsed and squirmed on the ground in agony. The Pure Seven regrouped. The figure of Germaine clawed his way out of the crater, with purple sparks of electricity surrounding his being. And ,Asmodeus smiled again. Another movement on the horizon caught my eye. The flames of guilt weren't the only things coming. Eight specks flew ahead of the storm. Seven glowing white angels and a red dragon: Moloch.

The maelstrom hit like a solid wall. A blinding darkness of flames scorched chaos around me. A scaled claw scratched my face and I lashed out with a cutting blow toward my attacker. Moloch roared in agony and whirled away, retreating quickly before I could connect a blow. I heard the clash of worlds, as The Pure Seven's primal war cries pierced the furnace. Beating wings and sprays of unnatural blood unfurled above me. The angels of Heaven met the angels of Hell. I turned to see the red dragon, Moloch, spearing toward me again, but a cracking cord of elemental power swung upward and caught Moloch's wing. Germaine swept the beast down to the ground.

To every side there was violence, but my focus narrowed to see only one thing: my enemy. Asmodeus was like a void of calm amidst the tempest. He hovered across from me in the air, grinning, pulling elements from every side of him so he swelled in size.

"The seeds of doubt have been sown, Michael," he rumbled as he grew. "And a harvest of sorrow will be reaped for you. We will meet again on the field of battle. But it won't be today."

With a clap of boundless thunder, his body turned into smoke and became one with the storm around us. I looked around in confusion to see the same had happened to his allies. My companions who had been locked in combat were now fighting air. The flames of Guilt swept past, and Hell started to simmer back to normal. I frantically searched to see what kind of trick this was, but our attackers were nowhere to be seen. Inexplicably they had retreated before any real battle had taken place.

It was over as quickly as it had begun.

23

THE MILLIONS OF HELL'S INMATES started to stir from their forced grief on the Great Lawn. I watched the guilt storm recede in its roiling horror, back below the horizon. The sudden appearance then disappearance of Asmodeus had left me shocked. Not only that, he had brought seven angels and his dragon Moloch with him. *How?*

I had braced myself for an almighty battle, but my father had fled before we barely locked horns. I knew there was more to it than showed on the surface. His words replayed again in my head.

The seeds of doubt have been sown, Michael. And a harvest of sorrow will be reaped for you.

Confusion still wracked my brain, but I forced myself to breathe and settle. I had to prepare myself for the fallout that might arrive in the coming hours. We would deal with it as it unfolded. I rose back up to the balcony where I had started my sermon. Some shouts of disorientation below had begun already and I realized I didn't have much time to control the crowd. Turning quickly, I saw with some relief that Marlowe stood firm, his sword out, blocking the way into the castle. He sheathed his blade at my approach and stepped aside, opening the doors. Smithy, Clytemnestra and Charlotte all looked up in fright, standing guard over our earthly bodies. All seemed in tact, save for their rattled appearance.

"It's over," I said in brief explanation. "He's gone. Come back out and close the doors. Marlowe, please go in and keep guard over our mortal shells. We'll need them very soon."

My friends all snapped unquestioningly to obey my command. They came out onto the balcony with me. I drew Charlotte to my side in the same position as before.

I looked down to see the majority of the souls on the lawn were now awake and in a state of panic. Some looked to the sky, others around at each other for signs of destruction. Germaine was looking around wildly, still confused at how fast everything had stopped. The Pure Seven were on the ground, all bleeding from torn wings and burnt skin. They whimpered as they healed. It was a paranoid state of Bedlam I had to cut off.

"Friends!" I yelled out to everyone present, letting the confident tone of my voice carry all the way to the city. "We have one won our first battle!"

The looks of fearful bewilderment on the faces of my people turned slowly to each other, questioning, then up again to me for answers.

"Asmodeus was here but we turned him back!" I boomed, hoping the announcement would be greeted with cheers.

The crowd remained mute, unsure how to react.

Germaine saw what I was trying to do and let out a rallying cheer in his myriad voices. The effect spread out like wildfire. Everyone started clapping and shouting in celebration, their reluctance forgotten. I nodded to Germaine subtly in thanks before continuing.

"What that deceiver tried to do here was an act of terror," I yelled. "He wanted to instill fear in your hearts and doubt in your minds, but he failed. We will take control of our own destiny. We will not bargain with evil. It is total freedom or nothing!"

Again, rapturous shouts of triumph clamored through the gathering. Their determination was also mixed with anger. Anger at what had happened. The situation was ripe to burst. I motioned for Germaine to rise back up to the balcony. Using his abilities, he lifted off the ground and cast a purple light to draw attention to the movement. The crowd roared at the display, shouting support for the one who had taken the leap to defend his leader from insurrection. He had survived taking on Asmodeus! Part of me was furious that he had gone against my wishes, but his actions had meant Asmodeus had been forced to show his true colors, before he could sow further seeds of dissent amongst the people. Germaine had helped by acting independently of my will.

The Pure Seven also pushed off from the lawn and spread their battered wings in flight. I could tell they needed longer to heal, but they at least had the strength to reach the roof, where they resumed their posts above us. As they touched down, Germaine settled back into his rank beside me. I raised his hand in the air in victory. The people below called up with enthusiastic congratulations. Touching Germaine's skin was like touching a live wire. His body was virtually crackling with energy.

"This is what the courageous look like." I yelled.

The crowd responded by raising their arms as well, screaming their support. While they were cheering, I quickly looked at Germaine. Peering into his eyes I saw a murk of clouds starting to bleed towards the irises. I reached up and put my hand on his face. He tried to shake away but I held fast, drawing what I knew was the problem out of his body. The Jewel of Blood wept its plasma out of his skin and into my palm. I let it solidify. My friend slumped backward, but I held him up with the elements, pushing healing into him as I turned back to the crowd. I put the Jewel back into my pocket.

"We must all have the bravery to meet our enemies the best way we know how!" I shouted.

The masses responded, seemingly not to have noticed what I had done to Germaine. I pressed on.

"If Asmodeus didn't realize that we have more than one elemental on our side, he does now. It will chill him to the marrow."

Continued shouts and claps rose upward in response. It was clear they now felt we had the upper hand.

"You have shown your support for me as well," I went on. "By refusing to turn away from your own personal desires for the eternal gain of everyone, you have shown your true allegiance. You are the legions. You are the army. You are the warriors who will end this reign of tyranny!"

I hadn't thought the noise below could get any louder, but the cries of fevered devotion struck a new pitch. I hoped Asmodeus could hear it and it shook him to the core. He had left quickly, without really trying to fight, but we had manufactured strength from his actions. I would milk his mistake of fast retreat for all it was worth. There would always be repercussions from his appearance, as emotion settled and there was time for questions, but the chance to dampen the force of those questions was now. I waited for the crowd's cries to die down before I finished my sermon the way I had intended from the beginning.

"You all know your mission," I said, with authority. "Your path is clearer than it has ever been in history. You have each been appointed a worthy general to lead you towards that fate. Your sins are your guide. Now go forth and spread the word to those who might not have heard. We are at war. We are united. Celebrate, as only you know how. We begin to prepare our forces in three days."

With that, I turned and left the balcony. The cheers followed me inside, while I waited for the rest of my companions to gather behind me in the castle. I shut the doors and, along with them, the cacophony of hellish rejoicing from the Great Lawn.

Marlowe was steady at his post: a true soldier. The others, including the Pure Seven, had all entered and were watching me. I pulled Germaine toward me and then lowered him to the ground. He looked up at me with relief and closed his eyes with exhaustion.

"This was not a victory," I said to them steadily, looking up from Germaine. "We have salvaged what could have been a disaster, thanks to your combined faith in our cause, but we won no ground."

I laid Germaine down on the floor and his chest heaved as he fell into a deep healing sleep. I was glad I had caught him when I did. The power of the Jewel of Blood he had ingested had almost overwhelmed his mind. I wondered if this changed things for our resurrection to Earth. I continued to flood repairing elements into him, as I stood again to look at my friends. They were waiting for the next step.

"Gather your thoughts on what you experienced in the last hour. Be prepared to tell me the brutal truth of what you felt emotionally at each turn," I said to them. "We'll meet soon in the War Rooms. First, I need to get out of this ridiculous jacket."

24

I LEFT GERMAINE IN MARLOWE'S CARE, knowing he wouldn't wake for a few hours. I had wanted to heal the Pure Seven also, but they refused, saying the pain they felt was a reminder of the enemy they would face again. They enjoyed the searing burns of Heaven's fire on their skin. I held off from asking questions about the other angels who had come with Moloch. There would be time enough for that once we'd been able to process what had happened. Smithy and Clytemnestra would ensure everyone was gathered in the War Rooms at the appropriate time.

I walked back upstairs towards our bedroom with Charlotte and Mary. I needed them both with me now, because I suspected Asmodeus had succeeded in seeding some uncertainty beyond his open words. These two would be the most honest with me.

We entered my chamber and I slid the black military coat from my shoulders. I turned and pressed it into Charlotte's hands.

"Thank you," I said and kissed her quickly so as not to draw a negative response from Mary.

Lotte nodded silently. I could feel she was holding back tears.

"Everything's okay." I stroked her cheek. "We will always have to deal with the unknown. We now need to understand what really happened today. I'm concerned there is more to Asmodeus' visit than we yet know."

I paused, watching both of them. Mary looked grim, clenching her jaws in determined strength. I beckoned for them to sit. They each took a place on an opposite edge of the bed, sitting apart from each other. I paced in front of them, explaining to Charlotte with as much detail as I could about what had happened once I had sent her and the others inside. I spoke of Asmodeus' offer for a treaty and of his offer to Mary and Clytemnestra of power for betrayal. The details of the actual battle were still chaotic in my mind. The seven angels. Moloch. Asmodeus' withdrawal into the storm

92

before any real fight.

"My biggest concern is his use of emotional elements. The effort may have bolstered his attempt at making us all doubt our cause," I said. "Could you feel it from inside?"

Charlotte nodded slowly and tears started to fall quietly. She was still wearing her black silk dress. The striking power of its beauty looked strange on someone who now looked so vulnerable.

"I didn't know what it was, but I could hear all his words," she said clearly, despite her tears. "They made me feel like we could never beat him. I started to think maybe we should just let The Guilt disappear and be happy. I was afraid that if he fought you, you would lose."

She started to sob. I went to her side and laid my hand on her shoulder, before hugging her close to me.

"You know I would never let that happen, don't you?" I said gently.

"I know, but there's more," she said, lifting her head to meet my gaze. "Worst of all, I started to doubt you." Her tears increased. "A deep feeling kept asking: why did he send me inside? Does he think I'm weak?"

I sucked in sharply, wanting to reassure her, but she continued.

"I wondered why Mary was allowed to stay out there with you. Do you trust her more? Do you secretly love her? She is more beautiful and confident than I am."

Mary's snorted her disdain at the words and I shot her an angry look. I knelt down and took Lotte by her hands.

"You know you are everything to me," I said, searching into her eyes to make sure she was hearing my words. "I fear losing you, that's why I try to protect you. I know you're not weak, but I'm afraid I'm not strong enough to keep you with me. I couldn't bear to lose you again." I looked across to Mary and hoped my next words would not hurt her.

"Mary is my friend. Of course I trust her, but you are the only one I could ever truly love as my partner. There is no other and never will be."

I squeezed her hands and let my nose rest upon hers. I felt her tears against my cheeks. Her breath was hot against my lips and I wanted to kiss her deeply, but there was no time to linger in her arms. I stood up.

"Mary," I said softly. She was looking down at her hands, picking at her nails furiously. "Mary," I said louder. "What about you? What are your doubts? We have to voice them so they don't take a hold of us."

She looked up at me with steely eyes.

"They are not doubts if they are real," she said, standing abruptly.

I took a step forward to comfort her, but she brushed my hand away and walked towards the door.

"I have no illusions about our relationship, Michael," she said. "But when the real battle comes, you cannot be looking over your shoulder at Charlotte. You're going to have to let everything and everyone go if you have a shred of a chance at defeating him. Nothing else matters."

Before I could reply, she turned and left, slamming the door. I started to go after her, but Charlotte grabbed my arm.

"Let her go," Charlotte said, keeping her voice soft but firm. "Trust me. She just needs some time with her thoughts."

"That's exactly what I'm worried about," I said, but instead of leaving I stayed. There would be enough time to make things right with Mary. I just didn't know how I was supposed to do it.

25

THE COUNCIL WERE ALL READY and waiting in the War Rooms. Mary was the only notable absence. Smithy stirred his large pot of tea. Marax and Clytemnestra were seated together, waiting patiently. Marlowe had brought in Germaine's sleeping form and had him laid out in a corner of the room. It reminded me of how inert he had been at The Perceptionist's for centuries. He would come back to us soon enough this time: this was just sleep. The Pure Seven carried in the mortal bodies, which I hoped would still be used for our pending resurrection to Earth. They were perfectly intact and surrounded by cool air to keep them fresh and ready. The evil angels arranged the bodies side-by-side along the table top. Our War Rooms now looked more like a morgue. I clenched my fists, resolute. The events of the day had only made me more determined to stick with our plan. We couldn't sit by and just wait for Asmodeus to attack us again. I had to remain on the front foot, not shrink away as I was sure he wanted.

Charlotte and I both sat, as always taking random seats around the table, rather than the head thrones. The others saw that we were getting settled and came to attention. Smithy continued to look around, waiting for our final guest.

"We will start without Mary," I said. "She already knows the crux of the problem we face."

Everyone fell silent and listened intently.

"Asmodeus came here to see if he could create divisions between us," I began.

"Divide and conquer," Smithy said wisely from his seat. "It's one of the oldest techniques of war."

"And he is the master of it," I replied. "He used not only words, but his ability to manipulate emotion. I'm sure you all felt it, as did I. It was an elemental manipulation to make us feel uncertainty and embed it in our hearts. Charlotte has said she felt doubt in my love for her. Mary wondered if I had the focus needed to defeat Asmodeus. I'm sure you're all feeling similar uncertainties after his ploy."

The nods around the table were at once a blow to my heart, but also encouragement that they were all still truthful. If we knew what the problem was, we could overcome it.

"Tell me then," I said. "What are your deepest concerns?"

Not one eye came up to meet mine. Everyone sat, with their heads down, not even looking at each other. The silence was heavy. I stood up.

"I'm afraid we can't win," I said, honestly. They all looked up in surprise. "I'm afraid that he is too strong for me and, if I fail, you will all be punished for it."

Again I was met with silence.

"But I own my fear," I continued. "I think it's constructive. I will never be complacent. I will never underestimate what we're facing. That is our advantage. Asmodeus is so used to victory and control that he may just slip. We can turn our fears and doubts into a tool to make us work harder."

Smithy placed his cup down to rest on the table. The spoon inside it tingled on the porcelain and made everyone look his way.

"I'm afraid of war," he said. "I fear that, even when we bring down the physical barriers, the symbolic divisions will still stand. Those in Heaven think they have earned their right to be in Paradise while others suffer. They will never accept a world where those who have sinned are not punished. I'm not even sure I like that idea. What ever happened to the concept of justice, where evil deeds are held to account? If there is no Hell, what happens then? Do people simply get away with doing bad things in life?"

I heard his words and the enormity of them struck me. We were hoping to rearrange a universe which had been built for a reason. From our side, down in the fire and guilt, it always felt as though we had the raw end of the deal. But we were far from innocent. Those in Heaven had led good lives. Yet, who was the judge of good and bad? One being who had selfish intentions? I had seen enough to know that not everyone here deserved eternal anguish. Smithy himself was a noble soul. Why should he suffer forever and ever? Charlotte certainly shouldn't be here. Her only crime was to love me. It seemed punishment from an "objective" stance failed to take account of the context behind the deeds. Clytemnestra was a product of her environment. We needed to break the cycle of lies and let people decide for themselves. There had to be a better way.

"Smithy," I said. "Do you have any coffee?"

He looked scandalized, as if I'd asked him for poison. Sliding a cup closer to himself, he poured in hot tea and then passed it over to me.

"You're not doing yourself any favors, if you're trying to build our confidence again, by admitting you prefer the evil bean over the sublime leaf," he said.

I smiled.

"You have made my point for me," I answered. "Things are not black and white in this world. You believe that tea is the only thing to drink, but others prefer coffee. Some people see certain actions as heroic, or brave; others think the same deeds are foolhardy or misguided. There is no universal perspective we can hope to reach and still live this existence as individuals. If we all see things exactly the same way, we are clones of each other. The only thing we can ask for is the ability to come to conclusions on our own, without being forced one way or the other. We need unity through diversity. Right now, we do not have that choice. We are bound to live here. If we were all allowed to have the chance to migrate to Heaven, some might choose to stay here anyway. But we must have the option and we will need to fight for it. It is a fight worth having."

Smithy pursed his lips sternly.

"As long as you don't drink coffee, I'm okay with that," he said gruffly.

I suppressed a smile and took a sip of the tea he had given to me.

"If that's what it takes," I said, "I'm willing to make that sacrifice."

He laughed. It helped me feel better that my moral compass was still with me all the way. The others seemed to feel their anxiety ease, and Clytemnestra looked up.

"I am the same as you, Michael," she said. "I fear it's a battle we cannot win."

The others all voiced their agreement, but did not look afraid as they said it. The mood was more of confession, where the weight of what they held inside was lifted from them.

"We cannot pretend it's going to be a simple endeavor," I nodded. "But let's look at where we are. We have a pathway from Earth to Heaven. We still have the Jewels of Blood to enhance our bodies. We have a group of powerful and intelligent people in this room, and a whole army of some of the finest soldiers in history. We are hardly helpless. Asmodeus didn't steamroll us out there. He fled! If we were easy targets he would have finished us then and there. There is a way to move forward. We have to keep our heads pointing in the right direction and we will make it happen. We have to. The alternative is not acceptable."

I could feel the swell of confidence return to the room. I wished Mary was there to share it, but she still had not arrived.

"Now," I said to the closest of The Pure Seven. "You know better than me what happened out there. Those angels: who were they and how did Asmodeus get them into Hell?"

"We do not know how they were allowed in this place. They are our divine balance," the seven replied in their eerie chorus.

I took a seat again and waited for an explanation, but none was more forthcoming. Clytemnestra cleared her throat.

"I think I know who they are," she said in her low growl.

We waited for her to continue. She looked intently at The Pure Seven, before pressing on.

"What our sinful friends here are trying to say, is that they were the seven Archangels of Heaven: God's private guard. They are Gabriel, Raphael, Uriel, Raguel, Remiel, Mikail and Saragael."

"It is from the book of Enoch," a groan came from the corner.

I looked over to see that Germaine had awoken. Marlowe looked down at him, but did not help him up. He watched as the alchemist stumbled to his feet alone and took a seat at the table. He settled himself with deliberate patience. He was groggy, but I could see the clarity in his eyes had returned. He was with us again.

"I have heard everything you have all just said," he croaked with a dry throat.

Smithy brought over a steaming cup of tea for him, pressing it into his hands with a strong nod.

"Clytemnestra is perfectly right," Germaine continued, after sipping the reviving liquid. "They are the seven Archangels of God. It is all written down in an ancient religious canon called The Book of Enoch."

I turned back to her for more information.

"That is almost all I can tell you," she said, shrugging her shoulders. "They are the first of the angels. Powerful. Other than that, not much is known in Hell about them."

"There is more," Germaine said. "If I may?"

"Please," I said, indicating that he had the floor.

"If you behold our seven sinful friends here, you will see the exact opposite of the seven Archangels." He stood, tapping each of them on the wingtip as he walked past them. At his touch, he said their names. "Lust, Gluttony, Avarice, Sloth, Wrath, Envy and Pride. Their reflections in Heaven are named after the seven heavenly virtues: Chastity, Temperance, Charity, Diligence, Patience, Kindness and Humility."

As Germaine voiced each of the virtues, the dark angels hissed in anger.

"They will always oppose each other. Absolutely," Germaine went on. "The battle was too fast to notice, but I'm sure they would have been drawn together to fight the one they hate the most."

"They live nothing but lies," The Pure Seven spat venom. Their colored wings snapped tight at their backs. "Those angels reject their true nature of desire, while we are truthful and succumb absolutely to the craving that is built into us."

"You are right," Germaine said to them. "If you have too much charity you neglect your own needs. Too much kindness and people take advantage. Too much temperance and you do not fully experience life's pleasures. But some might say that neither of you are completely truthful either," he continued carefully. "Too much lust and, just as with chastity, you cut off the option of a full love. Purity is a strange thing. An abundance of one thing is not necessarily healthy either way. A balance should be struck."

"Purity is truth," they hissed back as one, "if you let your soul be tainted by one side, you cannot hope to be honest with yourself."

"As Michael said before, most of us are not so black and white, or blue, or green, or red, in your case," Germaine smiled, resting his hand on Wrath's shoulder.

Wrath turned and looked at his hand as though it was unclean.

"No matter what you think, it's certain that you are destined to oppose these angels. You will have your chance again."

"We will be more prepared next time," they chorused.

"We all will." I said. "Now, does anyone know how Asmodeus brought them here?"

No one responded.

"Perhaps Mary is working on the problem," I offered, but the thought sounded weak in my ears.

My gaze was drawn to the earthy bodies, in front of us on the table. In particular, the beautiful corpse with flaming red hair held my attention. I felt warm inside, taking in the perfect structure of her face. We couldn't sit and wait for another attack on Hell. We had to meet Asmodeus head on. Our defence was a fast response. If we could reach Heaven and bring down the walls, then our armies down here could be prepared. I had promised them three days of celebration, but in the meantime we could pave the way to war. I had made my decision.

"Marax and The Pure Seven," I said, rising to my feet. The eight generals of Hell all snapped to attention at my movement. "Start to make your plans for training your legions. You have full powers to nominate other leaders within your group. I'm placing full control in your hands."

They each nodded their acceptance with set faces. I knew from their calm reaction that I'd made the right decision in making them leaders of conflict. I turned to the others, who all appeared stunned at my sudden call to action.

"Germaine, Clytemnestra, Smithy, Charlotte and Marlowe," I said to them, "prepare to be reborn. I'll be back in a few hours. We leave for the surface on my return. It's time to go to Earth."

26

CHARLOTTE DIDN'T EVEN QUESTION where I was going as I kissed her goodbye. She knew. I had to see Mary alone and make sure she understood my commitment to our cause. She had been the one who had helped me along this path. Mary and Zoroaster had coaxed me towards Truth. I needed her full support to continue. She was the only one of us who had been to Heaven before. She was our eyes in making sure we took the correct route. There was no replacement for her. There couldn't be. I didn't doubt her unshakeable support for what we were doing. My worry was that I would fail her when it mattered most.

It only took minutes for me to jet down over Smoking Gun and come to rest on the street at the front of Magdalene's Mansion. The footpaths were jammed full of people – intoxicated, celebrating the impending war. They were lost in their revelry, drunk on hope and possibility. Music beat from every shop front and casino on the strip. Traffic had stopped. People and demons alike danced on the roofs of their cars, passing drinks between each other. It was the first time I had been in this suburb and not seen overt hostility and violence. Everyone seemed happy. The effect of turning the focus on an outside enemy was incredible. Within, there was only support. Bickering and internal prejudice had fallen away, but only in favor of a stronger hate for someone else outside. Perhaps one day humanity could find a better way to get along indefinitely. Perhaps. I had to believe that was true or we were fighting for nothing.

I deflected any attention away from me with a shroud of elements. I didn't want to be delayed. Pushing the front doors of Magdalene's Mansion open, I swept inside. The foyer was also full of revelers. The lusty Oba was at the front desk, frantically taking orders, checking customers in and giving directions to rooms upstairs. Other demons were helping her as well. They were all run off their feet with requests.

Impending war proved to be a powerful aphrodisiac. There were as many women in line as men. It looked like some people weren't waiting until they got upstairs for the party to begin either. Couples, trios and foursomes were sprawled on couches and even the plush carpet, taking their pleasure on the floor. The ground was a mat of heaving, sweating skin. Hands groped upward for any willing body they could find. This house of lust looked every inch its name. Without pausing, I picked my way past the elevators and towards a long, red corridor. I knew where I was going and it wasn't up. There was only one place Mary would be: The Crypt.

Winding down the polished stairs, I readied myself to enter Mary's underground shrine for Judas. This was the first time I had visited here since we had exorcised the souls of The Pure Seven from Mary's body, releasing the keys to the gates of Heaven. Those keys were now lost to Asmodeus. In our search for the keys to Purgatory, Judas had stumbled upon an ancient trap set to guard them. He had been flooded by a liquid, which caused anyone who came within its touch to fall into a coma. His sleep would last a thousand years and there was nothing I, or anyone else, had been able to do to lift it. The fact had been a source of Mary's sorrow since then. Her focus on our mission and subsequent love for me had helped her get past some of that pain, but that had been shaken as well. She would always return here when the outlook seemed impossible, perhaps to remind herself that there was more to what she was fighting for: there was family.

The interior of The Crypt remained mostly unchanged. Seven empty coffins lay in a formation around a crucifix-shaped altar. At the head of the altar, an eighth coffin sat. Mary was kneeling over it. Above, a suspended sculpture of a dove emerging from a sunburst shone white light onto them. I cleared my throat, but Mary didn't look back. She stayed intent on her brother, who lay still in the coffin, breathing almost imperceptibly. I walked to her side, looking down as well. Judas' face was so serene. There was some consolation in the fact that in his state there was no suffering. He was removed from the world and all its pains.

I stood together with them for a moment, reflecting on how far we had come. My initial mission had indeed been selfish: to save my love. But then I had met Judas and Mary. After hearing their story, I realized there was much more to be done: there was greater meaning than my own desires and needs. No matter how pure my own battles seemed to me, they were still small compared with everyone else's collective struggle. I became lost in my thoughts, trying to think how I could end all this. How could I defeat the undefeatable? Mary's voice brought me back.

"Judas would tell me that I am being silly," she said, looking at me with a sad smile on her face. "He would say that personal feelings are nothing compared with the greater good."

It seemed uncanny that Mary had just echoed my own interior thoughts. It made me pause, wondering if there was more to her than I knew, but I pushed that aside for the moment.

"He's the perfect example of someone who sacrificed everything they had for what they thought was right," I said, coming to Mary's side.

Judas had betrayed his best friend, Jesus. But it was Jesus who had asked Judas to give him up to the Romans. He had only done as God had wanted.

"And look what he got for it," Mary said. "He's the most despised figure in history. In the end it was God who betrayed him, leaving him trapped in Hell. I wish there was a way to end all this suffering."

I reached down and touched Judas' chest.

"You know there's a way," I said. "It's the path we're on already. By the time Judas wakes from his slumber it will be the dawn of a new age."

"Or will he awake to greater darkness?" she said, turning to me for the first time. "Is this really a fight you think you can win, Michael? Are you willing to turn your back on everything you love?"

I took my hand away from Judas, staring at Mary. I'd already proven I could make hard decisions. I had torn down the walls of Purgatory and Heaven, thinking I was leaving Charlotte behind. What more did she want? I took a deep breath.

"I would give anything to bring Asmodeus down. You know that. Don't let his words get in your head. Having us doubt each other is exactly what he wants."

Her eyes turned hard.

"Perhaps I'm just being realistic," she said. "I think about what I could lose in this as well. Look at what I've already lost and it all might be for nothing. What if we don't win?"

I looked around at the shadowy corners of the room. The black shade crept like smoke towards the bright centre of the room. Everywhere there was light, darkness would try to consume it. Or was it the light trying to consume the dark? Perhaps neither could exist without the other and it was a battle that would never ultimately be won. The best we could hope for was balance. I took each of Mary's arms in my hands.

"Mary. What would Judas say now? Would he say we should give up?"

It was the best argument I could give. She looked down again at her brother and I saw her jaw set in determination.

"I can't promise you happiness," I said. "But I can promise that when the time comes, I will sacrifice all I have for this. Are you willing to do the same? I need you."

Mary tore her gaze away from Judas and stared back at me with tears fluttering in her eyes. The glassiness made her dazzling green irises even more luminescent. She swept towards me and clung to me in a fierce embrace. I wrapped my arms around her and held her tight. After a few moments, she went to move back, but I held firm again, squeezing her body into mine. She relaxed into me, clinging to me again with passion. There was nothing more physical than a strong hug, but the emotion arcing between us could have torn down worlds. I held her and it felt as though time slowed. Her scent, the warmth of her body; they all blended into a serene calm. She was with me again. Finally, I let her go. She looked at me sadly, as if she knew that was the last time we would ever hold each other in such a way.

"We have another problem," I said, breaking the spell of the moment. "I'm not sure our bodies can contain the power of the Jewels of Blood."

Mary nodded; she had already known what I was going to say.

"I saw Germaine, too," she confirmed. "He was close to madness after facing Asmodeus."

"I don't understand it," I said. "We thought the blood was safe. Maybe it's because his mind has been weakened too much from before."

"Will he be affected the same way in a body of flesh?" Mary asked.

I paused thoughtfully. "I'm not totally sure," I said slowly. "Body and mind are always intertwined. Our ethereal bodies here are stronger, but they are also more malleable."

She looked at me quizzically, so I continued.

"Think of our forms here like rubber, where those of Earth are more like wood. In Hell, we bend more easily to pressure, but can resist more force. Real flesh is more solid, but can splinter apart under too much strain. I think maybe his body here is too susceptible to the influence of power. It's giving way too easily, because it's been loosened. Perhaps a more rigid body would help."

"Perhaps, but not definitely," she countered.

"It's a gamble," I said, turning the idea over in my brain. "I believe it would at least take longer for his earthly body to succumb. However, it might snap eventually. Perhaps all of ours would."

I stopped and thought more on the consequence of that happening.

"If he loses his mind on Earth, it might not destroy his body completely either," I admitted. "He could run riot there and kill innocent people. The destruction that an insane Elemental would reap on the physical world would be like nothing existence has seen before."

"But we need him," Mary said. "You saw how much he rattled

Asmodeus. He took on Moloch. We can't give that advantage away lightly."

"I agree. That's the problem. How do you use a weapon you might not be able to completely control?"

I walked over to the altar, placing my hands on the cool stone. I wanted to wholeheartedly trust all of our allies, but there was too much unknown to be able to move forward with confidence. My friends could be our downfall if we weren't careful. Each of the seven empty coffins in the room stared back at me blankly. They held no answers. I looked up to the room and saw the dove hovering. Its image made me angry. It was supposed to be the representation of the spirit of God. That Mary had put it here infuriated me. Everything I saw reminded me of Asmodeus. I had to close my eyes and forcefully calm myself again. As I composed myself, another thought came to me. I turned to Mary again.

"Zoroaster can control the elements. How can he do it without the need for jewels or potions?"

She came over to where I was standing and leaned on the altar, looking up to the white figure of the dove in thought.

"You forget he was a prophet of God during his life on Earth," she said. "That comes with some gifts. It would have been the same when you faced Gideon. Asmodeus has given certain people talents. Zoroaster might not be anywhere near strong as you, but his thousands of years of experience have produced a wisdom and intelligence that give him perfect control over his abilities. You should understand more than anyone that knowledge equates to power."

Remembering Zoroaster made me wish we had him down here with us to ask for advice. But maybe he was more use where he was, carefully gathering some support for us there. Either way, it didn't present a solution to our current problem. I slapped my palm on the altar in frustration.

"What if," Mary's gentle voice sounded next to me, offsetting my anger, "we just delay introducing the jewels into our systems until we reach the gates of Heaven? At least that way we're giving ourselves time to travel from the Hellmouth to Jacob's Ladder."

"But we'll be helpless," I said.

"Hardly," she scoffed. "You still have the power to wield the elements. That will make our journey a lot easier. And we are all capable adults. You keep the Jewels of Blood safe and we will fuse them with our bodies just before we need them most: at the gates of Heaven."

I let the idea settle in my brain. It sounded reasonable. I would have to be on extra watch to make sure no harm came to our fleshy shells while on Earth, but I would not let my guard down anyway. It would be more a matter of convincing Germaine not to want the powerful blood sooner. I could feel he craved it like a drug. However, this seemed the soundest course of action. If we met resistance along the way, the jewels would still be there to draw on quickly.

"Okay," I said, not willing to stall any longer. "I want to leave as soon as we can."

Mary frowned, looking back to the coffin, which held her brother.

"I would like to say goodbye to Judas alone first," she said. "Alright," I sighed, nodding reluctantly. I had to understand that she still needed some space. "Please don't take too long. We'll meet you at Casa Diablo."

I turned to leave, but a strange intuition stopped me. I reached my hand in my pockets to feel the Jewels of Blood. Taking them out, I walked back and handed the pouch to Mary.

"Here," I said, pressing them towards her. "I need you to hold these."

She shook her head furiously, like I'd lost my mind.

"No!" she said. "Last time I almost lost the keys. We can't afford that mistake again."

I silenced her with a quick kiss on her cheek.

"If you can't trust your friends, who can you trust? Keep them safe."

Before she could resist further, I turned and walked away. I shouted back to her, so the words echoed around The Crypt.

"Say goodbye to your brother. Use him as your inspiration."

27

GERMAINE'S REACTION WAS MORE VIOLENT than I had anticipated. He took the body he had made for himself and cut off one of its arms, while the rest of us watched in surprise. Slicing away the other arm, he threw them at me. I blocked the bloody missiles with a sweep of my hand and the stumps fell to the ground. Without the protection of the cool air Germaine had cocooned around it, the skin began to blacken and blister in the heat of Hell.

"You see this!" he yelled, slicing off the legs as well and tossing them aside like rank meat. "This is what you're doing to all of us. You cripple us before we even begin."

He moved towards the next body when Marlowe stepped forward, drawing his sword and holding it above Germaine's head.

"That's quite enough," the African said in an icy voice. "Michael is right to hold off on giving us the blood."

Germaine flung his arms in the air in frustration and slumped to the ground. He looked up to each of us, almost on the verge of tears. We were all gathered in the grounds at the back of Casa Diablo, across from the Fount of Mercy. Its deadly green waters of sleep shimmered with a mix of the Hellish sky's red and black reflection. I had made the waterfall at the request of the false Bishop John. It would allow people to effectively commit a temporary suicide, passing through the curtain of water into a cave beyond. They would then sleep the same sleep as Judas, unable to awake for a millennium. Its construction had just been a diversion, though. Asmodeus had wanted me to build it to drain my strength before he attacked me. It now stood there, reminding me that I had to be on constant watch for deception. I should destroy it. It was dangerous. Right now, I didn't have time to undertake the task.

Smithy's helicopter was perched close by, ready to take us to the point of resurrection.

"You don't understand," Germaine said. "We'll be helpless."

"We'll be ticking time bombs," Charlotte snapped, making Germaine jolt. She was normally so calm that the venom in her words took him off guard. "At least if we meltdown in Heaven, we might cause some damage where we want to. We can't risk losing total control on Earth. That won't help anything!"

"Michael will protect us. It's only a short journey to Jacob's Ladder. We have to trust him." Clytemnestra backed her up.

"But he doesn't trust us," Germaine said, locking eyes with me. "If you do, then give us each our own jewel to hold."

He stood, holding out his hand. I hadn't told them that I'd given them to Mary for safekeeping.

"No," I said. "You'll get them when the time comes."

He let his arm drop. He was about to say something more when I cut him off.

"You can stay back if you like. You can help The Pure Seven and Marax gather the armies for readiness. They're already down in the city, dividing Hell into separate grounds for the legions. Those are your options."

His face fell into despair. I knew which choice he'd make. If he stayed here, there would be no blood for him at all. It felt unfair to dictate the terms like this, but I couldn't risk Germaine being tempted to take his jewel early. Now that he had a taste of what the jewels could do, he might not have the will power to exercise his better judgment. It could spell disaster. His reaction now told me this was the right thing to do. I had to show some leadership. Smithy walked to him and put a hand gently on his arm.

"Come on, mate. You're better than this," he said. "I know what you did for us back there on the Great Lawn. We need you up there with us. Please."

The pilot held out his hand. Hesitating, Germaine looked to each of us.

"We do need you," I said. "We just need to make sure you strike at the right time. You know deep down this is the only way. You felt the madness coming in towards the end of that battle, didn't you?"

Germaine hung his head in the face of reason. He knew this was the right way. It was the demons inside him that were struggling against it. I watched as, with visible effort, he calmed himself. Moving back over to the body he had maimed, he laid his hand on its torso. The basic elements sprung to his call and the body started to grow limbs once again. I added my assistance to the effort, so the shell was whole again in a matter of moments. Marlowe still had his sword out and ready. I placed a hand on his shoulder.

"Keep an eye on him up there," I whispered into his ear. "We'll need to be focused if we hope to get to the Aedicule of Ascension without incident."

My words seemed to settle him and Marlowe slid his blade back into its scabbard.

We were ready to leave, but Mary still hadn't arrived. While we waited, Germaine and I worked together to make a body of my own. He guided me in growing the flesh and organs, helping me construct the human face I had once owned, without savage teeth and red ears. Once finished we started to load the bodies into Smithy's helicopter. It felt strange, placing them in the cargo hold. I looked into the mirror of my other, lifeless face. This was the vessel that would carry me to Heaven. Germaine and I had already gone over the procedure with Clytemnestra. We were to fuse ourselves with the shells. Not just our souls, but our entire ethereal bodies as well. Because the elements of our current bodies were less rigid, we could push ourselves right into the earthly flesh. It would be almost like piloting a robot exoskeleton, while encased within. If we split our souls from our ethereal bodies completely, it would leave that side of us exposed and without guard in Hell. Once fused, we would ascend into the Hellmouth, and onto the material realm of Earth.

As the last of the bodies were loaded aboard, I turned to see Mary exiting the castle and crossing towards us. The way she looked reminded me of the first time I had seen her. She was dressed in scarlet, a shade darker than her hair. The aura about her was of immense dignity and otherworldly power. She wore a mask of deadly calm, which concealed all of her emotions. Since we exorcised the souls of The Pure Seven from her body, she had been freer with her feelings, but now she had returned to the demeanor of a businesswoman. She was once again the cool madam of the biggest brothel in Hell. It suited her. I smiled a hello and she simply nodded to acknowledge me. Without even so much as a glance at Charlotte, she walked up to Smithy and greeted him with a hug and a lingering kiss on both cheeks.

"Thank you for taking us all, Captain," she said. "We'd be nowhere without you. Would you like me to ride in the jump seat with you and show you where we're headed?"

Smithy blushed at the compliment.

"By all means, m'lady," he said, opening the door for her and holding out his hand to help her aboard.

I looked at Charlotte, who rolled her eyes at the display. She moved to get into the back. Germaine, Marlowe, Clytemnestra and I all piled in together behind her. Doing his preflight check, Smithy flicked his controls and the blades overhead whirred to life. In moments we were lifting off, hovering above Casa Diablo and flying away from the city. At first we took a similar path to when we had traveled to the Chinvar Bridge. We zipped over dark and teeming jungle, past scorched and uninhabitable desert sands. Instead of heading to Zoroaster's old monastery, however, we moved further to what I supposed was East. I could see Mary pointing directions to Smithy, but the noise of the helicopter drowned out what they were saying. I grabbed one of the headsets in front of us and put it on.

"We're not far," Mary said. "It looks like we're going to arrive with good timing."

Previously, Clytemnestra had explained the best time to make a surfacing to Earth was just before the guilt storm. During that time the air became thinner above. It was sucked toward the horizon for the coming blast. Any normal resistance above was weakened momentarily and a wormhole opened up, which would enable us to weave our way through to the material realm. I glanced at the watch on my wrist. Mary was right. We would be there with enough time to enter our prepared bodies and lift our party into the entry. We could only go from what the Necromancers had told Clytemnestra. In a sense we were running blind, but that was nothing new.

Easing the chopper to the ground, Smithy quickly shut down the controls. We disembarked, each moving to the back of the aircraft to heft down our cargo. Almost without ceremony we laid them in the sand.

"Okay," I said to everyone. "I want each of you to lie down on top of your chosen body. Germaine and I will soften their construction, so you can sink down into them. We'll then have to fuse your thoughts and emotions into them. I want you to empty your minds of any thoughts. Try to become empty yourselves so that you may fill your new vessel."

"That sounds like some kind of hippy yoga nonsense to me," Smithy said, looking up. "How am I not supposed to think about anything? That what it is to be alive."

I paused for a moment and thought. "Just pretend you're trying to go to sleep," I ventured.

"Oh," the old pilot nodded. "I can do that."

Letting them each settle on their respective bodies, I waited for them to get as comfortable as possible. With a silent nod to Germaine, we began our work. The process was fairly simple at first. All we needed to do was create a small amount of space between the atoms which made up the earthly bodies' construction. Then, with a nudge of pressure, like clicking two Lego blocks into place, we pushed the ethereal bodies down to meld with their twin. Once they had been matched properly, the body jolted

110

with a heavy twitch, as if awaking from a deep sleep. After that, I needed Germaine's ingenuity to complete the process. He talked me through how to take strands of ethereal thought and emotion and connect them to the physical. As the process came to an end, one by one, each of our party sat up rubbing their faces and looking at their hands. They looked woozy, as if they weren't fully in control of their bodies. Marlowe pressed up onto his knees and attempted to stand, but toppled again to the ground, swearing. Clytemnestra did the same, while Smithy giggled. He then smiled at the sound of his own voice and looked at his hands as if they were brand new.

"They'll take some getting used to," Germaine said. "But it shouldn't take long."

"It will be like driving a new car," I offered, seeing that they were finally beginning to get the hang of their limbs. "Once you know how it all works, it will become second nature."

At my words Smithy pressed off the ground and remained steady. He was obviously a natural at controlling foreign machinery. He walked over to me slowly and reached out, pressing his hand onto my skin.

"That feels very odd," he said, before looking around. "It feels like I'm wearing thick gloves. And I'm very hot!"

"You'd feel hotter if you didn't still have a layer of cold air around you," Germaine said, settling over the top of his body.

Before I could even offer to help, he had sunk down into his shell with ease. I connected his spirit to it, before lying over my own shell and closing my eyes. Feeling my way into my body, I swelled up, as if filling my lungs with air. As I breathed in, the flesh underneath me rushed in to fill my pores. As I breathed out, I became fixed inside it. The sensation was indeed unusual. It wasn't like before, when I had returned to Earth. That had been my true earthly shell. This one was alien. I felt heavy, weighed down with too much substance. It took great effort to lift my mass. It reminded me of the few times in my life I had fallen asleep with my arm underneath me. When I woke up, it felt as if the limb was dead, but if I waited long enough, I could eventually make it respond. Ever so slowly, it would come back and feel normal again. This body was the same: a piece of thick rubber that moved at my will, just not exactly how I wanted.

A flash of light on the horizon reminded me that we didn't have long to get used to this new state. I would have to gather us all together very shortly.

"Smithy," I said, the words echoing strangely in my head. "Can you help me up?"

My friend came over and heaved me to my feet, keeping me steady until I had the ability to control the flesh that encased me. Even my mind felt misty, as if I had enjoyed one too many Heinekens at Sloth's Lounge. I made a concerted effort to focus.

"Don't fight it," Smithy said next to me. "Relax into it. It will do what you ask, you don't have to wrestle it."

I listened to what he was saying. Rather than physically trying to bully my arms and legs into submission, I used my mind and muscle impulse instead. It made a world of difference. While still strange, the construction around me made sense. It was similar to controlling the elements. I supposed in a way it was the same thing.

"Everyone!" I said loudly, starting to feel normal. "Do your best to gather around me. We're leaving in one minute."

As I finished the sentence, the bloody flames on the far edges of Hell spluttered into guilty whips of light. I narrowed my vision and let the elements take hold. Looking skyward, I could see a black vortex begin to open directly above us: The Hellmouth.

Pulling air in tight and grasping Charlotte close to my body, I formed a bubble around our party and took flight. As we pushed upward, the black hole of the Hellmouth beckoned us within. The flames of Guilt licked at our heels and we blasted inside. At once, the rush of noise below ceased. We were enveloped into a new atmosphere that was familiar in the back recesses of my mind. Through the dripping darkness above, I could make out rock stalagmites hanging from a limestone cave. A shiver of night air breathed around my body. We had returned to Earth.

28

I SLOWLY LET MY PHYSICAL GRIP on Charlotte loosen, allowing her feet to touch the stony ground beneath us. The elements I had constructed sifted away as I released my hold on the others. I stood, blinking, waiting for my eyes to fully adjust. After the constant storm-laden sky of Hell, it took quite a few moments to get used to our naturally shadowed surroundings. A cool breeze blew through the cave, from what I assumed was an opening somewhere further up. The sound of crashing waves shuddered in an irregular heartbeat through the tunnel from which we'd emerged. All of us were silent, each in our own personal world, remembering what it was like to be alive in the physical realm. It hadn't been as long for me as it had for most of the others, yet still it felt unique. It wasn't exactly the same, since we were in borrowed bodies, but the actual sensation of air on bare skin was sharper than anything else on the other side. This was living.

After waiting and listening for anything unusual, I made a move to light the cave. Letting a soft yellow light filter out above us, I illuminated every corner. Crags of rough rock on one side contrasted with smoothly worn wall on the other. It was as if a craftsman had only half finished his work inside a living piece of art. I realized that the smooth area was closer to where we had entered, so perhaps it was the centuries of hot blasts of air coming up from Hell upon every Guilt storm that had created the phenomenon. After searching around for any danger, it became clear that we were alone. We were safe, for now.

"We have to assume that Asmodeus is watching our every move from Heaven," I said to everyone.

They all looked to me, slightly startled at the sound of my voice. I hadn't realized they were all just as on edge as I was, if not more.

"Anything could happen," I said firmly. "We're at his mercy while we're here. Remember, though, the worst that can occur is that your physical body will be destroyed and you'll be ripped back down to Hell."

"Or you could be put in a coma and imprisoned here indefinitely inside a useless body," Mary said. She started to move ahead, up towards where the cool air wafted down to greet us. Her words sent a chill down my spine.

"So death is preferable," Clytemnestra said, shrugging her shoulders. She started to follow Mary. "We should get moving, then. I'd rather be caught in the open air than another stifling cave."

In front of us, a jagged stairway was cut into the rock. It appeared to be a natural formation rather than anything man-made. I wondered how many feet had actually trod those stones over the centuries. Surely not too many souls had left Hell to visit this surface and it seemed baffling that anyone would want to go down. I did vaguely recall an old Greek myth about Hercules descending to Hades, but surely this wasn't the same place.

It was slow going, climbing upward in a new, unproven body, but the exercise helped me get used to my mortal form. I made sure I was last to go up, just in case something unexpected came from below. Smithy seemed to move with ease, while Marlowe was having the most trouble. It was unusual to see such a normally graceful killer uncomfortable in his skin. I kept the light surrounding us, not too bright to create notice from anything on the outside, but just so that we could see. Nobody spoke. The silence among us was oppressive. It was like the moment before something terrible happens in a horror movie and everyone in the theatre is holding their breath for the impact. It went on and on and nothing happened. Still no one let out a sigh of relief. We all knew the impact would come. I only hoped that since the world was so big, maybe Asmodeus would not notice us until it was too late. Perhaps he had foreseen this already and was just biding his time. The sense of being watched started to prickle under my skin. Maybe it was just paranoia.

Finally, our party surfaced onto a flat opening, which had two huge rocks on either side. The pathway led to a short drop which hung above the sea. It was night. A scatter of boulders spread out into the murky Mediterranean waters with its swirls of whitewater frothing amid the rocks below. There were no clouds overhead. A crescent moon hung in the dark navy sky. Dots of stars twinkled above. To the rest of the world this was just another peaceful evening in secluded, southern Greece. Over to the right, a lighthouse sat perched, overlooking its keep. A few boats, with lights on deck, were scattered on the horizon. None ventured close to shore.

"What now, Captain?" Smithy asked me in a whisper at my shoulder.

What now, indeed, I thought. We had been focusing so hard on the more complex details of this mission that the simple things hadn't been discussed. We had a least plotted our course in Mary's Chamber of Maps. It was a matter of getting from here to Israel, which lay in a direct southeast line, eight hundred miles away. The fastest way would be to fly, but I didn't want to draw any unnecessary notice. Seven bodies shooting through the air wouldn't only garner attention from Heaven; Israel's anti-missile defence systems would also potentially pick us up. I didn't want to be attacked on all sides. I also didn't want to deplete my energy for more important battles. The slower, yet lower profile crossing by boat would have to be the answer. I could easily manifest a vessel big enough to hold all of us, powering it with a surreptitious elemental wind. However, at a top speed of twenty knots or so, it would still take us almost two full days to get there. At least we would have plenty of time to plan our next move once we hit land.

29

CALM WATERS LAPPED THE BOAT'S SIDES as we plowed quietly ahead in the night. I had constructed a wooden craft for us, using my memory of the vessels I had passed daily in my life on the wharves of San Francisco. Getting the shape right so it would glide steadily had been harder than I anticipated. I had used the simplest, but most effective material I could think of: wood. Smithy had jokingly dubbed the boat The Ark as we had filed aboard. A single piece of fine-grained timber now comfortably held the seven of us, floating on the Mediterranean Sea. A large triangular sail billowed above, full of a steady airstream I used to push us ahead. I had tied off a perpetual mini-storm behind the sail, so I didn't have to constantly maintain concentration to keep us moving. Truth be told, I was exhausted from the resurrection. We all were. Having a real flesh and blood body to maintain was taxing. It was easy to forget such simple things. On top of that, my nerves were frayed. Every irregular bump or breeze sent my teeth grinding with nerves. It felt like we were sitting ducks, ready to be sunk at any moment.

I had arranged for some of us to sleep, while Mary, Smithy and I stayed up to keep watch. Marlowe was snoring loudly beneath a small housing I had made for us to gather in, away from the chill of the night. After so long in the furnace of Hell, even the mild weather of Greece felt cold. Germaine, Clytemnestra and Charlotte were all lying close together, staying warm while they slumbered. Smithy dropped a fishing line over the railing of the boat, hoping to catch some food. It was easier for me to manifest a rod than a fish.

Mary was kneeling towards the bow of the boat, in silent prayer. Her habit unnerved me. I knew she always whispered her fears to the winds in Hell. She said it scattered her feelings outward and gave them less power over her mind. However, on Earth I was afraid someone might actually be listening. I looked out to the inky waters around us with trepidation. The stillness of the night only served to put me more on edge. Moving towards the front of the boat, I quietly sat down next to her.

"Let's hope those prayers don't get answered," I said, half- joking, trying to lift my own mood.

She looked up at me with a cool stare.

"They never have been before. I can't see it happening now," she said, rocking back off her knees to sit with crossed legs. "Still, it helps me relax."

"I wish it did the same for me," I said. "I don't know what will happen when we get to the ladder. Do you think there will be resistance there to meet us?"

"Unlikely," she shrugged. "From what I understand, it was the path the angels used to visit earth and help with miracles. There hasn't been a true miracle on Earth for over a thousand years. We would have heard about it in Hell otherwise. As the world became less believing, those in Heaven deserted humanity to let them fend for themselves. Always judging but never helping. I used to watch closely from Hell myself, but eventually even I grew tired of the violence and sorrow being created here. There's enough of that below."

I knew she was right. War was a constant feature of the surface on this planet. Conflict was an innate part of the human mind. We were made that way: wolves to each other. What had changed was the level of devastation we could now create through science. Nuclear war, chemical weapons, biologically created disease: they threatened to overwhelm life as we knew it. A brief divine appearance in Israel, where we were headed, announcing from Heaven that the land belonged to everyone equally, might have stemmed the flood of death in the region. Still, Asmodeus hadn't stepped in. He only manipulated for his own ends, when it served a specific purpose. Conflict for him was entertainment. There was no greater good he wanted.

"Do you think he is us watching now?" I asked Mary softly. "I don't know," she said. "I think if he was, he would have acted already. Perhaps there is some unrest in Heaven. I would like to hope that Zoroaster has been able to raise some concerns amongst the good people there. Asmodeus may be dealing with a minor rebellion of his own. It would certainly explain any lack of action here and maybe even his fast retreat from Hell."

It was strange. I should have been happy that we hadn't encountered any problems yet. It was literally smooth sailing, yet experience had taught me that when things were too easy there was a sinister reason behind it. I could only sit tight and wait, hoping Mary was right in her musings.

"Can you speak Hebrew?" I asked her, changing the subject. "Of course," she said, raising an eyebrow at the strange turn of the conversation. "I grew up in this part of the world. The language may have evolved since then, but I have evolved with it. I can speak most languages. Every culture in existence craves sex. I cannot help feed their individual desires if I can't understand what each person wants."

"Good. So you speak Arabic as well?"

She nodded, the light of understanding glowing in her eyes.

"You want me to serve as our guide through Israel," she said.

"And Heaven as well," I confirmed. "We don't look like we're from around here, so our best cover is a tourist group, with you as our tour leader. The Aedicule of Ascension would have to be a popular tourist spot."

"I'm sure hundreds of thousands of pilgrims from all around the world visit there every year. That's a brilliant idea, Michael."

"It was Charlotte's actually," I said. "She mentioned just before she went to sleep that I should ask you to lead the way, since this is your homeland."

"She's smarter than she looks," Mary said.

I let the backhanded compliment slide. It wasn't the time for petty differences to get in the way.

"Good," I said instead. "Once we arrive at the shrine, we'll conceal ourselves somewhere and work out how to climb the ladder when there's no one around."

She nodded slowly, her eyes watching out toward the horizon, which had just started to crack with a sliver of golden dawn. We still had a day and a night to travel until we landed on the shores of Israel. The rapidly reddening sky of the morning reminded me of the old proverb: sailor's warning.

A cry from Smithy behind us made me jump to my feet and spin around. For a brief second I thought we were under attack, until I saw him hauling a flapping fish aboard the boat. It was a huge silver thing, with bright scales that flashed with the reddening light of the new morning sky. Smithy leapt down and grabbed it in his hands, as it gasped its last breaths on the deck. He held it up in the air in triumph. His old face crinkled into a genuine smile of delight.

"We're having seafood for breakfast!"

30

I SUCKED JUICY FLESH from the fish bones in my hands. Smithy's catch had been more than enough to feed all seven of us. Using the elements of fire, I had cooked the creature from the inside, keeping the meat tender and fresh. The meal slid gloriously down my gullet to warm my belly: another forgotten joy. There was no fresh fish in Hell. We all sat in a circle around the carcass, which still held plenty of sustenance to keep us going for the rest of the day. Sounds of messy eating filled the air, along with the occasional caw from some surrounding seagulls. Smithy had a satisfied grin on his face as he watched everyone eat. When someone had finished what was in their hands, he would quickly peel another strip off his prize and force it on them.

"Eat up, eat up!"

We took our fill and more, stretching our stomachs to the limit in a true show of Hellish gluttony. I leaned back on my elbows and watched the surrounding sea. No boats had come near enough to cause any concern. I had almost forgotten we could be swamped at any minute by some kind of force of God. The thought made me sit up again a bit straighter. My mind and body were both weary with the constant strain of worry. To cap it off, my full belly was making me hopelessly sleepy.

"So, Mary," Clytemnestra said, wiping her greasy hands on her pants. "What can we expect once we're able to get to Jacob's ladder and reach Heaven?"

The plan to make our way to the Ascension Aedicule disguised as tourists had already been meet by approval from everyone. Mary finished her mouthful before speaking.

"It's been a very long time since I've been there," Mary said. "Hell itself has changed so much over that time it wouldn't be recognizable now. I wonder if the same has happened in Heaven."

"If Heaven is supposed to be perfection, then it shouldn't change," I offered. "The only way to improve perfection is to expand it so more people can enjoy it."

"You may be right," Mary conceded. "If that's the case and it hasn't changed, there is a main city, where the majority of souls live. The walls around it are made from diamonds and gold."

"That's a bit clichéd," Marlowe snorted.

"The gates are, but the city itself is anything but. It's not all clouds and angels blowing on trumpets. The centre of the capital is God's home, a veritable city in itself. There is a huge basilica-style building with high, solid quartz domes. It is built on a rise so it looks over the surrounding metropolis. The central dome has entryways from the sky, from which the angels are free to come and go as they please. Some witty soul nicknamed it 'The Aviary'. God was so delighted with the humor that it stuck. Around The Aviary is another set of seven domes, each named after the Archangel who presides over the palace within. There are pink quartz statues above each of those palaces, in the angels' likenesses. Their wings are spread out in welcome to the new souls who are fortunate enough to be able to move into the city. Underneath this complex is a rabbit warren of tunnels connecting the palaces, where the little-seen servant angels can scurry around bringing news, food or entertainment wherever they are needed. At the foot of the city centre there are walls built out in concentric circles to the outer gate. Each circle is reserved for the citizens at a particular level of piety. The inner circle houses the earthly saints and prophets. The next, those who are candidates for canonization and high-holy men of earth."

"I suppose there are nine circles," I interrupted.

"God does have a flair for the poetic," Mary said. "Nine circles of Heaven, just like the supposed nine circles of Hell. But these circles are real."

I stood up, watching the clear blue sky and then turned to our sail, which was still pushing us in the correct direction. I needed to work my legs or I would fall asleep. I walked over to the railing and looked down into the sea. It was another forgotten world yet to be fully explored. Charlotte rose as well, coming to me and putting a concerned arm around my shoulders. She was watching my tired eyes with worry. She could tell I was struggling to stay alert.

"And what are we looking for once we get there?" Marlowe asked Mary. "How are we going to tear down the gates of the city?"

"We don't need to take down the gates yet," Mary answered. "We will need to worry less about the city once the armies of Hell are able to rise up. The goal is to destroy the filter that pushes lesser souls out of Heaven back down to the fiery pits."

I recalled what it had taken to destroy the barrier of Purgatory. We had used the keys made from the divine element and wedged them into the flow of the filter: a roaring twist of emotion and power. The filter swirled constantly to sweep away those ready to enter Heaven. Now the barrier between Purgatory and Hell needed to be dismantled as well. I had assumed that Heaven would have enveloped Purgatory in its eternal arms once we had destroyed the first filter, but I hadn't been able to witness exactly how that had played out. As usual, we were dealing with the unknown. This was as much a discovery mission as it was an attack, like a biopsy on a tumor.

"We need to somehow get our hands on the remaining keys to Heaven," I said. "We can use them the same way to destroy this filter. I don't think Asmodeus will have them simply on display, though."

"We may be surprised at his arrogance," Clytemnestra offered.

She tore off another slice of fish and put it in her mouth. Germaine had made her body with normal teeth and gums. There were no disfigurements that could give us away as inmates of Hell. She was incredibly beautiful, with olive skin and the bone structure of a well-bred queen. Her razor teeth had always dominated my attention before, but now I was struck by her stately good looks.

"There is another set of keys as well," Mary said, almost too casually. I nearly missed the gravity of her statement.

"What?" I asked.

"Matthew Sixteen Eighteen," Germaine said to us matter- of-factly.

We looked back at him blankly.

"As the Lord of Hell, you really should know your holy scripture better." He continued, as if reciting the words from a page in his mind. "And so I say to you, Peter, upon this rock I will build my church, and the gates of the netherworld shall not prevail against it. I will give you the keys to the Kingdom of Heaven. Whatever you bind on Earth shall be bound in Heaven; and whatever you let loose on Earth shall be loosed in Heaven."

"I will give you the keys to the Kingdom of Heaven." Smithy repeated, realizing the significance of the verse right away.

"They are the keys between Earth and Heaven." Mary added. "The keys to the holy city. I'm sure they'll be made of the divine element also. We just need to find Saint Peter."

"You make it sound so easy!" I sighed, my fatigue getting the better of my patience. "How do you propose we find him and how can we assume Asmodeus still trusts him with the keys?"

"Asmodeus cannot go against his own divine mandate handed down in scripture," she replied hotly. "Not only will Peter still have the keys, but I know where he'll be. Just as the stories say, he's always standing at the front gates of the city, making sure only the worthy enter."

Her words reminded me of the traditional image of Saint Peter at the 'pearly gates': God's bouncer. If Mary was correct, then perhaps our mission would prove to be as fruitful as we could dare hope. If she was correct. I felt my legs wobble a little beneath me. The body I was in badly needed sleep. I noticed that Mary and Smithy who had stayed awake during the first shift also had black bags under their eyes. Sensing my exhaustion, Charlotte tapped me on the chest lightly.

"It's time you got some rest, my love," she said tenderly.

"I cannot," I said. "I need to be ready should anything happen. I can manufacture sleep from the elements."

"You're no good to anyone dead tired," she pressed softly. "It's easier for you to just close your eyes. It will help pass the time for you. You're like a skittish cat at the moment. There are four of us to keep watch. I'll make sure there is always someone right by your side, ready to rouse you if anything seems off."

I blinked a long blink of the weary. Sleep. We had a huge day coming up. I needed to be fresh for the climb up the ladder. Accepting Lotte's offer, I crept under the shelter on the deck and into the shadows. Smithy also dragged himself away from the food and laid his new old bones out on the wooden deck near me. Mary followed. Surprisingly, she lay next to Smithy, snuggling up tight into his body, so he had no choice but to wrap his arms around her. The pilot looked to me with shock. I gave him a tired wink and then finally put my head down. I had thought it would be a battle to keep my mind still enough to rest, but I had barely closed my eyes before the grip of sleep rose up like pseudo death, dragging me into its black embrace.

31

I WALKED ALONE IN THE VOID, stalking on a carpet of elements. I looked around, afraid. I knew something was coming for me, but wasn't sure what. My eyesight was muddled so I couldn't see further than a few feet in front of me. Still I walked on, knowing that I had to keep moving and everything would be okay. I had to keep going at all costs. A blur of movement flashed to the side, but when I turned towards it, it disappeared. There was someone out there. Were they friend or foe? I started to jog forward again, into the uncertain Void. One foot after the other I stepped, my feet padding faster and faster. The blur to the side kept getting closer. It drew up so it brushed my skin, hands stroking my leg roughly, then my chest. I jerked away and pumped my legs to quicken my pace. I looked ahead and saw an opening of color. The Perceptionist was there, next to a swirling portal. His thousand eyes were all blood red, like The Furies'. In a fast movement, he wedged his hands in front of him and tore the fabric of the Void apart, creating anti-matter, which burrowed away to another universe. I saw its horrid darkness and tried to stop, but my legs kept going. Again there was the blur, brushing my body, harassing me at every step. The Perceptionist covered the entry to the portal next to him with dark matter, blocking the way. I tried to tell my legs to stop, but my body would not obey my mind. It just kept running headlong towards certain death. Again, there was a bump against my body. I tried to turn but not even my eyes would work. I was being propelled onward against my will. As I came closer to him, The Perceptionist stepped aside. With a silent scream, I tumbled into the black hole of anti-matter he had made. I reached out instinctively to hold onto something in the physical world. This time my body reacted. My fingers gripped onto a hand. The blur gave out a shout of surprise.

Jolting awake on the deck of the boat, reality rushed into my earthly body. It was night again and the waves lightly swished against the gunwales of the boat. I grabbed the hand harder, looking frantically to see what was happening. It was Germaine, his fingers had been searching inside the pocket of my pants. His frightened eyes looked back at my glare. He was a hapless child, caught trying to take a treat from the candy jar without permission. He seemed to brace himself for me to lash out, but I just let his hand drop.

"Soon," I whispered to him. "Be patient and the blood will come."

He started to say something, but I shook my head to silence him. I should have been furious, but when you expect someone to do something, you can't be mad, only disappointed you were right. Despite all his knowledge and power he was still a slave to desire. I couldn't blame him for being human. I was only glad I'd given the jewels to Mary for safekeeping, or it could have been a disaster.

"If you try that again, I will end your existence." I said softly, but sternly.

He looked down at his hand, as though it had betrayed him. He rubbed it on his clothing, as if it was unclean. I looked up to see Charlotte and Marlowe in conversation on the deck, both looking out in constant watch. Clytemnestra was standing alone at the stern. It must have been Germaine's turn to sit by my side in case anything happened.

"I think we're only a few hours away," he said tentatively. "You've slept all day and most of the night. As have the others." Sure enough, to the side of us Mary was still gently sleeping in Smithy's arms. He let out light snores, his chin resting gently on the crown of her head. I stood up quietly, doing my best not to rouse them. Shuffling onto the deck, I left the awkward moment with Germaine back in the land of dreams.

"All quiet on the eastern front?" I asked Charlotte and Marlowe as I approached.

The pair turned to meet me with tentative smiles.

"We have been lucky," Marlowe said. "The only movement has been the steady progress this Ark has been making."

Charlotte came to my side and gave me a quick kiss hello. She squeezed my arm with reassurance, letting me know silently that everything was going well.

"If you look hard enough, you can just make out some lights on the horizon," she said. "I think it must be Israel."

Casting my sight to the horizon, I squinted to see that Lotte was right. The faintest of shimmering light was starting to come into view. We would arrive soon enough. I checked to make sure the sail was holding firm and the wind was blowing true. All was as it should be. Asmodeus really must be distracted from our small party. If he was going to attack us, it surely would have been on the open ocean where there were fewer witnesses and we were more vulnerable. The fact that we were still all in one piece lifted my spirits. I allowed myself to be truly hopeful. Behind us, Mary and Smithy stirred.

"Time to wake up," I called back to them. "We need to get ready. It's going to be a challenging day."

The dark night lifted into a grey dawn, as we edged closer to the coast. I kept our steady pace, but created a cloak of elements around our boat to reflect any vision away from us. We would be invisible to any prying eyes looking out to sea. Dawn broke and the pink sands came into view. We all stood on the deck, watching closely. Charlotte's blonde hair whipped lightly in the wind. She was so calm on the surface. I wondered if on the inside she was feeling as restless as I was. As if by instinct, she put her hand over mine to settle me. We looked to shore together. Southward was a jutting rock wall, which fed out to sea and then bent like a protective arm, harboring ships within. On the beach itself, ramshackle tents were scattered on the sand, some just battered tarpaulins strung over driftwood frames. Thatch-roof shacks sat behind them. Arching over it all was a set of powerlines that followed the coast. In the distance stood wide apartment blocks. Domes of mosques broke up the rest of the urban sprawl.

"I think we are a little off course," Mary said. "This seems to be Islamic land. Perhaps Gaza. We need to continue north or we'll find it difficult to cross the border."

At Mary's direction, I steered The Ark to sail along the coastline. A few people were dotted along the beach, heading down to the water. Small waves broke, rolling into the shore. Our boat rocked sideways from the movement beneath us. As we travelled, the landscape stayed the same. Short saltbushes and green trees with streaks of brown on their prickly branches jutted from behind soft dunes. The buildings, however, changed in appearance along the way. No longer did onion-shaped mosque roofs dot the cityscape. As we drifted along the Israeli coast, the buildings became more modern; the marinas were stacked with new white boats; kite surfers littered the beaches, zipping through the waters on small boards attached by thick wires to their sails overhead. They looked like little puppets being controlled by their kites. We sailed further, putting some distance between us and the Gaza border. I watched closely for a good stretch to take The Ark aground.

"What's that?" Charlotte pointed out to me, as we drifted along steadily. Rising above the vegetation ahead stood an ancient structure, as if it had grown from the sand. Worn stucco bricks formed three archways; two short towers sat at the front, like old watch keepers looking out to sea. On closer inspection, I could also see a low steel fence surrounding the structure.

"It must be Ashdod-Yam," Mary said. "It is a sea fort built by the Assyrian kings almost a thousand years before Christ. This place was used as a harbor and trading yard in my time. We should land here. It's quite close to Jerusalem."

Adjusting our course, I turned the bow of our boat to face directly towards the fort. I could see a few people moving slowly through the ruins, their hands clasped thoughtfully behind their backs as they studied the rocks. Tourists. Perfect: we'd be able to blend in here and make a move into the city. The nose of The Ark gently sank into the wet sands of Israel. I maintained our cloak of elements, while my six companions jumped from the decks, down to solid land. They bent low out of instinct, grouped close together, carrying nothing but the plain clothes on their backs. We had to be light and ready to move quickly. Instead of leaping down myself, I let the structure of the vessel slowly dissolve underneath me, turning wood into sand at will. What was once our Ark was now simply a part of the beach.

We didn't stop to admire the ancient ruins of Ashdod-Yam. I was intent on our mission. We carefully made our way up the beach, skirting the fence surrounding the site and making our way up a wide sandy path between the trees. With no one to see, I lifted our veil, leaving us exposed again to the outside world. I half expected a soldier to leap out from behind a tree and question what we were doing, but no encounter came. Instead, we came out onto a bitumen road. A large roundabout sat before us, with a twisted sculpture in the middle. It was some kind of circle, sitting atop of a zigzagging rod. The word "shalom" was wrapped around the top. Two short palms stood to either side. On the other side of the road were white buildings with satellite dishes scattered on their rooftops. Occasionally, a red roof broke up the banal color scheme. Cars filtered lazily along the foreshore highway. Compared with the chaos of Hell, it all seemed so ordered and safe.

"Come," Mary said, assuming her role as guide.

I wondered what people must have thought, looking at our group. None of us looked like we belonged with each other, apart from perhaps Charlotte and I. We had an African warrior, a Greek Goddess, an elderly soldier, a half-crazed man with purple eyes and a redheaded Jewess in our midst. If we had walked into a bar, someone could have rightly asked if it were some kind of joke. We filed across the street, easily negotiating the traffic. Mary waved down a white taxi, which had black lettering on the side and a traditional yellow sign on top. The man inside wound down his window and Mary greeted him in a string of fluent Hebrew. He smiled at hearing a native tongue come from a group which was clearly out of place in this land. She seemed to explain what we were doing and where we needed to go. He yelled out to the rest of us in accented English.

"I cannot fit seven. Wait. I call another car. We'll have you to the Mount of Olives in two hours."

32

IT WAS A STRANGE FEELING, driving through the coastal streets of Israel. This was a part of the world I had heard so much about, but never visited. I had expected a soldier on every corner and ancient buildings everywhere. Instead, our surroundings were more like an arid version of Miami. Tall palm trees sprung up in uniform rows on the dividing strip in the middle of the road. Art deco apartment blocks were a feature of the architecture. As we continued inland, the surrounds gradually changed, as though we were slowly driving back in time. The four of us in the first car were all in a contemplative mood, silently witnessing history fly by our windows. The driver, a smiling Jew named Elijah, chatted about the significance of the sites while we made progress. Mary sat next to him in the front, occasionally making comment to him. Quite often he would exclaim in surprise.

He turned back to me in astonishment at one point, saying, "You have a wonderful guide. It's almost like Miss Mary was here during the holy times!"

Mary smirked back to me at the comment, but we said nothing. Charlotte sat by my side on the left and Smithy was on my right. The other three were trailing closely in the car behind us. Elijah kept a lively pace, but made sure he hung back enough so that we didn't lose our companions.

"Are you sure you do not want to visit the Dome of the Rock?" he asked us. "It's the first place most tourists want to see when coming to our city."

"We have a special tour tomorrow," Mary explained. "I will take them to the Mount of Olives today and explore on foot. We'll then stay close by and get in early, before the queues get too long and sun too hot."

The lie rolled off her tongue like an offhand comment. For someone who normally practised absolute truth, I knew it must have hurt her inside. I hoped Germaine would keep his tongue in place in the other taxi, or Marlowe might cut it out to silence him.

The road we were on wound around, past the Dome of the Rock, whose golden roof was shining like a beacon in the midday sun. At this distance, the tile work on the façade was a deep azure blue. It almost looked like God's thumb pointing in the air, amidst a fist of sand-worn stone. The old city swung by on the left, the ancient walls of its outskirts cutting us off from the bustle within. I could see Mary staring at the structure with a look of nostalgia in her eyes. She was continuously shaking her head slowly, as if she couldn't believe what she was seeing. Along the streets on the outside, old women in their formal headdresses mixed with the new generation of girls who let their flowing, black hair whip free. The younger women seemed to be making a subtle statement in their dress that said, 'We are moving forward in our own way.'

Still our car drove on. Elijah pointed excitedly to the right.

"This is my favorite sight in all of Jerusalem," he exclaimed, winding down the windows as if there shouldn't be anything separating us from what we saw.

Scattered along a rising mountainside was a clutter of white tombs. There were no fancy headstones as you might see in a traditional Christian cemetery. Each grave was just a rectangular stone block, some with black symbols scripted on their lids. From this distance I couldn't make out what any of them said, but the view from the car suggested that there were some quarter of a million graves resting along the rise.

"This is the old Jerusalem cemetery," Elijah said to us. "My great, great grandfather is buried there, and his father. More than a hundred and fifty thousand souls laid to rest at the base of Mount Olivet. There used to be more, except the Muslim dogs demolished many before we claimed it back."

He spat viciously out the window. I was startled at how quickly his friendly demeanor turned to one of hatred. He caught his action and smoothed it over with a nervous laugh, as though he shouldn't have said such a thing in front of outsiders.

"Of course you must understand," he continued, "there should always be respect for the dead, on both sides. I do not like to see old bodies disturbed so."

"Why?" Smithy asked him. "They are dead. They cannot be harmed now."

Elijah shook his head furiously at the comment, but kept a light tone in his voice, as if explaining something to a child.

"Maybe in other places that would be more true, but this ground has special significance. In the Torah it says that when the messiah comes, this is where the resurrection of the dead will begin."

If you believe the Christians, he has already come," Mary said next to him.

"Yes," he nodded. "And yet the graves lie still. It is one of the reasons we know the Christians are mistaken."

"Either way, it's a very beautiful place," Charlotte said quickly from the back seat, diverting any debate that might arise from the comments.

"It is," Mary agreed, wisely keeping her knowledge to herself. Elijah beamed once more at the compliment. He was obviously proud of his heritage.

"Oh, I think you'll enjoy these next sites too," Elijah said, as we drove uphill, ascending the Mount of Olives. "First is the Church of Assumption, which is the place of the Virgin Mary's tomb. Perhaps you were named after her?" Elijah offered to our guide.

"Oh no," Mary smiled softly. "Not after the Virgin Mary."

"Then perhaps the other one. Mary Magdalene?"

Smithy started to cough in the back seat, his face going red with the lack of air. I patted him on the back, helping him recover. Elijah looked back briefly, but once we had settled the pilot down, he continued.

"Oh, yes, you have the red hair of Mary Magdalene," he said. "She is said to have been a great person, very important to the Christian movement, no? She was so great, this building ahead was built in her honor. But you would know this, of course."

Ahead, a towering church arose from behind a row of green trees. The gold-plated tops of seven, Russian style minarets gleamed; crowning each dome was a golden crucifix. The building below was a tiered white and blue construction: one of the most beautiful buildings I had ever seen. It was now Mary's turn to lose her breath. Her mouth hung open as our car drove past. She muttered something under her breath, which sounded like, "Impossible".

"Yes, it is an amazement, no matter how many times you've seen it," Elijah said.

"When was it built?" I asked, knowing from Mary's reaction that it must have been erected long after her time.

"It was built in 1886, by Tsar Alexander III," he said, happy to showcase his knowledge. "It was a tribute to not only Mary Magdalene, but to the Tsar's mother, also called Mary. This is well before the communist revolution, of course."

"Of course," I nodded. "You're very knowledgeable for a taxi driver," I added.

"I love my city," he said. "This is the place of God after all. You see this building is still a fully used Russian Orthodox church. While there might be some tensions, Christians, Muslims and Jews all still have a place here in God's land."

I let the conversation fall quiet again at the mention of religion. Elijah was slowing the car anyway, as we drove into a more built up area. Old stone buildings, battered by time, lined the street. Here and there, scribbled graffiti marred some of the walls. It felt like this was a semi-derelict part of town. Elijah continued through a few twists and turns before coming to a stop.

"This is your destination," he said, pointing ahead.

There wasn't very much to see, other than a high wall, similar to many of the other limestone and dolomite walls we had seen driving through the city proper. We piled out of the car. After a couple of hours sitting cramped in the back, it felt good to stretch my borrowed body. The other taxi pulled up behind us, and Marlowe, Clytemnestra and Germaine rejoined our group. Their driver waited in his car. We were about to walk across the street to enter the building when Elijah tugged my sleeve. My body went rigid at the unexpected movement. I turned almost too quickly, ready to attack. Elijah backed up a step, frightened.

"I'm sorry, sir," he said, holding up his hands in apology. "I only meant to remind you that you hadn't yet paid us for our services."

The others turned back to see what was happening and I waved them forward to wait. Money. It was not something we had brought with us and I had no idea what kind of currency I should give him. Searching the ground, I saw a stray rock in the gutter. It gave me an idea. I bent down and picked it up, while checking to make sure no one was watching. Elijah frowned as I held it out to him, but then his eyes turned to wonder as the stone transformed to solid gold in my fingers. He let out a gasp and I silenced him with my serious words.

"You are to speak of no one about this," I cautioned, placing it into his palm and closing his fist around it. "My words are for you only. I am the messiah your people have been waiting for, but no bodies will rise from your cemeteries today. All you need to know is that the life after this one is full of freedom. By the time this gold has left your family's hands, no one on this earth will have to worry about suffering in the hereafter, no matter which God they pray to. My love is unconditional, unlike my father's. Go forth knowing that every religion is equal in my eyes."

With that, I turned and rejoined my party, leaving a stunned Elijah standing next to his taxi.

33

WE ENTERED THE INSIDE COURTYARD where the Aedicule of Ascension stood. I silently chided myself for my rash action. I had turned stone to gold and told a man I was the messiah. Religions had been started on less. He could be outside the building now, showing people what I had given him, saying God on earth was inside. I only hoped that my warning to tell no one would at least keep him silent until we had risen to Heaven. A small part of me rejoiced with amusement. Asmodeus would be rankled at any influence I might have on his master creation. Earth and man were his toys to play with and no one else's. It wasn't my intention to simply meddle, however, but chip away at any divisions he had created over the millennia. Sometimes small actions could have large effects, given enough time.

Our group fell into a line which snaked back out of the stone building. It was an unglamorous place for a major religious site. The wall that enclosed the courtyard was basic and inside was just dust and a single pathway leading inside the Aedicule. If this really was where Jesus had risen to Heaven, it had very little decoration compared with less significant places. Perhaps it was because of the constant strife in the region that something more awe-inspiring had not been constructed, when it might only be torn down again. Mary stood at the head of our party, the others in the middle and myself at the back. The line moved painfully slowly and my feet started to itch with impatience. We were so close. While we stood, I concentrated and let the elemental vision drip over my perception. The world around turned from a normal day into a marvelous construction of glowing molecules. All my attention was drawn instantly upward. With this view, it was unmistakable that we were in the right place. A wide, sparkling staircase of pearled atoms stretched out of the building and up steeply, into the sky. No beings walked up or down. It was a deserted

132

pathway to Heaven. The outline of the steps was clear. This was Jacob's Ladder! My vision snapped back as the line shuffled ahead again. My heart was charging a marching beat in my chest. Mary's flaming head disappeared into the Aedicule, while more people exited. Clytemnestra followed inside, then Germaine, then Marlowe. I stepped forward, almost pushing Charlotte to hurry her progress. Smithy looked back at us as he entered next.

"We're here," I whispered to Charlotte.

She flashed an excited grin back to me. This might only be the first obstacle, but it was one that we had been working so hard on. It felt like a victory in itself just to be at the base of the steps. Two more tourists exited the building and we were allowed through. Inside was a cramped, round room. The high ceiling gave an illusion of space and the windows, about ten feet up, flooded the structure with natural light. The walls were bare, but everyone's attention was on the floor anyway. Towards the far end, there was a shallow rectangular hole in the ground, framed by stone blocks. As we walked forward, I could see that inside was a single footprint, eroded slightly but clearly pressed into the smooth, white stone in the ground. This was the last mark Jesus left on Earth, before he rose above. The air was hushed with a reverent silence. All I could hear was the blood pulsing in my ears. I moved quietly to the side of the holy place, using my vision to see that the stairway we were looking for began right in front of where the imprint sat. It rose up and through the wall, which was made of bland elements of rock. The contrast with the pearl hue of another world couldn't have been more striking. Steadying myself, I resumed normal vision.

Touching Smithy on the arm, I beckoned him and Marlowe closer, saying in a low whisper, "This is the place. We need to somehow get the rest of the tourists out of here, so we can prepare to move to Heaven in peace."

They both nodded their understanding and I went over to where Mary and Clytemnestra were huddled on the other side, to let them know our intent. Before I made it to them, I heard Marlowe clear his throat loudly. The action made everyone in the hushed space stare his way.

"Excuse me, friends," he said calmly in his African accent, clasping his hands in front of his stomach. "I have a bomb strapped to my body. If you do not want to be blown up, I suggest you leave this building right away."

It was like all air had left the room. Color drained from every face present, before panic kicked in. Even those who couldn't speak English would have understood the word "bomb". One woman wearing a headdress screamed and bolted for the door. Her action snapped the rest of the people in the room out of their dread-trance and, with wild fear in their eyes, all scrambled for the door, trying to save their lives. Each of us stepped back against the walls to let the people out. Bodies bunched at the door as other people outside, not knowing what was happening, tried to push back inside for a look.

"Bomb!" someone else yelled.

The bottleneck that had been forming at the door broke free, letting the fleeing tourists scamper away from the imminent blast zone. Outside, frantic yelling rippled outward, carrying the word that there was a terrorist inside the building. As the last person hurtled out of the door, I sent a rush of elements after them, sealing the exit and leaving the seven of us inside. I piled a reinforcement of earth and wood on top, shutting off the noise and anyone fool enough to try and come back in. I turned to Marlowe with frustration.

"I was thinking of something a little less dramatic," I said angrily.

"It worked didn't it?" he smiled back.

There was no arguing with that. We were now alone: free to explore exactly how Jacob's Ladder worked. I beckoned for everyone to gather around as I walked toward the footprint in the ground at the base of the staircase.

"You cannot see it with human eyes," I said. "But this is where we begin our climb. It's a carpet of elements, stretching straight out of this wall. I dare say it will be quite a journey, making our way up."

"How does it function?" Clytemnestra asked, squinting towards the corner where I was pointing, to see if she could make anything out.

"I'm not sure," I admitted, knowing the others wouldn't be able to see what I could. "Mary?"

"The bible didn't give any instructions," she answered, not offering any help.

I reached out tentatively with my foot, where I knew the elements were sitting in their invisible state. As I let it drop, I felt my soul connect to a hard surface. Encouraged, I pushed off the floor and stepped up. The rest of the group looked on in astonishment. Could it be so easy? Charlotte was the first to move forward to try and join me. However, her foot went straight through, leaving me suspended above her. My feet were at her knee height. She looked up to me perplexed, then down at her feet, as though something must be swimming around her legs. I changed my vision and could see that the elements were sluicing straight through her physical body, as if there was nothing there. Around the edges of my own feet, the pearl color had solidified into a bright blue. I walked up one more step. As my feet left the bottom rung, the pearl color returned. The blue was once again exactly where I stood. It must have looked completely surreal to the others, seeing me stepping up and down an invisible pathway. Hell, however, had desensitized them to odd occurrences, so they kept their cool. I came back down to ground level, looking back again with normal vision. It didn't make sense. Why could I go up and not the others?

"Perhaps it's like the entry to my home," Marlowe mused.

I recalled that if you didn't know that the doorway was there when entering The Perceptionist's kitchen, you ended up stuck in a boxy, yellow room. Perhaps that was the answer. Marlowe was used to such things, so I urged him to give it a try. Again, his feet passed right through. Clytemnestra, Mary, Germaine and Smithy all took their turns. Nobody but me could walk upward. I even went so far as walking right up to the wall of the aedicule. Reaching out to touch the stone, the hard surface gave way, leaving a soft place for me to pass through, should I have desired. It was a mystery. No matter how hard I studied the stairway's construction, I couldn't figure it out. I turned to the others once again, becoming nervous that we might not find the answer quickly. Police would be gathering outside soon enough. We didn't need any distraction from our true course. I paced around the room. No one seemed to have any ideas, until Germaine spoke softly.

"It's the blood," he said.

The rest of us stopped and watched him, at first thinking he was using this as a pretext to be able to have his jewel. His eyes were clear, however, the look on his face half-amused, as though he had had an epiphany.

"It's the blood!" he repeated louder. "Jesus might have been human when he ascended, but he still had the divine blood in his soul just like you, Michael. The angels are made from the stuff of Heaven as well, which is why they can use it too."

Yes. The reasoning clicked perfectly into place and I knew that he was correct. It was time for us to use the jewels we had won from The Furies.

"Mary," I said, turning to my friend. "Would you like the honor of trying out Germaine's theory first?"

Germaine started to object, but Marlowe put a hand on his shoulder.

"Ladies first, my friend," he said.

Mary reached inside the folds of her dress and pulled out a single, scarlet jewel. She opened her mouth and put it inside, letting it sizzle into her tongue. A brief burst of power shimmered out from her body and she blinked. The whites of her eyes had turned red. We all took an involuntary step back at her appearance, unsure that her body would hold. Germaine shuffled nervously next to me. He of all of us knew what Mary must be experiencing right now. I held my breath with anticipation. She stared at her fingers for a moment, before looking up at us and smiling. The action gave me confidence.

"How do you feel?" I ventured slowly, remaining alert.

She paused for a moment, looking up towards the ceiling. Her vision traced down the wall and stopped just where Jacob's Ladder spread down to the earth.

"I feel great," she said. "Like this is the right thing to do. I can see everything."

I checked her body with my elemental vision. Everything seemed to be in place. There was a glow of power surging through her veins, but it was held in check by the flesh encasing her. A deep golden knot of energy throbbed in her chest. The structure of her mind appeared as solid as ever. Mary tentatively walked forward and I moved aside to let her through. She raised her foot and brought it down again. This time it held fast. Stepping up higher again, she looked back to us, holding out her arms.

"Behold, she can now fly like an angel."

The whole group let out a whoop of triumph. We had done it! Smithy clapped Marlowe on the back with uncontained excitement.

"Charlotte," Mary beamed down to my wife in triumph. "You're next. Come."

I gently pressed on Lotte's back to urge her on. This was a great moment and I was proud to be able to watch her take her place in this. She walked forward, holding her hand up to Mary, who descended the stairs, reaching again into her dress. As she neared the bottom of the steps, Mary took Lotte by the arm. As she withdrew her other hand from her dress, Mary's smiling face turned into one of pure rage. There was no jewel inside her fist. Instead, it was a knife, materializing from the elements. The sharp blade glinted with the same glow of murder that now shone in Mary's dark eyes.

"Here's your blood," she growled.

Before any of us could react, Mary plunged the blade into Charlotte's eye socket, sending a spurt of blood squirting into the air. Punching hard, she then struck Charlotte in the chest, who was sent gasping backwards with the knife still in her skull. Her body crashed into Germaine and the pair tumbled to the floor.

Mary turned on her heel and fled up the stairs in the confusion. She disappeared through the wall with the speed of a poisonous traitor.

34

MY MIND SWAM WITH INDECISION. Part of me wanted to go after Mary; the greater part needed to see if Charlotte was still with us. My love won out and I rushed down to her side. She bled onto Germaine, who cradled her in his arms. Marlowe swept past, lunging towards the wall. He hit solid rock. In his all human state, he had no chance of passing through. Staring down at Charlotte, I could see her face had already gone grey with death. Her one eye was glassy, no light inside. A look of surprised horror was frozen on her lifeless face.

"She'll be back in Hell when we return," Clytemnestra said abruptly. "You have to go after Mary. There's no time."

No sooner had she said the words, than a flapping of wings sounded in the air. With a thud, the forms of angels dropped down into the frames of the windows above us. Black silhouetted figures blotted out any light coming into the room. The space around us fell into darkness as we all watched in dread. One of the shadows shifted and a hand smashed through the glass of one of the windows, which rained shards on top of us. Another window burst in a shower of glass and a shining white wing started to squeeze through the small gap above.

"It's a trap!" Marlowe yelled.

He bent down and tore the knife out of Charlotte's blood-soaked head. Swiftly, he raked the sharp edge across his wrists, his own blood surging forth.

"We can't let them take us hostage," he panted. "You go. We'll make sure we die before they get us. Go!"

He gave me a shove, before handing the knife to Clytemnestra. She plunged it into her breast in one swift movement, her body collapsing to the ground. I couldn't believe what I was seeing.

"Go!" Marlowe yelled once again, ripping the knife out of

Clytemnestra's body and throwing it at Smithy.

Rather than hesitating any longer, I let my anger loose. Gathering all the hatred within, I blasted it up towards the windows, where the angels struggled to get inside. Their screeching pain was music to my ears. I locked the stairway in my sights letting the elemental vision take complete hold. I sprinted up the pearly steps, passing right through the elements of stone and into the outside world. As I rushed up, I could see golden forms of angels fluttering on my periphery below but only had eyes for above. The form of Mary, dashed up into the cloud-laden sky. I used my talents to increase my pace, swelling air behind me. I was soon flying. Blinking free of the elements, I trained my vision to see the normal world. The path beneath me might have been invisible, but my target wasn't. She was just about to retreat into a large, grey cloud above. I quickened my pace even further. Air whipped at my face as I reached an inhuman velocity. I was gaining. I would have that treacherous killer in my grasp shortly. Wrath boiled my blood.

A screeching just below me made me look down. An Archangel was hot on my heels, its muscled body flexed in rapid flight. I could see its wings were singed from my attack, but it didn't seem to affect its speed. Below, his brothers were also giving chase. I shot another blast of fire down, which glanced off the angel's shoulder. He swung to the side, slowing momentarily before he beat his wings forward again. A flicker of triumph flashed through my chest, seeing that none of the Archangels beneath me carried any bodies. My friends must have escaped their fleshy forms and were now roaring back to the underworld. What small amount of joy might have been inside was lost, though, when I realized that if I returned as well, all our hopes for a skirmish on Heaven were completely dashed. We needed the jewels that Mary had with her. I had to catch her at all costs.

Trying to block out my pursuers, I focused forward and upward again. I was almost at the clouds. Mary would be just beyond. Gritting my teeth, I tried to contain the rage inside me, ready to unleash it on that murderous traitor. I held my breath as the vapor of the cloud touched my skin. I slid right through its watery form, bursting out the other side. My heart skidded to a rupturing halt in my chest. I too tried to stop. Marlowe's words repeated briefly in my head. It's a trap.

Asmodeus hovered above, with Mary at his back. He unfurled an elemental net, ready for my headlong attack. There was nothing I could do. Instead of trying to turn, I made the split decision to attempt to break through. Shooting streams of fire ahead of me I did my best to weaken the weave. As I struck, I realized I had made an error. The net was made from spirit. Fire would do nothing. Like a fly in a web, I was caught inside the sticky net that Asmodeus had waiting for me. I struggled to break free, but every turn I made only served to tangle me further. I let a wave of hatred escape from my mouth, but it was met with absorbing love that Asmodeus sent down to stop it.

"Now, now," his voice splintered inside my brain. "You don't want to hurt that wonderful body of yours."

He squeezed his fist, and the web around me constricted, holding me fast so I could barely breathe. His obedient Archangels each rose into view, surrounding me on all sides. Up close they were beautiful. They were almost painful to look at, like staring into the sun. Their eyes, however, had a cutting effect, like a shark's: all black and unforgiving. They settled in the air around me, hovering around the net. Small burns from my attack healed quickly on their wings. Asmodeus saw the frustration in my face at the situation. I rattled the bonds around me again, but it did nothing.

"You should know by now never to trust an Iscariot," Asmodeus said. "Betrayal runs through their veins."

Mary moved out from behind him, watching me cautiously. I thought I might see remorse in her face, but there was nothing but contempt. She turned away and began to walk up the stairs. I glared at her back. She wasn't going to even give me an explanation.

"An explanation?" Asmodeus said, probing my mind. "I thought you might have figured that out already. After all, it's basic human motivation." He pointed back to Mary's retreating form. "Not only did you spurn her love, but you failed to protect her brother. She lost confidence in you and so she turned to someone she knew she could depend upon."

"She would never!" I started, but he laughed.

"Already in denial, I see. Judas is now safe in Heaven as she asked, with a constant guard of angels sitting on hand for when he finally awakes. It was very simple to visit Hell again and retrieve him, once I knew you weren't there. She prayed to me, Michael. Can you imagine?" He let a smile of glee flutter on his lips. "The whore on her knees for God. I granted her wish: safe asylum for eternity in rapturous Heaven for her and her family. Of course, I'll have to keep a close watch on them, but it's a small price to pay to have you as well."

I tried wrenching the shackles he had me in, my every muscle straining to break free. It was no use. My human body wouldn't allow enough leeway for me to move. It was too rigid. My body! A dawning inside me linked to Asmodeus' hateful gaze. He wanted to keep me like this. As Mary had said herself, the only thing worse than death was to be trapped unconscious in a useless shell. My father clapped his hands in delight at my realization.

"Yes," he said. "An unconscious god is basically a dead god. I can't have you running loose down there anymore. You're causing too many problems. Unfortunately, you're at the point where you're too powerful for me to destroy your soul, so I'll just have to keep it contained."

He flung a shower of elements down to suffocate my mind. Instinct took over. Rather than attack back, I retreated. I pulled back, away from my physical shell and down into my ethereal self. I shrunk as much as I could inside the flesh that held me. As the tumult of Asmodeus' attack assaulted above, I let out fire. Not outward, but within. Searing heat shuddered through my veins, bursting blood vessels and sizzling organs. The pain of it spasmed right through me. My emotion was still linked to the shell. However, as the mortal body around me burned, the heat released me from the pain. It did not hurt to burn. It felt wonderful. The furnace was now my home and I would be back there soon.

The last thing my living ears heard was a deep swearing frustration from Asmodeus. He screamed toward me, throwing water and spirit ahead of him, to try and reclaim my wasting body. It was too late. I had disintegrated it from within. As his clawed fists wrapped around my neck, the skin dissolved to cinders in his hands. I was gone already, my spirit tearing back down into Hell.

35

I WANTED TO INCINERATE THE UNIVERSE. Better yet, I wanted to swallow it up. I wanted to take a wrap of The Perceptionist's anti-matter and smother everything to oblivion, as though nothing had even been here. Everything that Asmodeus had created made me sick to my core. It would be better to wipe the slate clean than to watch him pervert everything further; make him start again and then cut it off as soon as an evil thought entered the world. Then I opened my eyes and saw Charlotte waiting for me. The deep look of concern in her eyes put a block on my hatred. She was sitting at my side, where my ethereal body must have just materialized into life. There was at least one good thing in this world. Lotte. Instead of ranting and screaming my eternal frustrations, I squeezed my eyes closed for a moment and then looked at her again as she knelt to look me over.

"Are you okay?" I asked, reaching up to stroke her face over her right eye where Mary's blade had entered on Earth.

"I felt no pain," she whispered. "Death was instant. It was just the worry I had to feel until you returned. Clytemnestra said this is where you'd be."

I looked around. It was the room in Satan's Tower that I had awoken in before, every time I had returned to Hell. I didn't know how it worked, but it was like the code of my soul was assigned to land again and again in this exact spot when I plummeted from above. There was still so much I had yet to learn. It was why I had failed yet again against my father. He'd had forever to create all the knowledge in the word. I had only had one lifetime to start to unravel it. It simply wasn't enough.

I hadn't been a complete failure, though. I wasn't in his clutches. It had been a small victory to be able to burn my earthly body away before he could render me trapped inside forever. Before he could hang me as a prize in Heaven. Rage started to rise again over my sense of hopelessness.

Heaven. Mary was now there. The traitor. She had taken the coward's way out and done what was best for her and her brother only. Normally I would try to see a situation from everyone else's view, but I did not want to get into Mary's psyche this time. She was dead to me and if I ever saw her again she would be dead to the rest of existence as well.

"Michael!" Charlotte's voice invaded my thoughts. She was shaking me lightly.

I must have closed my eyes again. What was the use? Why should I bother to open them again?

"Michael," Lotte's voice urged once more. "What are we going to do?"

My thoughts presented nothing in answer. I was blank. There was no way forward. I had been trained in my life to get back up when an enemy knocked you down: each time your back hits the dirt, you dig in your knuckles and push yourself back up. But this was not life; this was death. It was supposed to be rest, yet all I had received since first dying was constant torment. It was more of a psychological Hell than the realm that surrounded me. When would the struggle end? I should have just let Asmodeus render me unconscious like Judas. That way would be easier. I kept my eyes closed and shut off any noise from my ears. It was blissful nothing for a moment, until a teardrop dripped onto my face. It made me look up into my wife's pained eyes.

"Michael, what happened?" she sobbed. "You have to tell me." Her hand rested softly on my chest.

"We lost," I said. "It's over."

"No," she said, shaking her head. "I can't believe that. It's not in your nature to give up. You're still here. We're still together. We can work out another way. There is always another option."

I started to sit up and Charlotte helped me. It wasn't that my body was tired. It was my soul that was weary. She propped me against her chest and stroked my hair.

"Mary took the Jewels of Blood with her," I said slowly, explaining. "We can't make any more bodies. We can't use their power to help us overcome him. We can't get out of this stinking Hell."

I clenched my fists, digging my sharp fingernails into my palm so the physical pain would distract me enough from losing control.

"That's not all she took." Charlotte said, rubbing her fingers along my cheek. The tender movement offset the gravity of her next words. "The Pure Seven are gone as well. They never turned up to train the legions. Marax has been doing that all on his own."

The news made me sit up properly with a jerk. The Pure Seven as well! Asmodeus had said "asylum for her family". I had assumed that only meant Judas, but she had taken her sinful angels too. My father must have been desperate to allow them all to enter Heaven. The thought made me seethe. If he was willing to make concessions for pure sin, then what about the others who were struggling against their vices to become better? Why weren't they given the benefit of the doubt? It only reinforced that his unjust actions were completely selfish in motivation. The rage inside pushed down the sorrow I was feeling. It galvanized me. This wasn't right and someone had to stop it. I would have to be relentless in my pursuit of Asmodeus, if we had any hope of winning. Perhaps I could wear him down with persistence.

"What is Marax doing with the army?" I asked, waiting for more disastrous news.

"I don't know," she said. "That's all I've heard so far. We haven't been back for too long before you. The others are waiting upstairs to debrief properly."

"The others?" I asked, still rattled internally, but starting to try and formulate ideas in my head.

"Smithy," Charlotte said in response, "Marlowe and Germaine. Clytemnestra has gathered them together. We're ready to plan the next battle. We're ready for you to command."

I wanted nothing more than to stay where I was. I wanted to lie back down and hold Charlotte with me. The look of expectation in her eyes told me she wouldn't let me do any such thing. I slowly got to my feet, feeling the lightness of my ethereal being. Only my thoughts weighed it down. We had a war to wage. Only the end of time would stop that from being true. The only way forward, was up.

36

THE ELEVATOR RIDE UPWARDS helped firm my resolve further. Watching the floor counter reminded me of re-living my life through unbiased eyes the first time I arrived in Hell. I had shuddered with disbelief when I saw myself wallow in doubt and self-pity, sinking to addictions of drugs and gambling to numb the pain. That was not the person I was. I had risen above then and I would do it again now. Fuck Asmodeus. I would beat him, even if it took an eternity of trying. Charlotte didn't say anything to me as we rode up. She didn't need to. She just held my hand, showing me that she was still by my side, always supporting and guiding. Even pushing me if she had to. The silver doors slid open and my diminished war council turned around. The only person who smiled to see us was Smithy. The rest looked as grim as I felt. Clytemnestra stood at the window with Marax, overlooking the inferno below. He was pointing downward and explaining something in low tones. When he noticed we had arrived however, he stopped and turned.

"Lord Michael," he snapped a fast salute. "I heard there was trouble with your mission. Clytemnestra summoned me as soon as she returned. Your army has started training."

I looked around at the others. They all watched me, waiting for an explanation.

"What about The Pure Seven?" I asked him. "I am told they have also disappeared."

He paused briefly, but continued.

"I was hoping you would be able to tell me. When they didn't show up, I assumed they'd been moved to another, more pressing assignment. That is what I told the legions. In their absence I appointed lieutenants to begin organizing."

"Good. How did you appoint them?" I asked hoping the conversation would give me a few moments figure out how to explain what had happened.

"Each Legion of Sin put forth a leader when asked." Marax said simply. "Of the seven, only the Legion of Pride wasn't unanimous. Six leaders stepped up. I had them fight until someone remained victorious. Genghis Khan now heads that division. He decapitated the rest of his opponents." Marax indicated down below as he continued to speak. "The hordes are busy already."

I turned my attention to Hell City. It was a hive of activity: not the normal chaotic hub of traffic and vice I was used to, but streams of people marching the streets in formation. Even the cars moved with a semblance of order. The buildings around us were each topped with colors, denoting which sinful legion belonged in which portion of the metropolis. On some rooftops, flags were still being mounted. It was as if Hell was being split into nine massive sets of barracks: The seven deadly sins, the black and the white. It was mostly a change in outward appearance at this stage, but watching the movement below, I knew it wouldn't be long until every soul in Hell had found a new home amongst their fellow soldiers, who they would fight alongside. The internal shift of intent was heading in the direction of jihad. This was a city on the brink of holy war.

"Impressive," I said, still watching it unfold. "You've done very well, Marax. Better than us." I didn't wait to study his reaction, but turned, facing everyone. "Unfortunately, The Pure Seven are not on a mission," I said loudly. "Mary has betrayed us. She sold us out to be allowed into Paradise. She took Judas and the Seven with her. I was also supposed to be part of the bargain. They tried to catch me. Hold me captive, but I escaped."

Everyone's reaction was different. Clytemnestra nodded like she had expected as much. Marlowe bristled with anger as did Marax, who punched the window in front of him with frustration. Germaine stared into space, like he'd lost somebody dear to him. Charlotte stood by my side, forever in support. Smithy shook his head in disbelief. I felt for him the most. He had been starting to form a stronger friendship with Mary and that was now crushed. I understood he might not want to accept that it had been a pretence on her part to keep up appearances. Still, he remained sagely silent, waiting for me to go on.

"She has also taken the Jewels of Blood with her. All of them."

"No!" Germaine exclaimed, his eyes widening.

I held up my hand to stop him from continuing.

"Our original plans are gone. We now have to bide our time, prepare and find another way. Does anyone have any ideas? I want solutions, not problems."

"We can get more jewels." Germaine said quickly. "We can –"

"We cannot," I cut him off. "The Furies made it clear that what we had was the only blood they would provide. Besides, do you think another resurrection to Earth will lead to a different result? That path is now closed. Asmodeus knew we were coming and will now have it heavily guarded. Next!" I said, waiting for someone else to step up with a plan.

"We should go to Magdalene's Mansion and see if we can find any clues to how Asmodeus took Judas," Charlotte said. "If we knew how he came in, perhaps we can trace his footsteps out again."

"Yes," I nodded. "That's a good start. What else?"

The others looked at me crestfallen. In the beginning, a resurrection had been the most feasible plan. It had been the only one. If there was another path from Earth to Heaven we were ignorant of it. They were all grasping within themselves to see if a plan would rise to the surface.

"The army," Marax said, casting his eyes out the window again. "We'll need to tell them about The Pure Seven's defection."

I sighed. The news could crumble any sense of camaraderie we had built faster than it had been formed. Smithy seemed to sense my apprehension. He walked over to the window as well and rubbed his whiskered chin.

"The army is the best thing we have going for us at the moment," he said. "We can't risk that. I suggest we continue the pretence that The Pure Seven are off on an important mission. Marax, does anyone else know we have returned?"

"No one," Marax said. "Clytemnestra summoned me with a signal only she and I have used before."

"Good." Smithy grunted, finally meeting my eyes. "We should keep it that way. As far as the armies know, we're still working on bringing down the barrier for them to attack. We could be gone for months. For them, the longer we are gone the longer they have to prepare. It will be seen as a blessing at first while the units gain confidence. If unrest starts to show, then one of us can appear, saying we were killed during the mission, but the others were getting close. We can't lose morale."

"We also can't keep up the charade indefinitely," Clytemnestra added, once again turning her attention to the outside world, as though it might erupt at any moment.

"It will buy us some time," Smithy replied firmly. "It's what we need."

"But we're lying to them," Charlotte cut in. "Isn't this the kind of thing we're trying to fight against? Manipulation of the masses?"

Smithy went to Charlotte. He took her hands in his, with a sad, but determined look on his face.

"We have to use any opportunity we can," he said softly, squeezing her fingers with reassurance. He turned back to me, choosing his next words carefully. "We can split moral hairs during peace time. During war, the only ethical wrong is killing the innocent or torturing your captured enemy. As much as I hate to say it, the rest is fair game."

Smithy was normally the most conservative when it came to this kind of thing. It made me think this was the right way ahead. We couldn't act flippantly, but an extraordinary set of circumstances meant that sometimes rules had to be broken. The Pure Seven and Mary weren't here to object with their religion of Truth. They, who had ended up being the worst liars of all. Every single one of us was on our feet, looking out to a more unified Hell than we'd ever seen before. I wouldn't let that fall without a fight.

"Marax, make it happen," I said, making the decision. "If what you've done so far in a few days is only the beginning, Asmodeus should be afraid of what you can do in months." He snapped to attention again, living up to his name of general. He saluted and started to leave. "And Marax," I said to him, stopping him in his tracks. "If you find any spies among us, hang them upside-down from the closest power line and set them on fire. We need to make people understand that betrayal will not be tolerated."

"Very good," he growled, grinning an ugly smile.

"Marax," I added before he could leave. "Only if they are truly traitors. If there is any question, bring them to me first. No kangaroo courts."

He understood my warning. While it was important to make examples of anyone who was against the cause, I wouldn't have people persecuted for no good reason. The last thing we needed was pointless witch hunts. When he had gone, the others remained in stony silence. Still no one sat. Everyone waited on their feet in vigilance. I started to pace over the plush black carpet, walking back and forth, still agitated. I strode to the back wall, examining the bookshelf to see if there was anything there that jumped out as interesting. There were was mostly volumes of history. Nothing. I ran my fingers along their spines, thinking. Could I still trust people for advice, or should I rely on scripture instead? Who else could I trust? Mary's defection had shattered my faith in everyone except Charlotte. I didn't want any more surprises.

No more surprises? I almost started to laugh at my stupidity. Why hadn't I thought of this before? I spun back to my friends; they appeared hopeful at the look on my face.

"Phineus," I said to them, as if it was the most obvious thing in the world.

Marlowe's eyes lit up with understanding. "The prophet," he said.

"The Perceptionist might not want to tell the future for us," I said, the wheels of a plan spinning in my head. "But an old friend might. It will take away some of Asmodeus' advantage." I clasped my hands together, happy with the possibility. There were other things to do as well. We were back in action stations, where I worked my best. I turned my attention to Marlowe again.

"Take Germaine with you to help find Phineus," I said. "If he's in the same house as before, it's a dilapidated shack across the road from the Smoking Gun strip. Smithy," I continued, turning to the pilot, now really feeling the momentum of opportunity churn in my gut. "You go and find the cabdriver Mack. We need reliable people at our backs. I will go with Clytemnestra and Lotte to Magdalene's mansion, to see if we can dig up anything useful. We'll all meet back here as soon as we can."

Without pausing, I started walking toward the elevator, the depression I had felt at being beaten by Asmodeus now lost in the flurry of activity in my mind. You hadn't truly lost until you had given up. This wasn't that time. With a bing the silver doors opened. I turned back to see the others looking at me, almost in shock. I was exhilarated with the new spark of energy.

"Let's go," I said, ready to rip back into Hell.

Charlotte swept her arm out to indicate everyone's dress. "Didn't you just agree with Marax that we were supposed to be keeping a low profile? None of us can be seen in the open, or his story will be exposed."

She had a point, but the objection was nothing some elemental craft couldn't fix. I waved my hand quickly, using my skill to send an illusionary wave right through the group. Their outer appearances all morphed to distort their faces. Horns sprouted and ears grew. Marlowe's skin turned white and Germaine's green. I let Clytemnestra's hair shrink back into her skull and had several pig snouts sprout in its place. Her chin extended and hooked up like a caricature of a witch. I made Charlotte look like a short, blue lust demon. With a flourish, I drew my hand down over my own face, twisting into the shape of an animated Guy Fawkes' mask. In mere moments, we were all completely unrecognizable.

"I'm hideous!" Charlotte exclaimed, catching a reflection of herself in the elevator mirror behind me. "I look like Gollum and Smurfette's love child."

"Come on, Lotte." I said to her in mock seriousness, "I love you no matter what you look like."

We were on a new path. It felt good to have some purpose again, even if it was without a clear intention. We would find that soon enough. It would come with Phineus, I was sure.

37

I FELT INVISIBLE IN MY DISGUISE. For so long, people had stopped and stared everywhere I went, whispering behind their hands. Now, no one gave our trio a second glance. We were just another set of deformed ghouls stalking the streets of Hell. Open trucks rumbled along the road at a slow pace, allowing people to jump on and off their wide flatbed trailers. They seemed to be making circuits of the city, providing a sort of efficient public transport, which kept the bulk of other traffic off the road. There was a definite purpose to people's movements. No one was loitering or standing around. There were things to do. I wondered if this had been another idea of Marax's. He had really risen to the challenge. Some people were born for conflict: he was one of them.

Not wanting to risk any kind of flight which might draw attention, we ran for a truck. Each of us was hauled up by fellow demons onto the moving platform. A skinny pride demon, who had lifted me with some others, clapped me on the back as I found my feet.

"Where to, friend?" she asked in a high-pitched rasp, which sounded like fingernails grating down a blackboard.

Her violet-tinged skin was covered in hideous scars from head to toe, some freshly scabbed. A crooked smile hung on her lips, her mouth turning up on one side, the other drooping down in misuse. It seemed she only had control of the muscles on one side of her face.

"Magdalene's Mansion." I said, making my voice deeper than normal.

"This route only passes its closest corner," she said, licking her palm and smoothing back her blonde hair, which grew in tufts out of her scalp. "We're gathering supplies for Lieutenant Kahn." Marax's newest appointment, I recalled. "Kahn is the greatest leader in the nine legions," the demon continued. "He would rival even Lord Michael in hand to hand combat."

149

I could see the look in her eyes, challenging me to say any different.

"I'm sure he would," I replied as the truck rumbled forward. "What kind of training is he having you do?" I asked, curious.

Lotte and Clytemnestra bunched a little closer to eavesdrop. Any information on how things were faring on the ground might be valuable later.

"He's having us work with swords," the demon answered, her eyes gleaming. "Guns are for the weak, useless against the angels. We can clip their wings with wicked steel before we chop off their heads."

The thought obviously gave her great delight, because she let out a barking laugh. A sloth demon standing close by took notice and came forward. His eyes were half closed and he talked with a slow lisp. His skin was dead on his body, flaking off in places. Open ulcers wept stinking pus on his arms. I recalled the zombie-like state the sloths could revert to, once they became steeped in their languid sin.

"Swords are for close combat only," he said. His mouth was a mash of bleeding gums and rotting teeth. "Our legion is concentrating on more long range weapons. We need bombs to launch ahead of us to create destruction from a distance. Liquid hellfire can burn divine skin like nothing else."

"Missiles are for cowards," the pride demon hissed.

The sloth demon looked as if he was going to retort, but then seemed to lose interest, shrugging his shoulders and turning away.

"Sloths!" The pride demon spat with contempt, looking at his back. "Can't even be bothered having a friendly argument. They don't care about freedom. Having to make choices is too inconvenient for them."

"It will take all kinds to win this war," Charlotte said next to me, in her distorted form. "Having hellfire in our artillery sounds like a smart decision to me."

"Yes," the pride demon said evenly, "but our ground forces are the most important."

"You're right." I said and she smiled at me, pulling a face back at Charlotte like that was the final word.

"I'm Droog," she said, holding out her hand, which I shook.

"A pleasure," I said, not giving my name in return.

I turned my attention to the street that was moving past quickly now. Buildings were being repaired all over. The city was being updated like never before. Old shop fronts had been marked for renovations, graffiti was being whitewashed over before new color was added. This district seemed to be dedicated to Wrath. Red was being streaked everywhere and angry faces sat on all of the workers. They didn't seem disgruntled in their

150

labor, rather taking it on with a furious vigor. We went through some traffic lights into the next block, which had scaffolding wrapped around the first few buildings. Demons scurried up and down the frame, hauling sheets of steel upward, before bolting them onto the building to reinforce its defenses. The truck we were on started to gear down slowly, stopping in the middle of the road for no apparent reason.

"Why are we...?" Charlotte began.

Her question was answered with a chorus of agonized wailing and a thunderous crash from the guilty sky. Bodies dropped limp around us, crashing onto the tray of the truck and spasming in their visions of remorse, as the fire and smoke swept through. The constant roar in my ears filled me with deep personal pain. While I didn't have to go through my own guilt, the storm cut me deeply, reminding me of my failings to my people. Droog, the pride demon, was at my feet ripping at her own skin, tearing bits of flesh from her face with clawed hands.

"Ugly, ugly," she whimpered, "I'll win the next pageant, Mommy. Ugly. Ugly."

Her wounds split open, dripping dark blood at my feet.

Her scars wil never heal down here, I thought.

She was doomed to stay this way forever without our help. All around it was a similar story: glutton demons sticking fingers down their throats to vomit, greed demons crying tears of eternal loneliness as they'd chosen material gain over affection. Lust demons yelled out to lost lovers they had betrayed for fleeting pleasure. I brought my eyes up to Charlotte, who was looking around in horror. She had never been this close to people experiencing their personal suffering. I touched her arm and she jolted. At first she looked at me like a stranger, but then remembered my disguise. I brought her close to me and held her tight, putting my lips to her ear.

"We're going to put an end to this," I promised.

38

THE TRUCK STARTED UP AGAIN a few minutes after the Guilt storm passed. Droog still lay at my feet, bleeding from her self-inflicted wounds. As we started moving I bent down and helped her up. The slices on her face were already slowly healing into puckered scabs. She smiled at me as I let her go. One of the cuts opened up again, sending a dribble of crimson into her mouth, staining her teeth. Everyone gathered their senses from the assault. No matter how long you'd been in Hell, the experience of those hauntings was never dimmed. I was yet to meet someone who didn't dread it coming. I felt like a fraud not having to experience it myself, and able to protect only a few close to me from its relentless tentacles. Stopping it should have been my first objective all along. I resolved to begin working on a plan to seek out its origins as soon as we had returned from Mary's in search of what might already be a cold trail. There could be something, though. We couldn't lose hope. I had to keep moving, or the frigid hand of depression would squeeze my soul to incapacitating sorrow.

"This is your stop," Droog said, pointing ahead.

She was right. I wouldn't have noticed if I hadn't been told. Normally this intersection was marked with a towering golden statue of Asmodeus. I had never had the time to remove it. Now someone had torn off its head and arms. The rest of the body had been painted blue. We were deep in the district of Lust.

Clytemnestra, Charlotte and I all jumped down from the truck. Droog waved us goodbye and I raised my hand in return. There were still well-meaning people down here, despite their personal shortcomings. This part of the city was the same as the ones we had just passed through. Improvements were being made to buildings, demons working in co-ordination with each other to achieve them. A casino across the street was being cleared of its gaming tables. The neon sign above the place had been replaced with something more utilitarian. A plain black board with white letters read: Mess Hall. I hoped nothing like that had been done to Magdalene's Mansion. As we neared the site of our destination, I breathed a sigh of relief. The façade of the building was exactly the same: red, reflective glass with an icon of a dominatrix holding a whip embedded inside the clear paneling. This close up you couldn't even see the top of her legs as she arched up the entire height of the structure. We entered the foyer and were met by a line similar to the one I had encountered last time, winding almost right back to the door. Despite the owner's absence, they were doing a roaring trade. It reassured me that the employees here were oblivious to their madam's defection. The customers were being served with proficient speed and it wasn't long until we were at the front of the queue, facing Oba. She looked at me with such familiarity that I had to double check I still had my living Guy Fawkes mask in place. It was a skill of her customer service to make clients feel that they had been remembered.

"And what will it be today, sir?" she asked with a lick of her lips.

"We'd like to hire one of the dungeon rooms," I said. "I'm going to give my two girlfriends here a spanking they're not likely to forget."

I heard Charlotte choke behind me at the comment. Of course I had no intention of using the rooms, but I knew that they were downstairs in the basement, in the general direction of where we were heading.

"I'm sorry, sir," Oba said. "It's a two day wait for the dungeons."

"You're kidding!" I said, in disbelief.

"Ever since Fifty Shades of Grey came out we've had a surge of bondage requests," she smiled. "One of our most popular rooms has been hired out permanently by a rich socialite and it has contributed to the backlog."

"I thought perhaps with the war effort there would be fewer people coming in."

"We're busier than ever," Oba replied curtly. "With all this training and talk of annihilation, people need some pleasure time to blow off steam. I have a nice jail cell on the second floor if that tickles your fancy. It has manacles on the wall."

"Fine." I nodded, knowing we'd be able to bypass the elevators without too much trouble. I could use a cloak of elements to make us completely invisible; but I was enjoying the interaction a normal disguise gave us. It was helping me learn more and more about what made people tick down here. My people.

"That's two thousand dollars," Oba said.

Before I could express my shock at the price, Clytemnestra slapped a wad of cash down on the counter and pushed us forward. At least she was prepared.

I led the way down the halls. The secret of not being stopped seemed to be marching towards your destination with confidence. Ushering my companions through the long corridor, we came to the concealed door I was looking for. It had been locked, but I let a weave of elements trickle from my fingers and it slid open. We took each step downwards with care, trying to take in every fiber and chink in the walls to see if anything appeared out of place. There was nothing. It was the same as every other time I'd been here. When we arrived at The Crypt itself, however, we were met with a different sight. All of the coffins were gone. Charlotte and Clytemnestra, who hadn't seen it before, didn't appear surprised, but I hadn't known this room any other way. It looked so bare without their presence. The crucifix altar still sat in the centre. The dove's white light flooded down from above. We split up and circled around, each searching the shadows. There were no strange marks, no hidden trapdoors. It was only after we'd done multiple laps of the room that I stopped.

"Why would he have taken all the coffins?" I asked, thinking it strange. "Couldn't he just have taken Judas' and left the rest? The Pure Seven wouldn't need them."

Clytemnestra paused to ponder the question. Lotte moved over to the altar and took a seat on its stony surface. I couldn't look at either of them seriously in their present forms, so I lifted our disguises for the moment. Clytemnestra tapped her jagged teeth with black polished fingernails while she thought. Charlotte lay down on the altar, taking up the position of a corpse as if getting into character might give her some extra ideas.

"Maybe Asmodeus needed to transport them all inside the coffins?" Clytemnestra offered. "He'd certainly look very strange appearing in Heaven with seven evil angels as an entourage."

It did make sense. Having them enclosed in boxes would not only hide them, but would contain them until he was ready to set them free. If I put myself in his shoes, I would have done the same thing.

"So what does that tell us?" I asked.

"Not much," Lotte said from her prone position. "Lifting a few coffins wouldn't be too hard for an Elemental."

She was right. He could have easily made them dance along behind him, hidden in a reflective cloak of molecules. But what about raising them to Heaven? How did he do that? How had he come here multiple times without being seen by anyone? My stomach was doing back flips at the same rate as my mind. The apparent ease with which he'd done it made me nervous. We all sat there in silence, waiting for answers that didn't come. I did one more circuit of the room, to no avail.

"There's nothing here," I said. "Let's go up to Mary's office and see if we can find anything there."

I reapplied our disguises in the privacy of The Crypt before turning to leave. We drifted in contemplation back to the ground floor, finding our way to the main elevator and getting in. The numbered floors held no curiosity to me; it was the symbol buttons which contained the most promise. The first was the one with an ornate 'M' on it. That would lead to Mary's office. The other with the universal eye would take us to The Chamber of Maps. Looking at my watch, I decided to press the latter button first. The eye glowed with its red backlight. The effect made it look alive, watching.

"Isn't that the same floor we went to last time, with the giant globe?" Lotte asked me, curious.

"Yes," I said. "I have an idea that I want to test out. That globe normally reflects all the changes that happen in the realms as they occur."

"What are we looking for, then?" she queried.

I stared into space for a few moments, hoping that my hunch was right. If I was, it would indeed give some insight into a question that had been burning bright since we got off the truck.

"I want to see exactly where The Guilt comes from."

39

WE ENTERED THE MAP ROOM. Straight ahead, the massive sphere of the earth rotated on its invisible axis. At our feet, under the clear floor, was our own realm: Hell. It boiled in its sweltering madness; the constant dark clouds of the sky parted as we walked, to give us a proper view downward. I searched beneath, to see if I could notice the minor details of buildings being altered. From here I could only really see the change in color in the burgeoning districts of sin. Casa Diablo sat perched on Mount Belial as always. The rolling desert sands waited in their loneliness. Over our heads, Heaven shone. I understood that this portion of the room never changed. Mary had explained that this version of Heaven was a static representation only, yet Earth and Hell were connected somehow to this model. Anything that was altered in those worlds would be reflected here in this room. I glanced at my watch again. We would have a few minutes yet to wait.

"What are we looking for?" Charlotte asked

"I'm not totally sure," I said, surveying the room from wall to wall. "The Guilt seems to always come from the horizons, so we should keep our attention there to start with. Look for anything unusual. Is there one spot it comes from in particular, or multiple spots? Does it start above or below? Is their any pattern? Anything?"

They both nodded their understanding and we fanned out to the edges of the circular room. With our feet at the rims of Hell, the normal storm clouds retreated inward and bunched in the middle. We would have a view of the horizons without them concealing anything. I watched down. I had never known what was at the edge of Hell. Here it was displayed as nothingness in an outward bulge: a curved, featureless wall. In front of that wall were high mountains, masking this edge of the universe. They would be totally impassable by any normal soul. From the sub-ground level they towered up almost to where Asmodeus' cursed barrier should be at my feet. Here, though, that wasn't represented either. I supposed that was for practical purposes. If it had have been included in its normal form, you wouldn't be able to see down into Hell. It would have obscured the world you wanted to see. I made a mental note that, in essence, the floor we were standing on was the barrier; it was simply clear in this instance. At that moment a shimmer of movement appeared beneath me.

"Something's happening!" Clytemnestra yelled out to me from across the room.

"Here too," Lotte said.

"Watch closely!" I replied.

At the very edges of the walls, behind the mountains, dust and clouds began to gather. The heat whipped into a fury. Pillars of flames shot downward, sparking and flashing. In a turn of power, the light twisted into plumes of cyclic energy, forming tornados that squirmed like fiery, beheaded snakes. Their tails licked the ground, charring the earth. I switched my view to that of the elements, to see if I could perceive anything different. What I saw rocked me. I had known that The Guilt was sewn together from different elements of memory and regretful emotion; The Perceptionist had taught me this much. What he hadn't told me was where those elements came from. Looking at this, it appeared they were streaming down the edges of the dome, leaking from the floor I was standing on. At the edges of Hell on every side, they gathered in a tempest of the darkest kind. I peered around me, half thinking that the movement of the elements must originally be coming from this upper portion of the room, but it wasn't. The intensity of the phenomenon grew below, until it was set to burst. Then, with a rushing sound the storm advanced toward the city.

On cue, the real fires of torment burst into the room around us, blinding the rest of the display below. Smoke choked the air. I continued to watch with my perception of the elements: greens, browns and blacks flung about in chaotic spurts. A tumult of oppressive emotions swept by, laced with memory triggers. They splintered towards our bodies and tried to penetrate our hearts. All three of us were protected. We simply had to wait for it to subside. Finally, the last of the fire cleared. I dropped to my knees, looking back down to see if I could find where it retreated. The vacuum of Guilt sucked back towards the horizons on all sides, passing in a misty wave over the mountains as it dissipated towards the edges of Hell. The weave broke up so it became a loose wash of separated atoms, which absorbed up into the glass floor I had my face almost pressed against. Then they were gone. It was finished.

Sitting back on my haunches, I tried to make sense of what had just transpired. I gazed in a trance of thought. Lotte and Clytemnestra came to my side, both talking.

"It's like it was raining fire from the floor," Clytemnestra said.

"The storm just came from nothing, like the heavens openedup and dumped The Guilt on our heads," Lotte added.

Her words were like an electric shock to my brain. Asmodeus had said something uncannily similar when he had appeared last time: *The Guilt will sweep in from the heavens and all of these souls will be helpless.* My synapses started firing together with the cause and effect of it all. *It was like the heavens opened up*, Charlotte had said. In actual fact, Heaven itself had done just that! That was why I had looked around at the room thinking it must have been coming from around us. It was, but we couldn't see it. This representation of Heaven didn't reflect the change. My mind was crackling ahead, knowing the ultimate conclusion already, but following the steps just to make sure my theory could be justified. There was a reason Paradise was seen as a place of eternal rest. There was no more struggle: no more negative emotions to weigh on your conscience. That had never made sense to me when the most pious people on Earth always seemed the most ashamed at their natural impulses. They denied their desires, chastising themselves as being evil. Born sick. Surely that self-loathing didn't end with death, simply because their choices had been vindicated with the reward of a golden ticket to Heaven. Asmodeus must have been draining that guilt away, siphoning it to us! Hell was taking on the oppressive sense of culpability from those above. That poison was laced with our own memories, to make us think it came from within, but it was forced into our souls. Psychopaths who had never felt remorse in their lives felt it acutely down here. It was manufactured – an essential process to make Heaven what it was to its inhabitants and Hell what it was to ours. I could picture it in my mind, the swirling of the filter drawing out the negativity in the holy souls above, pushing it to the outer reaches of Heaven with an imperceptible centrifugal force. It would build up and build up, like clockwork, being trapped on the edges, until the downward force became so great it would sluice through the weaker fringes of the barrier, like liquid straining through a leaking sphincter: the feces of human emotion poured into our minds, like so much filth. That's how Asmodeus would have entered Hell: by riding that torrent of emotion down. The Archangels and Moloch had appeared at the head of a guilt storm. They had all retreated before it could fully dissolve. I could picture them struggling up the lessening stream of elements, squeezing their way back into Heaven before the way had been blocked off. No one down here would ever hope to find that exit; they were incapacitated when it was opened. That's why it had been so easy for Asmodeus to conceal himself. No one was conscious when he arrived. The small number of demons lucky enough to be free of The Guilt could have easily been avoided. That's why no one had ever stumbled upon this way out either. You were either unconscious during the tumult, or had the advantage of being in Hell without its main drawback. There would be no motivation to leave. It was a massive entry front, too: impossible to patrol, spanning the whole diameter of Hell. All these thoughts flickered through my mind like a hyper-speed movie reel. Clytemnestra and Lotte stepped backward when I leapt to my feet, almost exploding with the revelation.

"I know how to get into Heaven!"

I struggled to contain the ideas flowing through me. Both my companions peppered with me questions as I worked to unravel the thought process that had just run through my head. Hell was taking Heaven's guilt. It would rush down from above six times every day. When it did, the outer edges of the barriers of Hell were weakened, enabling Asmodeus to enter, or leave. This was our way out: a way for a lightning attack on our enemies that they wouldn't expect!

"The Guilt comes every four hours," I said to them, looking at my watch again. "If I'm right, I think this would be how long we would have to raid Heaven, if we used that pathway. Maybe less. We would rise up during one guilt storm and then be ripped back down to Hell during the next."

"Wouldn't the barrier bring us back right away?" Lotte asked. I shook my head, knowing in my heart that wouldn't be the case.

"The forces of the barrier would work to drag us back down, but the pressure would have to build up as it went," I said, "That's the only thing I can think of that can explain what we just saw. If I'm right, this wouldn't be an instant process. I don't think it works like when light souls float upward at any time in the middle. I think the heavier evil has to be purged with a strong burst down the sides. Before, it would have had the filter of Purgatory to do that job first. Someone in Heaven would go there before screaming into Hell. With the filter of Purgatory gone, it'll be be slower. Something we can work against."

I was almost jumping on the spot with the energy this was injecting into me. Charlotte put a hand on mine, trying to ease my manic state.

"Please calm down, my love," she said. "We have to take our time with this. Every time we have rushed headlong into an opportunity, we have been turned back. Let's think. What's the best way forward?"

"This is the right way," I said insistently. I knew it in every part of me. Asmodeus had made the slip of the tongue himself. He knew. It had to be how he came here; how he brought the Archangels with him. My gut was a warm fizz of excitement. That warmth was sparkling out to all of my limbs.

"Please, slow down," Charlotte said. "We have to wait for the others. If Marlowe and Germaine have been able to find Phineus, he'll be able to confirm our possible success by reaching into the future with his sight, won't he?"

"Phineus, yes." I let myself smile.

Charlotte was right. We had to regroup and move ahead with caution. He would be able to provide some details, which might be important. He might be able to flag some probable dangers by reaching out with his inner eye.

I kissed my wife on the lips.

"I'd be lost without you," I said. "Your comment about the heavens pouring The Guilt on us sparked my thinking."

"You did this yourself, Lord Michael," Clytemnestra said in her husky tones. "You were the one who said to visit this room. It was your good will to end our daily suffering which led us here. Let's get back to Satan's Tower and wait for the others to get back."

A gleeful picture of revenge entered my head. I could choke Asmodeus by feeding him Mary's tainted soul when I found them both. This time, I would have the upper hand.

40

WHEN WE RETURNED to the top of Satan's Tower, Marlowe and Germaine were already waiting for us. I lifted their disguises immediately, just to make sure it was really my friends who lay beneath. Phineus sat leisurely on a couch to the side. I was glad, but perplexed, as to how they were back so soon. I thought that it would have taken longer to track down the prophet and convince him to help us.

"We've been back for hours," Marlowe explained as we entered. "Phineus found us before we even left the building."

"I had seen that you'd find me," Phineus said from the couch, with a yawn. "I thought I'd relieve you of the trouble. I would have come sooner but Michael had forgotten to write me into his story again until now."

I looked at him oddly. It was always difficult speaking with someone who knew the mysteries of the unknown. He was a riddler by nature, which didn't help things either. I walked over to Phineus, holding out my hand in greeting. He looked well. The bloody bandage he had once worn around his face had been discarded. Instead, eyes like clouds on a blue sky stared up to meet mine; the eyes that I had helped him retrieve from Asmodeus. He was still an old man, though: a prophet dressed in the robes of his time. He smiled at me and rose from the couch, shaking my hand with a firm grip that defied his aged exterior.

"It's good to actually see you with my real eyes," Phineus said. "I've been trying to track your progress with my sixth vision, but it's been hard to get a read on you lately. Things are always changing."

"Good," I answered. "Let's hope Asmodeus is having the same trouble watching my future."

I beckoned for him to sit back down and he resumed his relaxed state on the couch. I joined him on the opposite corner of the seat, happy that he seemed in such good spirits. I looked up to the others.

"We've had some good fortune," I said. "We found something intriguing at Magdalene's Mansion."

"It had nothing to do with fortune," Clytemnestra said. "It was through hard work and thinking."

"Then you are fortunate you can think," Phineus said wryly to her. She started to speak again, but he stopped her. "Just hold that thought for a few moments," he said, raising a finger in the air.

We waited for him as the seconds ticked by. Just as I started to grow restless, he pointed to the lift, which announced a new arrival with its sharp bing. Smithy and Mack strode into the room.

"Now you won't have to repeat your story," Phineus said with satisfaction, "and I won't have to listen to it twice."

"Michael!" Mack boomed, rushing in to shake my hand. He took my fingers in a crushing grip, his strength almost sending me to my knees. To push through the pain, I clapped him on the shoulder in greeting. He was wearing black jeans and a grubby white t-shirt with the sleeves rolled up. A tattoo of a 50s style pinup girl was plastered over his thick bicep. On his forearm was more ink, depicting cars, flames and guns. His face split in a grin, showing a couple of golden teeth where he had replaced lost ones.

"It's good to see you again," I said, trying to smile back instead of wincing. I really was happy to see him.

"I didn't think you'd remember me," he replied, mercifully letting go my hand. "I've been slaving away in your army, driving trucks around the city. I'm glad my skills can be put to good use."

"How could I forget you?" I frowned. The memory of how he'd picked me up in his taxi and led me to meet Smithy was still fresh, as if it had happened yesterday. He had also had the nerve to drive me into Satan's Demise. Mack had guts, and guts were what we would need.

"Well, you're all famous now and everything," he began, but stopped when I shook my head.

"This is not fame," I said. "This is duty. I don't forget my friends."

He cracked his big grin again, which looked out of place on such a burly man. I wanted to speak with him more, one-on-one, but there were pressing tasks at hand. I let the others gather around as I explained the significance of what we had seen in The Chamber of Maps.

"I'm going to take a handful of us to the edges of Hell and rise up against the flow," I said. "If I'm right, which I'm certain I am, we'll have only a few hours to make it to the Gates of Heaven and assess a weakness. If we can't find anything, we'll be expelled, but we can rise again after the next storm – again and again if we have to. Asmodeus wouldn't dare stop that process and plug the breach; it would clog up Heaven with negativity."

Germaine furrowed his brow, thinking. "But Asmodeus said he would stop The Guilt when he came here last time. It was part of his treaty offering."

"He was lying," I said firmly. "All he wanted, was to cause a revolt; for the people to doubt me. In part he succeeded. We lost one of our closest allies to his deceit." The others went quiet at the mention of Mary; no one wanted to even speak her name anymore. I rose from the couch. "We'll go in our ethereal bodies this time."

"Why don't we use bodies of flesh?" Smithy asked, in an effort to figure out the best way to attack this next mission. "We'll be able to stay up there indefinitely that way. The weight of the vessels will stop our ethereal selves from being drawn back."

"I don't want to risk us being captured and trapped in those bodies," I explained, and paused to make sure I worded my next sentence the right way. "Smithy, you won't be coming on this mission. I need you to stay here. I want you and Mack to help Marax lead the armies." He looked hurt, but I continued before he could object. "You're the finest soldier I know. Your advice will be more valuable in Hell. We need to have the legions battle-ready as soon as possible for when we succeed up there."

I didn't add that because Smithy had refused to be protected from The Guilt it would burden our entry against the storm. This way was better. I couldn't hold writhing bodies as we rose. As it was, it would take all my strength to overcome the flow of the elements pouring downward.

"Mack," I said, turning my attention to the macho cabbie, "I want you to help with the city's logistics. You're not just a driver. You know these streets better than anyone. I want to make sure efficient routes are being used to supply the legions with what they need as quickly as possible. We need to be on high alert. You can pick your own team and Smithy will explain to Marax that you have my full confidence."

Mack turned around and looked down to the streets below, through the panoramic window that afforded us a bird's-eye view of the city. He started nodding.

"I can do that, Michael," he said. "We can start to plan attack paths as well. I assume if this barrier thing gets broken, we'll have to be able to climb upward? We'll need to establish points to take off from."

He was absolutely right. In my hurried state of mind I hadn't thought of that. With no barrier, there would still be the problem of physically migrating upwards. We would have to start by building an air force. There were some demons who had wings already. Smithy was the most skilled pilot Hell could hope to have. We had options. Trust in my friends was returning rapidly. They held answers to problems I didn't have time to consider now. I nodded to Mack that he was correct.

"We'll cut roads to the mountains at the fringes, then," he said. "Lucky we have an abundance of council workers in Hell. They won't be allowed to rest on their shovels here if I have anything to do with it."

"That's a great idea, Mack," Smithy said, everyone now gathering the buoyant feeling in the room. "We can establish airstrips at strategic points. That way, we'll be as close to the foot of Heaven as possible when we open up the territory. We'll be poised to strike."

"And you'll be the commander of the unit," I said to Smithy. "You'll have to pull together a fleet of planes."

His eyes glowed at the prospect. I could see the wheels of thought ticking behind his wrinkled face. Things were coming together. I had no illusions that roads and airfields could be built in a matter of days, even with all the legions of Hell working the task, but we were thinking as a team. We were planning like a united nation looking to overthrow an enemy. It would continue to reinforce the morale and direction of the legions. There had been a sharp swing in confidence since the defeat on Earth. I knew we had to act fast on this, but doubt about our change of luck crept into me. I had grown so distrustful of positive events that I wouldn't allow myself to believe things would work just yet.

My attention turned back to Phineus. He would be able to tell me if the future held good things.

"The future holds only darkness for you," Phineus said to me, anticipating my question with his talent.

My heart sank at the words, but he stood up and came to my side. He reached out and took my hands.

"When I say darkness," he said in a comforting tone, "I mean I find it hard to see. There is only one event which I can make out with any clarity."

"Tell me."

"I will show you," he said, gripping my palms.

41

PHINEUS CLOSED HIS SMOKY EYES and bowed his head in concentration. I felt the welling of his energy starting to creep into my skin. I put my hands over his, drawing in his power. Last time this prophet had shown me my destiny, I hadn't been ready. This time, I was willing to accept what I saw with an open mind.

As I relaxed, Phineus tightened his grip on me. With a whirl of internal color, a shudder of visions shot into my head. They flashed like the strobe of images I had experienced once before. This time, however, the tumult was so fast that no single thing could be taken in with detail. Frame after frame sped into the future, tumbling onward, until the series of events slammed to a halt. The final image held, to show me standing on the broken ridges of a deep ravine, facing Charlotte. I couldn't feel any emotion in what was happening. All I could do was take in the scene in the third person, standing outside myself.

My love struggled on one knee almost a full body length away from me, breathless with exhaustion, holding her hands on the ground to keep upright. Beads of sweat pearled on her face. I stood watching her, not going to her side. Howling winds of power thrashed above us and below, yet where we were was calm. I looked up to make out the blue sky of Heaven, obscured by a thin atmosphere of power, which contained the empty expanse around us. Peering into the ravine below was like looking into a black hole which twisted down into a point, showing the red spark of Hell far beneath. This was Limbo, the central realm, but it had changed. Gone were the grey plains and mundane buildings. They had been replaced with nothing: with space. All that remained were the jagged edges of rock on which we stood. The rest had disappeared. The old barriers which had separated the realms had been ripped apart. Yet something else stood in its place: a makeshift, vacuum-like space to separate good and evil.

Charlotte struggled to her feet in front of me, her face twisting with the effort of it. She swayed, trying to gain her balance and then firmed, looking up at me with hate in her eyes. The revulsion of her gaze made me step back. She looked around her quickly, as if searching for something, before staring back at me again. She braced her legs as if to pounce, her lip curling in a snarl. I watched her closely, waiting for her to strike, but she wavered. Her body wobbled again and her sneer fell momentarily. The hate in her eyes turned abruptly to a look of pleading. Her lips moved, but let out no sound.

Help me.

The features of my face hardened. All love left my countenance and was replaced with hateful anger. I took a step towards her and she recoiled. Pushing my hands out in front of me in a wedge, I strained with effort, every muscle in my arms bulging. My hand slipped forward and a tearing sound split the air. On one side of my fists, new elements were born into existence. On the other side, anti-matter sprang awake in its shimmering death. I had just torn the nothingness around me as I had once seen The Perceptionist do in his void. Charlotte turned to run, spinning on her heels in fear. It was too late. Before she had taken barely a step, I had wrapped the darkness into a ball and hurled it towards her soul. As the hideous weapon struck, her skin dissolved around her. All sense of anything that had made Lotte my love melted before my eyes. Her material nature bled away. Her soul disintegrated into the atmosphere of nothingness around us. The anti-matter ate away at her being until not even a speck of an element was left.

I stood looking at the space that had once contained the body of the woman I loved. A bitter tear slid down my face. My Charlotte was gone and there was no coming back.

42

I AWOKE FROM THE VISION, my eyes trying to focus. After blinking, my sight cleared. I was lying on the carpet with feet surrounding me. Looking up, the first thing I saw was Charlotte with an expression of hopeful anticipation on her face. That beautiful, innocent face I had just seen destroyed. She had run from me and I had torn her down like a heartless god. My love. My wife. My life. Gone.

Squeezing my eyes closed, I rolled over and buried my face into the carpet to muffle the scream of hopelessness that shuddered from my lungs. The scene flashed through my head again and I started to shiver. The emotions I had felt after Mary's betrayal came raging up inside me again. Despair. Sorrow. If there had ever been a time to contemplate taking my life, it was now. I needed to kill myself: to burn my ethereal body away like my flesh had been destroyed on Earth. I could do it. I could end this all with force of will. But I had no will left. It had been sucked out of me when I had witnessed what I would do. Every muscle and thought in me went limp. I didn't even feel the hands picking me up and propping me up on the couch. The emotional agony overwhelmed the rest of my senses. I was no longer coherent. Madness was threatening to wrap its tentacles around me and strangle all reason from my mind. I let out another wailing cry to try and push my thoughts away. Distantly, I felt a body hugging into mine, and a voice ask:

"What did you show him?" There was no reply.

He showed me the end of eternity, I thought.

The body pressed softly against mine, wrapping me in its arms. I could hear Charlotte whisper in my ear, her lips brushing across my cheek.

"Whatever it was, we can change it," she said. "It hasn't happened. We can change it."

There was some other murmuring in the background, but the only voice

I could listen to was the voice I would silence forever: Lotte's.

"It hasn't happened. We can change it," she repeated over and over again, rocking me in her arms.

Can we change it? I thought, with more internal panic. Having seen it with my own eyes had made it so real. Phineus was a powerful prophet: he wouldn't show me this lightly. If it was the only thing he could see with such clarity, then surely that was my destiny. Yet the outcome seemed beyond comprehension. I would *never* hurt Lotte. Ever. Each time I tried to reason it through, trying to pick the scene apart, the ending would crash its finality into me: Charlotte's pleading eyes; her turning to flee; her body bleeding away into darkness. I watched it again and again, until my own mind melted into darkness. I welcomed unconsciousness as some survival mechanism cut my thoughts to black.

43

THE ROOM WAS DARK when I came to again. Blinds had been drawn over the office windows. I was still cradled in Charlotte's arms. No one else was there. The only sound was the breath in her body that my ear rested against. The breath I would rob from her. My first thought was that I wished I were dead – Not this fake afterlife we had been given, but true death. I couldn't bear knowing that eventually, I would deliver just that to Lotte.

"We can change it. It hasn't happened," Charlotte said to me firmly, as she saw my eyes open.

I didn't believe her, but I didn't answer. I just looked at her face, trying to force a sense of calm within myself, at least enough to be able to speak. The quiet surroundings helped. A lack of movement within the room enabled me to still myself as well. Lotte watched me patiently, hugging me tightly, showing I had all support I needed.

"What did you see?" Lotte whispered softly, looking concerned. "Did you see your own death?"

I let out a sigh. I wanted nothing more than to lie to her, but I could not. If I owed Charlotte anything it was honesty. She had died because of me once before already. She knew every part of me. There was no hiding in the shadows from her. I held my breath for a moment before letting the words out in a rush.

"I killed you. I took dark matter and turned your soul into nothing."

There was a momentary look of confusion on her face, before it filled with compassion.

"Oh, Michael, that must have been horrible."

Horrible? Horrible didn't even begin to describe it. Just thinking about it again brought terror to my bones.

"How?" she asked, interrupting my thoughts.

I watched her, puzzled. She was still holding me, asking in a perfectly straight voice how I would murder her. It was like she didn't believe it. But she hadn't seen it like I had. The placid look on her face made me hurt even more. She trusted me completely and I was going to betray her. There was no shying away from this future. Deep in my bones I knew it was the truth. I wished I could just push the memory deep inside myself. Instead, I let it out in the open.

"I used dark matter," I said, not meeting her eyes. "We were in Purgatory, but it was like it wasn't there anymore. It was more like The Perceptionist's void. The barrier between us and Heaven was gone, but it was still divided by something. You were hurt, exhausted. You looked like you hated me. Then, you seemed frightened and begged me to help you."

I looked away to the covered windows, wishing I could escape from this reality. Charlotte's silence spurred me on.

"Then, I turned on you. You tried to run, but I didn't let you. I ripped the void around us apart and created anti-matter. I used it to burn you into nothing. I killed you, Charlotte."

My last few words were barely a whisper.

"We can stop it from happening," Charlotte said firmly, putting her hand on my chest. "We make our own fate."

"I will stop it," I said, finally meeting her gaze. "I'm going to kill myself."

An anger I had never seen in Lotte before twisted her features. Pushing me off her, she lashed out and slapped me on the face. I fell to the ground. She stood up and slapped me again as I cowered beneath her.

"Don't ever say that again!" she yelled, before her anger turned into hot tears. "I would rather die."

"You will if I don't!" I countered from the floor, afraid to stand up. I couldn't fight her. I didn't understand why she was acting like this.

"Do you really think I would want to live for an eternity, knowing that you ended your existence for me?" she said, exasperated. "How could you be so selfish? There couldn't be a worse torture!"

I hung my head in shame. I hadn't looked at it like that. I had thought I would be saving her. I needed to save her. Charlotte's life was worth more than mine. I was tainted, an ugly soul. She had something inside her I could only envy: total trust in humanity. That was what would save us all, not me and my hatred of Asmodeus. Lotte went on, the words flowing out of her like a rage.

"I'm not afraid to die, Michael. It would be nothing. You're only thinking about yourself; how you'll feel afterwards. If we can't change this, you'll be the one suffering, not me. Did you think of that? If I were dead I

170

wouldn't have to worry about you every day. I couldn't be lonely, because I would be nothing. I wouldn't miss you, because I wouldn't be. This afterlife has taught me that we shouldn't fear dying. Living forever is the greater horror, especially if you were to lose the one you love most. If we are to die, then let it be together for something bigger, not to save the other."

She brushed tears from her face, still furious. I didn't know what to say. Lotte continued, unrelenting.

"It could have been Asmodeus, you know, making himself look like me. Wouldn't that make more sense? That you killed him?"

I was absolutely taken aback by her fury. Charlotte was standing over me, waiting for me to answer. All I could do was stare at her transfixed. She had the determination and energy in her that I normally had. Her cheeks were flushed and her eyes wild. Her hair was pressed against the sweat that had started to form on her brow. She kept going with her argument, hammering the point home to me.

"It could have been any one of his angels that he disguised as me, trying to throw you off. This isn't a normal war. We aren't fighting an enemy that fights in the open. That vision is totally out of context. You don't know what happened before, or after. You don't even know when it's meant to happen, if it does at all. It could be thousands of years from now. You can't let something like that cripple you!"

She knelt down, gripping my arms and lowering her voice. "You're focusing too hard on the obvious, Michael. We're on the verge of a great victory and you're letting a small thing stop you. You missed the most important thing about this future!"

I didn't know what to say. She hadn't witnessed what I had. She didn't know that pain I felt just looking at her perfect face.

"How can you say I missed the most important thing?" I whispered, still having the image of me murdering her in my head. "You are the most important thing. You are everything there is."

"No," she said, standing up straighter, looking down at me again. "You said in your vision that the barriers were gone. Don't you see that? There was nothing between Heaven and Hell. We broke them down. We won."

44

CHARLOTTE STOOD NEXT TO ME as the others gathered on the rooftop of Satan's Tower. My wife, who had dragged me out of debilitating self-pity, was yet again the only reason I could continue. She was my true savior. The memory of the vision still hovered in the background of my consciousness like a stain of dread, but Lotte had cast enough doubt on its reality to keep me moving. The future was complicated. That much was clear. I had retold what I had seen to the others. After my collapse, Lotte had sent them to prepare for our departure, resolute that no matter what, we were pressing ahead. It did appear that in the scene I had witnessed we had pulled down the barrier that caused all of The Guilt in this Hell. The filter that separated Heaven and Hell would be no more, to be replaced with something weaker, which I was sure could be passed through by our armies. It was strange that even the certainty of the barrier being destroyed still didn't seem real somehow. It only remained a possibility. Even though I had seen it as the future, I knew we still had a lot of to work to do to make it happen. Destiny doesn't come to those lying in bed. Logic said that I should have felt the same way about the darker part of my vision as well, but I didn't. The outcome we fear is always the one that seems the most likely.

I looked up to the clouds, which were forever streaked with lightning. I would carry us to their edges, beyond the mountains in the far distance; to the end of Hell. There we would rise up to meet whatever fate lay in between now and the prophesied vision we had been given. Clytemnestra, Phineus, Marlowe and Germaine would be the ones coming with Charlotte and me. Smithy and Mack had gone with Marax to carry out the rest of the plans and continue the training of the legions of Hell. The remaining six of us now gathered together, with the furnace winds of the underworld whipping about us. Germaine stood firm, his purple eyes cold, without a trace of the madness inside them.

Marlowe stood at his back steadily, never far away from the beggar alchemist. Phineus waited to the side with the ease of somebody who always knew what was just around the corner. A slight grin hung on his lips. Clytemnestra looked fierce. She was dressed all in black, with her raven hair flowing around her shoulders. Since I had destroyed the dagger she normally had with her, she had replaced it with two small hatchets, strapped to each thigh. The razor edge of their blades matched the sharpness of her teeth.

"So, we are all clear on the path," I said to them. "I will use the elements to take us to where The Guilt enters Hell. Germaine will hold us together, while I move us forward. That way neither of us will become too drained. We'll await the storm at the base of the mountains. As The Guilt begins to form, we will push up through it, again with mine and Germaine's help."

Everyone nodded their understanding and Charlotte picked up my line of command.

"We're expecting to enter the edges of what was once Purgatory," she said, stepping forward. "From there, with the old barrier above gone, we will move as quickly as possible toward Heaven and the city we've been told about. Mary said that Saint Peter stands on the wall there, at the gates. That's our target. If we can band together to bring him down, we can take his keys and use them to destroy that last wall between Paradise and misery."

"Is that all we know?" Clytemnestra asked. "Do we have any kind of map of Heaven? Do we know how to make it to the city?"

"We do not," I shook my head. "However, we have Phineus. His vision will be able to help us on the right path."

"The closer the future, the easier it is for me to predict," the prophet said, backing me up. "I will be able to lead the way, I'm sure. Michael's path might be clouded, but I can follow everyone else's to make sure we don't get lost or divided."

His words injected confidence into the others. Talk of the future kept the uncertainly of Charlotte's possible death fresh in my mind. I did my best to push it back, reasoning it away as being only one possibility of many. Moving always helped clear my mind, so I stepped back and asked Germaine to stand next to me, ready to depart.

"Just keep us in formation," I said to him. "I'll do the rest." Summoning the necessary atoms around us, I pulled the air thickly together. Germaine wove his talents, locking each of us in a triangular grid as we lifted off the rooftop. I was the head of the spear; Germaine and Charlotte were just to the side and back; the other three made up the tail. With the winds rushing behind us, we surged forward. Hell twinkled below: the city streets showing the perpetual motion of souls, organizing and training. From this height, the division of the colored districts of sin looked something like a demented pie chart. Each wedge began from the base of Satan's Tower and spread outward through the city, the edges of each regiment clearly visible in the change of markings on every building. Mount Belial remained untouched, still the seat of my own rule. The Pit, where entertainment normally ran constantly, was dark.

Everyone was involved in this fight. Not a single inmate of Hell had shirked the calling of the legions. Satan's Demise was still black. No one was willing to disturb The Perceptionist's home, even for war. We pushed away from the city, jetting with growing speed over the blurring landscapes. Jungles and deserts spun by. Lakes of lava the size of seas boiled beneath us. Barren valleys of rock rose out of them as the mountain range in the distance grew larger and larger in front of us. Ridges so high on Earth would have invariably had snow on them. These remained void of life. They were jagged jaws of rock, spiking up into the clouds.

The flight was surprisingly easy with Germaine helping to hold us together. All I had to do was propel us onwards. With use and practice my ethereal body had grown stronger. I was unbounded by its potential, willing to face Asmodeus head on. I wasn't fool enough to believe it would be easy, but I also knew that I was no weak target. We really did have a chance in this. He had said himself that I was now too powerful to destroy. His words from Earth were a hope to me. *An unconscious god is basically a dead one.* If that were true for me then it would be true for him as well. He had also said Judas was yet to wake up, which made me think he couldn't overcome Zoroaster's creation of sleep. There may be a way I could use that same liquid to trap Asmodeus. If only I could hold him for long enough. Destroying this barrier, and The Guilt along with it, was our first aim, however.

Germaine brought himself upwards so he could yell over the wind that roared in our ears as we flew on.

"I have been thinking about the vision Phineus showed you," he said. "Did you say you thought there was some kind of void placed between Heaven and Hell?"

"Yes," I yelled back. "You've been in The Perceptionist's creation. It was almost identical, except there was still an outcropping of rock to stand on and some kind of pull downwards instead of being able to stay still in the nothingness. I could see towards Heaven, there was an atmosphere holding the void in. Underneath it was like a vortex spinning down to Hell. I'm not sure how, it all happened so fast."

I watched ahead, shaking the thought of killing Lotte from my mind once more. We were on a direct path forward. The massive mountain range before us seemed endless now, thick and foreboding. We were still a long way away, but their dominance overshadowed everything else, making them appear closer than they really were. We had to get to the other side of them if we were to get to where we needed to be.

"What you're describing is exactly how our master made his home," Germaine continued. "I helped him do it."

I turned my head then to Germaine in shock. He had helped The Perceptionist build The Void? I had always assumed our teacher had done it on his own. Seeing my reaction, Germaine let a wry smile touch his lips.

"Would you know how to do it again?" I asked, curious at the possibility this presented.

"It was my idea to begin with," he grinned. "Like any other vacuum, you create a seal and then have to suck everything out through an exit point. Once there is nothing left, you close it off. For The Perceptionist, we let everything escape, including space and time. We then added the elements we wanted back inside very carefully. It sounds like there was still some constructed matter inside what you describe. The most solid things, like ground and fully formed earth, always go last, which would explain why you were standing on some kind of cliff. Eventually it would be eroded away, leaving nothing at all. There would have been no elements around you in the air by then. That explains why if you created anti-matter, it would be able to exist without being cancelled out right away."

I peered back to the rest of our group, making sure Germaine's concentration hadn't wavered while we spoke. Everyone was still in formation. Charlotte gave me a reassuring nod that she was okay. My chest hammered with the potential of what Germaine had said.

"Do you think you could do it again? Could something like that erode the barrier?" I pressed.

He shook his head, his long, scraggly hair flapping backwards as we flew.

"The barrier is too solid. It would resist because it's under its own power. You would have to break it up first. I'm not even sure you could actually make a void, especially if Asmodeus was trying to stop you. I certainly don't have anywhere near enough power to do it. I planted the idea, but The Perceptionist made it happen. He had had decades of practice making smaller versions until we tried it on a large scale."

I let the conversation fall silent. Perhaps The Perceptionist would come to our aid after all, if I had truly seen what I thought it to be. For now, my attention had to be on getting up to Heaven through The Guilt. The mountains were upon us.

"Hold us tight, Germaine!" I said to him, knowing we would have to go up through the clouds.

He fell back and I increased my concentration. Our speed, which had been steady, quickened as the black foothills raced below us. I brought us to the right, going up, getting ever closer to the sheer rock face of this mammoth growth of stone and earth. The face of the mountain steamed with hot gases, escaping from deep within its fissures, but there was no other movement. I created a small buffer of air around us for protection and looked to the clouds above. I would have to hug close to the face of the mountain to make sure we didn't get lost in the darkness of the storm above.

A spark of light speared down and I zipped to the side, narrowly avoiding its sizzling energy. Thunder exploded in an instant, almost splitting my ears with the noise. Germaine pulled the formation even closer together, to make us a smaller target. I placed my trust in him to keep the others with us, training my eyes forward. Staying as close to the mountain as I could, we shot up into the clouds. I could almost feel the stone of the mountain below graze my stomach. We bumped upward in turbulence as the air bubble I had placed below did its job, keeping us from being shredded to pieces. I was nearly blind in the clouds, the thick black smog choking my senses, basically traveling by feel. Another bolt of lightning cracked, lighting a shadowy path ahead. We veered to the left to avoid an outcrop of rock. We must have been nearing the peak. Again thunder shuddered at our heads as I pushed on. The mountain began to fall away slowly and I let our altitude drop with the decline, keeping the speed constant. Abruptly, we burst from the bottom of the clouds. The sudden light startled me. As my eyes adjusted I almost stopped short. The end of Hell sat before us: a shimmering white wall. The solid mass was as smooth as a bleached eggshell, dead straight with no angles or end. If this was the true edge of the universe, then I had no idea how to get beyond. As we descended, I watched with the elemental vision, which showed nothing different. The wall was completely even, without a single gap in its composition. It didn't glow like the other elements, nor was it like dark matter. It was totally impossible to describe, except that I knew it was there and that there was no way through. I let my sight return to normal. The thing was stunning: featureless but beautiful. It seemed to be the opposite of The Void: pure matter condensed into something with infinite density and mass. Indestructible, immoveable; yet not created through any process I could fathom.

Our feet came down to the ground and we all stared up in wonder.

Almost no one else in all of history had seen this. Despite why we were here, I felt privileged to be able to witness something so rare and impossible. I looked around. All the others were as transfixed as me. Germaine had his mouth open like a circus clown. Marlowe knelt down in reverent respect. Clytemnestra murmured her astonishment. Only Phineus watched it with a calm face. He turned back to the mountain range behind us to get his bearings before returning his attention ahead. Charlotte moved forward, walking over to the mass. She reached out to touch it, pressing her palm against the surface. Turning to us, she frowned.

"You all have to try this."

We moved forward as one. I pressed my fingers tentatively against the wall. Puzzled, I took my fingers away and did it again. I watched the others, who were all doing the same thing. Each time my hand touched the wall it resisted, but there was no sensation that I was pushing against anything. It was as if I was being held back by an invisible magnetic force, but I could still see what I was touching. I could have spent years in this place trying to figure out its mysteries, but a deep hissing noise from above made me look up. High above, murky black and brown elements were seeping into Hell. I couldn't see the gap that they were coming from because it was hidden by the clouds, but it was clear the first movements of The Guilt were starting.

It was time to rise up.

45

MY COMPANIONS GATHERED TOGETHER. Our heads tipped upwards to watch the tempest of guilt begin to form. I had seen it with Charlotte and Clytemnestra in miniature back at Magdalene's Mansion, but nothing could have prepared us for the true scale of the force coming through. Energy rippled, boiling and streaming down, gathering in eddies and swirls in the clouds. The wind around us grew and grew until it howled in our ears and pulled at our bodies. The tornadoes started to form. They were like whirlpools in the clouds at first, lumbering into life before starting to twist faster. The first plume burst alight, spinning downward. The tail smashed to the ground jarring the earth at our feet, sending a tremor right through the ground and shaking the mountain. Rocks started to fall from the peak, adding to the thunderous violence all around.

"Quickly!" I yelled, my voice swept away by the wind before it had even left my mouth.

I had to physically pull everyone toward me with the elements to get their attention. We were now in a huddle amid the chaos of a category Hell maelstrom. I held Charlotte in one arm, tightly against my body. With my spare hand, I motioned for Germaine to hold everyone firm the same way, as one tight group. He nodded his understanding and pulled what elements hadn't been ripped into the tornadoes back towards us, to help keep us in place. The bond formed, but I could tell it was a major effort for Germaine to keep it steady. I moved to lift us off the ground, but there wasn't enough air pressure to rise up. Everything was being torn into the sucking storm, piling power into The Guilt that would soon explode over Hell. Our feet started to drag backwards, toward the closest fire-twister. I gripped hard to stop us, but the current of elements whipping past us was too frenzied to resist. Our group lifted up, skipping across the ground in a scraping motion, before Germaine held us tight again, helping our collective weight hold us back. We couldn't stay this way for much longer without letting the opportunity to push through the gap in the filter pass. I searched my mind wildly for ideas.

Snapping over to an elemental vision, I could see every ounce of ungrounded energy whipping up into the storm. The momentum it created was astonishing. The glowing molecules shot past us at the speed of sound, looking more like tiny comets than single atoms. I could tell we only had seconds to make a choice. There seemed no way we could do it, though. All the elements I could use to help us were becoming part of the tempest. Somehow I had to pull them back. My eyes locked on the tornado that was trying to suck us in and an idea came to me. It was a long shot, but if I didn't try we might be consumed by it anyway. I yelled out to Germaine again.

"Hold!"

He nodded as he saw my lips move and I could feel our bodies cling harder. Bending my legs, I pushed off the ground with all my strength, assisting the cyclonic winds to pull us upwards. Without the resistance of the ground, we started to spin into the air. The field holding us together slackened momentarily, and Clytemnestra's body started to slip outwards. Marlowe lunged up and grabbed her with a powerful arm, yanking her back again. Once more, I felt Germaine deliberately hold us in with what strength he had. If one of us was lost here, they might never be found again in this wilderness of rock and fire.

I steeled myself for the heat that was rushing up to us, and heard Charlotte scream as we met the flames of the storm's searing intensity. I shook the pain off, keeping my vision on the elements as we were tossed like a human tumbleweed into the heart of The Guilt. Elements of regret and pain lashed about us. Every other atom was there as well: earth, fire, liquid vapor and air. The wind carried us around one circuit of the twister and then another. I could no longer see the others, only feel them against me. Their features were lost in the torrent of elements sparking around us. Germaine held us with all his might. Now that the elements were closer I was able to gather some of them behind us, straining to pull them away from the storm, into my grip. I used their momentum to follow the raging flow upward and around, spinning in a dizzying cycle of anarchy. It took every ounce of skill I had to hold us on course, while I hoped Germaine could keep us united.

We rushed up to meet the clouds and the intensity of the tornado's pull started to lessen a fraction. I could now make out the break in the barrier above. It was tight against the shimmering white wall that stretched up and through. Pestilence spewed out into Hell. With a shuddering bang the storm started to move towards our city. I held for a split second longer as our mess of a group spun around one final time. With a wrenching effort I sent a blast of the elements behind us, launching like a slingshot in the direction of the wall that marked the end of Hell. The burst of The Guilt moving away propelled us even faster forward and up. I braced for impact, but as we hit the wall there was no pain: the unusual property of its construction shielded us from its touch. Instead, our impetus propelled us, skidding upward against the final elements sifting through the filter. Emotion squeezed around us and our group slithered though the closing gap like a screaming baby being born into a bleeding world.

The roaring silence that filled my ears seemed as loud as the cacophony of the storm we had left behind. Sprawled out in a scatter of bodies, the six of us rolled to a halt on a grey meadow of grass. We had made it through.

46

I ROLLED TO MY FEET in an instinctive rush. Marlowe had done the same and was peering around us for attack, shrugging off the tumble of the storm like it was nothing. I held my breath for another impact. Something. Anything. All was still. The gap had been shut off almost as soon as we had slid through. The white wall that marked the end of Hell continued upward next to us, into the sky of Purgatory. The grey grasslands around us stretched into the distance, seemingly unchanged. Above, the old filter that had once separated Purgatory and Heaven was no more. Instead was a ceiling of spirit and earth combined to make up a powder-blue sky. Searching around I saw the rest of our party had made it mostly unscathed. The heat of The Guilt storm hadn't done any severe physical damage, but the pressure of the pain around us had taken a toll. Clytemnestra lay on her side, breathing heavily, with her eyes wide in fright. Charlotte was sitting with her head between her knees. Germaine stared at the sky, gathering his wits. I knew he would have been drained from the effort of keeping us together through the tumult. Phineus scrambled to his feet next to Marlowe, using the African's body to haul himself up. He dusted off his robes and blew out a sigh of surprised exasperation.

"Not even I saw that coming," he said, his cloudy eyes locked on mine. "I think we were lucky you acted so quickly."

I nodded silently, moving to Charlotte's side to make sure she was okay. She flinched and looked up as I touched her back. I could see some small burns on her face healing rapidly. The fire of The Guilt didn't normally burn our ethereal bodies. In its pure form, so close to the source, it had done some damage to Lotte's, which wasn't yet as used to the heat as ours. I touched the red welts on her cheek, to assist her healing. She sucked in air, feeling the elements work. With my help her recovery was swift. She

181

swallowed to regain some moisture in her mouth.

"Thank you," was all she could manage. I helped her stand.

She clung to me, more for moral than physical support. Everyone's clothes were smoldering, but not burnt. Like all garments in Hell, they were clothes built to withstand incredible heat. Nevertheless, I sent a fine mist of water over our group to cool us off. Phineus smiled his relief. Germaine coughed on the ground and some blood escaped his mouth. I left Charlotte and went to his side, using the elements to heal him too, and let some extra energy flow into his body. His eyes regained their shine as I restored him. He nodded his thanks and stood. One by one I went to the rest. Marlowe and Clytemnestra both brushed me away, saying they didn't need to be healed. Phineus accepted an infusion of strength, although he didn't seem to require it. Finally I used the elements, which were abundant here, to help build my own stamina. The vitality I was able to draw into myself easily offset the energy it took to do it. We were soon all completely alert, ready to continue towards Heaven. Mentally I was still exhausted, but I knew that would pass as we moved.

"We can't linger," I said to my friends. "The flow of guilty elements will start again soon. If I'm right it will grow stronger over the coming hours. We don't know exactly how long it will take until it gets too strong to push against. Better we go now."

"This way, then," Phineus said without ceremony, and started walking into the meadow, directly away from the white wall.

Clytemnestra adjusted the small axes she had strapped to her thighs and continued after him. Marlowe took Germaine by the upper arm and led him into a marching pace. Charlotte and I followed. Two by two, we kept a strong pace over the drab grass: Phineus and Clytemnestra in front, Marlowe and Germaine in the middle, Lotte and I close behind. There were pieces of rubble here and there, the only remnants that marked the broken barrier which had fallen from above. I considered taking flight, but thought it better to let Phineus lead. He obviously thought the best way was to march right now, so I kept walking briskly, using the chance to study the sky. The construction was a beautiful light blue, speckled with silver; a mixture of light earthly elements and different kinds of spiritual strength. It looked like a crystal clear day on Earth, but with a galaxy of bright stars adding their light in as well. I couldn't see the finer detail because it was so high up, but the weave must have made up the ground level of Heaven. This universe was a strange place. Seeing how it was made in The Chamber of Maps had only given me an inkling of how it all really fit together. The sky seemed like it was still a separation to Purgatory of sorts. However, I thought that if I tried I would be able to break through

182

quite easily. Without knowing exactly what was on the other side I didn't want to risk it just yet. My intuition told me that where Zoroaster and I had destroyed the centre of the old filter, cracking its power source apart, there would still be a gaping hole leading upward. That hole we created would be in the outer reaches of Purgatory, away from the city. With luck we wouldn't have far to travel from where we were.

"Do you think there will be people down here?" Charlotte asked, looking at me earnestly as we walked. I remembered she had friends in this place.

"I have no idea," I answered plainly. "Perhaps some have chosen to stay. It doesn't have that same depressing feeling with the light of this sky."

She looked upwards, contemplating what I had said.

"It is beautiful," she agreed. "Still, the lure to see Heaven would be strong for people who have been working to make it there every moment since they died. I would be surprised if Zoroaster hadn't taken a majority to the heavenly city right away."

Surely she was right. I couldn't imagine that strange but charismatic man staying idle after we had brought down the barrier together. He always worked for the people and that wouldn't have changed between realms.

The meadow changed slightly around us. It wasn't the ground but the sky. In the distance, there was a distinct variation in color. The blue and silver above cut abruptly away to a burst of sunny gold. The heavenly light streamed downward, making even the grey grass glow with life. This was the breach that had cut through when the barrier had been destroyed. If I thought about it, there was most likely some kind of gap in this sky before anyway. The light souls from Purgatory, lucky enough to pass to Heaven, had been pulled up through the centre of the filter, so there must have been a space to emerge through. We had simply peeled back the first barrier, making the space larger at the top. The aura coming through cast new meaning into this mundane realm. Even here, at the fringes of its influence, small white flowers began to appear in clumps around us. After mere moments, we were walking on a soft bed of them. Through the light, still far away, I could just make out some kind of pathway that had been built to rise up beyond sight. It was a wide, winding ramp of stone. Zoroaster had indeed been true to his word. That was a new bridge between realms.

"Shouldn't we be trying to go faster?" Germaine said as he beheld the sight ahead of us.

The prophet leading the way didn't break pace, but he and Clytemnestra both looked back at the comment.

"If we do, we'll miss him," Phineus said and turned back into his march.

I looked at Charlotte in questioning, but she appeared just as curious I was. I caught up to the prophet, wanting a clearer explanation. He was almost running on his short legs; Clytemnestra moved easily beside him with her long stride.

"Phineus?" I asked, as I came to his side. "Who will we miss if we go too fast?"

He simply pointed up ahead. A small silhouette appeared through the golden light. It was a single figure, standing patiently with a bundle in its arms, looking away from us, up into the sky. It was impossible to make out exactly who it was through the glow, but Phineus made hope flood into me with his next words:

"The friendly man with the teddy bear. He has been waiting for us."

184

47

"DANTE!" I YELLED AS I RAN ahead to greet my old friend.

At first I remained cautious, but I could sense no deception. The comment by Phineus that this was a "friendly man" eased my worry. Dante spun around at the sound of my voice. His eyes were always wide and eyebrows raised high, so I wasn't sure if he was surprised to see me, or simply wearing his normal expression.

"Saint Michael!" he greeted me, waving.

He held up the teddy that he called Virgil in his arms and made it wave as well. Ever since I had first met him on the icy winter streets of Las Vegas, that bear had been at his side. He had lost his mind and even in the afterlife was yet to find it again. I recalled that he refused to admit Virgil wasn't real, since it had been his only friend and support through his troubled times. Dante stood in front of a raised group of cloud- like rocks. This was the place I had first entered Purgatory. Right below us, deep in the ground, was the very centre of Hell's filter. A few hundred meters away, Zoroaster's bridge of stone began. It was like a giant spiral staircase, winding into the sky. The heavenly light coming down was warm and comforting, streaming through the rough edges of a giant opening, which looked like a chasm spreading upward instead of down. The lip of the large tear spread wide, like the teeth of a great white shark. If it weren't for the illumination coming down, it would have looked positively evil.

"I've been…" Dante began as I neared.

"Waiting for me, I know," I finished his sentence for him.

"You always were very wise," he smiled happily, hugging Virgil to his chest and then looking into space.

"Why are you here?" I asked.

His eyes fogged for just a moment, like he was searching for a memory, before the spark came back and he remembered.

"We volunteered," he said, indicating the bear. "Mr. Zoroaster needed someone to meet you, to explain what was happening so you could be prepared for Heaven."

The rest of our party came towards us and he nodded to them in greeting, saying: "Hullo."

"This is Dante and Virgil," I said to the others as they came near enough to hear. Charlotte stepped in.

"We've met before," she said, holding out her hand to shake his.

"Oh yes, at the Truth School. You're beautiful," he said, taking her hand and kissing it. "We remember."

I introduced the others, who all hung back at a slight distance, wary, as I had been. Phineus was the only other one who approached, raising his palm in salutation. Dante paused, looking at the prophet's strange eyes before turning back to me.

"Zoroaster said that if I found you, you should come to him right away. He told me," Dante screwed his eyes up in concentration, "come low through the trees to the left of the city. Stop before you exit the forest. He'll have guards waiting to bring you to the camp."

My friend opened his eyes again and smiled, as though proud of himself. What he had said sounded foreboding, so I pressed him for more details.

"Is there anything else? What is it like up there?"

"Michael?" Marlowe said from behind me.

I turned to see the African looking steadily up into the light streaming down from above. He was squinting, but seemed worried. I followed his line of vision, but could see nothing different.

"Can you feel that? I think we need to get going," he said.

I stopped and concentrated. There was a very light pressure, starting to tug at my body, gently urging it to return the way we came. It must have been the start of the cycle of cleansing I had predicted. Searching upwards with elemental sight, I could see it. A fog of atoms was coming through the gap pierced in the ceiling of Purgatory. It mixed with the light, which was pink in this view, appearing to be some type of love. The darker elements flowed down through it and then outward in all directions, away to the edges of the filter that was concealed below our feet. I guessed that before we had destroyed the filter above those evil elements would have gone to the edges of it instead, before being pushed through the sides of both barriers into Hell. It explained why The Guilt had been stronger recently: it didn't have as much to push through now. The effect here against my body was like standing in a weak stream. It would become a river before too long, I was sure. Marlowe was right.

"You can tell me more while we fly," I said to Dante.

"Fly?" he asked, looking to Virgil, afraid. "But we don't have wings."

"You won't need them," I said kindly, before turning to Germaine.

He also looked skywards, studying the elemental construction of what was happening. His face was pursed deep in thought.

"Germaine!" I said, snapping him out of it. "The same formation as last time, but I want Dante next to me."

Germaine blinked slowly before nodding his understanding. He came in closer to me. Marlowe and Clytemnestra fell in also, like two prepared soldiers. Phineus adjusted his robes around him, so they wouldn't flap in the wind as we flew. I gave Charlotte a quick kiss on the cheek.

"Are you ready to see Heaven, my love?" I asked.

She nodded her answer.

Without waiting any longer, I let her go and brought us upward, whipping the elements thickly beneath us. As we lifted off, Dante let out a cry of surprise, looking down as the others came up as well. Germaine kept us in pattern and I surged ahead with Dante next to me, aiming straight for the chasm. We wouldn't need Zoroaster's pathway. Dante gripped Virgil tightly to his chest, squirming with fright as he tried to figure out what was happening.

"Relax," I said to him soothingly, as the cloud-like rocks below faded from view. "I've got you. I won't let you fall."

He watched me, his eyes bugging out from below his sweeping eyebrows. His nose was big and hooked, nearly touching his upper lip, which quivered as he tried to control his fear. I looked away for a moment, concentrating as we pushed upward. The flow of the dark elements coming down felt stronger as we neared. From this closer vantage point I could see the blue and silver sky that made up the ceiling of Purgatory was actually as solid as rock. There were clawed rips in it from the force of the final explosion I had created last time. The space was canyon wide, but because elements were being pushed through from the open air above it, the power of the current was greater as we passed through. Switching to regular sight, I kept the group steady and headed into the heavenly light. The love that was infused with the illumination coming down buoyed my mood. Making us go faster, I eyed the top of the opening. Now that my eyes had adjusted, I could see a stunningly white sky. A lush rainforest met the edges of the ravine on one edge, but I made our way to the other side where Zoroaster's path was cut into the ground. I didn't touch down, preferring to keep moving quickly, but made sure we glided only a few feet from the trail. As the pathway rose, the blue rocks of the ravine disappeared.

We emerged onto an immaculate lawn, long and wide, bordered on all sides by tropical trees. Rows of sapphire statues marked the edge of the forest. There were hundreds of them, immense sparkling replicas of cherub angels. Their innocent faces were all turned to the side, facing the same direction. Their baby fingers pointed the way. I looked to where they were facing. At the top of the wide stretch of vivid green grass, the row of statues formed to a point that opened onto a road glimmering like diamonds. The statues seemed to border it all the way into the distance. On the horizon, a shining city of white and gold rose up. This was the first thing the souls rising from Purgatory would see. There could be no mistake that it was the heavenly city we were heading to. The sight almost overwhelmed me with joy. I felt almost as if I was returning home after a long time away, knowing all my friends would be there to greet me. Nearly all of my friends, though, were at my side. I grew suspicious of the emotion, suddenly feeling exposed out here in the open. Without pausing further I increased the pace of our flight and headed for the trees to the left as Zoroaster had instructed. The palms rushed at as with speed as I spotted a gap.

Looking back, I yelled at Germaine, "Single file!"

In an instant he obeyed, snapping us together like a zipper. We threaded between two of the statues and rushed into the shelter of the forest. I had expected the interior to be dense and thick, but the trees were all arranged in symmetrical order, row by row, leaving only enough space for a single body to pass through the grid. The mathematical precision on such a large scale was sublime to behold. It was... perfect. The only thing stopping me from being able to see all the way to the end of the forest was the canopy above, blocking out the light. I flew on until we were deep inside, away from where we had entered.

Bringing us to a stop, I let our feet touch down, feeling more at ease in the shadows. The rest of the group landed with grace behind, except Dante, who stumbled into me. Propping him up, I held him at arm's length, making sure he was steady before letting him go.

"Holy shit," he said, wide-eyed, checking that Virgil was still in his arms. "That was much faster than when we came up the first time."

I looked over his head at the others, who were still in single file. I had to lift a little off the ground so I could see them all. Marlowe was at the rear, looking back to make sure nothing was behind us. I watched as he stepped across to the next row of trees before coming back and doing the same on the other side. He nodded that we seemed to be clear. Germaine and Clytemnestra fidgeted uneasily, while Phineus stood calmly. All was completely still apart from us. Charlotte looked cautiously to the side before catching my eye.

"We should keep moving," she said.

"It's okay," Dante replied, turning back to her. "There's nothing in here. Everyone is at the city. No one wants to be too far away from it."

"Why is that?" I asked.

He looked back at me and sniffed, hugging his bear against him. "Do you feel good?"

It was a strange question, but I thought for a moment before answering. Now that we had stopped, that feeling of wellbeing and confidence I had felt as we entered Heaven had subsided. The effect of it being gone left me nervous. I could also feel the pull of the filter lightly trying to draw me back to Hell.

"No, not really," I said.

"In the light here you feel good," Dante said. "It's not like that under the trees, where it doesn't get through. The sensation of light is even nicer near the city."

"Why?" I asked.

The old bum shrugged his shoulders. "People say it's the love of God. Zoroaster says it's a beautiful lie to keep people happy and stupid."

"And what do you think?" I pressed him.

"It feels fake. All I want is to see my wife and show her I can be not crazy anymore, but they won't let us in the city. Everyone is gathered at the gates, camping out and waiting. They say we should be glad that we're even that close. I don't like it, but if I get too angry I might go to Hell, so I try to stay content."

Dante's words made me feel like all my efforts so far had really been for nothing. It was one division after another with Asmodeus. The love of God. It sounded as if he was manipulating them with the elements to keep them sedated. If it grew stronger nearer the city, people would naturally be drawn there. He was keeping all his supporters in one place, but he was still keeping those he felt unworthy out of his precious capital. I needed to know more. Zoroaster would be able to tell me. I turned around, peering through the rows of trees.

"Are we heading the right way, Dante?"

"Yes," he nodded. "We just keep walking and we'll get there eventually."

Eventually wasn't quick enough. I prepared to take us all there now. No more delays. We couldn't afford to wait.

48

ZOROASTER'S GUARDS WERE WAITING at the edge of the forest when we arrived. There were two of them: tall shirtless men who looked like Vikings. Both had blonde hair, plaited in long braids down their backs, with beards to match. Neither carried a weapon, but their bulging muscles said their bodies were lethal enough. They greeted us with stoic nods. One, who had a jagged scar on his left cheek, spoke as we approached.

"You are Michael," he said in a question that wasn't a question.

"I am," I confirmed, watching him with care. "Please follow me," he said curtly.

Without another word, the two of them turned and started to walk back through the last of the trees. I looked to Dante for an explanation.

"They aren't very talkative," he offered and followed them.

Not wanting to fall behind, I waved for us to move forward. I could feel the pull of the filter growing again in strength against my skin. It was now like a stiff wind that made no noise, but pushed persistently against me. Keeping pace, Charlotte strode to be level with me, one row across. We were separated by a tree-length, so I saw her appear each time we passed a trunk. The others were right at our backs. We finally exited the forest and Lotte came to my side. Towering above us, the capital of Heaven shone in its soft, white illumination. It was built on a vast slope that rose at a steady incline back and up. At its top I could see the eight quartz domes Mary had described to us: God's Basilica. The central dome was higher than the rest. Distant figures of angels flew around it, going in and out. Around the basilica complex was a sweeping wall. The roofs of buildings could just be seen between it and another. In concentric circles all the way down, the city spread along the slope, its mostly white roofs and walls zigzagging between like a maze. Where the incline finished, a final barricade stood, capped with curved parapets. It looked to have no one guarding it. The height alone was enough to turn anyone back, blocking out from view what I guessed must be the first quarter of the metropolis. It was made from a solid weave of gold and diamond, without a gap or a break in its construction. At the bottom of the wall, white cloth tents had been erected in neat rows, creating another mini-city at the foot of the real one. Some tents had flags; others were bare. They caught the glimmer of the city above, but still looked dull in comparison. The tents were organized in the same circular pattern of the metropolis, with streets and pathways neatly laid out. It looked more like a regimented army had set up camp here, rather than the refugees of Purgatory who I knew were inside. It was a creation of Zoroaster's mind. Truth brought order – or so he said. The light coming from above washed over the entire scene and I felt the familiar emotion of content spreading into me. Pushing it away, I ignored the effects.

"Don't be fooled by what you feel right now," I said to the others, continuing my walk to catch up to the Vikings and Dante, who had just reached the first of the tents. "We are not here to stay. That happiness is an illusion. We will have the real thing soon enough."

Our group moved as one, covering the short gap between the forest and the tents in an instinctive crouch. The Viking with the scar inclined his head for us to keep following and began heading through the narrow streets of the camp. We barely drew a glance as we moved past the people milling inside. Their eyes were half-glazed, as if they were stoned, happy to drift through their surroundings without a care for anything or anyone. I saw Clytemnestra grit her teeth at the sight as I turned my head to make sure we stayed close. Everyone was with us in a tight huddle. Lotte touched my arm gently.

"What are you thinking?" she asked.

"I think Zoroaster will have some answers for us. He will know where the gate is and where Peter stands guard. That is all we need."

I was doing my best to keep my cool. If we got drawn into this camp we would waste precious time. I had to keep a strict focus, something Lotte seemed to understand well.

"He likes to talk," she offered. "Don't let him distract you." She had been in Zoroaster's presence more often than I, so I took the advice to heart. I would need to keep on my toes, despite his best intentions.

Our guides took an abrupt turn and strode down a side street. The ground at our feet was still vivid green grass, like the first lawn we had seen when entering Heaven. No matter how my feet trampled it, the blades would spring back up again as if untouched. Ahead was a tent slightly larger than the rest, grey in color with a flag above it showing a golden icon of a bearded man. He had flat eagles' wings spreading from his waist, and was holding a ring in his hands.

"The Faravahar," Charlotte said, still at my side. "It's Zoroaster's sigil."

The Vikings came to the tent and pulled the flap open, standing back to let us through. Dante went in ahead, with the rest of us not far behind. The interior was bare, except for a single round rug on the ground. The squat, turban-wearing man I had met once before sat on it cross-legged, writing furiously on parchment in front of him. He looked up at us as we entered, immediately dropping his pen and jumping to his feet. Dante, hugging Virgil close, bowed low in greeting.

"I found them," he said as he straightened. "I told you they'd come."

"Yes, good work, Dante. Thank you, thank you. Please sit." Zoroaster let the bum take a seat, before addressing the others and me. "So many of you, I didn't expect such a crowd without feeling the barrier fall."

He studied our party one by one. His scrutiny made me turn. Germaine met his gaze firmly, as though sizing up a powerful opponent. Marlowe stood to polite attention, with a wide stance, as if bracing himself against the flow I could also feel gnawing at my body. Clytemnestra hung back, looking outside the tent, forever on guard. Phineus had already taken a seat, cross-legged, making himself comfortable. It wasn't a good sign. Charlotte was right next to me as always, watching Zoroaster.

"You look terrible, Michael. Those ears have gotten worse," he said. "How did you get here? I'm surprised you were able to enter Heaven without me sensing it. Where is Mary?"

The questions caught me off guard. I had almost forgotten the manic jumping from subject to subject that characterized his conversation. I felt a stab of pain in my chest at the mention of Mary. He didn't know. I should have expected it would be the first thing Zoroaster would ask, but I wanted to move things along without a tedious explanation, which would only delay us further.

"I'm sorry, Zoroaster, we don't have much time," I said, naturally matching his staccato way of speaking. "We found a way up through the edges of the barrier. We only have another hour at most until we will be dragged back. Mary betrayed us so she could bring Judas to Heaven. I assume she is in the city with Asmodeus."

He furrowed his brow at my comments, staring at me intently. His gaze pierced into me.

"Hmmm, I can see you're telling the truth, but there's a strange knot in there blocking it all. There's something missing."

"Look," I said, my patience straining. "I'm sorry to be rude, but we really don't have time for this. Is there any way you can show us to the main gate of the city, where Saint Peter stands guard? It's important."

"Rude?" Zoroaster said, his smile returning. "The truth is never rude to me and I don't take offence at someone in a hurry. But I would like some more details. Why is it important you get there? You have taken me by surprise. Mary isn't the kind of person who would hurt her friends."

His split line of questioning had me at my wit's end. I was about to snap, when thankfully Charlotte stepped forward, calmly.

"Zoroaster, it looks like you have been busy since we left. Michael has also been busy, organizing the Legions of Hell and trying to bring down the final barrier, as we discussed with you last time. Do you remember?"

"Yes, Charlotte," he smiled. He turned backward and lowered himself to the ground again. The action made me furious, anxiety tingeing my need for the progress that didn't seem to be coming. I was about to object, when Lotte continued.

"We have stayed on that path. We had a plan to bring down the barrier, but Mary plotted against us to serve her own needs. She is now with our enemy. We found another way and are pursuing the same end: total freedom for all. Can you see I'm telling the truth?"

He squinted at her before nodding.

"Yes, but that doesn't mean you know all the facts."

"The fact," Charlotte pushed, remaining composed, "is that our goal is to find Saint Peter and use the keys of the gates between Heaven and Earth he keeps to destroy the final filter between Hell instead. All we need from you is to show us where he is, to save time. If you can help us draw him out into the open it would help us greatly. It is that simple."

"Yes, simplicity is preferable," he said. "I appreciate your directness, Charlotte. I have had my hands tied in a certain way since we came here, so I'm glad to have people without the need to play games."

"Games?" I asked, unsure of where this was heading.

"You would have seen that we have set up camp outside the city because Asmodeus will not let us in. Heaven has changed very much since I was first here. It used to be that people could roam its bountiful lands without restriction. It is a wonderful place, really. There are oceans in the shape of perfect circles and mountains that embody everything the mere hills on Earth try to be, but fail in comparison. Everywhere is the ideal form that creates the definition of existence for the rest of the imperfect universe, which is just a shadow of this place. I wish you had the time for me to show you."

I would have reminded him of time, but he seemed, mercifully, to be coming to his point. Anxiety bolstered my frustration. Every pull the barrier below made against my body was a reminder we were running against the clock.

"Now," he went on. "Asmodeus has changed the paradigm. Instead of letting people explore and settle where they like, he has built a device that draws them to this metropolis."

"God's love," I said using the phrase Dante had given me.

"Yes, I knew you would have noticed it. That love is now built into the walls of this city. It was there before of course, but now its gravity permeates everything and has become impossible for most people to resist. It's a subtle way for him to draw people in and build his own army without them knowing it. God used to rely on people's unconditional faith in him to do his bidding, but now he uses this beautiful lie to manipulate their need to carry out his whims. It is a symptom of his new fractured nature. He is really is Asmodeus now not God. It is something I cannot abide. He is making people happy, but he is doing so in the wrong way. On top of that, he shuts us out. He is using a delicate form of torture against my people, having them know that they would feel even happier inside the city, where the seat of his love is placed. They have family in there he isn't allowing them to see."

"Then why haven't you done something?" Germaine said, from behind us, speaking for the first time. "It looks like you are content to just sit here."

Zoroaster craned his neck to see the mad-looking alchemist standing behind me. He nodded, obviously impressed.

"You look like a strong one," he said to Germaine. "I hope we get to talk later, but I'm afraid if I don't continue what I was saying, Michael may explode with rage."

I clenched my jaw to stop myself from doing exactly that.

"We cannot directly confront Asmodeus," he went on, "because if we do, we will all be swept down into Hell. Some of the citizens in the camp don't mind being here. They're simply happy to bask in the false love where we are. Most are not so easily deceived, but they are scared. They do not want to leave a peaceful place for the realm of terror below that they have been told about. It is a game of chess I play, agonizingly slow. Non-violent resistance is all we have. It has been enough to stop Asmodeus from trying to rebuild the first barrier Michael and I took down, because our camp stands in his way. I have seen him and some angels take flight high up and out of sight once or twice, but they returned again within half a day. I would have felt it if he had tried to manipulate the elements here; I would have moved our camp to where he was and hampered his efforts with a passive shield of bodies. He hasn't forced the issue yet, but my only choice has been to stand firm and wait. If I openly resist Asmodeus it will give him the excuse he needs in front of the rest of the population to banish us from our place here. I am forcing a stalemate. If he acts against us without provocation, he risks losing his children's faith completely, no matter how much he sedates them with his charms. They are good people in the city. Some have come to the walls to shout down to their families here. They are beginning to question, but are blind to the truth he is shielding so well. Now that you are here, we can do something to expose it."

"That is why we came," I said, exasperated. "I come telling you we don't have time and you delay us. I appreciate you have stood in the way of him attempting to rebuild the barrier, but please, I beg you, we have to go now."

"Mary not being with you made me pause," he said explaining in his excruciating way. "And you need to understand, when you go to the wall I'm not going to be standing behind you."

"Why not?" Charlotte asked this time. I could see even her patience was thinning.

"Because you are from Hell, dear" he said, as if talking with a small child. "We cannot be associated with you. If you fail, I need to remain here to make sure the barrier isn't rebuilt. You will have the attention of everyone inside that city when you approach the walls. I have created a shield over this camp to make sure they haven't heard our words in case they are trying to listen, but rest assured, when you leave, Asmodeus will feel your presence so close to his home. You are lucky you found a way up that didn't alert him right away. That is one of the drawbacks of him gathering all his supporters in one place; he has lost his breadth of vision in all of Heaven. He is frightened of you, Michael, and it is causing him to make mistakes. Now, let's stop wasting time with more questions, shall we? Leave the camp from the very central avenue and head right for the wall. As soon as you exit, I'm quite certain Peter will appear. He won't be the only one either. I wish you luck."

49

NOT WANTING TO ASK anymore questions, we left Zoroaster's tent to head for the wall. It had only taken fifteen minutes or so to speak with him, but it had felt like a long, agonizing day. We still had time to complete our task, but there could be no more delay. I would have to bring Peter into the open in the most direct way I knew how.

The Vikings ushered our party through the camp. I turned to Phineus as we half ran, pushing against the ever-present pull of the filter that wanted us back in Hell.

"Do you see anything?" I asked the prophet. "Any danger, or anything I can use?"

"I see angels and a dragon," he said, puffed from the exertion of our hurried pace. "There will be fighting, but I cannot see the outcome. All goes white. I don't know what it means."

"Let's hope Asmodeus doesn't know either," I smiled grimly, "if he can already see the same future as you."

The others all drew abreast of me, so we were striding six across. Dante had said goodbye as we left the tent, wishing us luck. Part of me wished he had come with us, but I knew that he could not. As we moved with murderous purpose, we started to garner stares from the refugees of Purgatory. Some children gathered to watch, held back by concerned parents. It must have been a sight to behold: a sextet of warriors from Hell about to storm the gates of Heaven. Charlotte's hair was blowing backwards from the flow of the barrier. It exposed her ears, which had grown a deeper red than before. I knew mine would have looked the same, but darker and more deformed.

"Get ready for an attack right away," I said. "We have to assume they'll be on the offensive. We're at a disadvantage with them above us, but we still have a certain element of surprise. Asmodeus is used to knowing everything. It should tip him off balance if we catch him off guard."

Marlowe drew out his sword as we began to approach the final line of tents. Clytemnestra kept her hands close to her thighs, ready to draw her axes from their resting places. Germaine's fingers shimmered with fire elements, which he had drawn to be close for use. It was time.

The Vikings stopped short at the end of the camp, standing steady, not so much as looking at us as we left. I could feel a light touch of cold pass through me as soon as we left the last row of tents. It must have been the shield Zoroaster had put up. We were now in the open, nothing between us and the great wall, which rose before us like a living, diamond beast. Still there was no one on the parapets. A blast of light jetted into the sky from somewhere in the city. Someone knew we had arrived. Summoning a supernatural voice, I boomed upwards so I knew the whole capital would be able to hear.

"Peter!" I yelled. "Come out and let us into the city. We have come to claim our rightful places in the throne room of Heaven. Your new master has arrived."

50

A SCREECHING IN THE AIR heralded the arrival of the Archangels. Their brilliant white figures appeared in the sky as we craned our necks upward, looking to the top of the wall. They circled high, before spiraling downward and landing on the parapets above. Each left their wingspan fully open when they landed, displaying their dominance as they stared back down at us. The one in the middle spoke and pointed down to me.

"You do not belong here, Michael. Turn back to Hell before we destroy you utterly."

My companions shifted at the threat, each drawing themselves into readiness to receive some kind of barrage. I projected an air of confidence outwards, hoping it would steady them, and barked a laugh up at the angels.

"I will not stand here and argue with servants," I said, goading them. "Summon Asmodeus. Or is my father too scared to come and greet his son from atop a fortified wall? Is he cowering in his basilica with his gimp Peter and his whore Mary?"

The angel who had spoken looked back over his shoulder as if expecting an instant reaction from such open blasphemy. When one didn't come it started to speak again, but I shouted over the top of it, again making sure every citizen inside the walls would hear.

"Listen to me, those in Heaven: you who pride yourselves on humility; who hold charity most dear. There is a camp of people out here asking to be let inside. They are not evil souls. They want to see their families. They want peace. Yet you refuse them! What sort of kind hearts are you, languishing in the false love of a god who won't even let children inside your walls? Is that really divine justice? Are those the actions of someone who is all good?"

I paused to let my words sink in. Above, the Archangels stood ready,

198

their black eyes staring down at us. I started to walk from side to side, in front of my friends, pacing back and forth, always looking upwards as I continued.

"You need to question the false logic you have been fed your whole lives. What is the truth here, you supposed saints? Is your father and mine an all-knowing being? If he is, then why didn't he know I was coming and tell you beforehand? Don't you want to see your families down here? Do you not love them anymore?"

There was more movement on the walls and more faces came into view. Lesser angels began to appear, watching with softer eyes. People gathered to look down and see who was speaking to them - six human figures below, not the horde of hideous demons they might have expected. They wouldn't be able to make out our minor deformities from that distance, just as I could not make out their individual features without using my powers to assist me. I took their presence as a cue to press my point. They were listening. If I couldn't make Asmodeus come out with Peter, we would be swept away. As it was, I would need to use the elements soon to help hold us all in place. This was the final roll of the dice.

"I come here with an offer," I said. "Hell will not wage war against you, if you will accept us as citizens in your realm. We don't even want the city. We just want to be able to roam Heaven in peace. We can no longer bear false imprisonment and torture below. However, let those in the camp behind me, inside your walls. They deserve no less. They are not sinners. I make this offer now, once only. Ask yourselves, is it worth fighting over a paradise, which has no end? There is space for all, so why does Asmodeus block it off from some? Why does Peter stop good people from having the personal freedom of going where they please, even within your own city? I have seen the walls inside. Can everyone pass without complaint into the heart of the capital? What are they hiding from you?"

The glowing wall was full of people and angels now, but there was still no sign of my hated father, or Peter. The Archangels towered above the others, like giant guardians. They stood still, not attacking us. How could they, when I had just offered a treaty? I hoped Asmodeus was listening and felt as I had when he had done a similar thing in Hell. Why hadn't he acted yet? Phineus had seen a fight, so where had it come from? I had to bring them out now, or attack regardless. I looked back to my friends, who all held firm, looking up with the same determination in their eyes as I felt in my soul. I let my voice fall a notch, so it was still audible to all, but softer and friendlier.

"If you accept my offer of peace, then toss Peter out and I will leave you. If God were truly an all-powerful being, he would be standing up there with you right now. Instead he hides with his gatekeeper and stays silent. Perhaps he isn't even listening anymore. I know none of my prayers were ever answered before. Is it the same for you? Have you simply been giving out all this time, receiving nothing in return?"

A pulsing bright light sparked above and I heard a collective cry as the Archangels and people fell back to the side. On the wall, forming into a solid figure, was Asmodeus. He had come. To his right, an old man with a long beard stood, a hint of gold around his neck: Peter. Next to Peter was someone who made my blood boil with rage: Mary. Her red hair blazed against the light backdrop behind her. I barely even heard my father speak as my eyes locked on her face. I felt as if my body was being split apart from the hatred I felt.

"You are a lying demon from the bowels of Hell," I heard Asmodeus begin, addressing me, but really talking to his subjects around him. "You spew forth disgust and lies with every sentence you speak."

His words felt far away, like they didn't matter, they were just a distraction. Something else inside me was gnawing to get out. I focused intently on Mary as she smirked down at me. My insides churned and my sight snapped to see the elements.

"And like all demons inhabiting somewhere they don't belong, I will exorcise you from Heaven and cast you back to the depths of the dark pit," Asmodeus was saying.

Yes, exorcism, my instinct from somewhere deep down seemed to say. Memories welled up and flooded into my mind as I took in the construction of elements inside Mary's body. I began to understand. With understanding came cautious hope. There was a knot at the heart of her that I had seen once before. I had even seen it on Earth when she had ingested the first Jewel of Blood, but I had not recognized what it was then. I didn't want to.

Forgotten memories that I'd pushed down and sealed off leapt into my consciousness. I remembered The Perceptionist helping me to form a kind of secret intellect hidden deep within myself that would plan without the rest of me knowing. I saw myself almost in a trance, whispering in Mary's ear in The Crypt.

Betray me, like your brother betrayed Jesus. Help our cause. Hide the Jewels of Blood inside you and take them to Heaven. You will be my Trojan Horse.

Standing on the wall was our secret to destroying the barrier. Wrapped inside her was a knot of evil souls: The Pure Seven. They were keeping a package of bloody jewels safe, like they had once kept safe a set of keys. It was the same knot of sinful souls that had stopped Asmodeus from reading Mary's thoughts when they had been in Hell together. He had no idea what was next to him as he spoke. Mary wasn't smirking at me; she was smiling. She had placed herself perfectly. I realized all of this in the blink of an eye.

51

WITH A ROAR, I let my instinct take control, striking lightning into the depths of Heaven. Sending a crack of elements shuddering into the wall, I rattled the barrier the capital's citizens stood on. They cried out, holding on.

Mary took her chance. In the brief moment of confusion, she tackled Peter, sending them both tumbling down towards us. I felt a rush of elements come from behind me, as Germaine reacted. He pushed liquid fire toward Asmodeus, who was already looking to attack. The blast was enough to make Asmodeus roll to the side, while his Archangels took flight.

As Mary and Peter fell, I sent a probing hand of spirit deep inside Mary's body. Feeling the chord I was looking for, I yanked it free, spilling the souls of The Pure Seven out from within her and into the open sky. They shot upwards, wailing with hideous glee towards their twin opposites, who flew downward, trying to grasp at Peter. The collision sent the seven Archangels smashing backwards into the wall. The Pure Seven disappeared inside them, possessing the white angelic bodies with their corrupting natures. The Archangels' wings instantly turned grey as they wrestled the sin that squeezed inside them.

Peter and Mary thudded into the ground, the Jewels of Blood raining onto them as well. As one, my five friends ran forward to retrieve what was now ours. I projected my energies up, sending waves of hatred and pestilence into the sky. I thudded earth and air into the parapets above, attacking the lesser angels and people who still stood gaping like sheep, watching the carnage. I aimed a thick chord of special odium toward Asmodeus. He had no choice but to fall back with his subjects to avoid it, down behind the walls that protected them. His warrior Archangels flapped helplessly in the air between the top of the wall and the ground.

They were being attacked from within, reduced to nothing but frenzied beasts, scratching and beating at their own skin, trying to get the perfect demons out of their own perfect bodies.

I darted ahead to meet my friends, who were gathering up the red jewels from the ground. Germaine, of all people, had resisted and leapt straight at Peter, tearing the keys we needed from around his neck. Marlowe, right behind Germaine, decapitated the saint and kicked his head away so he couldn't oppose us further.

Mary's body was inert on the ground. Using the elements instead of a proper exorcism to pull out The Pure Seven's souls, had almost ripped her in two. I could see her healing quickly, however. She must've still had the power of The Furies inside her to be recovering at all. Still, she wouldn't be any immediate help in this fight.

"Swallow the jewels," I yelled to the others. "Asmodeus will be on us soon. We have to fall back."

Charlotte, who was closest to me, shoved the ruby-like stone in her hand straight into her mouth. As she did, Phineus let out a cry next to me. The sound brought my attention to the prophet.

"No," he said urgently, rushing to Germaine, but still looking at me. "They will be wasted on the others. You must feed the rest to Germaine. I have seen the effects."

I hesitated just a moment, but watched as he pressed the jewel he held directly into Germaine's mouth. The alchemist swallowed in surprise. I could see the injection of power instantly snap into his eyes. Clytemnestra followed the action, having two jewels with her. She offered them up and Germaine gobbled them in a fever. Marlowe held his firm, not willing to do the same. I was about to order him to hand it over, when a guttural scream of hatred filled the air.

Asmodeus was back on the wall. Flapping above him - the red dragon, Moloch.

52

THE SKY TURNED DARK BEHIND ASMODEUS as he stood on the wall, his gigantic pet circling above. It was as if Asmodeus sucked all the illumination from around him into his body. He sparked with a charge of electric energy as the force inside him grew. Raising his hands in the air, he drew the struggling Archangels upwards at his command, until they hovered in front of him.

"Be gone from what isn't yours to possess, demons!" he snarled, shooting a burst of light into the angels before him.

The impact jerked the souls of The Pure Seven out of the vessels they clung to. Their colorful forms hung for just a moment, grasping to get back at their enemies. In a sudden rush, the ghouls were ripped away in the wind of the filter that was now starting to howl in my ears. Without ethereal bodies to anchor themselves to, it was impossible for them to resist the pull for long. Their spirits sailed away in a streak of light, over the camp behind us and back towards Hell.

The Archangels regrouped quickly around Asmodeus, no longer hampered by the sinful souls that had been burrowing into them. Our advantage was gone, but we still had what we needed.

"Go!" I yelled to Germaine, who had the golden keys gripped in his fist.

Phineus and Marlowe held his arms, using him for support against the drag of the filter. Germaine didn't react to my command. He just looked up at me through a haze of madness. I could see the blood surging around his body. Had we done the wrong thing?

Clytemnestra took one of her axes and dug it into the ground for support, while looking up to the wall. She used her spare arm to reach out to Germaine, working to haul him backwards. He wouldn't budge. The other two saw what she was trying to do and started to pull as well. With the wind at their backs, they would be able to make a fast retreat back through the opening into Purgatory. Still, Germaine stood, unmovable. Charlotte was next to me, the only one who had taken the blood. She didn't know how to use the elements properly, but at least she had the extra strength that would help her resist the filter. I wanted to tell her to take the others back to the cloud-like rocks which marked the central power source, but I didn't have time. Our enemies were upon us. In a rush, Asmodeus and his followers attacked.

Diving off the wall, with his warriors at his side, my father speared down. Moloch tore in behind them. Asmodeus shot towards Germaine, propelling himself forward. In an act of desperation, I launched up to meet him, using every ounce of speed I had to hit them head on. As I flew upward, I pushed a charge of emotion to the outside of my skin. I was a human missile that would detonate on impact. Striking Asmodeus from the side, I crashed into his torso. He only saw me at the last moment, so intent was his focus on Germaine and the keys. He reached out and wrapped me in his arms, trying to absorb the impact. The emotion I had laced into my body struck like shards of shrapnel, sizzling into the Archangels and Moloch who were also mid-dive around us. They screamed as it hit them, twisting away from the blast. The brunt of the blow thundered into Asmodeus, but he held me tight. We fell sideways, grappling with each other, each trying to gain the upper hand even as we plummeted to the ground. With a crunch we struck the dirt, me on top. I used the momentum to bury him downward, striking in a flurry of fists and fire. I struck again and again, pummeling attack after attack beneath me. I lashed out with a speed I had never known, hammering relentless atoms of death into him. I was beating a god. He was limp beneath me, but I kept on, trying to tear at flesh that was impossibly strong against my attack. Only a few flecks of blood sprung from the wounded deity beneath me. Without pause I pulled him upward, lifting him over my head. His eyes snapped open at the movement and he started to struggle, but my instinct had a hold of my actions. Heaving with all my strength, I sent Asmodeus back into the air, slicing an atomic explosion of light after him. The effort sent him sailing over the wall, back into the city. It would buy us the extra moments we needed.

I looked up to see what was happening to the others. My hopes that they were getting away were dashed. The Archangels had them surrounded. Marlowe, Clytemnestra and Phineus all clung to Germaine, who seemed rooted in the ground, fighting a battle within himself. One of the angels advanced and Marlowe struck out with his sword, slicing through its wing. It howled in pain, falling back. Another struck out, clipping Phineus, who lost his grip on Germaine from the blow. It was as if the prophet's world had been turned sideways, while the rest of us were upright. He tumbled along the ground and away, sucked back down toward the abyss we had come from. I could feel the pull grow even stronger, but dug in my grip of the elements. I watched as Mary's limp body also started to skip along the ground, crashing into an Archangel as it went, before it lifted into the air, taken down to the abyss. Asmodeus' power to keep her in Heaven had been shattered.

I had to get Germaine loose, but first I searched frantically for Charlotte. She had moved away from the group; Moloch was stalking around her, snarling smoke and spittle. She held firm against the filter, but the dragon would consume her if I didn't do something. Leaping to my friends' aid, I whipped a cyclone of heated air against the wings of their attackers. The hurricane sent the Archangels scuttling backwards, right against the diamond wall of the city. They were pressed hard against the solid bricks, but Moloch roared, resisting the wind. I cut the intensity of the storm off, in case I harmed the others. Losing its interest in Charlotte, the dragon turned now to me. Digging clawed talons into the ground, Moloch started forward. Before I could do anything more, however, the terrible lizard burst apart in a shower of light and blood. I shielded my eyes as the glow increased in intensity and then abruptly fell. I ran forward, expecting Germaine to be at the centre of the attack, but as the shimmer of power settled I could see Charlotte staring at her hands in wonder. She looked up at me with her mouth open. I felt the same astonishment. Lotte had somehow used the elements to destroy the beast as if it was nothing.

Unanswered questions poured into me as I made it to my friends. There was no time to stop and ask. The Archangels paused in shock, but we had zero time to spare. The pull of the filter was too great against us and Asmodeus could come back at any moment. Clytemnestra lost her grip and was ripped away. There was nothing I could do. I had to get to Germaine. Marlowe clung to the alchemist, straining when I got there. Charlotte also moved forward and anchored herself on Germaine as well. The Archangels, who weren't affected by the filter like us, started to regroup.

"Germaine!" I yelled in his ear. His eyes flickered with some recognition. His body poured with sweat. "Germaine, you have to let go. We need the keys."

The precious items were gripped tightly in his right hand. Only the chain that had held them on Saint Peter's neck could be seen coming out of his fist. He turned his head to face me and said in a rasp of multiple voices.

"I need another jewel. I need more power, so I can make your void. You will need it to kill Asmodeus."

I looked to Marlowe, who still held his stone. The African held fear in his eyes at the prospect as well. He shook his head, as if he would rather let go of his grip on Germaine than on the Jewel of Blood. Seeing my indecision, Germaine reached out and touched me, sending visions and thoughts spiking into my head. The explosion of images explained to me instantly what words would take hours to do. Germaine understood the prophecy Phineus had shown me even more clearly than I. If I truly wanted to stop Asmodeus, I would first have to use anti-matter to destroy his body. For that I needed a void, one where I could use my darkest weapon without fear of unhinging the rest of Creation. Germaine could make that void for me, but he would need every ounce of power we could give him to do it. He would harness the destruction of the barrier of Hell to create something new in its place. It would keep the realms separate, but allow people to pass through. It would also destroy him at the same time. It was suicide. His single, clear voice finally entered my mind.

I could do anything with the power I hold inside me, he said, *but I choose to do the right thing. Maybe that makes me truly crazy. Please, let me do this. It is my destiny.*

"Marlowe," I croaked, emerging from my mind, knowing only a split second had gone by. "Give it to him. Now!"

Still clinging to Germaine, Marlowe reached up on my command and did what I asked. He shoved the jewel into Germaine's mouth. A reddish purple rush of light streaked right over Germaine's body as the blood passed his lips.

"Now run!" he whispered with absolute clarity in his eyes. "I will hold them off, before I do what I must. Trust me."

I chose to believe him.

53

LOOKING AT GERMAINE ONE FINAL TIME, I let go. The raging vacuum of the filter pulled me away. Marlowe and Charlotte followed. We tore backwards, now in the grip of the force of God. Keeping my wits, I summoned the elements at my call to pull my friends close, keeping us together.

I looked back, as Germaine held his arms to the sky. Thunder peeled a cacophony of doom. The air crackled with a hideous white heat. He became a power of his own, sucking every particle around him into his being. Even our own momentum slowed, as the pull of the filter slackened back toward his gravity. High above, on the wall, the dark form of Asmodeus reappeared once more, crouching low and looking down. I heard his desperate cry as he called his Archangels to advance. He knew if Germaine escaped with the keys, Heaven as he knew it would be lost. The Archangels started forward, but in a mighty stroke, like bringing a hammer down on an anvil, Germaine swept his fists to the ground. A splintering noise cracked the air as he struck. In a series of staccato explosions, dirt sprayed upwards, erupting into the sky in a widening geyser of blue lava, which raced towards the city walls. The devastation mowed right through one of the angels. The others were skittled away like autumn leaves in the wind. The inferno hit the city wall, striking with ruinous impact. The gilded structure disintegrated like a magnesium strip thrown into flame. What we had thought was an impenetrable gate was gone in a flash of light. The backlash of energy sweltered back out towards us, rippling in an atomic gale. I kept my eyes forward, wanting to witness as much as I could. In the anarchy that had been created I saw Asmodeus falling to the ground and Germaine being consumed by a cloud of ash and dust. Then the wave hit us.

I clung desperately to Marlowe and Charlotte as we succumbed to the tumult of elements thrusting us down. We span away, back towards Hell. Underneath us, I saw the tents of Zoroaster's followers ripping in the blast, peeling away or being flattened completely. I tried to control our fall, but with the pull of the filter adding to the flight it was all I could do to keep us bundled as one. The forest of palms flashed below us in a sea of green; the lawn with the statues of sapphire; down through the chasm of Purgatory. Like a barrel being flung over Niagara Falls, we hurtled through into a land of grey: spinning, helpless. I could hear Charlotte yelling in fright. I felt her body next to mine, but couldn't see properly in the blur. Marlowe pressed on my other side. I tried again to steady us enough to ride the storm with some semblance of control. Slowing our spiraling movement, I managed to stop our tumble so I could see again. Beneath us, the cloud-like rocks I knew Germaine would need to get back to, whipped by. The boulder-strewn meadow we had marched through streaked away. I turned toward the direction we were headed in and watched as the end of Purgatory appeared up ahead. Our impetus was too great; the filter pulled us in and there was nothing I could do. I whirled my body back again to watch for another sign of movement.

Had Germaine gotten away from Asmodeus? Did he have the power to resist this pull long enough to break through the cloud rocks and plunge the keys into the filter? Could he carry out his plan to create a void? I cursed myself for my blind trust. I should have kept more control. I should never have left something this important in the hands of someone else, no matter how powerful.

The thought was cut off as my mind started to fade. We must have been reentering Hell. Every other time I had been sucked between worlds against my will, I had lost consciousness. This time I fought it. I clenched my teeth and used my resolve to keep my brain alert. A flash of black clouded my eyes, but I blinked to keep them open.

The world fell silent. My touch numbed. Any idea of smell left my body. The only sense I had left was sight. My eyes beheld the elements all over, coming together in regret and guilt. Memories of goodness spun by, only to be lost amongst greed and envy. I somehow registered that I was inside the guilt storm of Hell. It cut through my body, making me one with the tempest. In an odd calm I looked for Marlowe and Charlotte, but they weren't there – at least not in a form I could see. The chaos had meaning to me now. There was method in this madness. It was the construction of a brilliant mind; brilliant, yet evil. Colors of red oceans shimmered below. We tore towards a destination we had been to many times. Black desert appeared. The storm swirled and spat its bile into all it touched. Then, it faltered. A wheel in the perfect machine slipped. The cogs started to unravel. A howl of wind began in a whisper, then the volume turned to full, mid-gasp. It screamed suffering in my ears. As the storm started to fall apart, my body pulled back together. Blonde hair began to flutter next to mine. An African man with white teeth and a beard, burst into life right before my eyes. In a visceral wrenching of sensation, the vivid nightmare of reality came back to life. Before I knew what was truly happening, my body crashed down, striking the hot sand. The consciousness I had clung to so hard wavered again for just a moment, before a glorious noise pierced my ears. It made me look up. The groaning sounds of twisting metal met the cracking of thick ice. I had heard it once before, when Zoroaster and I had blocked the filter of Purgatory. I let out a cry of elation, hoping beyond hope that a cataclysm had started that couldn't be stopped. I searched around to share my happiness and saw the body of Charlotte face down in the sand twenty feet away. The Guilt Storm must have released us as it gave way over the desert. The jam in the filter had caused the tempest to die before it could reach the city. Normally it would have flung us back to our allotted destination of rest, but we had been let go as it dispersed prematurely. I rushed to Lotte's side and rolled her onto her back. She sucked in the scorching air of Hell and her eyes opened wide. Bending down, I smiled at her.

"Look up," I said to her in excitement. "It's happening!"

While my love gained her bearings, I scanned around for Marlowe. The African was already on his feet, his eyes glued to the clouds above. I stared up again and knew why he could not look away. The lightning that normally forked obstinately above had stopped. I braced myself in case pieces of the filter began to fall as they had in Purgatory. For a long moment nothing happened. Then a breeze began to flutter. The clouds above started to shift. From the horizon inward, they pulled up, as if an invisible hand had grabbed the middle of a sheet and was lifting it to reveal us beneath. The folds of black mist crinkled together and zapped through into a throbbing circle of purple energy. Fine veins of the same color spread out to cover the pure blackness that had replaced the clouds. All the way to the edges of sight, a color like Germaine's eyes engulfed that static filter of Hell. I was frozen in awe, seeing a cosmic event unfold. The sky itself began to twist and spin. It went from purple, to red, to yellow, to green, to blue and then finally to white. Fine stars of black appeared, twinkling oblivion on a blanket of life. I felt the whole realm of Hell hold its breath. This was the Armageddon we had all wished for. Meteors answered our prayers. The white started to bleed down in a rain of rubble and light. A chunk of the debris slammed down over the dune from where we stood, sending a ripple of black sand our way. I pushed a shield of thick

DEICIDE

air around Charlotte and me, enveloping Marlowe as well. Safe in our bubble, we watched. I hugged Charlotte, happy in the destruction. Drumming a beat of hail, the meteors dropped. Their trail of descent started to pull inward, focusing on one spot, as a black hole formed in the sky. A vortex of nothingness had opened up on Hell. Purgatory spewed outward. With one last blast, a new atmosphere cracked into life. The impact sent us sprawling back onto the ground, despite the shield I had built.

I rolled to my feet, leaning back down to pull Charlotte up with me. Any pain that I should have felt was lost in gratitude. The faith I had put in a now vanished friend had paid off, despite my trepidation. The iridescent purple I had come to associate with a beggar alchemist filled the sky. Germaine had done it. He had sacrificed himself for us. It was a bittersweet victory. The world had lost an incomparable mind, but in return it had gained freedom. I hugged Charlotte close to me and wept.

The barrier between Heaven and Hell was no more.

54

MARLOWE INTERRUPTED MY EMBRACE with Charlotte with a light tap on the shoulder. I looked to him with glassy eyes. A wide smile hung on his face for a moment, acknowledging our victory, but it soon pursed into a serious look.

"We have not finished," my African friend said in a gruff voice. "You do know that."

Charlotte caught my eye and nodded as well. She stepped back, out of my arms, but kept her hand on my chest.

"Now that the barrier has fallen, the souls of Hell will be restless to invade," she said. "We should get back to the city to make sure they don't do anything too hasty."

The mention of the armies made me stare back towards the city. It was nothing but a glow in the distance. My friends were right. Smithy and Marax could only hold the demons' eagerness for so long. At the same time, we should make the most of the confusion we had caused up in Heaven. There was no better time to strike than now. However, I needed to regroup in my own mind. So much had just happened. The deception I had unknowingly planned with Mary; Germaine's selfless act of creating a new void; seeing that to destroy Asmodeus I would have to dismantle his body first with anti-matter. I had felt the strength of my father's body firsthand up there. Any other being would have crumbled into dust at my attacks, yet he had withstood and come back quickly. I feared now that even Zoroaster's potion of sleep wouldn't be enough to subdue him in his present form. We'd had surprise on our side last time. Asmodeus had been rattled, his focus torn. I doubted he would make the same mistake again. Nor would we be able to manufacture such a perfect series of events to fall our way. Without the Trojan deception of Mary and powers of Germaine, I struggled to think how I could defeat Asmodeus in hand-to-hand combat, should he be ready for it. There would be a way. There must be. We had overcome so much already.

"Michael," Charlotte said, bringing my attention back to the present world. "We should go back. We can debrief with everyone once we return to the city."

She knew me so well. Lotte only needed to look at me to know what was ticking behind my eyes.

"If everyone is there," Marlowe said. "Phineus, Mary and Clytemnestra were all ripped away in the storm before us. They could be anywhere out here."

"And The Pure Seven," I reminded him. "Mary wasn't the traitor we thought she was. She saved us."

I looked at Charlotte as I said it, but she turned her head away. Some things weren't accepted so readily. So much had happened. It would be better to let explanations wait until we had been able to reunite with the rest of our companions, if they had made it back safely. I peered into the sky again, seeing the stunning new vista above. A fine atmosphere of Germaine's doing was all that separated his void and us. Above that, Heaven waited for the taking. We had to get moving.

I started to summon elements of air around us, when Charlotte touched me lightly again.

"May I try?" she said softly, coming back to my side. She had a strong look of certainty on her face, as though she could do anything if she put her mind to it.

This was yet another surprise I had almost forgotten: Charlotte had used the elements to destroy Moloch.

"How...?" I began to ask.

"I know what you know, remember?" she smiled, tapping my temple with her finger. "I have seen what you've seen. I have been trained by The Perceptionist just like you have. I have your knowledge inside me. I simply never had the power to use that knowledge before."

I looked at her eyes closely again and saw behind them the strength of the Jewels of Blood infused with her spirit. She was indeed now a force to be reckoned with: perhaps still not as physically strong as I but certainly smarter. She had my knowledge and hers combined. Even without my memories, she had always been more intelligent than me. In many ways Lotte was now far superior to most beings in the universe. The realization made me want to kiss and hug her tight. I stood back, inviting her with a sweep of my arm to weave her newfound magic.

With a wriggle of each of her fingers, elements sparked around Lotte. They came together to form thicker and thicker strands of air. Marlowe came close to us, ensuring it would be easier to hold us in a tight formation. Blue and greens shimmered at our feet and we began to take off. It was slow at first, but as Charlotte gained confidence our speed increased. I thought I would have to give her some extra pointers, but I didn't. Lotte simply needed to become used to doing physically what she already knew how to execute mentally. She took us high up so we overlooked the rolling sands of the desert. I was able to make out Mount Belial in the far distance, which marked the beginning of the city from this approach. Over to the left, the Chinvar Bridge arched with its intense light into the sky, still holding its integrity to meet the void. Not far across from the bridge, the mouth of the black hole Germaine had created continued to rain rocks and other material down into the desert below. Seeing a strange shape fall from the phenomenon, I pointed over.

"Can you take us closer?" I asked Lotte.

She veered towards it immediately, whipping further winds at our feet to accelerate. I peered up into the black hole and another of the shapes fell through. Then another. I couldn't yet see exactly what they were, but the things were moving, not only down but also within themselves, as if they were wriggling. We finally came close enough to make out more detail and I realized with shock why the objects were acting that way: they were human bodies.

55

FEAR LEAPT INTO MY THROAT. This might already be an attack. I started to warn Charlotte but, emboldened by her newfound powers, she didn't slow our approach. Instead she sped up, sweeping lower to the ground to see the carnage. A steady deluge of people poured into Hell, plummeting into the desert sand. Other debris came with them, including white and grey silk tents. There was no order to their descent; they were simply scattered and broken, flailing in the air. This was no attack. It was Zoroaster's followers being cast down from Heaven. I gazed up, to see if I could make out anything behind the black hole, but there was nothing beyond the hundreds of bodies twisting downward in freefall.

We landed and the three of us kept going at a run. Up close, seeing the faces torn and bloody, it was clear they had been sent down with brutal force. Some of the people were still conscious. Their ethereal bodies healed. Others were out cold. They were heaped in a pyramid, looking like a pile of living corpses from a war zone. Marlowe reached the base of the pile first, kneeling down next to a child. He picked up the little girl up in his arms and carried her backwards, away from the still falling wreckage from above. The single action made me understand we had to help restore some kind of order for these people as quickly as possible. As it was now, they were thrown together in a mash of confusion and agony.

"Charlotte," I yelled, who was also dragging a young boy clear of the wreckage. "I'll catch the ones still coming down. You pull everyone else away from each other gently. Use elements of air to separate and water to cool. They'll be feeling the heat as much as any of their other wounds!"

She nodded her understanding, laying the boy back down. She kissed his forehead tenderly before standing again, focusing her talents forward. I left her to work, spreading a spirit blanket of my own upwards. Stretching it out wide, I created a net to break the fall of those continuing to come down. At first I kept the invisible weave flat, letting the bodies sink down softly. Then I had to create a slight dome to it, so the people would roll gently away from the centre, and slide to the ground clear of the others. Marlowe was busy also, running to those hurt worst, checking them and offering a kind word. No matter what he said it would be small consolation, but at least they knew they were in safe hands. Charlotte did her best to tease people away from the crush, giving them room to breathe. After taking some weight off the top, she then lifted the whole pile as one, spreading the people apart and lowering them down. I could see the effort was taxing for her, but she didn't need my assistance.

A flash of color made me turn my head to the right as seven flying objects caught my attention. Again I feared the worst, but very quickly realized they weren't the Archangels I feared. It was The Pure Seven: they flew forward at high speed, coming to our aid. They must have been close by and seen the skies open up as we had. The red and blue angel-demons already had a person in each of their arms, but the others flew forward to catch the morbid precipitation from the sky. We now made progress. People lay moaning all about us, writhing in pain. As much as the noise sounded like suffering, it heartened me. They would live. The pain they felt now was temporary. I held the net firm, picking up the overflow of those that The Pure Seven were unable to grab. The flood was mercifully slowing. Finally, the last of the bodies plunged into Hell and the rain from above resumed to a regular flow of single elements.

Easing away the weave I held, I searched around to assess the damage. It was like the aftermath of a medieval battlefield. Everywhere I looked, people lay bloodied and battered in the black sand. A few had found the strength to sit or even stand, but they were all shaken from the ordeal. The Pure Seven landed also, gathering around a single spot. It looked like Mary and Phineus were with them too. They were the two people I had seen red Wrath and blue Lust carrying when I first spotted them. I ran over to where they were, shouting for Charlotte and Marlowe to do the same. My friends came to my side, looking overwhelmed by the scale of what lay around us. Tears streaked Charlotte's face. She was pale from the effort it had taken to separate the bodies. Marlowe kept his calm demeanor on the outside, but his labored breathing gave his true feelings of horror away. We reached the others, who only had eyes for one figure on the ground. The Pure Seven stood in a semicircle, looking down. Phineus was with them. Mary knelt on the ground. It was Zoroaster, or what was left of him. One of his legs had been torn away from the hip, the other severed at the knee. One arm was just a stump of bleeding flesh. A tear in his neck looked like something had taken a bite from him. The most ghastly thing of all was that his eyes were open and he was smiling.

"He got the better of us," Zoroaster said, with a muck-stained mouth, as I knelt over him, "but I took a part of him as well."

An eye rolled out of his palm. The strength Zoroaster must have gathered to do such a thing was staggering. I had barely been able to make Asmodeus bleed, yet here was a whole eye. Phineus came forward, scooping down to pick it up. He held it in his fingers, as though it was evil to touch.

"That devil did this to me once," he said, "I hope he feels every shred of pain I had."

The prophet squeezed it in his fist, as if trying to make it pop. The eye held its shape, not budging under the pressure being exerted on it. I stood up, taking the wretched thing. The vile jelly was warm against my skin. Looking deep into its dilated pupil, I knew with a tingling feeling of hatred that it was watching us right now. Taking the thing in my hands, I held it outwards, showing my father through his decapitated sight all the pain he had caused here. I knew he would feel no sorrow for this, yet I showed him anyway. Finally, I brought it to face me, drawing my finger across my throat, to show that he would pay for his wrongdoing. Closing my fingers over it, I charged every ounce of will I had inside me into my fist. I poured disease into the eye, infecting it with malice. The stew of elements did nothing to damage the structure of the body part, but it was now so hopelessly corrupted I hoped it would never function again. Using my talents to assist, I then threw it away, driving it through the air and out of sight. I pushed enough molecules after it to make sure it carried the missile away to the edges of the desert, where it would roll into the lakes of fire. Asmodeus would feel that burning, no matter where he was in the universe. I prayed it stung him every moment of every day from here forward.

Remembering Zoroaster, I looked down again. His state was wretched but not without hope.

"Charlotte? Mary?" I asked the two women close by me to help. "You both have the power of blood. Lay your hands on him and project as much love outward as you can."

"Thank you," Zoroaster mumbled, his eyes clouding in and out of consciousness.

While The Pure Seven, Marlowe and Phineus looked on, the three of us gathered our strength and pushed in towards our friend. Atoms sang in my ears, hearing my call as they sprang forward, slowly building Zoroaster's body again. A leg began to form out of his hip. It wasn't the same as before, looking like a prosthetic limb. The corruption that

217

Asmodeus had used to do this must have been stopping it fuse properly together, but at least it was something. We pressed on, reforming the wreckage of his body in the best way we could, attaching a reconstructed arm and sealing the wound in his neck. Zoroaster gasped and flickered back awake. He reached out and caught my hand.

"That is enough," he said, groaning. Again, a smile flickered to his lips. "Go and tend to the rest of the people. We're going to have to pull them together. We must get back to the city, to your Legions of Hell. The occasion for sitting on the fence is over. It's high time we brought war to our maker."

THE LIEUTENANTS OF THE NINE LEGIONS of Hell all stood before me, ready to report. We were gathered in the top level of Satan's Tower.

Our party had made it back in one piece after a few days. At first, I had stayed with Charlotte, Zoroaster and Mary to heal the wounded of Purgatory while The Pure Seven, Phineus and Marlowe went ahead to the city to alert the others of what had happened. By the time we came to the fringes of the desert, Marax had sent out a small force to escort us back into the metropolis. The only person who remained missing was Clytemnestra.

During our time helping the people of Purgatory I had been able to get an explanation out of Mary about how she had been able to plant herself in Asmodeus' circle. At my secret encouragement, she had summoned The Pure Seven to The Crypt before our departure to Earth and invited them to reenter her body. They formed the Zoroastrian knot inside her as they had done once before. Because they knew the process, the evil angels were able to do so with only minor difficultly, wrapping their spirits around the Jewels of Blood. Mary had kept one of the jewels for herself in case she needed to use it on Earth. The middle of the story was plain enough, having lived it painfully myself. Her betrayal had been so real that we had all believed it. It had been required. Even now, Lotte kept her distance from Mary, not having fully regained trust in her.

While in Heaven, Asmodeus had kept Mary close, under the pretense that they were now allies. He was delighted to hear that she had stabbed Lotte in the eye, right in front of me. He had asked her to retell the story over and over. Asmodeus had kept his part of the bargain, keeping Judas safe in his basilica, but unable to rouse him from sleep, as I had suspected. My father kept Mary in sight at all times, always watching her. He had been furious when I arrived and he accused her of deception, but was unable to read her mind to prove anything. He had stayed with her and

Peter, away from the walls but, because of my constant goading, had no choice but to meet me or lose face. His pride had been his downfall. Asmodeus brought Mary and Peter to the wall with him, not willing to leave them alone together in case she tried something. That paranoia had cost him dearly. My plan had worked exactly as I had subconsciously hoped. If Mary hadn't been in the right place, we would have had no chance scaling the wall alone. When I released The Pure Seven they had been able to take out the Archangels in the confusion and give us the element of surprise we had so badly needed. Once they had been banished, however, they were easily ripped away in the filter. Having only light souls, The Pure Seven had been spirited all the way back to the city, where they were reunited with their bodies. Mary had taken them out of The Crypt and hidden them in a dungeon room, which she had rented under the guise of a "rich socialite". It was the dungeon we hadn't been able to hire when we had gone to search for clues. Everything made sense in hindsight. The unraveling of the story made it feel as though it had been fate all along.

When Phineus had been deposited back in Hell after their descent, he had been able to find Mary with his power of foresight. He had seen that The Pure Seven would come for her and knew it was his best chance for a fast return. However, there had still been no word of where Clytemnestra had fallen. She could be on the other boundaries of Hell for all we knew. It didn't sit well with me to leave her behind, but sending out a search party to trawl the depths of Hell was out of the question for the moment. We needed our strength centralized, ready to rise up and take Heaven. Someone could come back and look for her later, if she didn't get back of her own accord. I had every faith she would walk in any moment. She was the toughest person I'd ever met.

We now stood in the tower, The Pure Seven at the backs of their allotted Lieutenants. Charlotte was next to me. Phineus, Zoroaster, Mack, Smithy, Marlowe and Mary were seated to the side. My pilot friend had rejoiced when he found out Mary had not been a traitor. He said he knew it in his bones all along, but the true relief in his eyes said otherwise. I briefly informed them all of where things stood at this moment, not pausing to give them details on how or why, but keeping it simple: the barriers had been brought down. Asmodeus had cast the refugees of Purgatory out. We now had their allegiance as well as Zoroaster's. I was adding them to the Legion of White, placing Zoroaster in total command of the unit. Smithy had been caretaking the position while I was away, but now he had to concentrate on his new role: Captain of the Air Force. Every pilot, or demon who had grown wings and had the ability to fly, was now under his command, no matter what sin they came from. The only exception was The Pure Seven. I needed them to hold their legions as one. It was as though they were one mind; in battle that kind of synergy would be invaluable.

"The Legion of Pride is ready," Lieutenant Genghis Kahn said, stepping forward from the rest, their self-appointed leader.

He had retained his Asian features in the afterlife, looking almost human if not for the scars which ravaged his face. One side of his mouth had a tear that stretched right up his jaw, revealing barbed teeth on the interior. Blood oozed down that side of his neck, making him look fearsome. The other lieutenants stood behind him with eyes forward. Gluttony was represented by a demon called Savela, his head and belly swollen and orange; his feet black webs, long and flipper-like. Bewley fronted Lust. He was completely naked. Matted hair flowed like dreadlocks from his pubic regions. He carried himself with an air of confidence and ogled the females in the room with open desire. To the left of them was Kabatoff, an envy demon, rakish and tall. His green cats' eyes flitted to the others with hostility and suspicion. On the far right, the other three legions' commanders hung at attention. All were female. Rangda, the Wrath demon, had hair braided in stripes of red, black and white. Her eyes extended out of her head in boiling rage. Tusks jutted from her mouth: two hooking up, two down. Belphegor of Sloth watched indifferently. She was surprisingly young and model-beautiful, her only deformity the rotting skin which covered her shapely torso. Avarice was represented by Kai Ah Jecks. She was dressed in the rags of an old business suit, like some kind of failed real estate agent who pined for better times. Still, the ferocity of her yellow gaze held a cunning that I knew would help our planning. Marax was at their far left, watching to make sure they didn't embarrass him. This was his moment.

"Our warriors are superior on foot," Kahn continued. "I expect us to be the first wave through to lead the charge on Heaven. If, that's want the Lord wishes," he added, almost as an afterthought.

"You desire is granted, Kahn," I said to him. "I will lift your legion and two others through the void and into Heaven to begin the assault. Smithy's air force will come in behind us. He'll be able to match the angels in flight."

Smithy nodded his approval as I met his eye. He stood to rigid attention, his military training coming to the surface of his usually genial exterior.

"Marax, who else do you suggest for the initial attack?" I asked, turning back to the one who had formed this army into what it was.

The muscle-bound demon also took a step forward. His square jaw was clenched tightly, the sinews in his face flexed, even when he spoke.

"Wrath and Lust are the most aggressive," he said. "But my Legion of

Black is also strong and more dynamic in their abilities."

Kahn grunted softly at the declaration, but I silenced him with a dark look.

"I think perhaps four units would be better to begin with," Marax went on. "That would still leave Envy, Gluttony and Sloth as backup. The Legion of White can stay with Avarice to guard the city. We don't want to be caught without a base to regroup to if need be. This is still our home after all. We are at our strongest here."

It was clear he had thought this through even more than me, so I accepted his idea. We wanted to hold power over all the realms. Many demons would still want to remain settled down here, especially now that The Guilt had been stopped. With the barrier gone, that horrid device had been lifted from everyone's mind and Hell seemed more inhabitable now, at least for those who had lived through the darker age.

The end goal for me now was to take down Asmodeus. With his armies engaged in battle I would stand a better chance of getting to him; with his power eliminated, the will of Heaven would fall and we could restore everlasting peace for all. It would be a bloody fight to make that a reality.

"Mack," I asked the cabdriver, who leapt out of his seat at being addressed. "What about supply lines? We'll need artillery and ammunition to refuel the frontline troops. We can't fight with only our bare hands."

"There is no shortage of weaponry in Hell," Mack grinned. "The lords of war have been kind in their support: guns, rocket launchers, grenades, tanks. We have it all, laced with some hellish surprises for the enemy. What the legions can't carry themselves, I can truck out to a take-off point. We've managed to cut roads through the jungle to the beginning of the desert already. You'll need someone to lift them up, though. We don't have an aircraft big enough to raise that kind of firepower."

"I can do it," Lotte said next to me.

The demon lieutenants looked at her with raised eyebrows. Not everyone had seen what she was capable of. I hesitated for a moment, reluctant to commit her to the forefront of the battle. It wasn't that I didn't think she was up to the task; the vision of me destroying her was still lurking in the back of my mind.

"I can do it," she repeated fiercely.

"I will come back to help you after I have seen the first wave strike the city," I said, thinking of a compromise. "You will need help to bring the support legions up as well. Will you hold them steady in the desert until my return?"

A single nod of her head showed she would, but she wasn't happy about it. Looking again at The Pure Seven, I knew we would be able to coordinate this with deadly precision. Phineus silently stood and walked over to the windows to stare out to Hell. I watched him for a moment, but continued addressing the others, keen to mobilize our efforts quickly.

"Zoroaster. Are you willing to hold the city for us? I want you personally on Mount Belial, so you can see both our metropolis and the desert."

"I will do whatever is needed," he said. Normally jumping from subject to subject, Zoroaster had been single-minded since he had been cast down from above, in keeping his flock safe and supporting our cause in any way asked.

"Bewley, Rangda," I said to the lieutenants of Lust and Wrath. "Are you prepared to join the front line and storm Heaven with us?"

"We will gut those pious fools," Rangda spat between her tusks.

"And sodomize their dead bodies," Bewley laughed horridly.

The others gave a shout of support. The stage was set for us to take on Asmodeus and his angels above.

"Stop," Phineus said, still looking out the window.

Every eye in the room turned to the prophet, who gathered his robes around him as if a chill had just passed through his body.

"Your planning is for nothing. They will be here in a matter of hours. Heaven is bringing the war to us."

57

CONFUSION ENGULFED THE ROOM. The lieutenants all shouted at each other at once. Kahn yelled that we should go now and meet them head on. Kai Ah Jecks screamed back that we should fortify the city instead. The rest of their arguments were lost in an incomprehensible din of panic.

"Silence!" I boomed over the top of them, making them all stop and stare back at me. "This is what Asmodeus is trying for, to put us off balance. He won't succeed."

Only Marax and The Pure Seven held my eye. The rest looked at their feet like chastened teenagers. Phineus remained at the window, looking outward.

"Where will they come from?" I asked the prophet. "How many?"

He reached out and pressed a palm on the window, as if to give himself extra support. Bowing his head, his next words rang around the room, even though he spoke in a hushed tone.

"There will be many millions: angels of every kind. They will come from the same black hole as the refugees of Purgatory. Hell's desert sands will be awash with pure souls."

I stared outward to my city. Millions of angels. We had the numbers to match them easily. I would not fail my people. The others watched for my direction. Their stares helped my mind click into gear.

"Most of our plan will remain, with some changes," I said slowly at first, before gathering a sense of urgency. "We will march out to the desert to meet them in open battle. The Legions of Wrath, Pride and Lust will take the left flank. Marax and his Black will take the middle. Envy, Gluttony and Sloth will take the right. Smithy, you'll cover the skies."

"Aye, aye," he said, looking out of the window with a glint in his eye. He was ready.

"Zoroaster," I said, feeding off the confidence of Smithy. "You'll hold the city with the Legion of White and the Legion of Avarice. Mack?" I whirled around to the burly cabbie, who stood with his arms folded across his chest. "How soon can you have our army in position?"

"We have enough trucks to take maybe three legions out to the desert. That in itself will take just over an hour if I leave right now," he replied matter-of-factly.

"Fine, go." I nodded towards the elevator, urging them on. "Take Rangda, Marax, and Savela with you. Charlotte and I will carry the rest with the elements. I'd like to save as much energy as I can, so doing what you can will help. The Pure Seven can fly out to meet you."

The group left hurriedly while I spun to face the rest. Phineus was still at the window. Zoroaster, Smithy, Mary, Marlowe and Charlotte all stood in a row. The Pure Seven grouped with the remaining lieutenants, awaiting commands.

"I want you to all go down and assemble your legions as quickly as possible on the rooftops of the city," I explained to them. "We will lift you from there and take you to the front lines. Zoroaster and Avarice, secure the city while we move."

"I can help ferry the troops as well, sir," Smithy said with a military tone. "I have an idea. My planes will carry some out to the desert. The Pure Seven can help, but I'll need to leave immediately to get it ready."

"Go," I said with a grim smile, trusting him completely.

He rounded up Zoroaster, the evil angels and their demon offsiders, herding them out the door in a rush. Only Mary, Charlotte, Marlowe, Phineus and I remained. My heart drummed in my chest with the flurry of activity. Now I had time to take a breath, a whisper of anxiety filled my lungs.

"What else can you see, Phineus?" I asked the prophet, moving instinctively to Charlotte's side for comfort. Just a touch of her arm was enough to calm me.

"You won't be able to stay on the battlefield," he said, finally turning back to face me. His cloudy eyes had turned completely white with his power.

"But he's our greatest weapon!" Marlowe almost shouted.

"Four will be needed at Casa Diablo to face the Seraphim who will try to steal the waters of sleep from the Fount of Mercy," he said, in a trance of visions.

"Seraphim?" Charlotte asked.

"Monster angels," Mary said, looking concerned. "It sounds like Asmodeus is going to unleash all he has on us. The Seraphim are his secret pets that he keeps in his basilica. There are other ranks of angels as well: Principalities, Thrones, Dominions, Powers, Virtues and Cherubim. You already know the Archangels. Make no mistake, their army will equal ours in might."

I let out a long exhalation, gathering my thoughts. I had no choice but to take our legions out to fight. But we couldn't risk losing the Fount of Mercy to the enemy. Pausing for a few moments, a solution came to me.

"Once Charlotte and I have dropped the legions in position, we'll fall back to a vantage point where we might at least be able to assist the fight from a distance," I said, not wanting pull back from the heart of the battle. "As soon as there is any sign Asmodeus and his Seraphim are moving towards the city, we'll fall back to stop them. Marlowe, Mary and Phineus. Can you make your way to the castle and do your best to fortify it in the meantime? Azazel will be able to help you. I'm sure that house has a few tricks hidden inside that may help."

"I'll make sure we get there," Marlowe said, looking pleased to have a specific mission.

"Now, Mary," I said, turning to my flame-haired companion. "Tell me everything you know about these different kinds of angels. You have ten minutes, then it's time for war."

58

CHARLOTTE AND I STOOD ON THE ROOFTOP of Satan's tower. We could see that demons had already begun to assemble on the other buildings. They watched the skies, waiting for their transport to the pending battle. If I looked with elemental vision, I could literally see the mixture of tension and excitement that rose from them all.

The constant hum of trucks flooded upwards, with every vehicle on hand starting to exit the city. It was an organized flow, using every street available to avoid the bottleneck that would normally occur. Mack had coordinated it well. The stream of traffic curved around the base of Mount Belial and onto a new roadway which had been sliced through the jungle. The legions were moving to war.

Leaning in close to my wife, I took both of her hands in mine. I noticed she still wore the diamond engagement ring I had proposed to her with. It was bordered by another white gold wedding band. I squeezed her fingers tightly and looked into her deep blue eyes.

"No matter what happens," I said to her, "I will always love you with all I have."

"I've never doubted that," she whispered.

I hugged her like she was my anchor in this universe. Through everything, every twist of fate, painful setback and joyful moment, this woman had been the reason I wanted to go on. Even though we had been through Hell and back, I found myself thinking how lucky I was to have her. Not everyone had this kind of passion to draw upon when their spirits were low. Together we could conquer the universe. Together we would.

The buzzing of planes made me turn my head. A squadron approached from the back of the city where Smithy's airfield had been. I don't know how he'd done it, but there were hundreds, perhaps thousands, of different crafts blanketing the sky. Planes old and new flew alongside helicopters and zeppelins. Winged demons streaked between them, zipping like huge birds among the machines. Seven planes led the formation, trailing long ropes from their undercarriages. Clinging to a rope on each plane was one of The Pure Seven. As they neared the first row of buildings with people on them, the evil angels let go and took flight, screeching orders down at the demons gathering. The planes dipped low, letting the rigging attached to their fuselages drag downward onto the buildings. In swift movements, demons ran forward, hitching rides with each passing jet. It was mesmerizing to see. Every aircraft that flew by snagged at least a dozen soldiers onto their ropes. The Pure Seven circled back, unfurling ropes of their own to carry some to the battlefield. Within minutes half the rooftops were emptied. The plan was something only Smithy could have cooked up. His fleet now had strands of demons dangling beneath it, sweeping through the air in a stunt that defied common sense. It took a full ten more minutes for the air force to fly over. By the time they were done, Charlotte and I only had the equivalent of one legion to carry between us. The rest streaked toward the desert. It looked like hundreds of metal jellyfish were flying away, with tentacles of warriors to dispatch in the field. I gave Charlotte one last kiss and held her tightly.

"You gather them up," she said in my ear. "I'll take us forward."

Lotte let me go, focusing her attention back to our remaining soldiers scattered below. Sweeping the two of us upward, I sent out a signal of light so those who remained would know we were taking them with us.

"I'll carry you as well," I said back to Charlotte as we started to circle the city in a long arc, building a line of elements to draw up as we went. "You just concentrate on making us move."

Snapping my vision now to a pure elemental view, I pinpointed the brighter sparks of the souls I would need to gather. The technicolor personality of Hell itself swarmed below, ever-moving like a living creature. Letting all air exit my body I drew my lungs full, summoning further gas molecules along with it. Imagining each soul was as light as pure thought, I plucked them one by one into the sky with us. As hundreds became thousands in my grip, and thousands became millions, I felt myself sag under their weight. Wavering slightly, I renewed my efforts, telling myself that I was a god. I could hold humanity in my hands with ease. The power was there, I just had to use it. Mastering as many elements as I could, I let the atoms work for me. They took away the strain from my being. Lifting higher, I climbed up. They came with me willingly, making the burden easier to bear.

"Now!" I managed to say to Lotte, keeping my eyes on the vast weave I had curled around the masses ready to fight for us.

A movement at my side signaled that she was doing all she could to sweep us forward. A breeze brushed my cheek. It grew to a wind, then a storm. We rocked forward. My muscles burned from the strain of my concentration. My mind was on fire with meditative focus. The ground surged below us. Still I held firm, like trying to grasp a memory for as long as I could, before the oceans of time washed it backward. My body was weakening. I didn't know how much longer I could hold. Closing my eyes, I let my sense of feel take over completely. I became lost in the effort. Not seeing the masses that I held in my grip helped. They became one with my life force, hanging like raindrops beading at the bottom of my soul. Every single person there touched my core on a personal level. I felt their fears and their dreams. The united emotions threatened to overwhelm me.Blackness formed at the fringes of my mind.

"Lower," I heard Charlotte say next to me in a reassuring way. "We're here. Ease them down."

Blinking my eyes, I emerged from my internal fog to see with surprise that she was right. Beneath us were millions upon millions of demons, looking like ants, falling into rank. They formed vast units, square by square of military power. Trucks roared out to add to the army. Planes touched down on a makeshift airfield at the back of them. It was a testament to the unity of purpose we all held that this could be possible in such a short time. They all believed and, because they had faith, mountains had been moved to make way for our hordes. Inching downward, I lowered the souls in my grip so their feet touched the ground. All eyes looked up to me in wonder, witnessing mine and Charlotte's combined power to carry so many. It would give them courage for the fight ahead. Finally touching down ourselves, I collapsed in a sweating heap; Charlotte slumped down next to me. It was like I had just run a marathon with no training. Opening my pores to the elements of healing, I let my ragged breath soak up the welling energy of the army around me. Their collective zest made my recovery easier. Charlotte also seemed to recoup well next to me. Still, we stayed seated, a wide ring of demons all around, leaving us breathing room for the moment.

"Lord Michael!" a growling voice said, as Marax pushed his way through the crowd to approach. "I have never seen anything like that in all the years I have been in Hell! With you at our backs, we will be unstoppable."

"Remember, our enemy will have Asmodeus at their backs," I said to Marax, tempering his pride, so he would be sure to fight with the desperation of someone who could easily lose.

His face set in determination at my comment. This demon responded to challenges more than praise. I got to my feet, Charlotte doing the same at my cue.

"If Phineus was right, it won't be long before they arrive," I said to him with urgency.

"We are ready, Lord," he snarled.

"You have been leading this army from the start," I continued as if he hadn't spoken. "I want you to make sure they know what is at stake."

His face fell, as if to question what I was saying, but I ignored the look. I turned to look over the heads of our army, back to the city. A few miles off, I spotted a gigantic black dune, rising higher than the rest. The last of our army were gathered in front of it, ready to move forward. That was our fallback point.

"We need to create a line of extra defense between here and the city," I said sternly, turning back to Marax. "Phineus has foreseen that we will be needed on Mount Belial. We will stay as long as we can to assist, but it must be you who takes control of our force on the ground. You are our backbone. Make sure you stay strong."

"But I..."

"I will magnify your voice loud enough so all can hear. You will make a speech to quake the souls of Heaven. Is that understood?"

"Yes, Lord!" He snapped a salute and turned to go.

"And Marax," I said, stopping him before he left. "Do not disappoint me."

I watched the red demon march away, hoping I had used enough of the right motivation to spur him to greatness. The desert around us was abuzz with movement. People took their stations. Orders were barked by a chain of command I didn't even know existed. Others had done that work for me and they'd done it well. A truck rumbled by and then another. I would have stayed to watch my warriors assemble, but Charlotte tugged at my sleeve. She didn't need to say anything; it was time we took our place behind the army.

I let Charlotte take us both. She lifted us together and we flew with ease over the heads of the legions. Some stared upwards as we passed by, but most had their attention forward to the commanders bringing them into rank and file. We swept backward, onto the towering dune that overlooked it all. From that height, it looked like a carpet of demons had been laid over the desert. Stretching for miles on each side, the sands were teeming. I peered down, using the elements to assist my eyes, so I could see all the details. At the head of each organized square was a commander, holding everyone in place. Some legions had guns, others swords and knives. I spied Kahn, shouting words I couldn't hear to a frenzied group of warriors in front of him. Away to the side and back, I could make out Smithy, huddled with his pilots and flying demons, speaking in a measured way. I searched to the front to find Marax. He had walked out alone so he was separated by at least twenty paces from the very front line. I saw his mouth move as he went to speak. He furrowed his brow before trying again. This time, I sent a spiral of molecules whipping down to help him.

"Attention!" his growl rumbled up and over the legions. His call was greeted by a single foot stamp from the entire army, which itself sent a tremor through the sands below. "Today, we will do something many of us have only dreamt of doing since our deaths," Marax said, clenching both fists and shaking them above his head. "We will see justice!"

A short, sharp cheer of two syllables went up from the legions. The word rang from everyone's lips: "Jus-tice!"

"We have been living in suffering and guilt for centuries in this pit," the Wrath demon went on. "We have struggled against an oppressive system, which keeps us down by law!"

Again the two syllables beat out in a chorus that gave me goose bumps: "Jus-tice!"

"Lord Michael has stripped away the barrier which held us down. It was that same barrier which forced guilt upon our heads. Now we raise our heads high and we look up to Heaven and we say, no more! Today is the day to claim our rightful place, to be whoever we want to be and live where we want to live. Today we tear our enemy apart, so they cannot hold us down any longer. Nothing can stop us! We. Will. Rise. Up!"

A seismic roar came up from the legions, filling the sky with its clamor. The noise lifted my own spirits and made me look up to the black hole above. Right then, a flash of white light, then another splintered down. A different roar burst down into Hell. It was the sound of the militia of Heaven. Angels of every shape and size swarmed outward into the sky, like hornets from a stirred up nest. They had heard the call of Hell and answered.

Jihad was at our fiery shores.

59

THE POPULATION OF HEAVEN POURED into Hell. The masses shot downward, thundering into the sands. Their numbers blotted the sky, streaming outward like a billowing cloud of locusts. Every kind of angel Mary had described to me spun downward. Cherubim like fierce children flew into Hell. The Thrones were glowing wheels of flesh, covered in eyes, clattering down onto the desert floor. The Principalities were living rays of light, streaking in a burst of illumination. Their smaller cousins the Virtues were blue sparks of energy, darting to the battlefield. Not all of them could fly. The Archangels emerged and behind them, the fearsome Seraphim. They were giant beasts with six wings and four faces, seeing every angle of attack. Their bodies were bulbous, like swollen white bumblebees. The Archangels themselves were clad for battle in silver armor with blades attached to the edges of their wings, which made them look as though they had scythes protruding from their backs. The Dominions were last: worker ants with weak wings. They dropped from the sky, ready to meet our foot soldiers in hand-to-hand combat. The army of Heaven formed ranks of its own, squaring off against our legions. Not hesitating for a moment, the Archangels called for the charge forward. The demons responded, roaring a battle cry in return. The crunch of bodies colliding beat the air around us.

Behind the army of Heaven, another flash of light struck and I saw the Chinvar bridge form into a long arch. Different colored gases leaked through the atmosphere of the void above. It was the Powers: insubstantial angels that could choke you with their wispy souls. Emerging behind them, the human portion of God's army thundered down. We were being matched soul for soul. It was almost like Asmodeus had created more soldiers for this fight and had flung them down. I could not see my evil father, but my attention was drawn back to the battle as our forces clashed. Kahn broke forward, taking the ranks of the Dominions in a cry of hatred.

His warriors unleashed metal on wings, tearing at the flesh of their attackers like butchers to squealing pigs. Our air force scrambled, firing rounds of searing lead into the Cherubim, who screamed in a flash of blood. The Archangels burst upward and their evil opposites, The Pure Seven, shot in to meet them. Their collision exploded in a puff of feathers and scales.

It was utter chaos. Screams and shouts of death rose to meet my ears. Hammering shots from machine guns mixed with the ringing of steel on steel. The light beings of the Principalities and Virtues engulfed the Legion of Lust on the far side. Bodies burst into flames as they touched. Terrified screams of agony cried from bleeding souls. The Legion of Gluttony went to their aid, but was also consumed by the light. Both sides burrowed deep inside the other's lines. The armies were like two hands, with stretched fingers interlocking and combating each other.

From the back of the charge, I could see still more of Heaven sweeping in.

"We have to do something!" Charlotte shouted, witnessing the same thing.

I moved to call the elements, but my attention was diverted again as I saw a gigantic Seraphim burst right through the balloon of one our of air force's zeppelins. The tearing turned to an explosion. The flames engulfed angels and planes alike. The first Seraphim pressed onward, joined by its three brothers. They bullied their way through the air, scattering planes and demons in their wake. It was clear they were looking to break away from the fracas and head toward Mount Belial, just as Phineus had predicted. We would have to fall back, but I couldn't leave without doing something to help. My eyes were drawn to the fast approaching support of the humans and Powers of Heaven, who had descended on the Chinvar Bridge.

"The sand!" I cried to Charlotte, hoping to slow them. "We need to build a wall!"

She immediately understood my idea, reaching outward with her mind toward the small desert space between the main army of Heaven and their reinforcements. It was as if Lotte and I were dancing, spinning our talents as one to lift the black desert upward in a cresting wave. The molecules of the universe sparkled as we manipulated them. The dunes became a tsunami, rolling together like liquid, rising up and then crashing down, enveloping our target. They disappeared in the sand storm, their frontrunners buried completely. I would have let out a yell of triumph, but the sound caught in my throat as I saw the Seraphim rush across the last line of the air force and into free space. We might have bought our own army some time, but we had left our retreat late. I took one last look at the battlefield and saw unending violence. We had regained an upper hand on the ground. Kahn had cut a swathe of destruction inside the ranks of Heaven and was now hacking back out. Marax, in the centre with his Legion of Black, split the enemy forces in two. Above, the colorful Pure Seven locked horns with the Archangels, grappling each other in an even match. Smithy's planes shoot and rolled every which way, with angels and demons darting amongst them, ripping wings from aircraft or biting down into heavenly flesh.

"Come on!" Charlotte pulled me away, forcing me from the scene.

We rose up in unison, hot on the wingtips of our quarry. The Seraphim made haste towards Hell City. Their multiple wings pushed them faster than I could have thought possible. The faces on the backs of their heads looked back at us with contempt. We'd have to hurry if we wanted to stop them before they reached Casa Diablo.

Charlotte held next to me, matching the pace I whipped at our backs. We shot forth side-by-side, jetting through the skies, giving chase over the dunes toward the jungle between the desert and Mount Belial. As we reached the first trees we gained on the pack of fleeing Seraphim. Mount Belial was in clear view. Holding my speed, I unleashed a spray of liquid fire ahead of us, trying to clip the back of the last Seraphim in the group. Because of its 360 degree vision, the monster angel saw the blast coming. It beat its wings to fan the blaze away. My attack was swept off in the wind it created. Still, I smiled inside. The maneuver had caused the seraphim to slow. With a body that size, it would take precious moments to regain its momentum. The thing seemed to realize its dilemma the same moment that I did. The face pointed toward us looked more lion than human. It snarled. Instead of retreating with the other three monsters, it advanced. Its six wings locked together, propelling it towards our approach. I drew in elements to fling an attack its way, but the monster unleashed a hiss of inky blue gas at us. The spray reacted with the air, making the atoms I'd tried to pull together slide off each other. I saw Charlotte struggle to draw a weave and fail as well. In the momentary confusion, the Seraphim struck. Its body hit Charlotte and sent her plunging downward. One of the side wings caught me in the stomach, knocking the wind out of me. I span away, avoiding the swipe of the next wing that tried to connect with my head. The sight of Charlotte dropping caused anger to well up in me, pushing my pain away. With a growl of rage I whirled around, charging right at the Seraphim. It opened its forward-facing mouth to send another cloud of gas toward me, but I swung out with my fist, cracking it square on the chin. My forward momentum sent me colliding into the beast's underbelly and it grasped me in its massive human arms. The Seraphim squeezed its meaty hands, gripping me by the torso as I swung my own fists into its body. I laced my punches with hateful emotion to spike into its skin. The attack fell useless. Every element simply absorbed into the soft flesh of its swollen gut, as if giving it more strength. I let out a cry of agony as my ribs cracked. I kicked with my feet, again and again, trying to break free from the leviathan's death grip. I felt a rush of wind to the side and saw a flash of energy ripple up beside me. The Seraphim's four faces wailed. It let me go. A putrid smell invaded my nostrils as its body started to fall down onto mine. I steadied myself in the air, rolling to the side. The Seraphim slid past, limp, spiraling downward into the jungle below. I looked up to see Charlotte. She hovered in the air, covered in angelic blood, clutching three severed wings in each hand. Lotte had torn them clean out of the Seraphim's back. She let them drop. The fluttering appendages scattered away as she spread them apart with the elements.

"One down, three to go," she said fiercely, her chest heaving with the effort of what she had just done. She turned toward Mount Belial and a look of fear spread across her face. "I hope Mary and Marlowe are ready."

60

SCREAMS OF BATTLE MET US as we rocketed toward Casa Diablo. The three remaining Seraphim wreaked havoc on the grounds of the castle. The entire back lawn swarmed with demons. Azazel and his staff protected the house. Two of the three Seraphim advanced on the building, screaming murder into the sky, sending gas attacks streaming out of their many mouths. Marlowe grouped a small force against one, while Mary led a fight against the other. The third Seraphim hovered over the Fount of Mercy, flapping in the air above the bottom pool. A sucker-like tentacle extended out of its belly and dragged in the waters, drinking up the green fluid of sleep into its body. Its stomach must have been lined with the inky gas I had seen earlier, creating a barrier that stopped the beast from being affected. I saw the hideous potential of this right away. If it managed to escape, it could fly back to the battle and spray the toxin onto our legions, or worse, into our city.

I speared in to attack the angel, taking my chance of surprise. Creating a sawblade of metallic elements from the sky, I sent it cutting down through the belly of the beast. The edges of my creation bit into its skin and sliced downward, wrenching its body in two. In a splash of anguish and gore, it sunk into the depths of liquid sleep. The cry of pain its lion face made before bubbling below the surface turned the attention of the other two monsters. They saw Charlotte and me approach. We landed on the cliff next to the waterfall that splashed down onto their brother. The sight made them howl in anger. One of them pushed a plume of liquid from its mouth into the group of demons that were trying to fend it off. I saw Marlowe narrowly escape the torrent which made those around him go up in a flame of white. There was no time to catch our breath no matter how worn we were from the effort of the chase. We had to stop this threat immediately.

"Left," I said to Charlotte through heaving breaths. "We go together."

"Okay," she nodded. "Now!"

Leaping off the cliff, my wife fearlessly sparked ahead. Marlowe rounded on the Seraphim on the right, managing to skewer one of its wings with his sword. Azazel was next to him, running headlong into the beast's back, gouging his horns into the space between its wings. I followed behind Charlotte, knowing we had a serious fight on our hands. The monster we shot towards saw us coming, swelling up its abdomen to defend itself with a blast of air. Charlotte realized what it was trying to do and pushed her own weave of air towards it, dispersing the gaseous attack away to nothing. My wife's feet hit the ground and she rolled sideways as a wing tried to strike her flat. Lotte's blocking move paved the way for me. I came in at top speed, flexing my hands. Bowling into the Seraphim, I latched my fingers deep into its skull and tore upwards. The ripping of flesh felt beautiful in its intimacy as I plucked the thing's head clean off its neck. Stinking gas and plasma squirted out of the wound, as I pulled clear. The headless body flailed for a few moments, listlessly flapping its six wings one last time, before it crashed backwards. Without so much as looking at the ghastly head in my hands, I sent searing flame into it and burnt the thing to ash.

Touching down, I knelt, feeling exhaustion try to take over my body. I let the sounds of the continuing fight spur my motivation, closing my eyes for just a few moments. Looking up again over the lawn, I could see between the carnage. The final Seraphim swept a deadly row of wings against Azazel's advancing demons. They were all thrown backwards, bouncing like hapless dice. I searched around and saw Charlotte, reclaiming her strength and wits from our attack. Mary was close to her, but she only had eyes for the last monster. Mary let out a call to those around her and they regrouped. Marlowe and Azazel were on its other side, reforming their defense of the castle. I could see in the Seraphim's eyes that it knew it was trapped. Taking my time, I rose to full height, stalking on foot towards the hideous angel. It locked gazes with me, seeing my determination.

Without warning, the Seraphim bellowed blackness from every orifice in its body. Clouds of poison filled the lawn, spewing towards us. Charlotte, who was closer than me, threw up a barrier of air to stop the fog from overtaking our side of the grounds. The cloud rose up, hiding the Seraphim from view. I was about to launch forward when I saw it lift up high in the sky. Its body was half the size of before, having expended all its internal power in a desperate act of survival. The wings on its back buzzed, lifting it away in retreat, back out over the jungle. I prepared to go after the thing, when a voice stopped me.

"It cannot hurt us now," Phineus shouted from behind the group.

I turned to see the prophet, untouched by the fight. His eyes were shrouded in foresight.

"There is other work you must do," he said with the certainty of fate, "if you are to have any hope of winning this fight."

67

THE BLACK FOG that had hung over the grounds of Casa Diablo dispersed, as Charlotte blew an elemental wind to spread it away. The lawn was littered with comatose bodies that had succumbed to the poison of the Seraphim. Among them Marlowe and Azazel lay as still as death. The sight of my African friend claimed all my attention. I ran to him, ignoring the others who I knew were safe for now. Coming to his side I knelt down, letting the elements hold of my vision. A quick scan of his state let me breathe a sigh of relief. The effect would only be temporary, nowhere near as powerful as the waters of sleep, which still shimmered over to the end of the lawn. Placing my hand over my friend's mouth, I drew the gas from Marlowe's lungs. As the poison exited his body he spluttered awake, heaving to his feet and looking around wildly.

"It's okay," I said to him, trying to calm myself at the same time. "Only one got away. We are safe for the moment."

By now the others had gathered around. Mary was flushed from the fight. Charlotte was only a touch more composed, her blonde hair tousled and knotted. Phineus approached at a walk. The other demons who had escaped the gas held a distance. Bodies still lay around us, yet to be revived.

"What's happening in the desert?" Mary asked in a rush.

"I don't know," I said, feeling tired suddenly after the heat of the battle. "When we left we were winning, just. But anything could have happened since then."

"We have to get back there," Charlotte said with a sense of urgency.

I looked to each of my friends, who all looked back at me for direction. My eyes fell past them to the green waterfall we had come back to defend. It was a too much of a liability. I couldn't leave it as it was.

"I need to destroy the Fount of Mercy," I said breathlessly. "Azazel and his workers need healing. We need to secure this place, before rushing headlong back into the breach."

Phineus stood silent, his attention elsewhere. His eyes searched beyond this point in time. No matter what he was seeing, I knew those waters couldn't stay as they were, with a Seraphim still alive to use them against us.

"Charlotte and Mary," I said. "Do your best to heal those who have fallen. Marlowe, regroup the others in case there is another attack. Keep them clear from me."

Pausing to place a reassuring hand on Charlotte's shoulder, I walked toward the Fount of Mercy. My heart raced, my mind tumbling ahead in a game of chess I didn't understand. My gut was churning and hot. I couldn't stop. Not now. I came to the edge of the green pool. The waterfall thundered down from the cliff above. It was time to destroy this cursed creation of mine. In the depths of the centre, I could just make out the silhouette of the Seraphim I had cut in half. Closing my eyes, I let the feeling of the world soak in around me. Atoms brushed over me. Elements whirled. I summoned the molecules of earth from deep in the mountain below, twisting them, unseen far beneath. Using my mind, I made them churn and burrow downward into depths that would never be found, then away into the distance. I let the sinkhole collapse inward, lifting a funnel to meet the surface. With a gurgle, the waters in front of me drained away. I let every last drop siphon off, pushing the pieces of the Seraphim along with it. As I looked on, the waterfall above slowed to a drip, its source of flow severed. With one final flick of my hand, I sent a slice of air through the cliff above. It sparked an avalanche that rained rock down into the sinkhole. My construction crumbled, falling down and away far into black nothing beneath. Once the landslide had settled, I pulled what remained of the cliff right over the top of the hole. Sealing it off, I solidified the ground again, making sure the mountain was firm once more. I let grass grow from out of the destruction, restoring the lawn to what it had been before. No one would find those waters again, unless I wanted them to. They had been buried deeper than anyone else would even think possible, away from the mountain into a depth that might have even scraped the bottom of the universe. My stomach settled and a brief sense of peace washed over me. I had done this right.

The dust cleared, but I stayed where I was, watching out over the jungle. I felt slightly numb looking on. My brain and body needed time to recoup. Keeping on my feet, I stared outward. There was movement out in the desert that I didn't yet understand. A noise behind me made my head turn. Mary, Marlowe, Charlotte and Phineus had come out to the edge of the lawn. We stood on Mount Belial together, with our backs to the castle.

"Azazel is shutting the building completely," Mary said to me, her hands clenched at her sides from the stress of what had happened.

I nodded slowly, but kept watching below. The movement became clearer. Legions of demons were retreating across the sands, pursued by Heaven's warriors. They reformed at the beginning of the jungle, creating a new line of defense against the enemy, who had gained an advantage in my absence. The air was awash with color. The distant forms of planes, demons and angels looked like flocks of birds, attacking each other from within. A feeling of dread crept into my stomach.

"We have to help them," Charlotte said next to me, clutching my arm as if to sweep me back off the mountain.

"No," I said, shaking her off. "This is all just a distraction. Asmodeus is not down there."

Her eyes went wide with an understanding of what that meant. If this were indeed the true battle, my father would have been leading the charge. His absence meant he had more important plans brewing. There could only be one frightening possibility, but I didn't want to voice it.

"He is building a new barrier above," Phineus said, his words echoing my worst fears.

I looked to the prophet whose eyes had returned to their regular cloudy blue. The color draining from his face struck terror in my heart. Had he seen more than he was letting on? No matter what he could say, there was no choice but to rise to Heaven and face Asmodeus now. If he succeeded in rebuilding the filter, all would be lost. There was no way he could have done something so time consuming already, but without interruptions the task would be much easier. While the war raged here below, Asmodeus was creating that diabolical device anew. If he pulled it shut, his angels and saints would be drawn upwards, safe from any pursuit by the Legions of Hell. It wasn't his plan to defeat us. It was his plan to throw everything he could into delaying our ability to enter Heaven so he could recast the universe. It had to be stopped.

"I'm coming with you," Charlotte said, realizing what I had to do without it being said.

"You can't," I said to her, lowering my voice.

I shut the others out of my mind for the moment. The only thing holding my attention was the beautiful face of my wife. This might be the last time I would get to see it without other distractions. I took in the curve of her lips and her innocent cheeks. Her blonde hair fell over ears that I knew were dark red. She wasn't the sum of her body parts, however. It was the light behind her eyes that made her who she was. I could see that light sparking fiercely now, getting ready for an argument I couldn't let her win.

"I will not let you put yourself in danger of fulfilling Phineus' vision. I won't," I said.

She started to interrupt me, but I silenced her with a kiss.

"I won't," I repeated into her lips, before pulling away and gripping her upper arms tenderly, but firmly. "This is too important, Lotte. You are needed down here. You have to fight with the legions and use your strength to help turn the tide. You need to divert all the angels' attention away from me. I can't have anyone following me up if I have any hope of beating him. Promise me you'll do that."

Lotte glowered at me with hurt eyes. She knew the sense of what I was saying. If she didn't create a diversion, keeping the Archangels or the last Seraphim from coming to help their master, I would never succeed. I could see her grasping for an excuse, so I pressed my point.

"You know there isn't any other way. Promise me," I said softly.

She paused, looking out to the desert. Lotte watched the fighting for what seemed like an age, while I held my breath for her answer.

"No one will follow you," she said, finally staring back at me. "I'm not saying goodbye to you though, Michael. You will come back to me."

There was no way I could promise such a thing, so I kissed her again instead, pressing my lips to hers and letting them linger as our foreheads touched. I sighed with the sorrow of the moment, but hid it by looking back to Mary.

"Go to the city," I ordered her. "Get Zoroaster to bring every soldier we have out to the desert. They'll need everything we can offer in support."

Mary just bowed her head to show she understood. Her red curls reminded me of the blood that was now flowing out in the desert. She had been a true friend and I wanted to go and give her a hug farewell, just in case I didn't return. The moment didn't allow such personal comforts.

"Marlowe," I said, turning to my African friend.

I paused for a second. My stomach fluttered with a breath of possibility. I had grown to know the feeling since the revelation of how I had managed to hide Mary's plan of betrayal, even from myself. It was my instinct working in my favor. I listened and let it speak for me.

"Go to The Perceptionist," I said to Marlowe, "Tell him I am going to follow the path of the good shepherd, but that he must close the gate behind me."

"What?" Charlotte asked, her face twisting into fearful confusion.

Mary looked on in stoic silence, as though she understood what I was saying, but knew not to interfere.

"I will tell him," Marlowe said, never one to ask questions.

"What does that mean?" Charlotte asked, her panic showing.

"I don't know," I replied honestly, "but I have to keep the secret buried in me if I hope to defeat my father."

It truly pained me to keep anything from her, but I knew deep down the truth would come out soon. She would know everything in due course, as would I. Lotte saw the steely expression on my face and nodded again. She was a soldier of fate in this, just as I was. We had to create our own path.

"Are you ready?" I asked her, reaching out to take her hand.

"No," she answered, her resolute gaze returning to the battlefield below. "I could never be ready for this. But I will create your diversion. No one will come after you."

62

LOTTE AND I FLEW HAND-IN-HAND, across the first half of the jungle. It almost felt like we were Wendy and Peter Pan, flying to Never Never Land. But this wasn't a fairytale. There would be no happy ending.

The conflict on the desert sands took realistic form, ceasing to be far off birds and becoming a bloody massacre. Smells and sounds rose up that could melt a person's soul. I let my grip on Lotte's palm loosen, our fingertips sliding away. I smiled, turning my head to her for what I thought could be one last time. She nodded back firmly. There were no words to be spoken. Anything but the language of her eyes would have been worthless. Drawing a shroud of invisibility from the elements over me, I watched Charlotte go on her way. The cloak I had made would never be able to fool an angel up close, but it would be enough, so long as Lotte kept her end of the deal.

I swerved in the air, directing myself to the edge of the battle. Below, the sands swarmed with demons, fighting recklessly to hold their ground. The full might of Heaven now pushed their backs against the jungle, but I could see our legions fighting valiantly. I spotted Smithy's Apache helicopter showering a chorus of angels with bullets, which detonated as they hit. Hellfire engulfed the pack of Cherubim, who plummeted down, becoming living missiles of flame. Our ranks on my then crumbled under the pressure of the Principalities and Virtues. The beings of light cut demons down wherever they shone their glory. The insubstantial forms of their bodies made it difficult to resist in any real way. I paused, wanting assist my people. Then Charlotte struck with all her wrath. She hit the earth like a dark star. In a spray of sand, an earthquake rattled the entire scene, sending both armies toppling. Not stopping for a moment, she sprang back into the air, directing her charge right at the remaining Seraphim. It circled the Archangels and Pure Seven, who were still pitched in an even struggle. Charlotte turned herself into a brilliant ball of fire as she speared up. She blazed right into the Seraphim's belly, splitting through and out the other side. The monster burst alight, completely gutted by a fire which burned from its insides. Lotte rounded on the Seraphim and, in a howl of elements, pulled its body completely apart, sending sprays of gas and blood over the heads of the Archangels below. They looked up, pausing from their fight with The Pure Seven. Charlotte had their undivided attention: a true Elemental in their midst. The danger she presented could not be ignored. They peeled up towards her, screeching hatred. The Pure Seven were in hot pursuit. The sinful angels gripped their nemesis' ankles to hold them back and pulled them once again into hand-to-hand combat. Charlotte, seeing she was clear, summoned a cloud of molecular energy over her head, ready to launch into our enemies.

A curdling cry from right beneath me drew my attention. I looked to see a new force surging from out of the jungle towards the main battle. I started to rush down to stop them, when I recognized the figure leading their charge. She had raven-black hair and was wielding twin hatchets, screaming blue murder into the sky. It was Clytemnestra with The Furies at her side. The women of the Necropolis trailed out behind them: millions of wondrous Amazons coming to the aid of Hell. Their assault lurched into the fray, causing confusion amongst Heaven's troops, who hadn't seen them coming. My heart lifted with purpose. I watched again to see Charlotte blast a wave of atomic destruction into the angelic forces. I had to leave. Hell was in good hands.

Resuming my flight, I carried myself as fast as the elements would allow. The desert swept below. Mutilated bodies littered the surface, victims of a battle that had left them for dead. There were angels and inmates of Hell, all starting to painfully heal. Coagulating blood of different colors drew back out of the sand and into fallen soldiers. Their wounds knitted together. Dead eyes opened. Those who had regenerated enough to stand already make their way back towards the battle. The sight made me realize that this fight could go on forever. An army that couldn't be cut down was an army that wouldn't stop. Both sides would be at each other's throats until someone called a truce, or a higher being intervened.

Eyeing the black hole in the atmosphere above, I carried on, hammering up with speed, ready to enter the void. I drew every ounce of acceleration I could, hoping my momentum would carry me through up to Heaven. Little resistance met me as I went up. A few stray elements swept past as I arrowed into the space. As soon as I passed through the buzzing purple entry, an overwhelming sense of emptiness met my body. I shot inside. A cliff of solid rock towered up on my right. It was a sheer wall that rushed past as I went up. My impetus began to slow. There were no longer atoms of air I could use to help propel me forward. I wasn't able to grip onto anything, or push off a surface to continue my flight. This really was a void, even more so than The Perceptionist's, which still contained the elements he wanted at his call. The gravity of the vacuum, which was still pulling final earth elements out into Hell, worked against me. However, my speed was enough that I continued up. I had almost slowed to a stop when I reached the roof of the void. Stretching upward, I shoved my arms into the purple field which contained the nothingness below. The elements within allowed me to dig inside it and pull myself through. As my head entered the thick layer of power, a whispering came into my ears. It was the essence of Germaine. He wasn't completely gone. The powerful consciousness that had defined his spirit was still alive. It wasn't totally coherent, but I knew he was there and I felt he had welcomed my presence. He existed as a worldless being in this atmosphere around me. It was like liquid you could breathe in. My desire to move forward stopped me from pausing any longer to feel my way around. No matter how much I wanted to stay, my real duty was above.

Swimming onward, I gathered what elements I could at my back. The light upward began to grow bright as I reached the surface. My body broke free and I entered a flow of atoms being manipulated by someone else. Wading through thick strands of elements that tugged at my soul, I knew this was the incomplete filter that my father was trying to reconstruct. Asmodeus was near. Hate, guilt and regret swarmed at me. There was no power in it yet, but the potential was clear.

I pressed on, against the atoms that were being pushed downward with the talent of a true maestro. Searching up and peering through the tiny gaps in the construction, I spotted the source. The jaws of the entry to Heaven were right around me. At the top, Asmodeus wove his magic. He was in a trance of creation, vibrating with the light of his labors. Like a silent shark breaking the waters of a black ocean, I burst forth from the flow, elements dripping from my body. I pushed every shred of emotion at my call in front of me as a battering ram. Glee entered my soul for a fraction of a second. I had caught him off guard. I would cut him down like the deadwood he was. But, as I struck, a zapping of intense electricity pierced my ears and I was blown clear of his body, flying further into the sky. It was as if the energy he was using to create the filter had repelled me, like a magnet of similar poles. The shock caused my body to go limp and I rag-dolled, head over heels, crashing down onto the immaculate lawn of Heaven. I rolled on the ground for a moment in pain, twisting as if my skin was being melted away, while sapphire statues of angels looked on. Through the agony, I felt a tap of energy snap closed. Heaving myself to my knees I looked back toward the entry to Hell. Still standing, the figure of my father turned. As Asmodeus faced me fully, I nearly gagged in revulsion. One side of his face had been ripped away and hadn't healed. Black plasma oozed forth, bubbling out from his stinking soul; it was a grisly wound from his previous fight with Zoroaster. Where his right eye should have been, a blue dot of pure energy glowed in his head. His other eye was a beacon of red destruction, focused right on me.

"You have interrupted me yet again," he said, his voice full of malice. "This will be the last time."

63

ASMODEUS TORE TOWARD ME with godly speed. He rushed in, gripping me by the hair and lifting me up. I was swung like a broken pendulum, down into the ground. My body thudded into the dirt, forcing every ounce of air out of my lungs. Whipping atoms of hate in his hand, he shot them into me as I desperately grasped to defend myself. I had hoped his efforts in building the filter and his injury would have weakened him, but there was no sign of fatigue at all. Power leapt out of him like an eternal spring of supremacy, straining to break me apart and scatter me to the wind.

I slapped his attacks back with desperation, trying to get away and create some space to counter. It was all I could do to stop him from flaying my soul away one element at a time. Rolling over on the ground, I kicked up but he punched my foot back down. I whipped a blast of spirit to push him away, but he sucked the elements into his own power and pushed them into my body. The tentacles of death wedged between my consciousness and began to expand. My grip on reality started to falter. In one last gasp of instinct, I stopped fighting. Instead, I expanded my self outward so his attack fell through me. I lifted up blindly over him, flipping to my feet and locking myself back whole again, reeling at my own ingenuity as I struggled to keep my balance. Asmodeus span, also stunned at what I'd done. I remembered The Perceptionist's teaching: there was no way I could beat a creature who could see what I was going to do. I had to let my mind stop and my intuition take control. Allowing the knot within me to loosen, synapses in my very pores started to spark with impossible swiftness. Before I even knew what I'd done, a blast of light detonated from within me, sending Asmodeus sprawling to the ground. The fright in his normal eye spurred me on. In a hurricane of vitality I descended upon my father, sending fists and elements in to slice at his very essence. He scrambled backwards, as I had done from him only moments before. With every element in my soul I pursued him. Scuttling in retreat, he fired a counter attack into me, pushing himself back towards the edge of the opening to Hell. I blocked his feeble attempt and leapt in, grabbing his throat so I could look into his broken face as I ended his existence.

Squeezing at him, I pushed my life force into him. Still, he resisted, his superior body naturally repelled my best efforts at getting under his skin. Gathering as much strength as I could, I reached up to pull more elements around me. The move was a mistake. I had thought about it too much. With a jerk of his fists, he impaled his arms into my chest. I slumped. Blood flowed out of my mouth onto his face.

"So close to a god, but still a human soul," he laughed malevolently at me, as my life bled all over his smile. He rolled over so I was pinned beneath him. "I am impressed," he sneered. "You definitely pushed me. Still, it wasn't good enough."

Asmodeus wrenched his fists inside me, pulling at the life chord that held me together. There was no release I could undertake. No attack I could now launch that would save me.

"A pity," he said, enjoying his victory. "We could have made such a team. But what am I going do to with you? The stuff of your soul could be used to help heal my face and create a new eye."

He squeezed my insides, wriggling his fingers right into my spirit and scratching it apart. I choked in agony, and would have blacked out – if it wasn't for the sound I heard next.

"He's not your soul to take," a voice said, quivering with rage from behind both of us. "His heart belongs to me!"

Asmodeus looked up in alarm at the words. His hold on me loosened as he pulled his hands from my chest to meet his attacker. It was too late. With a sparking chord of elements, a chain of pure hate wrapped around his neck and flung him off me and away. Scrambling to my knees I pulled myself up and looked down into the gateway of Hell. Asmodeus hurtled back through his unfinished filter, into the void, Charlotte strangling him with her passion.

64

I WATCHED IN DREAD as Charlotte and Asmodeus disappeared into the cycle of elements below. My love had saved me from certain destruction, but had signed her own death warrant in return. I stumbled for a moment, instinctively pulling strength from out of the air around me. I had to stop this.

Digging my hands into the edge of the opening as if I was on a diving block, I propelled myself down after them. I made myself as sleek as possible, tucking my arms at my sides, torpedoing back into the void. The incomplete filter shot past and Germaine's atmosphere roared by. My eyes cleared to see Asmodeus and Charlotte. They crashed down onto the single cliff that remained below, rolling from the fall. I speared forth toward them in a dive I couldn't really control. The pair below rounded on each other to fight again already.

Turning so I was as flat, my body fell between them, thudding an impact into the cliff top. Elements of earth showered upward as I struck. Both Charlotte and Asmodeus stumbled back. I groaned, rolling to my knees hopelessly. I tried to heal myself, but there were no elements on hand to do so. I had to let my ethereal body recoup on its own. Ignoring the crippling pain as it did so, I struggled to get back to my feet. My arrival had made Asmodeus and Charlotte pause. They stood off against each other, staring loathing into the other's face, with me caught in the middle. I saw Charlotte flick her hands as if to send atoms toward our enemy, but nothing happened. Asmodeus did the same, instantly realizing his error. There was simply nothing there to command. Keeping my wits, I gripped the earth beneath me, rolling it into a rock missile that I shot at my father. He blocked the move easily. The attempt was like throwing confetti at a tank. The primal elements split apart and floated away, drawn down toward the black hole below.

Asmodeus looked around, weighing up his options, while I steadied myself properly. Charlotte came to my back, holding me up. I wanted to ask her why she had broken her promise, but there was no time for words. My father peered over the cliff, looking as though he might jump at any moment and take his chances in Hell. Using the earth at our feet as a weapon was out of the question. Something so pitiful against fellow Elementals would do zero damage. He looked up to us again and smiled his hateful smirk.

"We seem to be at a stalemate," he said, clasping his hands in front of him.

I knew he was buying time, trying to see a way out. He wanted nothing more than to go back above and finish his filter, but we were a thorn in his side that would fester until it was removed. I took a single step towards him. A churn in my guts made me pause. The warmth inside me grew. The prophecy of Phineus rose into my mind. My final training with The Perceptionist came forth in a flood. Asmodeus had felt it too and his smile fell. True fear captured his face. He turned and ran. I reacted, sweeping Charlotte back away from me. Pushing my fingers in front of my body in a horizontal prayer, I tore through emptiness. My instinct caught hold and my hands dug inside nothing. I could feel my skin prickle under the fabric of the universe. Beneath, searing heat and freezing cold swirled together, but did not cancel the other out. I spread my fingers wider, to create space. With all my strength, I pushed my hands further forward. The rip sent a wave of elements out one way and pure darkness the other. The new life I created sparkled upward. It shimmered in its positive goodness: the building blocks of Creation. But it wasn't those elements I was interested in. It was their opposite: the seeds of Destruction. My mind clutched onto the dark matter, forming it into a javelin of annihilation. I watched calmly as my father fled. There was nowhere he could hide. Asmodeus took one final look of desperation back and cast himself off the cliff to escape. I sent my weapon after him as he fell. The darkness caught up with him in a blur. Evil forked into his back. Not even his body's strength was a match for its subtraction. In a hiss, his skin dissolved to become one with the void. His spirit zapped into oblivion. Every element of his soul withered away to become the gift of nothing. In moments it was over.

My father, Asmodeus, was finished.

65

I SPAN BACK TO CHARLOTTE, who I'd knocked down in my haste. She sat, staring at the space where Asmodeus had been and was now nothing. I rushed in, lifting Lotte to her feet and hugging her. We had done it. We had done it! I held her close, whispering in her ear.

"I love you. We're safe," I said, feeling the weight of all of my fears evaporate away in a single phrase.

Her hands clung at my back. Her lips met my skin, wet on my neck and then my mouth. The intensity was increased by the joy we both felt. She pulled back to look me in the eyes.

"How did you...?" she began, with tears falling onto her lips.

"It doesn't matter." I hugged her against me, burying my face into her hair and smelling blessed victory. We were together. We had won. "You came after me," I whispered. It wasn't said as an accusation. It was pure gratitude.

Her palms nestled softly against the back of my neck. Her fingers rubbed up along my twisted ears. I wondered strangely if they would go back to normal now, without all of the separation Asmodeus had created. It would be a brave new world with us leading the way.

"I couldn't let you do this alone," Charlotte said. "The war was being won when I left. Clytemnestra and The Furies came..."

"I saw," I cut her off.

Our conversation was a rush of half finished sentences, even though we had all the time in the world now. It would take getting used to – Peace. Without Asmodeus to stir more conflict, we could convince the angels to lay down their arms. They would be forced to surrender. There was no power they had now to oppose us for long. Hell would dominate the realms.

"Michael, I..." Lotte started to say, but the words died in her mouth. Her eyes went wide as she focused on something behind me. "No," she choked instead.

Her reaction made me turn. A speck of light was forming inside the void. It turned from inside out, gathering brightness by split seconds. It came from nowhere. No elements were used to build it. It was a power of its own, growing from within. A horrible voice whispered all around us.

I created myself from nothing, you fools, it said, *I will not be subdued so easily*.

I froze in shock as the light built into a brilliant white ball. It streaked toward us, gathering speed to attack. My only thought was to put myself between it and Charlotte to protect her. Stepping forward, I lifted my arms to meet the light, but hands at my back shoved me sideways. *No, Lotte!* I thought as I stumbled and fell. My love had pushed me away.

As my back hit earth, I looked up, just as the white soul of Asmodeus pierced inside Charlotte. It disappeared within and a gut-wrenching scream issued from my wife's lips.

66

CHARLOTTE'S BODY CRUMPLED as the soul of Asmodeus possessed her.

"No!" I leapt to my feet, the single word repeating itself in my head over and over.

Hopelessness wracked my spirit. This couldn't be happening. I wouldn't let it. My wife collapsed on the ground, shrieking and raking her nails against her face, trying to eviscerate the evil that had just entered her. She went mad, tearing at her hair, rolling and writhing in agony. In desperation I lunged at Charlotte, holding her down. Using my elemental will to search inside her, I grasped to rip out the corruption of Asmodeus. My hands fumbled over her body as I worked, but it was no use. This wasn't a normal soul possessing her; it was the ultimate power of a god who had spawned his own existence. I could see his light totally envelope Lotte. It became one with her soul, fusing its hatred inside her love. The toxicity of his spirit infected everything that made her who she was. In grief and impotence I held her, but then her hand reached up and lashed out at my face, scratching me. The action jolted me to look into her eyes, which were now full of a loathing that repelled me totally.

"She is mine now," the mouth of Lotte spat in a gurgle of wickedness.

Again her hand reached up to scour across my face, but I fell back, pushing myself clear. I stood, stumbling backwards in pure horror. Asmodeus had taken ownership of Lotte. I could still see her life force struggling against his, but it was losing and I was powerless to help.

The vision of Phineus came alive around me: the prophecy I had known would come true, but refused to accept. My love struggled on one knee almost a full body length away from me, breathless with exhaustion, holding her hands on the ground to keep upright. Beads of sweat pearled on her face. I stood watching her, not going to her side. Howling winds of power thrashed above us and below, in Germaine's atmosphere yet, where we were was calm. Charlotte struggled to her feet in front of me, her face twisting with the effort. She swayed, trying to gain her balance and then firmed, looking up at me with hate in her eyes. I stepped backwards slightly with the revulsion of her gaze. She looked around quickly, searching for some elements to use against me, before staring back again. *This is Asmodeus*, I told myself. She braced her legs as if to pounce, her lip curling in a snarl. I watched her closely, waiting for her to strike, but she wavered. Her body wobbled again and the sneer fell momentarily. The hate in her eyes turned abruptly to a look of pleading. My wife was back for a flickering instant. My breaking heart bled out compassion towards her. I wanted to help, but anything I could do would kill her. Asmodeus was part of her being. I struggled within myself to fight for a solution, but not even my instinct answered the call. Lotte's lips moved, but let out no sound.

Help me.

I turned hard inside. All love left my body and was replaced with vengeful anger. He would not have her. I knew she would rather die than live possessed forever by that devil. It was the only way. I took a step towards her and Asmodeus inside recoiled. If I could create dark matter again, I could end Lotte's pain. There was no use resisting fate any longer. Pushing my hands out in front of me in a wedge, I strained with effort, every muscle in my arms bulging. My hand slipped forward and the sound of the universe tearing once again split the air. On one side of my fists, new elements were born into existence. On the other side, anti-matter sprang awake in its guttering death. The body of Charlotte turned to run, spinning on her heels. It was too late. He wouldn't have her. Before she had barely taken a step, I had wrapped the darkness into a ball and hurled it towards her soul. As the hideous attack struck, her skin dissolved around her. All sense of anything that had made Lotte my love melted before my eyes. Her material nature bled away. Her soul disintegrated into the atmosphere of nothingness around us. The dark matter ate away at her being, until not even a speck of an element was left. I stood looking at the space that had once contained the body of the woman I loved. A resentful tear slid down my face. My Charlotte was gone and there was no coming back. She wasn't like Asmodeus. She hadn't created her own consciousness. Lotte had been born of this world and now had returned to the darkness behind it. There was no return from the oblivion in which she rested. I fell to my knees in soul-crushing despair. My life was now worthless. Asmodeus had beaten me. At least Charlotte was free. She had once said she would rather die than exist without me. I had granted her that wish. I was glad she wasn't here to see what I knew would happen next: my utter failure.

I didn't even open my eyes. I just waited for the feeling to take hold. The air grew warm around me as I felt the indestructible soul of Asmodeus reform. There was no way to kill the unkillable. No way to outsmart the all-knowing. It was over. His cursed whispering started as soon as his form seeped through my skin. He wormed himself through me, bonding me with his sordid essence. I didn't fight it.

My son. His smug voice sang disgusting noise through my brain. *You tried so hard. You fought so bravely and it was all for this? You could have at least let your true love live on. You could have learned to let me rule Heaven as her. You would have had eternity to heal the pain of it. I would have given you Hell.*

I didn't answer. There was nothing left to say. All existence was meaningless. Utterly meaningless. Good did not triumph. The hero didn't win. The innocent were murdered for no good reason. That was true reality. Life created by Asmodeus was something I would be glad to relinquish, if I could. But now I was trapped within myself. I could feel his thorny soul attaching to me, digging its spikes right through every part of my soul. I truly would be his puppet.

I'm glad I have this body, though, Asmodeus went on in his noxious whisper. He made me stand up, flexing his new ethereal body and making me dance. *Charlotte was beautiful, but you have more animal strength. I will be able to make this body impervious to anything. Who knows, I might even go down to Hell and tell them I, Michael, won. Why would they doubt it?* He walked right to the edge of the cliff and looked over. *Yes, I like that idea. It will be amusing. I will be the perfect actor, so sad that my lovely Lotte had been destroyed in the process. Oh, but Mary will be there to comfort me. She will give her body to me. Her nakedness will ease my pain. You can enjoy it too, my son, I will let you watch from within.*

Even this torment didn't spark anger in me. I was beyond caring. There was no use in resisting. All that brought was more suffering. He dug in further, deeper and deeper until he came right to the core of me, clutching onto me, growing inside me with every breath. I felt him prodding at the knot within, that The Perceptionist had helped me form once. Little good it had done.

So here it is, Asmodeus said in mirth, *this box of intentions that hid away your future from me. Very clever, Michael. Very clever. But still, it didn't work. Maybe I can use it myself. Yes?*

He tugged at the emotion that had been wrapped around my deepest thoughts. The tangle gave way at his touch, revealing what I had been planning all along and not actually known myself. Smiling bitter triumph with my own lips, I said in my own voice with perfect control.

"I have you now, Father."

67

NO! THE STUNNED SPIRIT OF ASMODEUS rasped from inside me. It was too late for him. He was in too deep. He struggled to back out again, but I held on, sucking the elements of my soul tightly together. He resisted and I locked onto him, like a host knowing that the parasite within was really a prisoner. His strength battered against me. It was a struggle to keep him from escaping, but I stayed firm, wrapping my elements of energy over the barbs he had dug inside me. Every breath was ragged and every movement a war. Our spirits fought each other. If I let this go on forever he would eventually gain the upper hand. But it wouldn't go on forever. With an immense effort, I lifted my foot and stepped out into space, over the edge of the cliff. Nothingness embraced us, as I embraced the evil being inside me. I hugged him tight like a lost lover. His voice swarmed, choking at my brain. I smiled as we fell.

The vacuum of the black hole caught the body that contained the both of us, drawing us back to Hell. We swept down, bursting into the realm of fire, which I had come to call home. With each scramble Asmodeus made to break free of me, I held him. It wouldn't be long. My eyes beheld the war still raging on the horizon. I couldn't tell who was winning, but that didn't matter. They couldn't fight forever. They would eventually figure that out, even if it took eternity. Again, Asmodeus shifted inside but, by now, even he knew the futility of it. He, who could see the future so close.

I arched my head to watch the ground come up. On the desert sands there was a gap of rock: a round circle of fragile stone that contained a sinkhole underneath. When I had drained the waters of sleep away, I had pushed them deep through the earth to rest somewhere no one would ever find them, unless I wanted them to. That place was here, where a body freefalling from Germaine's void would crash down. It had been my hope that I could do it before Charlotte could come to help, but in the end I had failed. Asmodeus would have beaten me in Heaven had she not arrived. It had been fate and she took her role willingly. She had laid down her life just as I was doing now. She had made this plan possible. The waters of sleep would make sure my body lay inert forever, lost inside a pool that would drown it on every side. With Asmodeus and me attached so hopelessly, there was no chance we would ever emerge.

I could now see a figure with a thousand eyes watching us come down. My master, The Perceptionist, had received my message and understood, as I knew he would. I had paved the way. He did not have to interfere. All he had to do was let us fall. He could then seal the gateway behind and bury us deep: forgotten in the shifting sands of the black desert. Asmodeus saw The Perceptionist too and let out an unintelligible cry of anger through my mouth. He knew he had finally been defeated.

I saw my teacher nod in pride, as my plummeting body cracked through the rock. His student had done what had seemed impossible. I had taken down a god. An avalanche of stone came down with us, through the sinkhole. I turned my attention inward, ignoring the rubble tearing at my skin as we fell into the darkness. I let my soul grin at my father, who was still bellowing in fury. His soul tangled in mine. There was no way out for him. The gurgling voice of Asmodeus was cut off, as liquid met our body. I didn't even hear a splash. The only thing that met my ears was a beautiful silence, which meant I would never have to listen to anything ever again. I would never wake. I would never be. In that way, I at least shared the fate of my love, Charlotte. We were both lost to oblivion, but oblivion was sweet. Our suffering was at an end.

EPILOGUE

I AM WATCHING YOU, AS I WATCH THEM.

I do not interfere. I simply stand sentinel with my thousand eyes.

God Asmodeus and his son Michael are frozen forever. I have concealed them where not even the most powerful of souls will be able to look.

You are now free to do as you wish. There is no one to stop you but yourselves. As humans, you were created with the gift of free will, but because of the manipulation of higher powers your gift was not true. Now the opportunities are open. They are endless. God is dead. Everywhere you turn now, there is nothing but unbridled choice. You have total responsibility for yourselves. There is no one to answer to; no higher justice or purpose than what you can conceive in your own minds.

Does this sound liberating, or does it place a burden upon you? Some only foresee darkness when they are asked to rely upon the goodness of others, who have no fear of divine punishment. For many, this freedom seems a gift with sharp edges on all sides: you can spill blood with it, or cut a path that opens the way for something more. Even now the war goes on in Hell. But you can bring it to an end, if you want it.

I believe goodness lies hidden somewhere within you all. I believe perfection is there. I see brief flickers of this potential, but you have an evil side which needs to be overcome. True justice is not doing what is right because you are forced to; it is doing what is right because it is good. True beauty does not lie inside a well-proportioned object; it lies within a pure action. That is perfection. I hope to see it unfold one day, but all I will do is watch.

The rest is up to you.

"The good shepherd lays down his life for his flock. The hired man is not the shepherd and does not own the sheep. So when he sees the wolf coming, he abandons the sheep and runs away. Then the wolf attacks the flock and scatters it. The cowardly man runs away because he cares nothing for the sheep, only for himself. But you are not just sheep and I am not a cowardly man. I am the good shepherd."

JOHN 10: 11-13

For more of Tim's writing visit www.timhawken.com

www.ingramcontent.com/pod-product-compliance
Lightning Source LLC
Chambersburg PA
CBHW010539100726
47903CB00011B/3063